When the Spider Strikes

E. C. Pecha

Contents

Chapter One

A cloudless sky covered the ocean. The full moon floated among the stars, a luminous centerpiece accented by the spots of light. Nolaton City's skyline cut into that beauty where it curved around the coast, the sharp edges of fifty-story buildings stabbing into the night.

Officer Katherine Dell had lived in the city for a decade, but she was still unnerved by the commotion. Cars honked constantly, even now in the middle of the night. Smog billowed up from the sewers. Newfangled neon signs blinked from the windows of shops and restaurants with hypnotic requests to buy their goods. Eat a hamburger. Drink an old-fashioned. See a picture show. Most nights, the barrage left her dizzy. At least tonight the colorful pleas of downtown flashed from a distance.

She leaned against the brick wall of a seafood processing plant. Streetlamps flickered as gas met flame, offering glowing patches of relief from the dark. The trash can in the alley next to her overflowed with waste, and the odor of rotting clamshells turned her stomach. The workers had gone home yet the docks still teemed with life. After sunset the harbor became a hub for dope peddlers and kidnappers, and anyone lurking around at this time of night likely had ill intentions.

A ship rolled into the harbor and bellied up to the dock. Men in dark clothing crept over it and caught the bow and stern lines. Once secured, they pulled crates off the deck and popped open the lids. Katherine's eyes narrowed as she watched from her safe distance. She might be able to peek at the contents if she climbed the fire escape, but right now they were none of her concern. Her job tonight was important, and she had to stay focused.

Bodies had been washing up on shore, dead prostitutes, and the police had received a tip about a man with a distinct birthmark seen dumping someone in the water. The precinct had been buzzing with the news, discussing ways to catch the killer. Officer Henry Williams came up with the idea for a sting, and as Katherine was the only female officer on the force, she was volunteered for the role. Though the heavy makeup made her feel like part of a bad circus act, she obliged. It was worth it to save lives.

The wind blew her loose curls into a frenzy. She swept her hair aside, prying a lock free from her lipstick, and draped her jacket over her shoulders helped to keep out the cold, though she had no help from the rest of her skimpy outfit. She had pulled an old red dress from her closet for tonight, one that she hadn't worn in at least five years. It had been her favorite once, her go-to garment for a night on the town. Beads glittered in a diamond pattern down the front, and the saucy hemline hit just below her knee. It was a dress for wearing out dancing, and for spilling cocktails on after a few too many. It was a size too small now and the unforgiving fabric constricted her, but the tightness helped to further her desired effect. She pushed her chest up and sucked in her stomach.

Her cigarette burned her lungs, and a cough escaped her throat. She took a few deep breaths of fishy ocean air, then another drag. It had to look natural — *she* had to look natural — or this whole plan would fall apart. She hitched her skirt up higher to reveal rolled-down stockings and dangling garters. Goosebumps spread along her thighs, but that ought to help entice her target.

A man stumbled toward her along the boardwalk. "Miss?" From her vantage point, Katherine took stock of his features. Short. Dark hair. No birthmark. Not her guy.

"Miss?" he said again. He approached, swaying with each step he took. With each "excuse me" and "hey, miss," his words slurred more. Great, just what she needed, some boozehound pawing at her.

"Hey, I'm talking to you." He was right in front of her now, so close she could get sauced from the whiskey fumes pouring off him. He put a hand on each of her shoulders to steady himself. "How much are you charging?" he said. At least that's what it sounded like, as half the consonants were missing. Over his shoulder, Katherine saw another man step onto the boardwalk. Tall, sandy blond hair, sharp features, an oblong birthmark across his cheek. Bingo.

"You can't afford me. Beat it." Katherine blew smoke in the drunk man's face as she spoke. He pushed himself off her shoulders and stumbled away, cursing her. She tossed her hair and stuck out her chest in the direction of the birthmarked man; hopefully he liked redheads. He noticed her and his eyes drank in her form as he approached.

"Looking for some company?" She angled out her hips to accentuate her curves, beads on her dress shimmering in the light.

"If a pretty gal like you is offering, I can't turn you down." He leaned in, his hand on the brick behind her, trapping her against the wall.

"Wanna do this down the alley?" Katherine flicked away her cigarette. The ember glowed on the cobblestone, then faded to ash.

"Wherever you want, dollface." His lips hovered by her ear, making the hairs on the nape of her neck stand at attention. He moved closer, pressing his body into hers. His closeness disgusted her, but she swallowed her disdain. At least the plan was working.

She pushed him back to arm's length, then beckoned him toward the recesses of the shadows, away from the harbor lights. He followed a few paces behind her, and she listened for any sign of trouble. Between his footsteps, she heard a click that didn't belong. She glanced back.

He had flipped open a knife.

She kept her pace steady, an attempt to demonstrate she had not noticed the weapon. If he believed he had the upper hand, she had a better chance of completing her mission. He quickened his steps and caught up to her, threw his arm around her neck, and pressed the blade against her throat. But he'd underestimated her strength just as she hoped he would. She grabbed his wrist and twisted the knife away. He dropped the blade and cried out in pain as her nails dug into his flesh. She hauled him around, spun his arm behind him, and kicked the back of his knee. He collapsed into the grit of the alleyway.

"Officer Katherine Dell with the Nolaton City Police. You're under arrest." She dug into her coat pocket and took out her handcuffs. Officer Henry Williams and Detective Crenshaw ran to her from the shadows.

"Good work, Dell." Williams let out a laugh and ran his fingers through his hair.

"Thanks, Williams." She took the compliment, though his tone rang with surprise. He must have underestimated her strength as well.

"Why don't you head home, Dell? You need your beauty rest." Detective Crenshaw, the lead on this investigation, smirked at her.

Katherine scowled at him. There was plenty of work left to be done, and he wanted to send her home? "But don't you need—"

"We can get your report tomorrow."

"But I can help—"

"Do you really want to go to the station wearing that, sweetheart?" Crenshaw motioned toward her dress and rolled stockings. He had a point. It would look ridiculous to her fellow officers, even those who were aware of this plan.

Williams gestured to her heavy makeup. "Yeah, some of the guys are scared of clowns." He grinned at his own joke.

Katherine rolled her eyes. Williams's vanity was only outdone by his arrogance, and he always had to be the center of attention. Based on his stories, the local floozies fell for his charms, though Katherine could never figure out how they could be so dense. Sure, Williams was a good-looking man — tall, broad-shouldered, well-built, chestnut hair that was always in perfectly in place, big hazel eyes, and flawless olive skin. Looks were the only point in his favor, though. He was loud, rude, and painfully obnoxious.

"You're just jealous, Williams. Next time you can play the alley cat. I'll even let you borrow my dress." She gave him a little wink.

He snorted in return. "Are you kidding me? The whole city would flock down here to get a piece of this." He tapped his chest as if showcasing the merchandise. "There would be riots in the streets."

Katherine shook her head, and though she tried to suppress it, a smile crept onto her face. She turned her attention away from Williams and back to Crenshaw. "I'll go wash off this layer of paint. Try to get some beauty rest yourself; you need it more than I do." She turned on her heel and sauntered toward the boardwalk.

The police car she had arrived in was parked a few blocks away, and as she made her way toward it, disappointment settled over her. When would the men on the force see her worth? Would she ever be given the chance to run her own cases? She contemplated the unfairness of it all on her way home to the arts district.

Katherine walked up the crumbling concrete stairs to her apartment, grateful that none of the neighbors would be awake to see her provocative appearance.

Her home hadn't changed much since she had first moved to the city ten years ago. A crystal lamp sat on her bedside table, and sheer curtains covered her windows. Most of the flat surfaces were bare except for a thick layer of dust and a browning house plant. Flies congregated near her kitchen sink, nibbling on the crumbs on her dirty dishes. A pile of laundry had built up in the corner of her bedroom, and she peeled off her dress and threw it carelessly on top. It was a far cry from the orderly home she had grown up in.

As a girl, she had lived in Lavendale, a three-hour drive up the coast from Nolaton. Her parents still lived there, in a lavish house beside the ocean. Lavendale was a lovely town, but not nearly as exciting as Nolaton. Her parents had often brought her to the big city on weekends to enjoy the cuisine, the shopping, and Katherine's favorite: the theater scene.

Photos hung on the wall of her bedroom. She fixated on the oldest one — her at age seven, cheeks splattered with freckles and missing her front teeth. Standing with her parents outside The Regal Theater, a performance arts center with a focus on classical ballet.

Katherine had studied ballet as a girl; her parents had insisted she become well-versed in arts and culture. She'd learned how to play the piano, and became nearly fluent in French, but as she got older, music and language lessons had fallen by the wayside. Dance inflamed her passion. Her parents wanted her to settle down and marry a man with good prospects, but Katherine couldn't contain herself to that.

Ten years ago, at the age of eighteen, she had informed her parents that she would be moving to Nolaton to pursue her dreams of becoming a professional dancer. They were aghast, but Katherine reveled in the irony. If they hadn't pushed her into ballet to begin with, she would not have found her calling. She had packed her things and left the comfort of her hometown, and never looked back. After a few months of waiting tables by day and auditioning at night, she landed a contract with The Regal Theater.

Though she loved dancing, she'd had to give it up. After the tragedy she suffered, police work took precedence. The stage still called, but justice screamed louder. The people of Nolaton deserved a safe city, and Katherine had decided that she would rather spend her life making sure they had it.

Headlights shined through her window as cars passed by, and people shouted at each other on the street below. She was often woken up by drunken shouting from the theatergoers frequenting the nearby bars after a show. Annoying as it was, she couldn't be too upset; she and her girlfriends used to go out drinking and dancing at all hours, at the speakeasies before Prohibition had been repealed. These folks were just having a little fun.

She slipped on her softest pajamas. The cotton graced her skin, soothing the places where her too-tight dress had dug in. She stepped over to her bathroom sink. Rust crept from the faucet, the stain growing larger with each passing month. It would be simple enough to scrub it away, but Katherine's energy was running low. She washed off her makeup and rubbed cream into her pale skin; the sea air had left it dry. It felt good to be herself again. She rolled her hair and clipped each curl at the base of her neck.

A murderer slept behind bars tonight thanks to her efforts. Why, then, did her heart sit empty in her chest? Crenshaw would get the credit since he was the detective on the case. Williams would get a pat on the back for his help with the sting. Katherine's efforts, as always, would be dismissed. That didn't matter, though. She hadn't become a police officer for the recognition. She'd done it to accomplish exactly what she had done tonight — to get murderers off the street. To make sure no one else had to carry the pain of losing a loved one.

She sat down on her bed, staring at the ring in the dish on her nightstand — a massive oval ruby, Katherine's favorite gemstone, with a smattering of diamonds on either side set in gold. She'd had to take it off tonight; it could have scared away their target. For a moment, she considered leaving it off altogether, but that didn't feel right. When she accepted the ring, she promised to wear it forever, a symbol of her devotion to the man she loved. She placed it on the ring finger of her left hand. The ruby gleamed up at her.

She twisted the ring so the ruby faced her palm. Katherine preferred to wear it backward so it looked like a simple gold band — not nearly as eye-catching that way. Wearing expensive jewelry in the city meant getting robbed. Some women wanted flashy engagement rings to show off to their friends, and Katherine understood the temptation, but the display wasn't worth the risk. She cared more about the man who had given it to her than the gem itself. Her heart fell as she thought of Joey. He should be here, keeping her warm. Instead, he lay buried in the cemetery.

She turned off the light and pulled her quilt over her shoulders. Her eyes floated shut, but sleep escaped her. She caressed the pillow on the cold side of the bed. The weight of Joey's absence sank into her chest like an empty vase, hollow and heavy.

Shrieking laughter floated up to her window from the sidewalk below. Light flooded the room again as she pulled the chain on her lamp. The noise outside died down, yet Katherine still could not relax. She threw her blankets off and knelt at the side of her bed. Her scrapbook was just within reach under the mattress; she pulled it out and flipped through a few pages. Newspaper articles were haphazardly pasted to each page, highlighting the crimes of Nolaton's most prolific murderer.

She sat cross-legged with the book on her lap, the hardwood floor cooling her bare calves. She had devoted each page to a different victim, and the book was jammed full. Forty or fifty victims that she knew of, starting fifteen years ago. That meant that the Spider was killing three people per year, on average — some years only one or two, some years five or six. It was enough for a pattern to emerge, but too sporadic to know with any certainty when the Spider's next strike would come. Katherine opened to a page in the middle.

Alice Agatha Thurgood. Gambling addict. Found dead near the casino she frequented. Stabbed through the abdomen. An opal necklace she had worn every day was missing, as was her pocketbook. Katherine flipped the page again.

Gabriel Lawrence Perkins. Bartender who claimed he won the lottery. Shot through the head, found inside the car he had purchased with his winnings. His gold watch was absent from his wrist and no wallet was found on him. Next page.

Arthur Reginald Fitzgerald. Stockbroker who lost everything in the Black Tuesday crash of '29 suddenly had enough money for a nice vacation. Found in the park with his throat slit. His new Italian leather shoes were gone as well as his billfold.

Her colleagues thought Katherine was crazy for believing the rumors. The higher-ups on the force saw these murders as unconnected random events in a crime-riddled city. They were so similar — bodies found out in the open, an expensive trinket missing from each victim — but that alone wasn't much of a tell. Lots of murders happened in the city, and surely some of the killers would rob the bodies and then skip town.

Katherine understood their doubts, but she held on to her hunch, and with good reason. Of all the murderers Katherine wanted to put away, this perpetrator was top of the list.

The media had been obsessed with the rumors about the infamous hitman called "the Spider" when Katherine had first moved to Nolaton in 1924. The papers speculated about different murder cases, trying to forge connections between them.

The strangest part about the newspaper reports was the interviews that would surface with people close to the victims. They would report that the victim had acted strangely for weeks or months before their deaths, that they complained about being followed by two similar-looking men. The interviews described them the same way; they always wore dark gray suits and lurked in the shadows, earning them a nickname — the Gray Suits. As soon as the victim was killed, the Gray Suits would disappear.

Katherine had been curious about the reports, but her new theater friends in the city dismissed her concerns. They'd said it was just a story to scare folks into staying home at night, that the crimes were probably muggings gone wrong. In the face of the pressure, Katherine had decided to dismiss it too. That is, until she saw the men in gray following Joey.

Her ruby twinkled in the lamplight as she flipped to the next page in her scrapbook. The edges of this leaf were soft and crinkled, much more so than the others. Joseph Robert Callaghan, a poor boy who bought a lavish engagement ring. Found outside the theater with a bullet lodged in his chest. His hat, his favorite hat, missing. The gray homburg with the purple liner that he wore every day. The hat that belonged to his father. No one would have mugged him for his ragged old hat.

Katherine shut the book and hugged it to her heart. Guilt flooded her. Joey must have gotten mixed up in a bad crowd and borrowed money from the wrong people to buy her ring. Then when he couldn't pay the debt, the Spider struck. If she had never met him, never loved him, maybe he would still be alive.

Chapter Two

Officer Henry Williams walked into the station lobby, slicking his pomaded hair back. Though he had gotten home late at night after the sting with Crenshaw, he'd made the time to press his shirt and shine his shoes. He needed to look sharp any time he wore the uniform, but especially today. This afternoon was the big parade celebrating the founding of Nolaton City and several officers from their precinct would be marching, including Henry. It would be a good day, seeing the people of Nolaton come together.

His smile faded when Officer Katherine Dell entered the lobby. All the guys at the station liked Henry; they'd laugh at his jokes and listen to his stories. Dell, on the other hand, treated him like a stray cat — a nuisance to be shooed away. She always had a sour expression on her face, like she was biting into a bad piece of grapefruit. Now, her pinched mouth scowled at him. Her dark eyes narrowed in his direction. She brushed a frizzy red curl out of her face.

"Williams." Dell gave him a quick nod.

"Dell," he replied with his own tense nod.

Dell pushed past him and hurried to the stairs. Henry chuckled to himself. Why not have a little fun with her? He followed her, picking up speed until he got to the stairs just behind her. She was only a few paces ahead, glaring backward in his direction every few steps, and he took the stairs two at a time to get ahead of her. She took her last stair, then quickened her pace down the hallway.

They were striding shoulder to shoulder, marching as quickly as they could without breaking into a run. She took the lead for a second, but Henry turned into the break room, cutting her off. He dug through the cabinets and found what he was after. He held up a bright red coffee cup with a rush of victory.

Dell stomped in after him and balled up her fists. "That's my cup."

Henry pretended to inspect it inside and out. "I don't see your name on it."

"It's the one I always use."

"Why? Because it matches your hair?"

"Give it to me." She reached for the cup, swiping at it like an animal. Henry was half a foot taller and he held his arm straight above his head, keeping the cup out of Dell's reach.

"Give me that cup!" Dell jumped in the air for it.

Henry backed away, still holding the cup aloft and laughing at the spectacle Dell made of herself. With a low growl, Dell burst onto her tiptoes and got her hand on the cup. Williams did not let go. She tried to pry his fingers loose, but he kept his grip.

"If it isn't my two favorite officers," said a voice behind them. They both froze. Lieutenant Robert McAlister leaned on his cane in the doorway, and his stare put fear into Henry.

Dell relinquished the cup with a huff.

Henry straightened up, clicked his heels together, and pressed his shoulders back. "Hello, sir," he said in his sweetest timbre.

"Are you done boxing each other for the heavyweight title?" McAlister glared at Dell, then Henry. Henry gulped, cursing himself for letting the lieutenant see that childish display.

"Sorry, sir," Dell mumbled as her chin dipped down.

McAlister pressed on. "Williams, you still training the new guy?"

"Yes, sir. Peterson's been doing well under my wing. I take every opportunity to show him the ropes." Henry grinned.

"Why don't you work on that instead of your fighting moves."

Henry deflated. He looked at Dell, waiting for McAlister's punishing tone to lash out at her as well, but the lieutenant remained silent. Why would he let Dell off the hook? He must have higher standards for Henry. Maybe that wasn't a bad thing; there was a spot open for another detective on the team. And while every officer in the precinct was vying for the position, the general agreement was that Henry would be given the promotion.

"I hope this won't affect my chances at getting the detective spot," Henry said.

"I'll be making an announcement about that at our meeting on Thursday. In the meantime, I want you to keep assisting Crenshaw with his caseload. Is that something you can handle?"

"Yes, sir," Henry said.

Dell had wandered over to the cabinets while they were talking and grabbed a regular white coffee cup. She poured her coffee. McAlister caught her attention.

"Fix that run in your stockings before the parade, Dell."

"Will do, sir," Dell said, turning red and angling her leg to see the torn patch on the back of her calf.

McAlister went back to his office.

"Will do, sir!" Henry imitated in a high-pitched mocking voice. Dell stuck out her tongue at him. "That wasn't very ladylike," Henry said.

"Enjoy your coffee," Dell said as she took a sip of her own. Henry picked up the coffeepot. Empty. Dell had taken every last drop.

"Hey!" he shouted, and Dell smirked at him as she walked out of the break room.

The city center bustled with life. People from every corner of Nolaton City came out to the party to celebrate the city's founding. Blankets and chairs full of happy families dotted the sidewalk, some still wearing their Sunday best. Kids ran through the closed-off street, fighting with fake swords. An elderly couple shared cotton candy.

The parade was set to start in fifteen minutes. A hand mirror sat on one of the floats, and Henry figured the owner wouldn't mind if he used it. He checked that his hair was still in place, no spinach in his teeth, nothing stuck to his face. He smiled at himself, satisfied with the view.

A woman sauntered by, looking up at him with a coy smile. Henry smiled back — those blonde ringlets and her tight shimmering gown got his attention. She plucked the mirror from his hand and looked at her own reflection. She fluffed her hair, then looked back to Henry and winked. A zap of excitement hit him — the blonde was followed by half a dozen other women, each one as gorgeous as the last. The Miss Nolaton contestants. They gathered next to the glittering parade float for the pageant, waving and blowing kisses to the crowd.

The sight mesmerized Henry. He floated closer to them, hoping to get a phone number or two, but that plan went sour when his brother Benny came around the corner. He had convinced Benny to meet him for the parade, but his mopey face was a reminder that Henry's life was different now. Henry had responsibilities and could no longer run around with any gal who struck his fancy.

"Benny, come on." He waved for his brother to pick up the pace. Benny kicked a piece of litter with each slow and dragging step. Being fourteen was hard for everyone, but especially for Benny.

They grew up on a Midwestern farm, but the dustbowl had desecrated the land. On top of that, both of their parents had passed away. They had two other brothers, but they were both wandering from town to town, smoking reefer and getting into trouble. Benny had nowhere else to go when their mother passed, so Henry took him in. Henry hoped Benny would enjoy the excitement Nolaton had to offer, but he felt trapped in the steel tangle of the city. While Henry was happier in Nolaton, Benny missed the farm and craved the independence that a country life provided.

They'd been having the same argument ever since Benny moved in. Henry had a long list of rules, the first of which was to get an education, but Benny insisted on making his own money now.

Henry's finances had tightened with Benny's arrival. The farm was worthless and the land was auctioned off for next to nothing. Their parents had no savings to leave them. Henry had done fine on his own, but with an extra mouth to feed he was struggling. Benny often brought up the pile of unpaid bills stacked on the kitchen table.

Benny kicked the litter into the street and stared at a shop window. What had him so entranced? Whatever it was, Henry was tempted to buy it; if it would make Benny happy, any price was worth it. He walked over and saw that Benny wasn't staring at an item, but a sign that read "Help Wanted."

"No," Henry said before Benny could speak. "Let's find you a spot to watch the parade."

"I don't want to watch a parade. That's kid stuff." Benny spoke through pursed lips, his changing voice cracking like a needle scraping a warped record.

"You *are* a kid. Come on. It'll be fun. You can make some friends in the city."

"I don't want to make friends. I want a job, and they aren't easy to come by." Benny started toward the shop door, but Henry clapped a hand on his shoulder.

"If you want to help out a few days a week after school, and after your homework is done, then go right ahead and apply." Henry stuck his hands on his hips.

Benny crossed his arms and pushed out his bottom lip exactly the way he had as a toddler. Henry stared at his brother's scrunched face and watery eyes. Seeing him miserable made him feel like a failure, but he knew what was best for Benny.

"You're not dropping out of school, not to be some two-bit shop boy. End of discussion." Henry dropped his hands to his sides. A burning pit of guilt opened inside of him as Benny glared at him.

"Don't pretend like you know how I feel. You get to live the life you want but I'm stuck here, away from everything I wanted." Benny turned his face away. It had only been four months since Ma passed, and the sting hadn't faded for either of them.

"I'm sorry. I know this isn't what you wanted, but you're here now. I'm in charge and I need you to listen to me. You're not getting a job."

"I'm sick of feeling like a burden. I want to help." Benny gave him a hard stare. Henry's frustration subsided, and anguish took its place. Sure, his life got more complicated when his brother moved in, but hearing that he felt like a burden was a stab to the gut. Henry cherished every moment they spent together, even the difficult ones.

"You're not a burden. Far from it. Listen, there's a big promotion coming up at work and I'm sure they're giving it to me. They're gonna make me a detective! Ain't that something? Once I'm making more money, we'll be set. You have nothing to worry about." Henry put his hands on Benny's shoulders. Benny folded his arms. Henry continued, "Remember all those cardboard shacks we passed on the way here? Do you know what those are?"

Rows of makeshift homes had been built in the corner of the park. The structures tipped and tilted, looking like they might collapse at the slightest breeze.

"That's where people who don't have jobs live." Benny's mouth twitched into a confident smile as if he had outsmarted Henry.

"Not exactly. It's a shantytown. People who live there are down on their luck and have nowhere else to go. We've got it better than them, don't we? We've got a roof over our heads, food in our bellies—"

"For how long?"

"You don't have to worry about that. I'll worry about the bills. You go get an education."

"What if I want more out of life than sitting in a classroom?"

"You'll get it after you graduate." Henry checked the time and cursed. "I need to get in line. Meet me in the park after the parade."

Benny kept his arms folded and stared as Henry took his position.

"You can't tell me what to do, Officer. I'm old enough, and I can get a job if I damn well please," Benny shouted. Henry was not going to reward him by reacting. He stared straight ahead. After a few moments, he couldn't help but glance over at Benny. He expected a salty stare in return, but instead, his brother was deep in conversation with a stranger. The man was abnormally tall and thin, almost skeletal. He bent over to whisper in Benny's ear.

Henry almost stepped out of line to intervene, but before he made his move, the last of the officers filled in the gaps. Officer Dell blocked his view with her wild hair. He scoffed and tipped his body forward to peer around her. Benny stood alone. Henry looked around but couldn't see the man anywhere. Given how tall he had been, that seemed odd. Perhaps he'd stepped into one of the shops. The music started, and the line moved forward. Henry checked again. Benny was alone. Henry let the moment go and decided to enjoy the parade.

Sometimes, Nolaton felt cold. People avoided eye contact as they crossed each other's paths. Neighbors got into scuffles over rambunctious pet cats. Drunken disturbances kept people awake. Criminals crept past under his nose.

Today felt different. People smiled as the balloons floated by and clapped for a local dance troupe as they performed through the streets. If every day was like this, his job would be much easier. Then again, he would lose opportunities to prove himself.

He thought of the promotion, imagining a shiny new badge pinned to his chest. McAlister had to pick him. No one else's record compared to his. A smile nearly cracked across his face, but he remembered the lieutenant's words. Look professional and dignified. The city needed to know the police took their jobs seriously. Looking straight ahead, he marched forward with a stoic expression.

A little girl in the crowd squealed and waved as the police passed by, and Dell broke the rules and sent a small wave back to her. The little girl fell into giggles. Henry shook his head. Unprofessional. He hoped McAlister had seen that.

The parade ended in the park. The officers stood at attention near the tree line. Concession stands popped up in a grassy clearing, and kids tugged on their mother's coats, begging for popcorn drizzled with butter or caramel apples that would glue their mouths shut. Henry groaned at the prices. Fifteen cents for a hot dog? They must be out of their minds. He would have to take Benny home to eat. That would be all right — he wouldn't risk getting ketchup on his uniform that way.

A large stage had been built in the center of the park. Mayor Herbert stood in front of it, greeting his constituents with hearty handshakes and his signature belly laugh. The people of Nolaton loved Mayor Herbert. He had been mayor for over twenty years, winning each election in a landslide. His family was one of the wealthiest in America, but while a man like him could stick up his nose at the masses, Mayor Herbert didn't play those elitist games. He was a man of the people, though he certainly enjoyed his wealth — his mansion sprawled over a hill near the ocean, and half of shantytown could fit inside.

McAlister went over to the mayor and whispered, pointing at his watch. The mayor looked surprised, then took to the stage. McAlister waved over the other officers. One by one, they also made their way onto the stage, forming a line shoulder to shoulder behind the mayor.

"Good afternoon, Nolaton!" The mayor's words boomed over the crowd. Though he spoke into a microphone, his voice would have carried without one. "What a lovely parade. It gives me such pride to be the mayor of the greatest city in the world. Seeing our people come together to celebrate the founding of our city is truly terrific.

"I have heard the call of the citizens, and I have delivered on my promise for better infrastructure. Before winter strikes, Nolaton will have a new bridge over the bay. Construction is nearly complete. Be proud, Nolaton! Proud of our hardworking men, and proud of our city.

"Another thing to celebrate: my wife, Daphne, and I are about to celebrate our thirtieth wedding anniversary. Come up here, darling," he said, beckoning a woman with an upturned nose onto the stage. She smiled and waved as she joined him, as though she was still on a parade float. The crowd applauded.

"Now go enjoy this beautiful day in this beautiful city!" said the mayor. The crowd dispersed, forming lines at the food stands or playing games on the grass. A group of city workers attempted to sign up volunteers for various projects: picking up garbage from the streets, tutoring children after school, planting flowers in the park. Every passerby waved them away. Henry was not surprised by the lack of interest. Times were tough, and most people were out for themselves.

Benny might be interested in the planting project, though. One day of volunteering wouldn't hurt his grades and might help him make some friends. Henry looked around for his brother. He saw Officer Martin dump apple cider on himself. Dell, for whatever reason, was talking to the dancers. Where was Benny?

Henry's mind spun with possibilities. Had he run off somewhere? Had that skeletal man done something to him? His breath quickened as a prickling sensation of dread crept across the back of his neck. Henry called out, with his hand cupped to his mouth.

"Benny!"

"I'm right here," Benny said, annoyed. He sulked behind a tree, ignoring the crowd. Henry jogged over to him. Benny hid his face in his hand as if embarrassed by Henry's display. Henry felt another twinge of guilt at his overreaction but was relieved that Benny was safe. However, that skinny man would not leave his mind.

"Hey, who was that fellow you were talking to before the parade?"

Benny bit his lip and stuck his hands in his pockets. Did he not know who Henry was referring to, or was he hiding something? After a long pause, Benny piped up.

"Oh, he was just asking when the parade was gonna start." Benny stared off, refusing to meet Henry's eye, a telltale sign of lying.

"Are you sure? Is there something you need to tell me?"

Benny turned pale and shook his head. Something was off about the situation, but if he pushed Benny to tell the truth, he risked pushing him further away. Maybe the best course of action was to let it go for now and find a better time to approach the subject.

"All right. Let's have some lunch before I head back to the station."

Once McAlister gave the go-ahead for the officers to depart, Henry took Benny home.

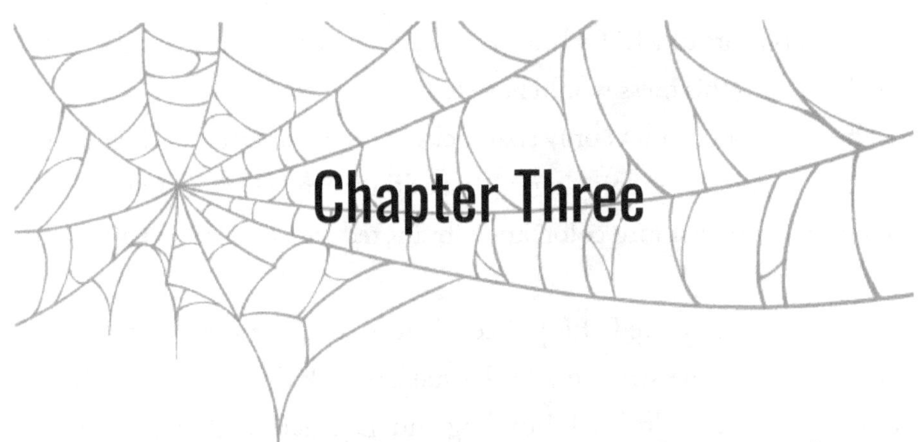

Chapter Three

Two days after the parade, Katherine stood in front of the mirror, fastening the brass buttons of her uniform. The state-issued uniforms only came in men's sizes, and as the only female police officer in her precinct, Katherine was the exception. She had altered the top herself, trimming extra fabric and putting in darts to make the shape more closely conform to her natural curve. She donned a matching skirt that she had made from scratch, and her revolver and a pair of handcuffs dangled from a belt looped around her waist.

Though this was her only day off this week, she couldn't let her work sit unfinished; she had reports to write and filing to do. There was usually no time to take care of that after a day on the beat, so often her unscheduled days wound up full of clerical work. She didn't mind. Going to the station was better than sitting at home alone. Today would be short anyway. She had plans to meet her friend Vera for lunch in a few hours.

She pinned up her hair, wrapping the curls around her finger then sticking them close to her head. If her job would allow her to put it up in a dancer's bun, muscle memory would take over and she'd have her hair up in ten seconds flat. But the style would create a knob that a criminal could grab on to and the vulnerability was not worth the convenience. Though time-consuming, her chosen style was safer. Her thick mane battled the pins, escaping their grasp and flinging them off. She threw up her hands and tossed the remaining pins aside. At least it was all up, though each section was more of a frizzy bump than a curl. Perfect hair would take too much time, so this mess would have to do.

The police station was only six blocks from her apartment. She walked out into the sunshine, enjoying the last of the warm weather. The few trees in the city had burst into color, and vibrant red and gold leaves painted her path.

Skyscrapers engulfed the police station, and the marble-columned museum across the street made the station look diminutive. Katherine stepped inside the old brick building and gave her badge a quick polish before pinning it to her chest. She pranced up the stairs and sat down at her cramped desk.

Crenshaw had taped a note to her typewriter. In his sloppy handwriting, he chastised her for neglecting to type up the report on their sting operation at the docks. Katherine glared at the note, then balled it up and tossed it in the waste bin. She hadn't neglected to do it; it wasn't her job! This type of secretarial work was often dumped on her, yet none of the other officers were treated that way. Williams was the supporting officer on the case, which meant he was supposed to make the report in this instance. Katherine had put herself in danger, used herself as a piece of meat to put their suspect behind bars. The least Williams could do was string a few words together.

Frustrated as she was, however, she saw no point in arguing. Williams wasn't scheduled to work today, and the report wouldn't take long. She might as well get it done so she could move on to tasks that actually belonged to her.

She plunked away at her typewriter, huffing as she tried to ignore the madness around her. Two of her fellow officers bellowed to each other across the station about a stolen car. Katherine did her best to drown them out with her own thoughts. The loud conversation turned to last night's football game. Katherine rolled her eyes but shrugged it off.

She tried to stay focused on her report, but her mind drifted to her bottom desk drawer. Her collection of files called to her, those old cold cases that interested no one but her. The ones that reeked of the Spider. Was there any point in flipping through them again? Of course not. Nothing new had been added in the last few months.

When she first joined the force, she looked through those cases daily. As new files were added to the stack she would pore over them, looking for any connection that could help her solve the murders. Her habit had died down as the years went on, though the material circled her mind constantly — an ever-present specter of Nolaton's dark underbelly.

Tempting as it was to reopen the cases, she did not have the authority. Only a detective could lead a murder investigation, and Katherine considered herself lucky to be on the force at all. To dream of being promoted to detective was downright foolish. And then, even if she was promoted, McAlister would not let her open a cold case without good reason. Her hunches would not suffice. Her only hope was to wait for the Spider to strike again, within their precinct's jurisdiction, and be selected as the supporting officer on the case. Then she could prove the truth behind the rumors. So far, her luck had run dry.

She put the finishing touches on her report just as Mrs. Bobern came by with the mail cart, bumping it into Katherine's elbow as she passed. Mrs. Bobern popped her hand to her mouth. "Sorry, dear!"

"That's all right." Katherine gave a sweet smile. She couldn't blame Mrs. Bobern for bumping into her. Her desk was crammed into a busy corner and other station employees often whipped around too fast and stepped on her toes. Officer Martin had once dropped a bowl of soup into her lap.

"Wait a minute. Did you mix up your schedule? According to this, it's your day off." Mrs. Bobern pointed to Katherine's schedule, which hung on the wall next to her desk. The weekly plan contained a mix of day shifts and night shifts, but today — Tuesday — was blank.

"I just stopped in to get a few things done." Katherine turned back to her typing.

"Well, don't work too hard. A young lady like you should be out enjoying life." Mrs. Bobern drifted away with her mail cart. She wasn't the only one in Katherine's life who made such suggestions. Yes, life was short. Katherine was painfully aware of how short it could be, but it wasn't always easy to find moments of joy. The weight of grief held her down and stole her happiness.

Joey would want her to be happy, but how could she be without him? She vowed to try and have a pleasant day even if it seemed impossible. She owed him that, at least. Katherine got up and gathered her things, then left to meet Vera for lunch.

She opened the station door, and the late October sun hugged her skin. Katherine embraced the sunlight, hoping to hang on to the memory when the warm weather was gone. Winter always snuck up faster than expected. She stepped out of the station into the city streets. On her way to the restaurant, she passed The Ophelia, a theater devoted to Shakespeare and other classic plays. Childhood memories of seeing *A Midsummer Night's Dream* warmed her as much as the sun. The wind picked up a few bits of litter, which frolicked their way across Katherine's feet.

She rounded the corner and saw Café Amore, the place where she and Joey had their first date nine years ago. From the outside, it had looked like a quaint restaurant for the average joe, a brick building with a hand-painted sign. When they had stepped inside, however, they were met with linen tablecloths and fresh flowers in vases. Candles flickered around the dining area and the light bounced off polished silverware. They were seated near the kitchen and the color drained from Joey's face as he opened the menu. Katherine figured out why as she opened her own. Neither of them had realized how high the prices would be.

Katherine had reached across the table and taken Joey's hand. She didn't need the café's expensive lobster or tenderloin steak to be happy. She just wanted to be with him. They had decided to split a slice of apple pie and made fun of their snooty waiter between bites.

Katherine shoved the memory down, pulled herself away from the café, and continued on. Still deep in thought, she bumped into a man in a shabby coat.

"Watch it!" He dusted himself off, and Katherine took a step back.

He was in a line that twisted around the next block, and as Katherine walked farther, she saw that the line ended at a booth run by a church. People entered empty-handed and came out holding loaves of bread wrapped in linen. They cradled them in their coats, trying to hide the bundles from view. No one wanted to be seen taking charity. A sense of helplessness took hold. As a police officer she could make positive changes for the city, but she couldn't ensure everyone went to bed with a full stomach. She shook off her guilt. Nothing could be done about it now. She should enjoy her lunch outing.

She met Vera at Cucina Dolce, a new Italian restaurant by the water. The restaurant was decorated in a winery theme, the walls covered with art deco grapes and bottles. Vera was already there, holding a table for them. Vera was the first friend Katherine had made in Nolaton.

They had auditioned at The Regal on the same afternoon, and though they were both vying for one opening, Katherine found herself drawn to Vera's fun-loving nature. Vera wound up getting the role, but another spot opened within weeks and Katherine landed it. When Katherine showed up on her first day of rehearsal, Vera ran to her, welcoming her with a hug. After rehearsals, they would go to jazz clubs or speakeasies late into the night. Katherine rarely went out anymore, but Vera sure did.

"Katherine! Where have you been?" Vera got up and wrapped her arms around Katherine.

Katherine hugged her back, then checked the time. "I'm only five minutes late."

"I mean in general. I haven't seen you in weeks. You haven't been in class." Vera took a weekly ballet conditioning class near Katherine's apartment and Katherine joined as often as she could, but work had been too busy lately. "You've got to come tomorrow. Maureen will be there. And Phyllis! They miss you."

Katherine hadn't seen Maureen or Phyllis, more friends from her dancer days, in months. She pictured her work schedule and tried to recall today's date. It clicked, and her chest constricted. Grief squeezed her windpipe with unrelenting hands while guilt bubbled behind her eyes. How could she have forgotten? She knew abstractly that it was coming up but hadn't realized the anniversary was tomorrow. The thought of flitting around a ballet class with the weight of it on her chest was awful. She had to visit him.

"I don't know about tomorrow. I have to work at night, and I have plans during the day." Katherine looked away, not making eye contact.

"Come on, it'll be an hour, tops. You can't make time for your old friends?" Vera stuck out her bottom lip in a pout. She had a point. It might be nice to take her mind off things. Friendly faces and a little exercise wouldn't hurt either. She could go to the cemetery afterward.

"All right. I'll be there." She forced a smile.

"Swell!" Vera exclaimed and shook her shoulders with glee.

They were seated next to a large picture window. Outside, several men were constructing the mayor's new bridge. They poured concrete, adding flesh to the steel skeleton that hovered over the bay. It looked like they were putting together a puzzle. Katherine and Vera watched them work for a bit as they caught up. Then Katherine scanned the menu and decided on a mushroom risotto. Vera pointed to the wine list.

"Let's get a bottle." Vera smiled mischievously and Katherine laughed. Perhaps the décor influenced her suggestion, but knowing Vera, she probably would have tempted Katherine even if they weren't surrounded by painted grape vines.

"It's the middle of the day."

"Loosen up, will ya?"

"I don't know…" Katherine had no problem with drinking. When she had first moved to the city, she broke the Prohibition laws quite frequently. That had been before her career change. Once she became a police officer, she had gone years without touching a drop. She had to respect the uniform. Those laws had been revoked last year, but she still felt uncomfortable with a glass in her hand in public.

"Come on, Katherine. You didn't drink with me for how many years? And now you finally can and you're turning me down?" Vera put on her pouty expression again.

"I'll have a glass with you. One glass!"

"Attention everyone. Hell has frozen over." Vera meant it as a joke, but she said it a smidge too loud. A few other tables looked her way.

"At the rate you're going, it'll thaw out quick," Katherine teased her. They both laughed. The waiter came over and took their order, a sweet white for Vera and a rich cabernet for Katherine.

"So, you sent that twit packing?" Katherine asked. Vera's boyfriend of six months had been running around with multiple women behind her back. Her longest relationship had crumbled, and Vera was crushed. She had tried to keep it going, but after a few more weeks of his hijinks, she had ended it.

"I finally came to my senses. I don't know what I was thinking letting him string me along. That cheating bastard. I just hope he's happy with one of those other gals."

"I hope he's miserable." Katherine smirked. Vera cackled.

"Why can't a nice man come along and sweep me off my feet? Is that too much to ask?"

"You'll find someone." Katherine had given this platitude to her friend many times before, but she believed it every time. Vera was beautiful. Her cocoa brown hair spiraled down around her ears, and her voice chimed like a bell. If only she would stop dating shifty men with wandering eyes.

"How about you? Anybody special in your life?" Vera spoke with hesitation. Katherine found the question foolish and insensitive. Vera knew the answer; it hadn't changed in the last five years, and if it had, Vera would be the first to know. Katherine looked down at her left hand, where her upside-down ring graced her finger. "Why do you wear it like that?" Vera spun the ring around, revealing the large ruby. "Look how gorgeous this is. Don't you want to show it off?"

Looking at the ring in its proper position made Katherine nauseated. She undid Vera's adjustment, spinning the gemstone back down toward her palm.

"It's safer this way. Criminals are less likely to hold me at gunpoint over a gold band." Katherine pressed her lips together, trying to hold back tears.

"Is that the real reason?" Vera took Katherine's hand.

Katherine's throat stiffened. The waiter set their wineglasses down and Katherine took a sip, then thought for a moment.

"It's hard to wear it. It's harder to take it off. I don't know how else to explain it," Katherine said, looking into Vera's eyes.

Vera took both of her hands. "Katherine, he's gone. You have to accept—"

An earth-shattering crash shook the table, cutting off the end of Vera's sentence. Outside, half of the bridge had fallen. Chunks of rock and steel plummeted into the water and pounded onto the ground. The workers screamed and ran out of the dust plume to avoid the debris.

Katherine jumped up, while other restaurant-goers clung to their seats. The waiter grabbed the phone on the wall and spoke to the operator. Katherine could barely make out his words over the commotion, but she heard him say "police," "accident," and "right away." Her colleagues were coming, but how long would they take? Katherine looked down at her uniform, then back up at the calamity. People could die while they waited for the on-duty cops. Katherine would not let that happen.

"I'm sorry, Vera. I have to go."

Chapter Four

Katherine ran to the scene. The chaos came to her in fragments. A man with his arm trapped under a fallen beam. Another, knocked unconscious and lying in the silt. One man pulled under the water by debris.

Katherine sprinted to his side, but the man who had been pulled underwater was dragged clear by a colleague. He coughed up water as he crawled onto land.

The man with his arm trapped tried to jerk himself free. Katherine ran to him and tried to lift the beam off him, but she wasn't strong enough on her own.

"Get outta here, lady. It's not safe," a voice called from several yards away. He barreled over to her. Katherine guessed he was the foreman, from his clothes.

"Officer Katherine Dell with the Nolaton City Police." She pointed to her badge. The foreman looked surprised, then snapped back into action.

"Grab that side, I'll get this one." They took hold of the beam and lifted it as high as they could; it only came up a half an inch, but that was enough for the trapped worker to free himself and roll away.

Sirens cut through the air, as police cars and ambulances drove onto the scene. Officer Henry Williams jumped out of his vehicle. He had on a department-issued helmet and chest plate. He surveyed the area, probably looking for the best opportunity to play the hero. Who could he save the most easily, yet the most dramatically? Anything to get commendations in his file.

Instead, his eyes landed on Katherine.

"Dell? What are you doing here?" He ran over to her.

"Same thing you're doing." In her head, she added, *But with better intentions.* Katherine darted to the next injured person.

"You don't have your safety gear!" Williams called after her.

Katherine barely registered his comment. It didn't matter. Gear or not, she was there to help. She ran to the shore where most of the debris had fallen. A young man lay at the water's edge. She hadn't seen him before; the angle of the ground had hidden him from view. A steel pipe protruded from his chest. Blood bubbled from the wound, spilling into the water. His unfocused eyes tensed as his hand swept over the blood. Katherine called for help, pleading to her fellow officers, but no one would listen to her. They were all too preoccupied with their own emergencies.

"You're going to be all right." She looked around for something, anything, that could stop the bleeding. All she had was a handkerchief, hardly enough. She pushed it against his wound, but the blood soaked through in seconds. He opened his mouth to speak, but no words came out. A smaller section of the bridge crumbled above them, and a sharp chunk of cement dropped to smash against Katherine's arm. It carved a gash into her biceps, the pain making her gasp. A man in a long white coat ran over to them, bandages and medical instruments sticking out of his front pocket.

"We need to get him to an ambulance." Katherine kept pressure on the man's injury, her own blood trickling down her arm. The doctor looked between Katherine and the man with the pipe through his chest.

"Ma'am, I don't think there is anything I can do."

"Well, try something! Wrap your bandages around the pipe and..." She looked down at the injured man and watched the light leave his eyes. They rolled back as his last breath escaped him. The doctor ran off without a word, a pragmatic decision to help the survivors. Katherine closed the dead man's eyes, then wiped the blood from her hands onto her skirt. She pushed through the horror and found another person to help.

The next morning, Katherine lay in bed reading the newspaper that had just been delivered. Photos of injured workers covered the front page. In the center was the smiling face of the young man Katherine had tried to help. A blurb featured quotes from those who knew him, including a heartbreaking message from his mother, who must have been the one to submit his photo. This was the worst part of Katherine's job. This was no one's fault; no murderer to catch. It was an accident, plain and simple.

Katherine willed herself to get up, get dressed, and go to ballet class like she had promised Vera. Her body would not cooperate. She flexed her muscles and tried to pull herself up, but a weight crushed her chest. It trapped her, pushing her into the bed. Physically she was fine, besides the cut on her arm, yet a fog of exhaustion held her down, like she was preserved in amber. Her mind would not communicate her desire to move. Instead, it forced wretched thoughts into the forefront of her consciousness.

Why bother getting out of bed? What was the point of carrying on without Joey? Would anyone be that devastated if she were gone? Why not allow the despair to take over, to drag her into death? Wouldn't it be better to shed her physical self and join Joey in the beyond?

Katherine shut her eyes tight in an attempt to reset herself. Why was her own brain attacking her? Why was it rooting for the fog to win?

If anyone knew about her affliction, they would have her institutionalized. Doctors would shave her head and stick wires to her scalp, then shock her with electricity until the demon was exorcised. If that didn't work, they'd lobotomize her and leave her to drool in a padded room.

She couldn't let that happen. Her mind was playing tricks on her, but she had to fight through. Of course she would be missed if she were gone. Vera would be devasted. Her parents would suffer the loss of their only child. Even her colleagues on the force might feel a fleeting sadness. Friends and family would collapse inward, just like she had when Joey died. She could not do that to them. The people of Nolaton needed her too, whether they knew it or not. Murderers wouldn't put themselves behind bars.

She wiggled her toes, then her fingers, until she felt the blood flow through them. She was still alive, whether she liked it or not.

Class was only an hour, then she'd make her stop at the cemetery, and after that she would start her night shift. She willed herself to push through the day. Get up, get dressed, and go. Her feet hit the floor. She threw a dress into her bag along with a satin slip to wear underneath; she would change into it after class. For class, she needed to wear her knee-length tunic. As she pulled her pajamas over her head, she thought of the first time she met Joey.

She was nineteen. The dance company had hired her for the back line. Though she was thrilled to get chosen at all, she had dreamed of a front-and-center lead role.

The theater had been empty. Most of the lights were off. The other girls had gone out for drinks at a local speakeasy. She stood on the stage, trying to master a complicated combination, but the final jump kept throwing her off-balance and onto the stage floor. She would have to contend with the bruises later, but that night she was determined to succeed. Flinging her arms wide, she took to the air, and this time kept her center. At last, she landed on her feet. She threw her arms up in victory. Feeling elated, she went to change.

She flipped on the lights in the dressing room. The other girls had made a mess, but Katherine was able to dig out her street clothes from the pile.

She slipped out of her rehearsal tunic, peeling the damp crêpe from her skin, humming a song from the show as she undressed.

The door flew open. Katherine screamed. A man stood there looking shocked. Katherine covered herself with her hands, curving her body away from the new janitor. He covered his eyes, but in the process, he dropped his mop and the handle hit Katherine square on the head.

He apologized, his arm still wrapped around his eyes while he swung around with the other, grabbing for the mop. Katherine was afraid he would hit her so she handed the mop to him. He swore he didn't see anything, apologized again, then hurled himself out of the room at top speed.

The air had changed. It fizzed like soda pop, like his presence had carbonated her surroundings. She replayed the scene in her head, finding it funnier each time. She dressed, then headed out of the changing room. The swish of a mop drew her backstage. Her head slipped between the split of the curtains.

The janitor was good-looking. Slim, but toned. Dark brown hair, bordering on black. Tan skin. Sweet-faced. Her feet shuffled toward him without a second thought and she introduced herself, startling him in the process. At least he held on to his mop this time. He told her his name was Joey. A pink flush spread across his cheeks and he wouldn't look her in the eye. She told him not to worry. He had given her a great story to tell the gals. He turned an even brighter pink then.

They bantered a bit. He was shy but funny. He joked that all the great fairy tales start with a janitor barging in on the princess. After a few minutes of their playful back-and-forth, Katherine had left him to his work, smiling as she floated away.

The next day, Katherine found a slapped-together bouquet of red roses on her makeup table. They looked suspiciously like the roses that grew on the bushes outside the theater. She unfolded the note next to the vase.

Dear Katherine,

I hope that mop handle didn't hurt you too bad. If it gave you brain damage, maybe you'll let me take you to dinner? Who knows, maybe we'll live happily ever after.

—Joey

Nine years later, Katherine still had the note tucked away in her dresser drawer. She couldn't bear to look at it, but she still remembered every detail. With a sigh, she pulled on her practice togs, threw her coat on overtop, and dragged herself from the apartment. Clouds formed in the sky above. An electric, earthy smell mingled with Nolaton's usual must. The air was thick with the promise of rain, and she had forgotten her umbrella. Was it worth turning around to get it? She blew out a puff of air. She could barely get herself to class. If she went back up, she wouldn't leave. She would have to risk the walk without coverage.

The clouds stayed intact as she pushed the studio door open. Several dancers stretched at the barre. One woman held her leg in the air, her ankle parallel to her ear. Katherine used to be that flexible. Maybe if she came to class more often, she could get that back. A moment later, Vera walked in with Phyllis and Maureen.

"Katherine!" Vera called in her windchime voice, waving her whole arm in the air. Katherine smiled and waved back, only mildly embarrassed. They greeted each other with hugs.

"It's been too long!" Phyllis said. Maureen nodded in agreement.

"I know. It's hard to get away from work." Katherine pushed her lips into a smile.

Vera opened her mouth to protest but was cut off by the instructor whistling to call the class to attention. The room fell silent. Madam Chernoff seemed intimidating to those unfamiliar with her, and Katherine had cowered through her first class many years ago. She'd soon learned that the stern brow and pursed lips were no more than parlor tricks.

"Start in first position." Her voice echoed against the wall of mirrors. Katherine moved in rhythm with the others. It was tough at first; her body was unaccustomed to this movement. As her muscles stretched and flexed, it became easier. Once she warmed up properly, the lethargic fog lifted as her heartbeat quickened and the movement came more easily.

She reached her arms forward then backward. She held her fingers in a gentle curve. Her knees bent then straightened. Moving her body in this way felt like coming home to a hot meal. She twirled and kicked and lunged. A sensation spread through her, like crystals catching light. Joy. Real, unabashed joy.

Madam Chernoff led them in their cooldown stretches, then announced class was over. The dancers pulled towels from their bags to wipe their sweat, then went to the changing room.

Vera smiled at Katherine as they dressed. "That was wonderful, wasn't it?" Vera clipped her stockings to her garters.

"It was exactly what I needed. Thank you for pushing me to be here."

"I'm always happy to push you. Say, you owe me a glass of wine, don't you? Want to stop for one?" Vera playfully shimmied her shoulders as if trying to hypnotize Katherine with the movement.

"I could go for a glass!" Phyllis put on a new layer of lipstick and smacked her lips together to get an even coat. Maureen nodded in agreement as she buttoned up her dress.

"I don't know. I have to work tonight and..." The fog descended over her again. "...and I want to visit him this afternoon." Katherine closed her eyes as a lump formed in her throat. Vera gasped.

"It's today, isn't it?" Vera put her arm around Katherine. "I'm sorry. I forgot. Do you want me to go with you?"

"That's all right." Katherine brushed her off. "I'd like to go alone. I'll walk with you on my way to the trolley."

They changed into their street clothes and headed to a nearby restaurant. The clouds darkened, but no rain fell. Maureen babbled on about her new show and Katherine wanted to give her the attention she deserved, but a voice caught her ear.

"Step right up, folks!" A greasy-haired man in scuffed shoes had set up a folding table down the street. He pulled out a pack of playing cards and laid three facedown on the table. A crowd formed around him while the man shuffled the three cards, holding one up every few seconds to show his audience what it was as he rattled off a rapid-fire patter.

"Step right up! Find the lady with the ruby red heart. She's shuffled up among the spades. Step right up. Double your money back. You, sir! Fancy a chance to make some cash?" He pointed at a portly man in the crowd, who opened his mouth in surprise and took out his wallet. The guy running the game shuffled the three cards. The portly man thought for a moment, then picked the center card.

"It's your lucky day, sir! Queen of hearts. Who's next?" The man pointed at Katherine. "How about you, miss?"

Katherine had seen this hustle a dozen times — a hustler sets up a makeshift casino and lets their accomplice win the first hand. The crowd thinks they have a real chance, but when the hustlers have a mark in front of them, the dealer switches out the winning card for another spade.

She narrowed her eyes.

"Gee, I'd love to. Let me grab my change purse." She pretended to dig in her pockets, acting flustered by the search. "Sorry, gentlemen. I must have left my money at home, but I did find this." She pulled out her police badge. Both of the culprits' jaws dropped.

"Pack it up!" the portly man whispered to the dealer.

"You're lucky I'm off duty. I'll let you go with a warning. If I ever see you out here doing this again, it's a night in jail." Katherine tucked her badge away. The men stumbled out weak apologies as they folded up their table and vanished.

"Katherine, that was incredible!" Phyllis stared at her, open-mouthed and wide-eyed.

Maureen and Vera applauded.

"What do you mean?" Katherine winced at the admiration.

"You just took down a criminal organization, and you're not even on duty." Maureen had a look of reverence.

Katherine stifled a laugh. She had to deal with hustlers like them all the time and it no longer fazed her. To her friends, it must have looked much more dramatic. "I told you it's hard to get away from work."

"It's different from the world of dance, that's for sure. Do you ever miss it?" Maureen asked.

"All the time." The answer popped out before Katherine had a chance to think. It was true. Katherine craved the stage, but work ate up too much time for her to even take a small role on the side.

"I'm sure the company would take you back," Vera said. This wasn't the first time she suggested Katherine switch careers again. It was tempting, but Katherine couldn't give up her badge. Not with all the evil going unchecked in this city.

"I'm sure they would," Katherine spoke with finality.

The ladies said their goodbyes and parted ways. Katherine walked toward the trolley stop. On her way, she passed a cart full of flowers. Katherine dug fifty cents from her pocket and handed it to the woman tightening ribbons around the stems. "I'll take that one, please." She pointed to a bouquet containing roses, lilies, and something wild she couldn't identify. The colors harmonized: burgundy, violet, a touch of sunshine yellow. The beauty of the blooms mocked the city's gray smog.

"For someone special?" The woman wrapped up the flowers. Katherine thought about her answer for a moment. He had been more than special. Joey was a rainstorm on parched earth. A fire on a cold night. The first bite of bread in an empty stomach.

"Yes. For someone special. Thank you." She took her bouquet and walked a few blocks to the trolley.

The ride was a blur of faces getting on and off the car. Katherine's stop came up sooner than she realized, and she stepped off the trolley near the church. Katherine stared up at the darkening clouds passing over it. Jewel-toned stained glass depicted the faces of angels, glowing in the few beams of sunlight that peeked through the clouds. Raindrops began to fall, pelting the angels. She wanted them to assuage her guilt and fear, but the endeavor was fruitless. How could they answer her prayers when their mouths were made of glass?

She walked around the building, her shoes squishing into the wet grass. Row after row of stone markers lay before her. She glided between the tombstones, numbness spreading in her chest. And there it was, his name carved in the small block of cement: Joseph Robert Callaghan. Born September 1, 1907. Died October 24, 1929. A part of Katherine died that day too.

"Hi, Joey," she spoke softly. "I brought these for you. I got all your favorite colors." She laid the flowers next to his name, then knelt down. Mud soaked her legs. Her throat began to swell, and her eyes misted. Through her welling tears, she read his date of death again. Five years to the day. She thought of his smile and his kind eyes, the ones that had instantly drawn her in. She remembered his cackling laugh, an unabashed display of delight. Five years since she had heard it. Five years since his arms had wrapped around her.

Her mind went to the day he proposed — June 12, 1929, the best damn day of her life. She had just returned from an all-day rehearsal, walked into her apartment, and there he was, already on his knee. The little sneak must have picked the lock. Though she was exhausted, she had run to him. Surrounded by vases full of red roses, he held the ring out for her to see. Her joy was cut by confusion. The ruby ring must have cost a fortune. She asked how he could afford it, and he stumbled over his words. When she realized how uncomfortable she made him, she brushed her question away.

It didn't matter. What mattered was the life they would build. She kissed him and said yes, and he slipped the ring onto her finger.

Except, after they got engaged, Joey started disappearing at odd hours. He would miss his shifts at the theater and cancel their dates last minute. His eyes sunk deep in his face and his skin lost its glow. Something had gotten ahold of him. He refused to tell Katherine what he was up to, and even after months of his odd behavior, he apologized and promised it would stop. Yet, he still wouldn't give details.

Not long after that, the Gray Suits seemed to appear wherever Joey went. Katherine saw them lingering outside the theater one night while Joey mopped up. They had gone to pick their wedding cake at a local bakery, and the same men took a table in the back. Joey said she was imagining them. She didn't know if he really couldn't see them, or if he just wanted to push the problem away.

Looking at his grave marker, she took a moment and a few deep breaths, then dried her tears. Her feet began to move away from the grave, each step heavy with mud and grief. Another trolley ride brought her back home.

She entered her apartment and stared at the spot where Joey had knelt when he proposed. A clap of thunder echoed through the apartment. She went to her bedroom and took her scrapbook out from under her bed. His page was easy to find, as its crinkled edges caught against her fingertips. She crawled back into bed with the book. Rain pounded from the sky. She watched the drops run down her window, then stared back at Joey's photo in the newspaper clipping.

Five years since he had been found in an alley in a pool of blood that had poured from his chest. Five years since he had been murdered.

Katherine checked the time. Only a few hours until her shift started. She would have to pull herself together in time to go to the station, but for now she let herself fall apart.

Chapter Five

The next morning, Katherine ached with exhaustion, and not just from yesterday's dance class. An afternoon of crying and a ten-hour shift had left her numb, like her face was made of smoke. She hadn't eaten much but was far from hungry. She made herself eat a piece of bread. It turned to dry dough in her mouth. She churned it through her teeth and forced it down her throat. After a sip of water, she left the apartment.

Lieutenant McAlister would lead the monthly all-staff meeting. Katherine arrived at the station with plenty of time to spare. Her desk, as always, was littered with papers that needed filing, and not all of them were her responsibility. Most of the time it was easier to do the tasks rather than track down the men who dumped them on her. She wanted to get an early start and make as big of a dent as she could in the pile. She had only just picked up a stack to organize when McAlister whistled and called for the meeting to begin. Katherine smacked her papers back down on her desk. Hopefully he would keep this short — just announce that the badge was going to Williams and let everyone get back to work. She shuffled over to the growing crowd in the bullpen and stood in the back.

Katherine hadn't given much thought to the promotion opportunity; she didn't have much of a chance at it. Katherine smirked at the very idea of herself in a suit, barging onto crime scenes and taking charge. The looks she would get if she introduced herself as a detective, a leader on a case! No one would take her seriously. They barely took her seriously as an officer.

The only thing that worried her was how insufferable Williams would be to work for.

The rest of the officers filed in, chatting excitedly about their cases. A few of the detectives whispered to Williams and gave him a thumbs-up in support. Williams nodded to them with a grin that grated on every one of Katherine's nerves. The newest officer on the force, Peterson, leaned over and said something to Williams, but Katherine could not make out the words. Williams laughed, then launched into a story in a much louder voice than was necessary.

He told Peterson about a daring chase that had led to capturing an arsonist who'd set fires in a dozen different buildings. How Williams had leaped from a fire escape and chased the criminal for several blocks before tackling him to the ground and arresting him. Other officers turned to listen, though Williams had bragged about the same damn thing a dozen times before.

Katherine rolled her eyes. That arrest had been what — three years ago? And Williams conveniently left out the fact that the arsonist had been an eighty-year-old who had lost his faculties. The old man thought he was out in the wilderness and needed to light bonfires to survive.

"Let's get started." McAlister tapped his cane on the ground like a gavel. The crowd went quiet. "First off, I want to reiterate that the Volstead Act was repealed almost a year ago. Like it or not, alcohol is legal now. Quit trying to bust up bars and breweries."

Heads turned toward Officer Martin, who often got confused by the laws. Rumor had it that just last week he threatened to have a restaurant shut down for offering a bottle of wine. His wife was so embarrassed that she bought the bottle and drank the whole thing herself.

Crenshaw piped up from the middle of the crowd. "Any news on Romano?"

McAlister heaved an annoyed grunt at the interruption, but answered the question anyway. "For those who aren't aware, we're on the lookout for Tony 'Bones' Romano. He's in cahoots with the Boss, but that's about all we know."

Katherine furrowed her brow. Detectives were privy to information that wasn't shared with low-level officers like herself. She had never heard of this Tony "Bones" Romano guy, though "the Boss" sounded familiar. He was a major player in the criminal underground, but beyond that, she was unclear on the details.

"I'm trying to track Romano's whereabouts, but he keeps slipping through my fingers," Hanson said.

"Probably because he's so damn skinny," Crenshaw said. This elicited a laugh from the detectives, though Katherine didn't get the joke.

"Keep on that and keep me informed. If there are no more pressing matters to discuss, I'd like to talk about this." McAlister motioned to Mrs. Bobern, who handed him a leather box. The officers leaned in to see what was inside, but the lieutenant kept it closed.

"As you all know, I'm looking to bump one of our officers up to detective." McAlister stared at the group. Peterson swiveled around and smiled at Williams, who stood up straighter. "Though most of you are doing fine work, one smart, courageous, dedicated officer has stood out above the crowd. This officer will make our department proud. Congratulations, Dell. You're the Nolaton PD's newest detective."

Open mouths and blinking eyes turned to her. Murmurs mingled with the hum of the radiator. Katherine went blank. She couldn't possibly have heard that correctly.

"You're making me a detective?" Her words came out in squeaks.

"No, I'm making you lead chorus girl. Come up and get your badge." McAlister waved her forward. Katherine floated to the front, tingly and light-headed, but she kept on her feet. Mrs. Bobern seemed to be the only one happy for Katherine, the only smile in a sea of scowls.

Katherine turned toward the lieutenant. She didn't expect a smile from him, as she'd never seen one on his face under any circumstances. Today was no different. Deadpan, he flipped open the box revealing a gleaming brass badge in a style similar to her old one. It said "POLICE" in large letters across the top with the city crest underneath and had the same badge number, but there, curving around the bottom in glorious bold letters, it said "Detective Dell."

"Thank you." She couldn't look McAlister in the eye. Now, with the badge in her hand and standing up in front of all her colleagues, she was frozen. As elated as she was, it didn't feel real, except that she held a detective badge with her name on it.

"Meeting adjourned." McAlister tapped his cane on the floor. The other officers scattered to their desks, grumbling to each other as they went. Katherine stood still. She couldn't keep her eyes off the badge. Detective Dell. She'd have to get used to that.

Detective Dell is on the case. Detective Dell wants answers. Detective—

"Your new office is right here, across from the filing cabinets. Go practice your high kicks." McAlister pointed to an open door. She couldn't stand there all day, could she? Without a word, she walked into the office and shut the door before looking around. All hers. Midnight blue wallpaper striped with gold. Deep crimson carpet. A dark walnut desk with decorative inlays. She sat behind it. *Detective Dell would like to see you in her office.*

She opened and shut the drawers, imagining them filled with her case files. She would have to move everything from her old desk. A smile broke over her face. She would never have to scrunch herself into that cramped corner again. She wouldn't have to listen to the asinine conversations of the other officers as they passed by. *Detective Dell can shut her door and drown out her loudmouth coworkers.* Just as this crossed her mind, she heard a knock. Probably Williams coming to hassle her about getting promoted over him.

"What's the password?" She leaned back in her chair and stuck her feet on the desk.

"Is it 'let me in or you're fired'?" Though his voice was muffled behind the door, that gravelly tone belonged to the lieutenant. Katherine bolted upright and opened the door.

"Good guess." She held the door open for him as he entered the room.

"I wanted to speak to you in private. You were brave when that bridge fell, helping all those people."

"Thank you, sir." Katherine smiled.

"Brave, but stupid." His face somehow became more stern than usual.

"I shouldn't have jumped in like that—" Katherine started, but McAlister interrupted.

"Damn right you shouldn't have. You didn't have your gear. You had no protection, no backup. Hell, you weren't even supposed to be working."

Katherine hung her head, then a thought struck her.

"If you're upset with me, why did you promote me?"

"I won't lie to you, Dell. It was a close call between you and Williams. I'm still not sure I'm making the right choice."

Katherine winced. How close had that call been? "Then why me?"

"When you saw that bridge fall, you did what any decent person would do. It was reckless and you're lucky you didn't wind up in worse condition, but you put the citizens of Nolaton before yourself. That's what a good cop does. That said, this new badge of yours comes with stipulations."

Katherine bit her lip. Could she get comfortable in this new position, or would it be taken away before she had a chance?

"We have rules and procedures around here. They are in place for a reason. You run your cases by the books or I'm bumping you back down. Do you understand me?"

"Yes, sir." Katherine looked at the carpet.

"I'm serious. Don't think I've forgotten why you joined the force in the first place."

An icy stab hit Katherine's chest. They had an unspoken rule never to bring up their shared pain. Katherine didn't like that rule being broken.

McAlister knew how badly she wanted the Spider behind bars, but like most people in the city, he didn't believe there was a hitman to catch, only a string of muggings gone wrong. Yet, he had hired her anyway. Her lips tensed, barricading any words she might say in response. McAlister pressed on.

"I had a hell of a time convincing the chief to hire you in the first place. How do you think he reacted when I wanted to promote you? Prove to him that you can handle this and that you'll stay focused on the facts of your cases. Facts, not hunches."

Katherine kept her eyes down, trying to control her circus of emotions. Moments ago, it was all smiles and glee over her promotion, but now the gravity of her new role sank in. If she stepped out of line, she wouldn't be the only one in trouble. McAlister had vouched for her, and he would get chewed out by the chief, or worse. She would hate for him to get in hot water over her actions. For his sake, she would have to play by the rules.

Chapter Six

Rita Davis slipped on her leather gloves, then turned the doorknob. As Walter promised, the door opened without a fuss. She slid inside and nudged the door shut. He had left it after his shift just like he said he would — no alarms, and no lock to contend with. Her stomach twisted with nerves. No matter how many jobs she pulled, she was always scared of getting caught. If she was lucky, this would be her last heist. Just this one last burglary, then she and Walter could pay off the debt she owed to the Boss, and they would be free from his threats. She glanced at her watch. Already past midnight. No time to dawdle.

Gas lamps in sconces lined the walls. Rita switched on the one closest to her just enough for her to see the jewelry cases. Floor-to-ceiling windows stretched the length of the shop, and now that the light was on, anyone passing by could see inside. She crouched down to stay out of sight, then slithered into the showroom.

She tried to peek inside the cases and remain hidden from the windows but found it impossible. Though she could get the job done faster if she stood, she couldn't risk being seen. Instead, she crawled over to a promising case. She reached up and slid the glass aside and tried to feel around for what she needed, but she couldn't tell through her gloves what she might be touching. She grabbed a few items at random then, like a claw crane game at a carnival, and dragged her hand back.

A square-cut diamond ring, a string of pearls, and an emerald bracelet fell into her lap. Each piece was valuable, but she had to follow orders. The Boss's client had requested only pearls. The ring and bracelet went back into the case, falling haphazardly into the display. She slipped the necklace into her bag.

Rita slinked from case to case, grabbing what she could and returning the unneeded items. A pair of teardrop pearl earrings made the cut, along with a pearl bracelet and a pearl hairpin. She got her hand around something round, too big to be a ring. She tossed her brunette curls out of her eyes to better inspect the item. It was a beautiful brooch, a large pearl surrounded by diamonds. She had never owned anything that nice. After everything she had done for the Boss, the least he could do was let her keep it.

She pinned it to her dress, wishing she could look in a mirror. She would have to take it off before the meeting, though; flaunting her prize in front of him would not be smart. And she would have to sell it in the days to come. She and Walter would need the cash; new lives didn't come cheap. For now, though, she enjoyed the sparkle — that little sample of the upper-crust life that she had never tasted. Her hand climbed up once more and grabbed on to what could have been either a wide bracelet or a watch. That too went in the bag. Satisfied with her haul, Rita slithered back toward the employee entrance, staying low. She shut the door, straightened up, and brushed herself off in the alley.

Her shoes pinched her toes and had carved blisters on her heels. They'd originally belonged to an old roommate, and Rita had taken them when they'd been left behind, never mind that they were a size too small. She took what she could. After a few painful steps, she pulled them off and carried the shoes in her hand. She would have to avoid the ever-present broken glass scattered on Nolaton's streets as she made her way to the Boss's headquarters.

She clutched the bag and shoes to herself as she twisted through the alleyways. The smell of fish wafted toward her on the ocean breeze as she got closer to her destination. She ducked into the shadows and saw the door with the green paint peeling from it, exposing the rust underneath. She put her shoes back on, though her toes were still throbbing, and rapped her knuckles on the door, knocking the code to enter.

The hinges creaked, and the door swung open. The skeletal face of Tony "Bones" Romano hovered in the doorway for a moment before he motioned her inside.

This place always made her shrink. It could have been the concrete floors, or the constant drip of the pipes. Perhaps it was that rusty iron smell. Or it was the Boss sitting at his desk, oiling his revolver, a cigar smoldering in the ashtray next to him. He caught her eye and motioned her over.

"I've been waiting." His eyes burned into hers.

"I'm sorry. I—"

"Dump it." He pointed to the bag. Rita tried to stop her hands from shaking as she tipped the contents out across his desk. The Boss glanced over the pile. He set down the gun and wiped his hands, then took a puff of his cigar. The ash lit only from one side. The Boss pulled it out of his mouth and examined the end, rubbing the stubble on his chin. He snapped his fingers at Tony, his most loyal lackey, and called him by the nickname his sickly appearance had earned. "Bones, matches." The Boss held out his hand expectantly.

Tony fumbled around in his pockets but came up empty. "Sorry, Boss. I don't know where I put them."

"Well, figure it out and make it snappy."

Tony hurried from the room. The Boss set down his cigar and continued polishing the walnut handle of his gun. He squinted up at Rita, also expectantly. She sprang into action, pairing up the earrings and untangling the necklaces.

Tony ran back in, holding a box of matches in the air. He presented them to the Boss with a smile. The Boss snatched them from his hands and lit one, then picked up his cigar and puffed it back to life. Smoke surrounded him in a wreath as he stared at Rita, unblinking.

"What is it?" She tipped her head.

"Nice brooch." The Boss gestured to her chest. Rita froze. That damn pin was still stuck on her. She'd forgotten to take it off. "Ain't that a nice brooch, Tony?"

The skinny man peered at the brooch pinned to Rita's dress. "Very nice, Boss. Very nice."

"Family heirloom." Rita bit her lip. A stupid, obvious lie. She had no family to rely on, let alone anyone in a position to give her an heirloom. If she did, she wouldn't be working for the Boss. She kept her eyes on the pile of pearls, trying to avoid his gaze.

"Odd. It looks brand-new to me. Hey, Green." The Boss whistled. Franklin Green, a wild-eyed man, walked in from the back room. The little hair he had stuck up at odd angles. "Tell me, does that brooch look old or new?"

Green twitched as he rambled his answer. "Brand spankin' new. If I didn't know any better, I'd—"

"Shut your trap." The Boss turned back to Rita. He put the rag down but held on to his gun. "Remember, I can send Green to deliver a message anytime. Tell me the truth."

Rita curled into herself. When the Boss wanted someone dead, he sent Green to deliver the hit to those awful men in gray suits. Those men would then investigate the person and plot the murder with the Boss's hitman. Soon after, the target would turn up dead. Rita glanced down at the brooch. Defeated, she did as she'd been instructed.

"I thought I could keep a little something for myself, seeing as how this will clear my debt." Rita's insides quivered as she gestured toward the hoard spilling across the desk between them.

The Boss sneered, revealing his yellow teeth. "Clear your debt? Honey, this won't even come close. Even with this included…" He flung his massive arm at her and tore the brooch from Rita's chest. Her dress ripped, but she grabbed the piece of torn fabric and covered herself. "…you're a long way away from getting out of the red."

"But…but that doesn't make any sense. How am I still short?" She had been pulling these heists for years, getting extravagant things for the Boss to sell. With all the stuff she'd stolen, she'd got to be in the black by now.

"You think I put every dime I make off you toward your debt? Not to mention the interest. A man's gotta make a profit."

Rita squirmed. She'd thought this was it, that after tonight, she was done. She'd had plans, for her and Walter to go wherever they wanted, where her past wouldn't follow her.

Her eyes filled with tears. "Can you at least tell me how much more I owe you? Or give me some idea of when I can quit?"

"What, you think this is a bank? You think I'm gonna send you a loan statement each month? It's over when I say it's over. You ain't gonna cry, are you?" The Boss puffed on his cigar.

Rita shook her head. Crying would make her look weak, an easy target the moment she stopped being useful. Despite knowing that, she wasn't sure if she could stop herself. Her jaw stiffened as terror bubbled inside of her, and the Boss leaned back in his chair. He unfastened the pin of the brooch and dug out the grit from under his fingernails with it. "You'd pay it off faster if you took bigger gigs."

"How much bigger?" She strained to speak around the lump in her throat. "I've gotten thousands of dollars of stuff for you. How much more are you gonna ask of me?"

The Boss opened his desk drawer and pulled out a slip of paper. "I'll make a deal with you. I got a hefty order from my biggest client, same guy you got these pearls for. If you fill it, you'll pay off a good chunk of what you owe."

Rita read the list. *Landscape painting in ink. Gold statue of a dragon. Three vases. Two tapestries.* What the hell did it mean? Her mind raced, searching for answers. Confusion must have been evident on her face.

The Boss leaned across his desk. "My top client went to the new Ming Dynasty exhibit at the art museum, and he liked what he saw. Decided he had to have some of it for himself. Fortunately, the museum has a job opening right now; I hear they could use a new security guard. I'm sure Walter would like a new job, wouldn't he?" He moved the brooch to his next fingernail.

Rita's face grew hot at the implications. The Boss had come up with this system three years ago and had been running the con with them ever since. Walter would take a job somewhere using a fake last name, leave the door open at the end of the night, and allow Rita to clean the place out. Sure, Walter would get fired, but they couldn't prove he had been involved in anything unseemly — he could claim he simply forgot to lock the door. Then they'd move on to the next heist. Walter would lie about his experience at job interviews, making himself out to be a top candidate. The Boss's lackeys would pretend to be Walter's references and give him glowing reviews or pull a few strings to get him hired. So far, it'd worked, but how long could they keep it up?

"Art museum? Ain't that right across from the police station?" Rita asked. Was that a risk worth taking?

The Boss stared at her. "What's your point?"

"I can't do this. I'll get caught. If I'm arrested again, I'm going away for a long time," Rita rambled while the Boss cleaned under his thumbnail with the brooch pin.

"Then don't get caught."

Don't get caught, huh? Like it was that easy. He's not the one out there risking his neck. He's not the one with a death threat over his head.

Rita's face hardened, and a rock plummeted into her stomach. She needed a new approach. Maybe the best she and Walter could do was survive. It might be time to turn themselves in.

"What if Walter and I are locked up in prison, huh? How would your hitman get us then?"

"You think you're safe in the slammer? That poison can't slip into your food? A bomb can't go off in your cell? You're only safe if I get my items."

Tears burned her face as they poured from her eyes. She flung her hands out and begged for mercy.

"Please don't make me," she gasped out between stilted breaths.

"Enough," he barked. "You don't get to decide what jobs you take. You owe me money, you follow orders. Got it? Until your debt is paid off, I own you."

In one swift move, he grabbed her hand and stabbed the brooch pin into the back of it, the metal grazing her bone as it sunk in. Rita screamed as burning pangs shot up her fingers and forearm. "Tell me what you're gonna do," he said calmly.

"I'm—" The brooch pin was still stuck in her hand, a throbbing heat surrounding the wound. "I'm gonna do what you say."

"Tell me what you're gonna do."

"I'm gonna tell Walter he's gotta get that guard job."

"Is he gonna get the job, Rita? Is his interview gonna be good enough?"

Blood trickled from her wound, filling in the gaps between the diamonds on the brooch. "He's gonna get the job."

"And I'm gonna get my money?"

"You're gonna get your money."

"What happens if I don't get my money?"

"You get the Spi—the Spi—"

"That's right, sweetheart. I send the Spider after you and your little boyfriend. You end your miserable lives as nothing more than flies caught in a web."

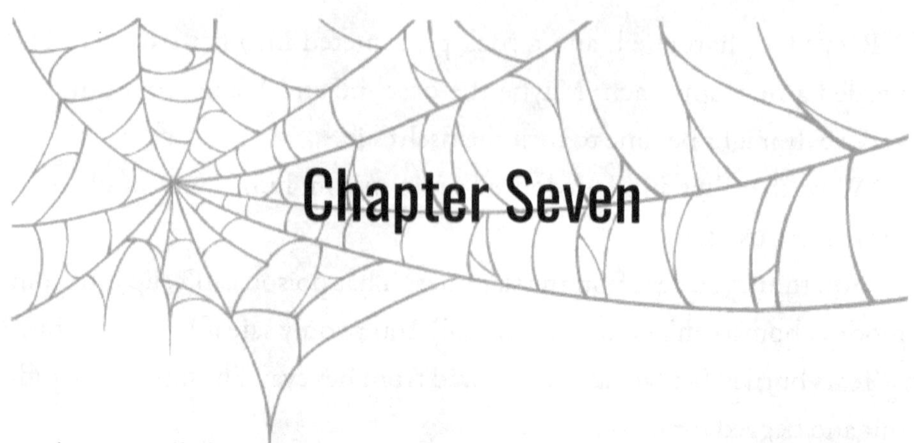

Chapter Seven

Katherine pulled her belongings from her old desk — a half-empty tube of lipstick, cranberry red. A note from the dance company gals wishing her luck at her new job. And, of course, those files from the bottom drawer. She threw her things in a box and carried them to her office.

She was sitting behind her desk and organizing her new drawers when McAlister walked in.

"Ready for your first test?"

Katherine jolted upright in her chair. Was he giving her a case already? *First test.* What would happen if she failed?

"I'm ready for anything." She tried to sound confident, but a waver in her voice betrayed her.

"There was a break-in at Bailey Jewelers, down on Third Avenue. Hanson took the case this morning, but I want you to take over. He's got other priorities. Go grab the file from him when you get a chance."

"Can do."

"You'll have to pick a supporting officer."

Katherine fought the urge to roll her eyes. She couldn't think of a single colleague she wanted on her team. How strange to be on the other side of the decision. An officer, one whose name she couldn't come up with, walked past her office door. For lack of any other option, Katherine pointed to him as he walked by, though she had no intention of actually working with him.

"Keep me posted." With that, McAlister walked out.

Katherine tingled with nervous energy. Her first case. Time to prove that she deserved her badge.

She marched over to Detective Hanson's office. He was scribbling notes in a logbook and didn't seem to notice her. She knocked on the door to get his attention, and he glanced up, then went back to his paper. Annoyed at being ignored, she stepped inside, forgoing an invitation.

"I don't mean to interrupt, but I need one of your case files." Katherine waited for him to respond, but he kept scratching with his pen. His graying temples flexed, and his eyebrows knit together. He'd never been her biggest fan. When Katherine had first been hired, she'd overheard Hanson tell McAlister it was a mistake, that criminals wouldn't take her seriously. He refused to let her work on his cases, and he didn't so much as make eye contact with her. Now here she was on the same level as him, yet the dynamic had not changed.

"McAlister wants me to look into the burglary on Third. He said you have the case file," Katherine said pointedly, hoping that name-dropping the lieutenant would yield results.

Hanson made a show of writing a few more characters, then spun in his seat to face her. "I don't need help, doll. I'll take care of it." He waved her away, but she stayed put.

"It's my assignment." She crossed her arms.

"I'll talk to McAlister about that," Hanson said with a threatening tone. His bottom desk drawer was cracked open, and she spotted file folders inside. A shadow fell across the label, but Katherine squinted to read the title "Jewelry Store — Third Ave." Hanson gave her a few more glances as he worked, probably wondering when she would give up and walk away.

That was fine...if he only thought of her as a ditsy broad, she could at least use it to her advantage.

"What are you working on?" She leaned over Hanson, pretending to look at his notes, but she bent too far and knocked his steaming coffee cup into his lap. She flung her hand across her lips in faked surprise. "Oops!"

Hanson leaped up. "Come on!" With a frustrated groan, he took out his handkerchief and blotted at the mess.

"Sorry! I'll help clean up," Katherine said, keeping up the ruse. She took out her own handkerchief, the one with the lace trim her mother had given her last Christmas. She'd never much cared for it, and now was a perfect time to ruin it. She dabbed up the drops that had hit the floor, and the edge of the drawer. With Hanson focused on his trousers, Katherine slipped the file under her arm.

She continued cleaning until Hanson shouted at her. "Get outta here, you clumsy—"

Katherine never heard what followed "clumsy," as she shot across the precinct to her own office. As she thumbed through the file, it appeared Hanson hadn't done a lick of work on it, only a brief phone call to the store's owner. Sure, he was a busy man and he was in charge of some of their most egregious cases. Still, this jewelry store deserved peace of mind and Hanson wouldn't make it a priority. No wonder McAlister wanted Katherine to take over. She would gladly do the legwork herself.

Yellow rope encircled Bailey Jewelers, obscuring a sign that read "Closed until Further Notice." Katherine snorted out a laugh. Was the sign really necessary? Most people would get shooed away by the mean-looking beat cops protecting the area and take the hint. The key to the shop was in the file folder she'd swiped from Hanson, and Katherine unlocked the door. Though sunlight streamed through the windows, she flicked on her flashlight to be sure no clues were lurking in the shadows.

For a place that had just been robbed, it looked, well…normal. She didn't see any of the usual signs of a robbery — no cut locks, broken cases, or window glass strewn on the floor. If Katherine didn't know any better, she would swear she was in the wrong shop. Plenty of jewelry remained in the cases; most seemed untouched, even matching the cards next to them. Some pieces had been knocked out of place, but not stolen.

The case closest to the door was in fine condition. Typically that would be the one with the most damage. Katherine made her way to the back of the store, playing her light over the different sections. Odd. Here too valuable pieces had been left behind. She opened the register, amused by the *ding!* it made when the drawer sprang out. The cash register had a few bills in it, another abnormal detail as most thieves would pocket the money. This wasn't an everyday smash and grab by a petty thief. This had been purposeful, premeditated. Maybe the crook had been after something specific.

Katherine stepped behind the counter. She opened the cases and shined her light inside. She took a tub of powder and a soft brush from her pocket. Dipping the brush into the tub, she swirled the bristles over the glass and edges of the cases. The ridges of a fingerprint would stick to the powder, if there were any. She found none that raised her suspicions. Nothing on the register, or the doorknob. The thief was clever.

She checked the list of stolen items. Bracelets, necklaces, rings, brooches. Why had the thief left so many items behind? There must have been a method behind what was taken. Katherine read the placards again. This time, a pattern emerged. Diamonds, emeralds, and sapphires all sat in their cases. The pearls, however, were gone.

The lock on the front door was intact, so the thief must have broken in through the back. She shined her light on the doorknob and inspected the mechanism. Odd. No sign of forced entry.

She walked into the back office. The owner, Sigmund Bailey, kept it tidy. He had a picture of his family on his desk, all well-dressed with dignified expressions. Bailey sported a thin mustache and shiny shoes. His wife had long blonde hair, each curl pinned up and piled on her head. Their young son looked like a smaller copy of his father, sans mustache.

Katherine opened his desk drawers. She pulled out file after file, careful not to disturb what appeared to be a rigid method of organization, but found nothing helpful. After putting them away exactly as she found them, she moved on to the next drawer. It contained records from the night of the break-in. Katherine read over the work schedule for the week. Apparently, Bailey only hired men, unless his female employees happened to be named Michael or David. Katherine read the name of the man who had closed up shop last night, Walter Smith.

Walter had filled out his closing checklist, something it seemed employees were required to do every night, given the stack of them that filled the drawer. Walter's didn't look any different than the others. Dust the lamps — check. Clean the glass — check. Vacuum the floor — check. About thirty more cleaning tasks followed, all with checkmarks next to them. Lock the jewelry cases — check. Lock front and back doors — check.

But he couldn't have. The lamps were dust-free, true, and the glass was shiny and devoid of fingerprints or smears, but the condition of the doors proved that he couldn't have locked them before the burglar struck. Perhaps this Walter fellow hadn't locked up. Perhaps he completed his checklist after stuffing his pockets with valuables. He hadn't worked there long, only a week. Maybe he'd taken the job there just to rob the place.

Katherine took one last look around. She paced the back halls and behind the counters, looking for anything out of place. Satisfied with her investigation, she decided to get back to the precinct. Her finger hit the switch to turn off her flashlight, but as she did so something caught her eye and she flicked it back on. A curly brown hair about ten inches long lay coiled on the carpet.

Strange. She bent down behind the register and moved her flashlight closer. The shop was surgically clean, and Walter had supposedly vacuumed during closing, so it couldn't have been there long. Katherine didn't suppose Michael, David, or Walter had hair like that. From the photo she knew Sigmund Bailey had tightly cropped short hair, so he didn't fit the description. It couldn't belong to his blonde wife. A customer, maybe, but how did it get all the way back there? Katherine picked the hair up and pocketed it. She would have to talk to Bailey. Maybe he could shed some light on the situation.

Bailey Jewelers reopened the next day. Katherine had called to let them know the police had concluded their search and arranged a meeting with the owner.

After perusing her closet that morning, she realized she didn't have anything appropriate to wear. Now that Katherine had been promoted to detective, she needed to dress the part — her new role called for smart skirts and blouses, no more brass-buttoned uniforms. She walked to a local shop specializing in women's clothing. Next door was a shop that sold menswear, with hats on display in the window. A gray homburg sat on a mannequin head. Katherine's heart sank as memories streamed through her.

She'd tried to buy a new hat for Joey, but he'd refused to get rid of his old one. Despite the fabric rips and loose threads, he wore the same homburg every day. It had belonged to his father, who'd passed away along with Joey's mother when Joey was young. Wearing his hat had made Joey feel connected to the man he could barely remember.

Katherine stared at the hats in the window until the shopkeeper took one from the display for a customer to try on. She swallowed hard to rid herself of the memory, then walked to the women's shop. A bell dinged as she entered.

"Welcome!" The young woman behind the counter had a bubbly nature that made Katherine think of Vera. "Can I help you find anything?"

"I'm looking for something to wear to the office." Katherine glanced around, apprehensive. The store carried a lot of flowered frocks and shirtwaist dresses, trimmed with butterfly sleeves or little capelets. These clothes would look swell for lunch with the gals but would look ridiculous on a working detective. Perhaps she should have picked a different store.

"I have the perfect thing. Wait here." The woman bounced to the back of the shop, then came back holding an elaborate dress made of pink cotton accented with brown seams. It had sleeves that puffed to double their size. Katherine cringed as she imagined running after a criminal, her arms billowing like taffeta parachutes trying to catch the wind.

"Do you have anything simpler?"

"How about this?" The shopgirl held up a turquoise blouse and blazer. A long bow dangled from the neck of the blouse. In Katherine's mind, the imaginary criminal pulled on it, yanking her to the ground.

"Still not quite right. I had something more functional in mind."

"Functional? Aren't you typing all day?" the woman asked, still holding up the blouse and blazer. Katherine wasn't a damned secretary, even if the men at work treated her like one. As proud as she was to get her detective badge, her trepidation lingered. Would anyone take her seriously? Would she be underestimated for her whole career?

"My job is a bit more active than that. I can't have any extra fabric in my way." Katherine took the bow in her hand, highlighting the part that gave her pause.

The shopgirl frowned. "Oh, all right. Well, we have a section in the back you might like. It's not the most glamorous selection, but they are practical..." She led Katherine to a rack of simple suits, and Katherine picked a few to try on. The skirts fit around her legs but left room for her to run. The blazers padded her shoulders but hugged her around her arms. She chose three versions of the same cut: one black, one blue, and one gray with a plaid pattern just for fun. The shop employee's eyes narrowed.

"Are you sure you don't want to jazz these up with some jewelry? A necklace might be a nice touch." The shopgirl showed her a long gold chain. Katherine's fictional perp choked her with it.

"That would get me killed." Katherine smiled as the shopgirl gaped at her. She took another glance around the store and pointed to a black hat with red netting. "I'll take that, though," she said. The young woman rang up Katherine's purchases without a word.

Dressed in her new black suit and hat, Katherine stepped into the jewelry store. The place had transformed overnight. Every piece of jewelry glistened on its proper stand, though the cases looked sparse. It seems the employees had shifted their inventory to cover up the gaps. The man behind the counter polished the glass cases, white gloves on his hands. That must help keep the shop smudge free. His nametag read "David."

"Anything catching your eye, ma'am?" he asked.

Katherine did notice a lovely pair of ruby earrings, but she wasn't here to shop.

"I'm here to see Mr. Bailey. Is he available?" she asked. The employee looked confused by the request. "I'm Offic—I mean, *Detective* Dell. I'm supposed to meet him here to talk about the burglary." The employee looked less confused, but wheels still seemed to be turning in his head. Katherine simply smiled, allowing him to process the information. A female detective. What a concept.

"I'll see if he's ready." David walked to the back. Katherine waited for a moment, and as she lingered a couple came into the shop. Arm in arm, they walked over to a display of wedding rings. Giggling, the young woman pointed toward a platinum-mounted square-cut diamond. Katherine's shoulders sank as she fiddled with her own ring. Hopefully this couple would have better luck than she did.

David came back around. "He'll see you in his office, just back there." He opened the half door that separated the "employees only" area from the store itself.

Katherine followed his lead and peeked into the owner's office. Mr. Bailey had the phone clamped to his ear. His cheeks puffed and his face reddened. He saw Katherine, did a double-take, then waved her in.

"Yes, I'm perfectly aware of that," he said in a clipped British accent, "but the fact of the matter is that I have been a loyal customer for seventeen years and I demand restitution."

Katherine felt out of place, standing awkwardly as he shouted into the receiver. They had arranged to meet at this time; perhaps the call had caught him off guard or taken longer than he'd anticipated.

"Yes, yes, I'm not an imbecile." He let out a grumbling sigh. Katherine busied herself looking at a collection of books perched on a shelf. She skimmed the spines but didn't dare pick one up to read. She got the feeling Mr. Bailey would not appreciate that.

"You've done your inspection. I've given you a detailed list of the stolen items, and I've filed a police report. What more is there to do? I demand to be compensated."

He must be speaking with his insurance company. Mr. Bailey looked up at Katherine and scowled. "Listen, I can't talk now. I have an appointment, but I will call back and I *will* get my payment from you in full, or I *will* get my lawyer involved." He rattled the receiver back onto the hook, then gave his full attention to Katherine. "Now who the devil are you?"

"I'm Detective Dell. I'm here to investigate the burglary." She held her chin up and straightened her spine. A smile broke across her face. It felt good to say those words out loud. Mr. Bailey recoiled as if Katherine had confessed to having leprosy. She deflated.

"I'd rather speak to that man I spoke with the other day. Oh now, what was his name, Sampson or Danson or..." Mr. Bailey trailed off and scoured through the papers on his desk.

Katherine scowled. "It was Detective Hanson you spoke with before—"

"Yes, that's the fellow!"

"—and if he's the one assigned to your case, your insurance company won't pay you a dime."

Mr. Bailey stared at her a moment longer, his lips pursed into a frown. He cocked his head to the side. "You're a woman."

"Good eye." Katherine placed her hands on her hips.

"I want to speak to an officer of the law, not a secretary." He clicked his tongue and shook his head.

Katherine whipped opened her coat to reveal her badge clipped to her blazer. "You are speaking with an officer of the law, Mr. Bailey. I assure you, if you want this investigation done correctly, I'm your gal."

"Well, I, uh. It's quite unusual, but...well. All right, then," Mr. Bailey stuttered. Katherine flipped to a blank page in her notepad and took the little pencil from its holder on the side.

"Whose job was it to close up shop on the night of the burglary?" Katherine already knew the answer but wanted to see Mr. Bailey's reaction for herself.

"Walter Smith," Mr. Bailey spat out the name as if it muddied his mouth. "One of our newer employees."

"So, he hadn't worked here long?" Katherine scribbled down notes.

"He had only been here a week and after the incident I let him go. I couldn't believe what he'd done. He left the back door open, and the jewelry cases unlocked. I can't understand it. I really can't." Mr. Bailey's face turned red again as he recounted the story. His mustache puffed as if it could pop off his lip.

"How do you know he left the back door open?"

"I chastised him the next morning when he had the audacity to show up for his shift. He confessed that he'd forgotten to lock up."

"Did he have much experience in this business? Is it possible he made an innocent mistake?" It seemed highly unlikely, but she wanted to cover her bases.

"Eight years at a jewelry shop a few towns over. At least that's what he told me during his interview and his references confirmed it." Mr. Bailey dug out his interview notes from his drawer. Katherine took the page and read over Walter's extensive list of references. She wrote down Walter's address and phone number in her notebook as well.

"That level of experience was the only reason I took the chance on hiring someone like him." Mr. Bailey looked at her from the side of his eye as if sending a coded message. Katherine searched her mind, but found herself unsure of his meaning. Mr. Bailey caught her uncertainty and grumbled. "Well, you know, someone of his *complexion*. I have high standards for my employees and prefer to hire those of favorable heritage."

Katherine put it together. Mr. Bailey didn't only exclude women — he also kept his staff Caucasian. It seemed like a foolish policy. The police force had integrated a few years prior, and it only made them stronger. But she was there to take his statement, and she was in no position to argue about his policies.

"What did he look like?" Katherine hoped Mr. Bailey would keep his description respectful.

"Medium height and build. Dark hair and eyes."

"Any distinguishing marks or features?"

"He had a mole next to his right eye. Or was it the left? No, it was the right eye."

As Katherine jotted her notes, Mr. Bailey pressed on.

"He knew nothing about the business. He kept asking idiotic questions — like what a cabochon setting is. Can you imagine?" Mr. Bailey scoffed. Katherine had never heard the term herself, but from Mr. Bailey's reaction, she gleaned that someone with years of experience in the jewelry industry should have known. Had Walter forged his references?

Mr. Bailey jumped up and paced the room. "If you ask me, that boy took the pearls himself. Yet the dolts at the insurance company are blaming me — if you can believe it! They seem to think I robbed my own store. They are accusing me of fraud! A respectable businessman like myself would never dream of doing something so lowbrow. The nerve. As soon as I can prove—"

"Mr. Bailey?" Katherine snapped him out of his trance. He took his seat, and the redness faded from his cheeks.

"I apologize. That's no way for a gentleman to act. You can't imagine the stress I'm under." He put his hands to his temples in a gesture of exhaustion.

Katherine rolled her eyes. She had to ask one last question, then she would let him return to his tantrum. She bent down to look him in the eye. "Your theory makes sense, and I think it's worth pursuing. There is one other thing I wanted to ask you. Do any of your employees have curly brown hair?"

"Well, David, who you met out front, has a bit of a curl, doesn't he? But he's one of my finest employees and I hardly think he was involved."

The man up front had a short-cropped cut. Katherine stifled her laughter at the mix-up. "No, no, Mr. Bailey. Long hair, about chin length. Would anyone with hair like that have been behind the register yesterday or the day before?"

"That's odd. I don't know anyone with hair like that. No one who would be behind the counter, at the very least." Mr. Bailey scrunched up his face in thought.

"It's probably nothing. Thank you for your time today and good luck with the insurance company." Usually, this type of interaction would end with a handshake, but most men felt uncomfortable shaking a woman's hand. Mr. Bailey would be no different. She gave him a small nod and left the office.

She paused and gathered her thoughts outside the store. This Walter guy must have lied to get the job. Odds were that he was the thief — it was simple enough to be true. Yet that hair would not leave Katherine's mind. Maybe an employee's wife had hair like that, and it got stuck to his shirt. Or a customer had leaned too far over the counter... For all she really knew, it could have blown in on the wind. McAlister would undoubtedly tell her to forget it, but she couldn't let it go.

A week later, Katherine walked to the station, her feet clomping on the cobblestone. Halloween had come and gone. A group of rambunctious teenagers had smashed jack-o'-lanterns against the station door. Fortunately, they had the foresight to blow out the candles first. Though the building's maintenance crew had cleaned most of the mess, pigeons picked at the remaining chunks of pumpkin. Katherine shooed them away before entering the lobby.

In her office, she ripped off a page in her calendar and chucked it in the wastebasket under her desk. How could it be November already? She hadn't made a lick of progress on her case. Walter remained her top suspect, but she hadn't been able to track him down. His phone number was disconnected, and when she visited the address Bailey had given her for him, she found that the house was merely a shell, an abandoned shack in the middle of town. A neighbor confirmed no one had lived there for years.

She had called around town to see if any pawn shops wound up with the pearls. Her luck ran dry, however. How odd that only pearls were stolen. If Walter only got the job to rob the place, why not take everything he could carry? Maybe he was afraid of taking too much and getting in more trouble than necessary. Or perhaps he thought if he only took a few items,

Mr. Bailey wouldn't notice. That couldn't be right, though. He would have settled all the jewels back into their proper place if he wanted to be inconspicuous. And that would still leave the question of why only pearls went missing.

Katherine had also called the other jewelry stores in Nolaton and the surrounding area, about twenty in total. She thought this may be an ongoing scheme, that Walter pulls the same heist in different shops. None of the owners had heard of Walter Smith, however. Well, two of them had hired other men with the same name, but neither matched her suspect's description. They were both Caucasian and neither had moles near their eyes.

She had looked up criminal records, military records, government employment records, anything that could lead to her suspect. She came across plenty of Walter Smiths, but none were her guy. Who was this fellow, and where was he now? And why, when the place was otherwise spotless, did Katherine find a long brown hair behind the counter?

Her phone rang, and the whirring bell made her jump. She picked up the receiver and greeted her caller.

"Is this Detective Katherine Dell?"

Katherine smiled. She would know that voice anywhere. "Avery Thurgood, as I live and breathe." Her old friend worked as a reporter for the *Nolaton City Gazette*; most of the articles in her scrapbook had been written by him.

"I heard a rumor that a woman on the force got promoted, and I figured there was only one gal they could be talking about."

"The rumors are true, and I couldn't be more thrilled."

Avery's voice lowered, getting somber. "Does this mean you'll be taking on murder cases?"

An uncomfortable tingle buzzed in her abdomen. He wasn't asking the question in a general sense — there was a particular case he was looking to reopen. Katherine rubbed her ruby. She wasn't the only person in Nolaton who had lost a loved one to the Spider.

"I'm not sure. I may be assigned to fresh murder cases once I gain some experience."

"But not cold cases?" Disappointment rang in his voice.

"I can't make any promises. But if I find a way to reopen Alice's case, you'll be the first to know."

Avery sighed, the sound of his breath crackling on the line. "I was hoping for a better answer than that."

Katherine glanced at the Bailey Jewelers file. Her first case, and she had nothing to go on. If she couldn't solve a simple burglary, McAlister would never allow her to reopen a murder investigation. At this rate, he might not even let her keep her detective badge.

"I want justice as badly as you do. For Alice. For Joey. But you know what it's like here. I have to prove myself before I can get that." The line went silent as though the wire had disconnected. Katherine listened for the dial tone but heard Avery heave a sigh instead.

"You've been the only person I could talk to about her death," he stuttered, sounding defeated. "I suppose I thought, since you had more authority now, maybe...I don't know..."

"I understand completely." Katherine had no one to talk to about Joey either; no one wanted to dwell on the topic, especially if she brought up the Spider.

"I'm sorry. I shouldn't burden you with this."

"No apologies necessary. I'm doing everything I can to find her killer. Trust me, Avery. I will not give up."

A long pause followed. Avery broke the silence.

"Say, why don't we get a cup of coffee sometime and catch up?" His jovial tone sounded forced. It wasn't an invitation, more of a signal to end the call. They ended every conversation that way, agreeing to meet for coffee or a bite to eat, and never once following through. Any longer conversation always wound up on the difficult subject of the Spider, and Katherine thought about that enough on her own.

"That sounds swell." They said their goodbyes and ended the call, then Katherine bent over to pull out those old Spider case files from her desk drawer.

"You hear me, Dell?" said a booming voice. Katherine, startled, looked up from the drawer and saw McAlister in the doorway. She needed to get in the habit of closing her door.

"Sorry, sir. I...I was distracted." She smoothed the front of her suit coat in order to look professional. His sudden presence made her nervous.

"I was just asking how your case is going. Anything of interest?"

Katherine shrank into her chair. She hadn't found anything concrete but debated mentioning the hair she'd found at Bailey Jewelers. McAlister might dismiss it as nonsense, but then again, maybe he would offer valuable insight. She gave him the basic details of the case, then decided telling him about the hair was worth the risk.

"There is one thing I found. I don't know if it means anything..." Her head dropped as her confidence faltered.

"What is it?" he asked. She found her strength and told him about the hair.

"I just don't know how it would have gotten there unless the real thief is a brunette woman." Katherine chuckled. She didn't quite believe that herself, but it was possible.

"That's far-fetched," McAlister said, just like Katherine thought he would. "If I were you, I'd keep pursuing this Walter Smith character."

"I'll do my best, sir." Though her best had proved insufficient.

McAlister clicked his cane on the floor as he walked away.

Katherine felt like a puff of smoke dissipating on the breeze. With no clear direction on where to take this case, she might have to mark it unsolved. Her first case, and she was butchering it. She rubbed her temples, trying to refocus. Maybe a cup of coffee would help. She stretched her legs, then walked over to the pot and tipped the dregs into her favorite red mug. She had to find Walter, no matter how much work it took. That's what McAlister wanted her to do — find him, question him, get him to confess, lock him up. Case closed. Katherine took a sip.

The hair kept nagging at her.

There had to be more to it. Mr. Bailey expected his store to be squeaky clean — dusted, polished, vacuumed. Walter had done everything that was asked of him on his closing checklist, except for the locking up part. That hair hadn't appeared out of nowhere, and it couldn't have come from Walter himself. Someone with chin-length brunette curls must have crept in after he left. Maybe Walter wasn't taking the goods himself. Maybe he was leaving the door open for someone else.

But who?

Chapter Eight

Rita stared at the nearby luxury apartments as she walked through Shantytown. The apartments were supposed to provide their tenants a view of Nolaton Park, a green refuge from the concrete and smog. Instead, lopsided structures filled the center of the park providing temporary homes to those who had lost their permanent ones. Out-of-work people had to make camp somewhere, so they built houses out of cardboard, tar, sheet metal — anything they could get their hands on. The grass turned to dirt as more and more folks fell on hard times and had to trample through the park to find themselves somewhere to call home.

The inhabitants of the apartments couldn't have been happy about that, but Rita didn't care about them. Sure, they had to stare at the evidence of poverty, but Rita had to live it. The have-nots tried to make the mud patch as habitable as possible. A man with graying hair sat outside with a bucket of water and a razor. He stared at his reflection in the bucket as he ran the razor down his face, making do without a hot towel or shaving cream. A young woman had tied an old newspaper to a stick and used it as a broom, sweeping the dirt from inside her shack. Their makeshift neighborhood paled in comparison to the shimmer of downtown.

In the heart of the city, signs lit up above the stores and in the windows, advertising things Rita could only dream of. A large billboard in the center of the city featured a woman in a fur coat holding a cigarette in a long, elegant holder. The blinking lights called on the viewer to purchase the same brand of tobacco. Rita wondered what it would be like to see the ad from the luxury apartments, to dig through her pockets and find enough change for a pack of smokes. To be able to choose which brand she would prefer. It seemed absurd. She couldn't even scrape up enough for a loaf of bread. She shook off her thoughts as she and Walter reached the plum tree.

They scrounged for fruit there every morning. This late in the year, most of the plums had rotted or been eaten by the other residents of Shantytown. Way up at the top, however, purple fruits clung on.

"Careful!" Walter called to her, and Rita laughed at him. Every damn morning he worked himself up into a frenzy thinking she would fall, yet she always kept her footing. Even as kids, he would lecture her to be safe.

Rita had been six years old when Walter's family moved to the apartment next to hers. Walter had just turned six as well and he spent most of his time out on the balcony with a book, avoiding his older brother, who liked wrestling better than reading. The outdoor sanctuary hadn't been enough. Neighbor boys would throw sticks and rocks at him, teasing him about his scrawny legs or his fear of bees. Rita liked that Walter was quiet, and the books he read made him fun to talk to. And she liked that he looked different from the other kids; more like her.

Her parents had been penniless immigrants, her mother from Mexico and her father from Scotland. They'd come to this country intending to find a better life, but instead, they'd found each other. Drunken brawls were commonplace in Rita's childhood home, and when her parents tired of leaving bruises on each other, they would turn their fists on Rita. The balcony had been her sanctuary as well.

One breezy summer day, she decided to pay Walter a visit. She stepped onto the top bar and nearly lost her balance. As she waved her arms in frantic circles, Walter had cried out for her to stay safe. The drop from their first-floor flats wouldn't have caused much damage, and Rita found her footing and leaped to him. She knocked him over when she landed, but

Walter hadn't seemed to mind. He'd beamed up at her, arms and legs still splayed from the impact. From then on, they'd been inseparable.

He would read to her, and she would chase off the bullies.

Now, Rita's job was to secure their breakfast. She wound her way up the trunk, curling her bare toes around the smooth bark. She hoisted herself up to the top of the tree and snapped off a luscious piece of fruit.

"Ready?" She held the plum out for Walter and he held out his hands, prepared to catch it. Just as she released it, their neighbor George ran over and knocked Walter out of the way.

"What's the big idea?" Rita dangled from the branch and looked down at the man who had just stolen her boyfriend's food. Walter brushed himself off but kept quiet. His neck disappeared into his shoulders, just like it always did when he wanted to avoid confrontation.

George sneered up at her. He had built his tin home right next to their cardboard one and harassed them daily — he didn't think a white man like him should have to live next to two people he thought of as lesser, no matter they were all in the same pickle. He shook the plum in his fist as he shouted at them both. "This tree doesn't belong to you. You don't have the right to take these away from hard-working people." George took a massive bite from the plum, claiming it as his own.

Rita scowled at him. "This park is public property. We have as much right to it as anyone else. And last I checked, you were just as jobless as the rest of us." Rita swung her body out from the branch and stuck out her tongue at him. George huffed and walked away.

Rita pulled herself back into the middle of the tree and plucked two more plums, then threw them to Walter. This time, he caught them. Rita made her descent, jumping to the ground once she was close enough. Walter handed one to her.

"Why do you have to talk back to him like that?" Walter took a bite of his fruit.

"Why do you let him push you around? He shouldn't treat you that way."

"Well, no. But that doesn't mean we should egg him on. I don't want to make him angry."

Rita bit into her plum. Walter had a point. She suspected the Boss had paid off some of her neighbors to keep an eye on them. Last year they'd been sitting in their shack and discussed running away to Lavendale to live with Walter's brother. The Boss summoned her the next day and reminded her of the consequences if she ran. If George was the one feeding him information, all he had to do was slip a nickel into the nearby payphone and tell the Boss she was disobeying him. If she or Walter tried to leave Nolaton, he would have them killed.

Rita had first worked for the Boss as a teenager. Her parents' drinking got worse, as did their violence, and she was an easy scapegoat, the unwanted bastard child. At sixteen, Rita could no longer handle the beatings. She'd packed a bag and taken the trolley as far as it would take her.

That first night, she'd watched the sun set over the ocean. The temperature had dropped and left Rita shivering. People passed by, avoiding eye contact. They probably assumed she was a vagrant — and maybe they had been right. She had no job and no one to rely on.

Tony had approached her in that alley, promising to lead her to a man who would help her. She followed him almost half a mile, then watched him walk to a rusting green door on an old warehouse. A few moments later, he'd walked out with another man. This man was larger, his broad shoulders spanning twice the width of Tony's, and he called himself the Boss.

The Boss offered to lend her money, enough to get an apartment of her own. All she had to do in return was work off the debt. Like a fool, she had taken the deal. At first the Boss hadn't asked much of her, just delivering messages or making phone calls. Then after a few weeks he prodded her to do more dangerous tasks — robberies and burglaries. She had refused and demanded to know how much more she owed him. She would have rather gotten a real job and paid him back the honest way.

But he wouldn't let her go. He wouldn't tell her the dollar amount and had said if she tried to quit, he would have the Spider kill her. She had heard him order hits before, so she knew he wasn't bluffing. From then on, she was trapped. If she did not pay him what she owed, or if she ever crossed the Nolaton city limits, he would make her pay with her life.

Now, plum juice ran down Rita's arm and broke her out of her memories. Rita and Walter finished their breakfast as they made their way to their slapped-together mess of cardboard and tar. The makeshift structure was barely big enough to fit the two of them and did little to keep out the cold, but it was home.

Walter held open the cardboard flap that served as their door. Rita ducked inside and Walter followed. They didn't have much inside, only a few blankets to sleep on and a bucket for washing. And something new — in the middle of their dirt floor, a rock had been placed on top of a note. Walter picked it up and read it, nodding as he took in the contents.

"I got the job at the museum." The words came out of him like a gust of wind. Walter had interviewed at the museum and presented his forged references, saying he had four years of experience as a guard a few towns over. One of the Boss's lackeys would have taken the phone call from the museum, then delivered the note. Rita's insides twisted. If they could pull off this heist, she'd be that much closer to getting out of the Boss's organization.

Walter let out a heavy sigh. "I know I get nervous every time, but this museum gig really has me sweating. Trying to pull this off right across from police station...I don't know how we're gonna do it."

Rita wrapped her arms around him and kissed his cheek just under that little mole by his eye. Walter deserved better than this. He could have left her when she got tangled up with the Boss's schemes. He could have run off to Lavendale after he graduated high school. But he would not leave her side, no matter how dangerous her situation became.

"You can do so much more with your life," she told him. "You shouldn't have to take these jobs and ruin your reputation. I've been a dead weight for too long. You deserve a good life." She pulled away from him and picked at a loose fingernail until it ripped off and bled. She gasped, shocked by the sting of it, but that was all *she* deserved, loneliness and pain.

Walter scooted closer and took her hand, stopping her from doing any more damage to the torn nail. "That's impossible without you. You're in this trap, sure, but none of it is your fault. We'll get out of it together. Then we'll really start our lives. No more cardboard shacks. We'll stay with my brother in Lavendale until we've saved enough for our own place. We'll get married, have kids. We'll get a big dining room table, set with fancy china and crystal candlesticks." He gave her a playful nudge. She looked into his beautiful brown eyes and fell into the fantasy he was creating.

"I'll fry up pork chops and make mashed potatoes." Rita broke into a smile.

"With extra butter?" Walter returned the expression.

"Of course. And green beans. And great big dinner rolls to soak up the gravy."

"The kids will wolf down every bite. Then we'll have dessert."

"Pecan pie. With ice cream on top." Rita's favorite.

"Then we'll sit by the fire, and I'll read the kids a story."

"As soon as we're out of this trap, we'll show the world what we're capable of."

If only she hadn't been so stupid when she was younger, maybe they'd already have what they dreamed of. She laid her head on his shoulder, wondering if the life they envisioned would ever come true.

Chapter Nine

After Henry had been denied the detective badge, McAlister had requested that he play the support role on the bridge collapse investigation, led by Detective Crenshaw. The consolation prize did little to lift his spirits. He should be leading a case of his own, not taking notes like an office girl.

He and Crenshaw had arrived at the Department of Urban Planning, a dingy building with a musty smell to match. They had a meeting with Victor Barnes, the man in charge of the bridge construction project. Crenshaw knocked on Barnes's office door. A gravelly voice called from inside.

"It's open."

Crenshaw pushed the door wide, and the two men walked into the windowless office. Smoke swirled off of Barnes's cigarette and hung thick in the air. His walls had turned patchy yellow in spots, likely from tobacco stains. Crenshaw shut the door, then sat in the only metal chair across from Barnes's desk while Henry remained standing.

"You're here about the bridge." Barnes said it more as a comment than a question.

"That's right." Crenshaw nodded. Henry took the cue and nodded as well. Even that small participation made him feel somewhat useful, like he wasn't just there for decoration.

"I don't know what the hell happened. Those city council blowhards voted to fund the project, the mayor signed off, then they barely gave us the funding. What were we supposed to do? We had to buy cheap materials. This ain't the first project that's given us trouble. You know the women's prison they built downtown last year? I'm surprised it's still standing. Couldn't even put up a decent guard wall. They got a barbed wire fence around it. Can you believe that?"

"Eh, that ought to hold the gals for now. There's more funding coming, right?" Crenshaw asked.

"That's what they tell me but I haven't seen it yet." Barnes fell into a fit of coughs, then cleared a wad of gunk from his throat. Henry tried not to gag while the department head continued. "Here, I'll show you the account statements for the bridge."

Barnes desk drawer gave an ear-splitting squeak as he flung it open. He held his cigarette between his lips as he grabbed a haphazard stack of files. Wrinkled and torn paper jutted out of the pile. "See for yourselves, gentlemen." Crenshaw gave part of the stack to Henry. He scoured the documents but couldn't find anything out of place.

A knock on the door caught Henry's attention. Barnes groaned and cursed.

"Come in," he said, then mumbled, "I forgot about the damn photo."

Before Henry could ask what he meant, the door flew open revealing Mayor Herbert himself. *Holy moly.* Henry blinked hard. He had seen the mayor speak and heard him on the radio, but never thought he'd have the honor of being in the same room with him. Another man stepped into the room holding a Kodak box camera with a leather strap on top.

"Mr. Barnes! It's a pleasure to see you." Mayor Herbert grabbed Barnes's hand and gave it a violent shake. Ash fell from Barnes's cigarette and landed on the desk, leaving a tiny burn mark. The mayor turned to Crenshaw. "And you must be..."

Crenshaw stood up and set his papers down.

"Detective Crenshaw, sir. It is a privilege to serve the city of Nolaton."

The mayor turned to Henry and extended his hand. Henry threw his stack of papers on the desk and gave the mayor a firm handshake.

"I'm Henry. Uh, Williams. Officer Williams. And it's also my privilege as well to..." Henry let his hand drop and kicked himself for stumbling over his own name. Damn it. His only chance to make a good first impression on the mayor and he blew it.

"Gentlemen, I want to thank you for looking into the terrible tragedy that has befallen our glorious city. I know you will not rest until the citizens get their answer as to why our beautiful bridge fell."

Henry took the chance to redeem himself.

"We won't give up until we find the truth." That sounded pretty good. The mayor needed to know they were taking the case seriously. He was a great man, and this was an awful blow to his legacy. He deserved to know what happened to his pet project.

"I'd like to get a photo with the officers in charge for the evening paper to show the citizens of Nolaton the hard work you're doing."

"Whatever you want, Mayor." Barnes flipped open his pack of cigarettes, pulled one out, and lit it with the end of his last one.

The man with the camera lined them up in front of the desk, Crenshaw and Henry on either side of the mayor. Mayor Herbert adjusted the jacket of his three-piece suit.

"Now, try to look somber." The mayor pasted on a frown and Henry did the same. Crenshaw kept his usual scowl, but it fit the mood. The camera man turned the winding key to get a new section of film in place, then pushed the exposure lever to snap the picture. The flash went off brighter than Henry expected, but the stars quickly cleared from his eyes. The mayor stepped away from the desk and bid the men farewell, then made his way toward the door. Crenshaw pulled a sheet of paper off the chair and showed it to Barnes.

"What's the story behind these cash withdrawals?" Crenshaw pointed to a statement with several negative numbers.

The mayor backtracked, giving Crenshaw a hard stare.

"Cash withdrawals?" The mayor ripped the document from Crenshaw's hand and looked scandalized. Beads of sweat formed on his forehead, and he mopped at them with a monogrammed handkerchief. "Oh, my heavens."

"Everything all right, Mayor?" Crenshaw stood at attention. Henry glanced over the mayor's shoulder to see the offending transactions.

"Well, yes and no. There must have been an accounts-payable mix-up. These transactions must have gone to other projects and been recorded in the wrong ledger. Yes, I'm sure that's what happened. Simple clerical errors with disastrous results. Terribly tragic.

"I'll have words with the Accounting Office." Barnes saluted with his newly lit cigarette as the mayor wandered out of the office.

"We'll have to take these statements to the station and copy out some of the information for our records. We'll get the originals back to you as soon as we can." Crenshaw gathered up the needed papers while Barnes nodded.

"Take what you need."

As they left the urban planning office, Henry looked over at Crenshaw. Did he buy that story? Was this catastrophe really caused by a few accounting mistakes?

"What's your next move, Detective?" Henry tried to keep his tone polite.

Crenshaw shrugged. "You heard the guy. He'll look into it."

"Sure, but doesn't this all seem a little odd? That so much money flowed from one account to another, and nobody noticed? Who messed up this badly?" Henry threw his arms wide.

"Probably a secretary. Mistakes happen." Crenshaw scoffed. "We'll let him sort out where the money went and add that to our report. That's about all we can do."

Henry didn't want to drop the subject, but Crenshaw's tone made it clear that he should. Crenshaw was the detective after all. As much as it pained him to keep his mouth shut, Henry needed to respect Crenshaw's rank.

A few days later, Henry sat at his desk typing up a report. It was an open and shut case — a purse snatcher had grabbed an old woman's bag, tried to run, but got caught in the strap. He'd fallen and knocked himself out on the pavement. Sometimes they made it too easy.

Henry hit the keys a bit harder than he needed to. Peterson sat by his side, watching him work, but for once Henry didn't want the attention. It wasn't Peterson's admiration he was after. Henry had a meeting with McAlister in ten minutes. That was the man he wanted to impress. He had to if he was gonna make it in this city.

He'd moved to Nolaton when he was eighteen. Though he had been raised as a country boy, he hated farm life — the stink of the animals, the dirt, the mud, the bugs. He'd dreamed of getting a high-paying job, becoming a lawyer or stockbroker. Henry wanted to wear a suit and tie to work instead of mud-soaked leather boots and denim. He had no one to vouch for him in Nolaton, and after a few months in the city, barely had a dime to his name. While fellows from better backgrounds were heading to college or landing internships at their uncles' law firms, Henry settled for the police academy. Police officers didn't make much, but there was plenty of room to rise up the ranks.

Now that he had Benny to worry about, Henry had to prove to the lieutenant that he deserved the next promotion. Hell, if he was lucky, he might even convince McAlister to give him Dell's spot. She had to slip up sooner or later.

Henry's phone rang. He checked his watch, noting that he only had a few minutes before his meeting, then picked up the receiver.

"Nolaton City Police, this is Officer Henry Williams."

"Good afternoon, Officer. This is Mrs. Costwell. I'm wondering when we can expect Benny back in class. Poor thing must be awfully sick to be out so long."

A nervous jolt ran through Henry. He didn't know Benny had missed school. He hadn't seen Benny in days but had thought nothing of it. Henry worked odd hours and assumed Benny was home when he was at work. "Benny hasn't been sick, Mrs. Costwell."

"But your note said he was feeling poorly and needed a few days to recover."

"I never sent a note. Exactly how much school has he missed?" Henry tried to keep his volume down. Mrs. Costwell did not deserve his anger. Benny on the other hand...

"I haven't seen him all week. He'll have a terrible time catching up if he misses much more."

"Thank you for calling. I've got to go." He hung up the phone, then picked it back up and dialed home. Henry's mind swirled with dangerous scenarios that his brother could have fallen into. The phone rang once. Then a second time. Then a third. He clutched the receiver so hard his knuckles went white.

"Hello?" said a screechy voice on the end of the line.

"Benny?"

"Henry? Why are you calling?" Benny sounded exhausted.

"Did I wake you up, sleepyhead? Sorry to disturb your afternoon nap. Any particular reason you're not in school?" Henry tapped his foot as he waited for a response. Benny stayed silent. "I have a very important meeting at work, but as soon as it's done, I'm coming home. You stay put." Henry slammed the receiver down.

Henry glanced at his watch again. He was a minute late for his meeting. Damn it. He grabbed a notepad and ran to McAlister's office. The lieutenant sat at his desk, making a show of checking his own watch.

"I'm sorry, sir. I got a phone call." Henry took a seat.

"I don't need excuses. I need you to respect my time," McAlister huffed.

"Sorry, sir." Henry looked down, chagrined.

"Well, don't waste any more of it. You want to know why you didn't get the detective spot, right?"

"Yes, sir. I work hard. I put in extra hours. I'm smart. I'm capable…" The words stumbled out.

"Dell has those qualities too. What makes you special?"

"What makes *her* special?"

"That's not what we're here to discuss. What do you bring to the table?" McAlister folded his hands on his desk.

Henry launched into a speech highlighting his accomplishments, trying to make McAlister see the talent he recognized in himself. "You want to know what I bring to the table? A four-course steak dinner. With the other guys, you're lucky to get a bologna sandwich."

McAlister's mouth nearly twitched into a smile, a sign that the speech convinced him, or at least that his attempt at humor had landed.

"But can you solve a case? If you're in charge, can you bring in a criminal?"

"Of course I can." Henry puffed out his chest. They stared at one another in silence for a moment. A clock ticked on the wall, each click of the second hand grating on Henry's ears.

"Here's what we're gonna do. You're ready for a bigger challenge. Detective Darwood's workload has gotten too heavy. He's been working on this string of apartment burglaries on the east side but can't dedicate the time that the case needs. I want you to take it over."

"A detective level case? And you'll put me in charge?" Henry leaned forward and patted his knees, ready to pounce on the challenge.

"Darwood's done half the work already, but you take the lead from here. Bring in the crook. Show me what you can do."

"Then I get the badge?"

"Then we have another discussion. I'm not taking Dell's promotion away without good reason. She's a smart gal and she can handle more than you'd think."

"What do you mean?" Henry noticed a glint in the lieutenant's eye like he had more to say about Dell but wanted to keep it hidden. That got Henry thinking — what was it that made him so eager to hire the dame in the first place? Before he could pry, McAlister continued on.

"...but I'll level with you. I thought she'd get her case solved quicker than this. If she's not up to snuff, well, I've got to do what's right for the people of Nolaton." McAlister gave Henry a knowing look. Henry grinned, accepting the wordless challenge.

The men shook hands to close out the meeting, and Henry smiled wider as he made his way to the door. As he pushed the door open, he was greeted by the team of detectives. Dell's fiery mane stuck out among the men's cropped hair. Henry pressed his lips together, a determined glimmer in his eye. Soon enough, it would be Henry lining up with the detectives.

Chapter Ten

Katherine scrambled for a notepad then sharpened a pencil, kicking herself for being unprepared. She was so accustomed to ignoring the detective meetings that she'd almost missed it now that she was supposed to be there. As the rest of the team lined up and chatted casually, she darted over to join them. A few of the detectives bored into her with unfriendly stares. Katherine felt like a tacky rug in an otherwise pristine parlor. As she wallowed, Williams left McAlister's office with a stupid grin on his face. Katherine squinted at him. What was he so happy about?

"Gather 'round, men." McAlister pointed to the open space in front of his desk. Katherine figured she was included in "men." The detectives filed into the lieutenant's office and formed a horseshoe around his desk. Katherine found a gap between Hanson and What's-His-Name with the curly mustache and tried to push through but was jostled back. She looked for another spot, but the men stood shoulder to shoulder and wouldn't let her into the line. With a sigh, she resigned herself to a place in the back of the room.

"Tell me what you've been working on. Wallace, you're first." McAlister pointed to him.

Detective Wallace launched into a detailed explanation of a fatal hit and run. He had two major leads and was taking a suspect in for questioning that afternoon. He stood up straight and his voice carried through the room. McAlister nodded his approval. Katherine went numb. Was she supposed to prepare a presentation? Why hadn't McAlister told her? She wished she could crumple herself up and crawl into the air ducts. No one would notice her absence. Detective Something-Or-Other spoke next, his delivery just as flawless as Wallace's. He would be leaving to arrest his suspect right after the meeting.

"Good work. Get that crook pinched." McAlister scanned the room. Katherine hoped his gaze would land anywhere except her.

"Dell, what have you got for us?"

The line parted, giving the detectives a view of Katherine. Every gaze burrowed into her. Katherine bit her lip as she tried to steady her nerves.

"I've been working on the burglary at Bailey Jewelers." Her voice faltered. She wasn't sure what to say.

"And?" Detective Hanson scowled at her. This had been his case originally, and Katherine was making a mess of it.

"And I...I don't have enough evidence to make an arrest yet, but..."

"Keep working on it. Hanson, what have you got?" McAlister was impossible to read. Was he upset with her, or simply moving the meeting along?

"I got a call about a couple of guys prowling around the harbor. One of them fits the description of Tony 'Bones' Romano." Katherine snapped out of her self-pity. She had heard that name before. "I can't say for sure it was him, but I'd like to keep an eye on it."

"I wonder what they're up to this time," one detective said.

"If it was Romano, we need to stay vigilant." McAlister grunted with disgust. Who was this Romano guy and why did the lieutenant find him so repellent?

The other detectives gave their updates, then McAlister dismissed the meeting with the tap of his cane. The men filed out of the office. Katherine tried to step up to McAlister's desk but risked getting trampled. She waited for all the detectives to leave, then got his attention. She started to apologize for her poor performance, but McAlister cut her off.

"Good, you're still here. I want to get you up to speed on Tony Romano. For years he's been working with one of the bigwig crime lords in town. You ever hear of the Boss?"

Katherine nodded.

"He's bad news, involved in pockets of illegal activity all over Nolaton. Been around since the days when Irish mobsters ran Midtown. Ah, you're too young to remember that. Anyway, he's got to have a headquarters somewhere here in town, but we can't figure out where. He's an odd one; sometimes he'll send his guys out to rob high-end places, but they only take certain items. It's never a typical burglary, never the stuff you'd expect to be targeted. It's almost like he's filling custom orders."

"Like my jewelry store case?"

McAlister stared at her, and his eyes went blank. "What do you mean?"

"My thief only stole pearls. They moved other things — there were sapphires and diamonds out of place — but they only took the pearls." Nerves turned to excitement. If her case was related to the biggest crime lord in town, no wonder she hadn't solved it yet. He'd have the resources to keep his people out of sight. But she could do it. Getting McAlister one step closer to the Boss might earn her the right to reopen a cold case.

"I didn't know that. We didn't get any reports of the gang casing Bailey's place, but I suppose they could have slipped under our radar." McAlister rubbed his chin as he contemplated this. "I may have handed you a case you're not ready for."

"I'm ready, sir. I can do this." Katherine's jaw clenched as she braced herself to have her first case ripped away. She couldn't quit now, not after all the work she had put in. McAlister stayed silent. Seconds felt like hours while she waited for his response.

"You don't get it. This guy is dangerous. If you cross him, he makes you pay." McAlister looked down at his cane. Katherine tried to read his expression. A glimpse of fury had flashed in his eyes as he spoke about the

Boss. Fury...but also fear. What made this "Boss" character so dangerous, and why would someone as tough as McAlister be afraid of him?

"If someone that terrifying is roaming the streets of Nolaton, I'll do anything to stop him."

"Don't you dare!" McAlister snapped at her. "Believe me, I'd like nothing more than to see that dirty scoundrel behind bars, but I'm not sending my least-experienced detective after him. He wouldn't think twice about putting a bullet in you."

Katherine scoffed, undeterred by the threat. She could put a bullet in him just as easily. If this man was such a menace, she would be proud to give her life trying to stop him. She held her breath while the lieutenant pondered his next move. How humiliating would it be to have her first case fall out of her hands? The men on the force would never let her live it down.

"Then again, we don't know for sure the Boss was involved in the break-in at Bailey's. I'll let you keep working on it. But if you get a whiff of the Boss's involvement, you tell me that instant, and I'll give it back to Hanson."

McAlister dismissed her, and Katherine sprang to her feet, heading back to her office determined to find answers. If the Boss was as bad he sounded, then there was no question in her mind — he and all his thieving minions needed to be caught.

The trees in Nolaton shed the last of their leaves as the mid-November cold snap hit. Only a few gold specks clung on to the branches. A streak of orange hovered above the horizon but the night sky descended upon it, indigo consuming the remaining rays of sunlight. Katherine stared at the display as she walked to work.

Two weeks had passed since the detective meeting, and still, Katherine did not have her answer. A man named Walter, whereabouts unknown, had left a door open at his workplace. A brunette woman's hair had fallen behind the counter. Pearls had been stolen. No matter what she tried, no new information emerged. She ran a finger over her badge and the smooth brass squeaked beneath her touch. How long would she keep it if she failed to solve her first case? And what were the odds of solving a burglary now that so much time had gone by?

She passed a bistro and did a double-take. A couple sat at an outdoor table drinking port and sharing dessert. They looked just like her parents, but if they were visiting the city, they would have called, wouldn't they? She hadn't seen them since last Christmas; her mother had called months ago to wish her a happy birthday and make sure their check had arrived. Other than that, they hadn't spoken. She approached them, ready for their faces to morph into strangers as she got close. They only became more familiar.

"Mother?" Katherine tried to hide the hurt in her voice. Her mother's face flushed as she looked down and fiddled with her bracelet. "Father?" He grumbled in response.

"What are you doing here, Katherine?" Mother finally looked up at her.

"I should ask you the same question. Why didn't you call?" Her mother and father looked at each other.

"We're just here for the day doing some shopping. I got some lovely new dresses." Her mother unzipped a garment bag and showed off the lace gown hanging inside. "And look what your father got me for our anniversary." Mother showed off a pearl bracelet that hung from her wrist. Katherine gritted her teeth. The bracelet only served as a reminder of her case. It also did little to assuage the hurt.

"You drove three hours to go shopping?"

"Well, of course, dear. The shops up in Lavendale don't have nearly as much variety." She looked Katherine up and down, taking in the clean-cut suit she wore. "Are you meeting someone?" Mother's voice wavered.

"No. These are work clothes."

Father mumbled something under his breath. Katherine ignored him.

"I see. Still working at the police station, I take it?" Mother did her best to sound polite, but Katherine picked up on her mother's implied criticism.

"I'm still a cop. In fact, I just got promoted to detective." Katherine dared to unbury a hope kept deep inside, that her parents would be proud of her career accomplishments. The tingle of self-worth left as quickly as it came when her mother's face twisted in disgust.

"Promoted? Why? Are you running low on funds, dear?" Mother rummaged through her handbag. Her parents used money as a bandage for Katherine's wounds. Sure, it was nice not to wonder how the rent would get paid, but the financial support only drove a wider wedge between them. Money wasn't nearly enough to replace the love she craved.

"You wouldn't have to work if you settled down." Father stuck a bite of carrot cake in his mouth. Katherine glared at him. "It's true," her father said through the thick icing. He swallowed the bite and spoke more clearly. "If you would come with me to my alumni events, I could introduce you to—"

"I'm not interested." Katherine's face grew hot. She started to storm away.

"Wait!" Mother placed a hand on Katherine's arm, and Katherine stopped. Though she dreaded continuing the conversation, she felt guilty ignoring her mother's call. "You're right. We should have called."

Katherine blinked hard at her mother, amazed the pompous woman had admitted to a mistake.

"Why didn't you?" Katherine ached to know the answer. Were they embarrassed to be seen with her?

"We thought you wouldn't want to see us." Mother looked at her husband. Years of unspoken words lingered in the air.

"I want to see you. I only wish I wasn't subjected to a lecture every time."

"We only lecture you because we're concerned about you. This is no life for a young woman of your background." Mother gestured to Katherine's suit.

Katherine smoothed her coat. "It's my life, and I am living it how I want. What's wrong with that?"

"You're not happy, Katherine. It's hard to see you so morose."

"What you want wouldn't make me happy. Life isn't about expensive dresses and wealthy men." Katherine glared at her father. He opened his mouth for a rebuttal, but Mother intervened.

"What would make you happy?" She took Katherine's hand, her touch warmer than expected.

Katherine thawed and contemplated the question. Perhaps she would be happy if her father had kept his classist views to himself all those years ago. Maybe then Joey would still be alive.

Joey's dream had been to go to medical school, but he couldn't afford it. Another mark against him in her father's book. Katherine didn't mind that Joey didn't have two nickels to rub together, but her father had. He wanted her to marry a doctor or a lawyer, someone who would take care of her — he still did. After dinner with her parents one night, Katherine had overheard Joey ask him for permission to propose, but her father had scoffed at the idea. He'd told Joey that without a decent ring, he could forget it.

That night, Joey had tried to end their relationship but Katherine hadn't allowed it. Joey had said he would never be good enough for her. Katherine insisted that was nonsense and begged him to reconsider. Then he'd said that he needed to clear his head and went to a speakeasy.

Katherine never got the full story from him, but something important changed that night. Within weeks, Joey was on his knee in Katherine's apartment holding out the expensive ring. Katherine had asked him countless times how he could afford it, but he'd always dodged the question.

And now she may never know the answer.

"I'm as happy as I'm going to get," Katherine told her mother. She deflated as the truth of her statement sank in; she had to make do with the lonely life she had. Her mother dropped the topic, though sadness radiated from her. They said their farewells and Katherine resumed her journey to the station. Pain resonated in her chest, her heart an empty chasm.

Katherine poured coffee and sat at her desk. She took out the Bailey Jewelers case file and studied her reports yet again. The words scrambled on the page as the fog rolled into her mind. She stared at her ring instead.

Those old Spider case files called to her from their drawer in her new desk, but she resisted the impulse to take them out. If she wanted the chance to work on them, she had to prove herself first. She looked back at the Bailey Jewelers case file and tried to focus.

Hours later, after failing yet again to figure out Walter's whereabouts, movement caught her eye through the window of her office. She snapped out of her trance and stared at the museum across the street. All of its lights were off, and a dim streetlamp offered the only illumination. She switched off her office light to see what caught her attention more clearly. She could barely make out the form, but a shadowy figure stood near the side entrance. The person slid closer to the museum door, which brought her farther into the pool of yellow light. A woman with curly brown hair, the same sort of hair that Katherine found in the jewelry store. The woman opened the museum's side door, which must have been unlocked, then slipped inside the building. Katherine bolted outside.

Chapter Eleven

Rita slid through the museum door. According to Walter, the Ming Dynasty exhibit was through the lobby and to the right. She ran to the spot, the other artifacts in their cases blurring as her focus narrowed. She checked the list. *Landscape painting in ink. Gold statue of a dragon. Three vases. Two tapestries.*

A satchel hung from her shoulder, and she planned to fit as many items inside as she could. She had scavenged a few pieces of cardboard out of a warehouse trash can near shantytown, which she would use to protect the breakables. Walter had done his part — detached the landscape paintings from their heavy gold frames and unlocked the artifacts cabinets.

She moved as swiftly as she could, opening the glass cabinet that held the vases. One depicted a cliff with birds flying overhead. Her fingers coiled around the neck, and she nestled it in the satchel, then propped a piece of cardboard up to it. She chose two more, one with a craggy mountain and the other with a twisting tree. Part of the vases stuck out from the bag no matter which way she placed them. She would have to be careful not to chip the exposed porcelain as she made her way back to headquarters. She tucked the dragon statue on the side of the vases then cradled the paintings and tapestries in the remaining gaps.

She ducked out of the museum, then looked around to make sure the coast was clear. Heat coursed through her belly. Across the street, a door opened and a red-haired woman darted out of the police station. She couldn't be a cop, could she? The streetlamp reflected off the badge pinned to the woman's chest. Damn it.

Rita fled. The woman chased after her, gaining ground. Rita pounded her feet against the pavement, zigzagging through the museum's courtyard. She jumped over leafless bushes. The vases bounced on her hip and nearly fell out of the bag. Rita gasped and steadied them with her hand but kept running.

The cop must not have anticipated Rita's leap. She came to a halt in front of the bushes and ran around the row. Rita careened down the closest alley and headed for the back street. A waitress stuck her head out the back door of a restaurant and threw a bucket full of dirty water onto the concrete. Rita flung herself inside as the door shut, barely avoiding the splash.

"Who the hell are you?" The waitress took a drag from her cigarette. Rita shushed her. Her eyes pleaded for mercy. The waitress rolled her eyes. "Just don't touch anything. The health inspector ain't too keen on strangers roaming the kitchen." She squashed a cockroach with her shoe.

A fist beat on the door. That cop must have seen her slip in.

"What now?" The waitress slogged over to open the door but Rita stuck her hands in front of it, imploring the waitress to ignore the noise. The waitress groaned, grabbed a tray, and made her way to the front of the restaurant.

How long would that cop wait for her? A steady drip fell from the faucet onto a tower of pots and pans. Rita curled up tighter. The bell over the restaurant's front door jingled. Rita could hear the rise and fall of a woman's voice in the front of the restaurant, asking if anyone had seen a brunette. Rita nudged the back door open and slithered out. She ran down the back street toward the harbor with the satchel held against her side. With any luck, the cop hadn't seen her escape.

Rita knocked the new code on the rusting green door. Tony let her in. She panted as she dug the stolen goods from her satchel and set them on his desk. The Boss blew out a puff of cigar smoke and watched her unload the merchandise. Rita's lungs burned from the run and the haze in the air. He picked up each item for inspection and nodded his approval, then stared up at her.

"Good start, but my buyer called a few minutes ago. He wants to add a jade pendant to the order, a birthday gift for his wife."

Rita's guts twisted into knots. He can't change the order last minute. Breaking back into the museum would be damn near impossible. Rita had to make him see reason.

"I almost got caught by a cop. They've probably got the place roped off already. I can't—"

The Boss pounded his fist on the desk, and the vases shook from the impact. Rita grabbed them in turn to steady the motion.

"Not good enough. I'm running a business here. I can't do that if you're not filling my orders." He cracked his knuckles, the popping sound reverberating in the otherwise silent warehouse.

"I can get the pendant, but I need more time. Give me a week and I can try to come up with a plan." Rita couldn't imagine how she would pull it off. After tonight, Walter would be fired so she would have no one to disarm the security system or leave the door unlocked.

The Boss stood up, his hulking form towering over her. "More time? My buyer wants his items *now*. The exhibit is closing in two days. You don't have more time. I am not losing my best client over this. You get me that pendant, or I'm calling in the hit."

Rita went numb. "You said as long as we stay in the city, and do what you say—"

"No, I said as long as I get my money, I'll keep you alive. If you don't fill my orders, how are you gonna pay me back?"

"I...I don't know."

"Get the job done, or I'm sending the Spider. I'll have your little boyfriend killed first so you can feel the sting of losing him. But don't worry. I won't make you suffer long after that."

Rita ran from the warehouse with tears streaming down her face. It would be impossible to break in again; she was sure of it. Yet, she had no choice. She had to try. If she did nothing, Walter would be killed. She'd die too, but that didn't matter. She deserved that fate for getting into debt with that brute to begin with, but Walter...sweet, sensitive Walter...he deserved a happy life in a real house with hot meals and a loving family. All she had given him was heartache and struggle. And danger. If she didn't get that damn pendant, Walter would wind up dead in an alley just like the Spider's other victims.

That cop would almost certainly have the museum locked down by now, but if not, she could sneak back in while the alarms were still disabled. Now that she had dumped the rest of the goods with the Boss, she could take the trolley back and check the premises.

She hopped on a car and rode until the massive, marble-columned building was in sight, then stepped off at the nearest stop. She had to be careful. If that cop was still around, she'd throw Rita in jail. No way she could get the pendant from behind bars and Walter would be killed for sure.

She ducked down an alley a block away from the museum, then peeked out and saw what she feared. Cops set up sawhorses with yellow rope stretched between them. That red-haired woman stood with her hands on her hips, watching as the officers sectioned off the area. A man with a camera took photos of the side door where Rita had entered, then went inside, probably to take photos in the exhibit.

She couldn't go in now, but she would have to come back soon. Odds were stacked against her for miles, but tomorrow night, she would come back, maybe break a window or jimmy a lock and sneak inside. The alarms would go off and she would almost certainly get caught, but she had to try for Walter's sake. For Walter's life.

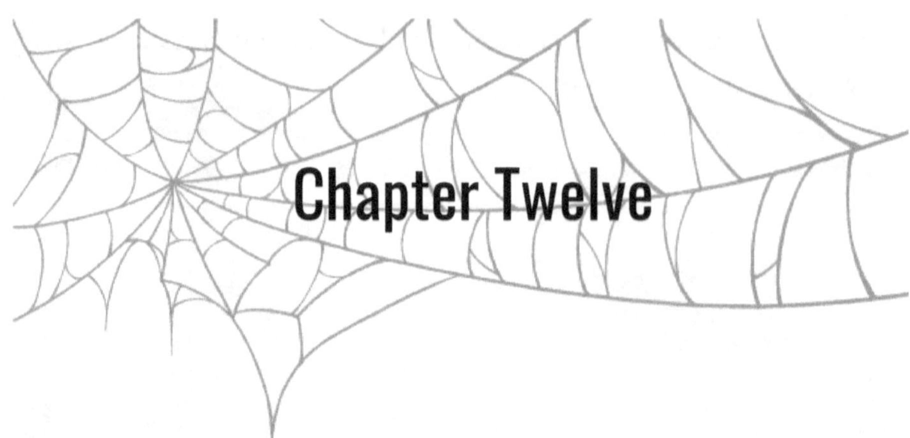

Chapter Twelve

Katherine's mind wheeled with speculation as she walked to the station. The woman who had escaped her clutches last night — could it have been the same woman who'd robbed Bailey Jewelers? She had strolled into the museum without breaking the lock and the alarms had not gone off. Had Walter taken a job there and left the place open, just like he did at the jewelry store?

During their investigation last night, they found that only Ming Dynasty artifacts had been stolen. Was this another of the Boss's orders getting filled? If these thefts were connected, she was one step closer to solving her case. Then again…she might have let her one opportunity to catch the woman slip away. She planted herself outside the station and looked across the street.

The museum stood out as the most grandiose building for a mile, stretching nearly the length of the block. The stone structure had been decorated with vines carved around the edges, and marble columns towered over the street below. Normally visitors in their daytime finery would file in and out through the gold-trimmed doors from open to close. The police presence scared them away today. The side entrance had been roped off and a couple of beat cops prowled the area.

Katherine turned to go inside the station. She was so lost in her thoughts that she almost ran straight into Williams. The entrance to the station lobby was only big enough for one of them, and he motioned for her to go in.

"Ladies first," he said with his condescending grin.

"Thank you." Katherine forced a smile.

"What's all the commotion across the street? Someone get murdered?"

"No, there was a burglary." She regretted saying it as soon as the words came out of her mouth. Since she had just arrived at work, she would have no way of knowing about the break-in unless she had seen it happen. She did not want Williams to know about her blunder. She quickened her pace, hoping to lose him before he asked any follow-up questions.

"A burglary, huh? Rat bastards are stealing from our greatest institutions now?" Williams took wide steps to catch up with her. Katherine wrinkled her nose, cursing herself for getting into this conversation.

"I didn't realize you were such a fine arts fanatic. I've only heard you talk about football games and jelly doughnuts." She ran up the stairs. Williams didn't seem to take the hint, hurrying up the stairs after her.

"Hey, I'm a man of culture. I went to one of those plays with all the singing and dancing in it once. Didn't care for it, but I went." Williams puffed out his chest.

"Well, aren't you a regular thespian?" She spoke with a flat tone.

"A what?" He deflated as if he'd been insulted.

"Never mind." Katherine held back laughter.

"So you're on the case?"

"What case?" Katherine moved to open the station door, then paused. "Oh, the museum. No, I'm not." Katherine wanted to take it, but McAlister had been clear when they spoke last night. The case seemed to be tied to the Boss, so a more experienced detective needed to be in charge. Hanson would lead the investigation, and knowing him, he wouldn't let Katherine anywhere near it.

"Then how do you know it was a burglary?"

Katherine froze. She didn't want to tell Williams the truth, but he could easily find out if he asked around the precinct. Still, she took a moment to think up an excuse, a way of pushing off her embarrassment. Her mind spun, but nothing came to her. Williams gasped.

"You saw it, didn't you?" Williams raised his eyebrows.

Katherine's face grew warm, a sign that her reddening cheeks were betraying her. Williams let out a cackling laugh. "You did! See? I am a good detective. Thief got away from you, huh?"

"Keep your voice down. Yes. I saw the burglary." She broke eye contact and stared down at her badge.

"How the hell did he break into that place?"

"I think *she* may have had help."

"A lady on the lam, huh? What kind of help?"

"It may be related to my jewelry store case, believe it or not." Katherine looked back at him but still could not look him in the eye. Her humiliation was too potent.

"Same crook?"

"Same technique, that's for sure. Her accomplice gets a job somewhere, then leaves the place unlocked for her."

"So tell the museum they've got a crooked employee." He spoke as if his idea was a brilliant revelation, something Katherine never would have thought of herself. Did he think that little of her? Williams held the door open for her and she trudged inside toward her office. How on earth was she going to get this thief behind bars?

Katherine went to the break room for her morning coffee. A few officers stood near the pot with steaming cups in their hands. They looked at Katherine, whispered to each other, and laughed. As Katherine opened the cabinet to grab her favorite cup, another officer strolled by.

"I heard about your big takedown last night, Dell. You really earned that promotion." He fell into a fit of laughter, and the officers in the break room joined in. Katherine slammed the cabinet shut. Coffee no longer sounded appealing as her stomach churned. She had been the laughingstock of the station since she joined the force but would be ridiculed now more than ever.

She stomped over to her office and shut the door. Plenty of crooks had gotten away from other cops and the rest of the men showed support, saying *You'll get the next one* or *It happens to everyone*. But now that she lost a thief, they used it as proof of her incompetence. She laid her head on the desk and heaved a sigh. If she had just been a bit quicker getting across the street last night, McAlister would be patting her on the back and assuring her that he chose the right person to promote. The men wouldn't be using her as a punchline, well, not for that at least.

With the museum burglary in Hanson's hands, she may as well give up on her jewelry store case. If it was the same duo, Hanson had a decent shot at getting the crooks behind bars. He was a good detective, though it pained her to admit it.

No, she was being ridiculous. She stood up, snapping out of her melancholy. If it was the same duo pulling off these heists, then she and Hanson had no choice but to work together. Whether he liked it or not, she was his equal now and he had no authority to dismiss her the way he always did.

Katherine marched to Hanson's office, let herself in, and took a seat across from him. He put his newspaper down and his mouth sloped into a frown.

"Something I can help you with?"

"Yes, actually. I'd like to know what you've found out so far about the museum heist." Considering how he had filed the Bailey case away, Katherine assumed he hadn't even started the new case, but wanted to establish her interest early.

"What do you want to know?"

Katherine picked up on his scathing tone but would not allow him to intimidate her.

"Everything."

Hanson grumbled, then to Katherine's surprise, grabbed a file from the stack on his desk. He opened it and pointed to a page of notes. Why was he so agreeable? Maybe he had a bigger heart than she realized and took pity on her. Or maybe he thought he'd get another splash of hot coffee in his lap if he didn't play nicely.

"Here, I called the museum this morning and this is what I found out." Katherine scanned the paper, barely able to make out Hanson's chicken scratch. A note at the bottom caught her eye — a description of the guard on duty at the time of the break-in. Male. Dark hair, skin, and eyes. Medium height and build. Mole near his right eye. Name — Walter *Carson*. His description matched that of Walter Smith exactly, except for the last name. Was it the same man going by a different alias?

"We done here?" Hanson snatched the file back and put it to the side, then grabbed another stack and plunked them into Katherine's arms. "Go stick these in the file room for me." He lifted the newspaper and ignored her scoffs of protest. Katherine scattered the files on his desk and walked out empty-handed.

Chapter Thirteen

That evening, Henry and Peterson parked a police car outside an old brick apartment complex. They'd made a breakthrough in the apartment burglary case, and Henry had narrowed down this building as the one most frequently hit. If the perp showed up again, they'd get the bastard. Then Henry could flaunt his victory in front of McAlister and take the badge from Dell.

Daylight faded into night. Henry let out a sigh. There was nothing on the planet more boring than a stakeout. But if this panned out, it would all be worth it. Peterson sat up straight and scanned the area with binoculars.

"First stakeout, Peterson?"

"Yes, it is." A few minutes went by in silence, then Peterson said, "How long do these things usually take?"

Henry laughed. "You're in for the long haul, pal."

Peterson sank back in his seat and tapped his foot.

"So we might be here all night, huh?"

"When you were a kid, did you bug your parents every five minutes on trips?" Henry put on a mocking childish voice. "Are we there yet? Are we there yet?"

Peterson playfully punched him in the arm. "Knock it off. I'm just excited. This'll be my first collar."

"I'll hand it to you, that is exciting. You gotta let me do the heavy lifting, though." Henry gave him a knowing look.

"What do you mean?" Peterson tilted his head.

"I mean, don't go flying out of the car at the first sign of trouble. Let me handle this and follow my lead."

"Will do. You're the expert after all."

Henry grinned. Not enough people had that level of respect for him. He liked that about Peterson.

"Hey, I meant to ask you..." Peterson trailed off for a moment. "I know this sounds silly, but I had a date with a gal last night and she mentioned something about the Greenhouse Killer."

Henry laughed. He too had heard that myth when he first moved to town.

"Yeah, it's a story floating around Nolaton about a guy who kept bodies in his greenhouse, except there's no proof it ever happened."

"I thought it sounded fishy. Terrible place to hide a body. The smell alone..." Peterson shuddered.

"Have you heard the one about Chophouse Joe, the guy who would marinate his victims' hearts in steak sauce?" Henry looked over, eager to see the rookie's reaction at the gruesome scenario. Peterson's face twisted in disgust.

"Don't worry, that story is total baloney too. Oh! Another good one. Have you heard about the Spider?" Henry spoke with a warbling tone like he was telling a scary campfire story to a group of boy scouts. He wiggled his fingers, mimicking spider legs.

Peterson laughed. "Haven't heard that one either."

Henry folded his arms. "It's this ridiculous conspiracy story, nothing more than a rumor. Supposedly the Spider is this hitman who services the criminal underground. Somebody borrows money and they can't pay it back, you hire the Spider to off them."

"Wouldn't it make more sense to keep them alive? That way you have a chance at getting your money back?" Peterson asked. Henry let out a chuckle.

"That's not how the world works, my young friend." Henry ignored the fact that he was only a few years older than Peterson. "It's about power. If you have a death threat dangling out there, you control the situation."

"Creepy." Peterson shuddered.

Henry chuckled again. "Needless to say, anyone with half a brain can see it's a bunch of hooey. The media tries to connect all these random murder cases to the Spider, probably to sell more papers. Doesn't matter what it is. Shootings, stabbings, bodies found on the south side or the north side. Totally unrelated crimes with no evidence tying them together."

"They don't think these unrelated murders might be unrelated?" Peterson mimicked Henry's chuckle.

"Well, I'm sure the newspapers know it's malarkey, but if they're scrounging for a headline, it's a story they can fall back on. I'm glad you see the folly of it, Peterson. We need more guys with common sense on the force."

Several hours later, both men sank into their seats. Henry scanned the area with binoculars. The sun had made its descent and the lamps sparkled to life. The dim glow shined off the metal fire escapes and window ledges. Henry put the binoculars down.

"No sign of him. You dozing off, Peterson?" Henry nudged him with his elbow.

Peterson's head had been dropping steadily to his chest. He popped back up with a jolt. "Nah just...stretching." Peterson rolled his head from side to side much more vigorously than before. Henry laughed at him.

"Good. I didn't bring a blanket to tuck you in."

"Can I take a look?"

"Sure, why not." Henry handed over the binoculars. Peterson stuck them to his eyes and searched. He spent a few moments panning back and forth, then stopped. He gasped.

"I saw something."

Henry jerked the binoculars out of his hand. Peterson pointed to the second floor of the building and Henry found the spot. A man dressed in all black stood on the fire escape. Henry could just make out his shape. The thief glanced around, then dug a pry bar out of his pants. He jimmied open an apartment window.

"Go!" Henry shoved open the car door and crept out. Peterson sprang from the car.

"Hey, stop!" Peterson yelled to the criminal. The thief froze, then hurried down the fire escape.

"Shut it, will you? We wanted to sneak up on him," Henry steamed. They had the guy, and the rookie wrecked it. His first big case, blown. Now McAlister would never promote him.

But just when Henry thought all hope was lost, the thief shot around the corner of the building.

"We got him. Come on." Henry indicated for Peterson to go one way while Henry ran the other direction. The thief must have caught on that they were trying to corner him, and he climbed up a fire escape ladder. Henry followed, close on his trail. The thief flung a leg over the ledge and hoisted himself onto the roof. The pry bar slipped from his hand and fell to the ground. Henry pulled himself up onto the roof. The thief stood still in the center of the roof, surrounded by a haze from the exhaust vents. He stared at Henry with wild eyes, and Henry took a few steps toward him.

"Nowhere to run. Nowhere to hide." Henry took out his handcuffs. The thief backed away toward the edge of the roof. He looked down, shrugged at Henry, then dove over the side. Henry ran to the spot and peered over the side, expecting the worst.

The thief was smarter than he looked. He had jumped into a delivery truck bed full of romaine lettuce. He climbed out and ran down the alley. Henry took the same dive and landed in the produce, squishing a few heads of lettuce under his feet. He hauled himself out, scraped the vegetable fibers from the bottoms of his shoes onto the cobblestone, then ran after the crook.

The thief slipped on a patch of broken glass. Henry pumped his legs and put on a burst of speed. The thief sprang up, but Henry had already gotten close enough to grab his arm. He pushed the thief to the ground and slapped handcuffs on him.

Peterson, huffing and puffing, jogged to the pair. He held the pry bar in his hand. "We got him!" Peterson jumped in the air and pumped his fist.

"Damn right, we did." Henry smiled. He imagined his conversation with McAlister, telling him that he'd made his collar before Dell made hers, convincing him to give Henry her detective badge. He deserved it more than she did, didn't he?

Chapter Fourteen

Now that Katherine had evidence to support her theory, she spent the day tracking down any burglary cases that involved men named Walter. Her search didn't turn up much as most of the Walters in their records were thieves, not accomplices. She did manage to dig up a case from '32 in which a Walter Miller was fired after leaving the door open at an antiques shop. No description of his appearance was given but Katherine wondered if it was the same man.

Her eyes watered from the strain of reading small print all day. She rubbed her temples to stave off a headache, then turned her chair to face the window and enjoyed the view of the sky. The sun had set and stars twinkled overhead, diamonds on a velvet black background.

Then movement snagged her attention just as it had the night before. Exactly the same way, in fact. A woman, that same woman, stood by the same door looking just as delinquent as she had last night. She wouldn't dare break in a second time, would she? Her accomplice had been fired according to Hanson's report.

Katherine sprang to her feet as the crook stepped into the light and began to pick the lock. The station hallways blurred as she ran past. Alarm bells rang from across the street. That woman must have gotten inside the museum and tripped the security system.

Katherine dashed to the museum and ran through the still-open side door. With the bells pealing, she couldn't hear the thief's footsteps and had no idea where she might be. Was she picking up more Ming Dynasty artifacts, or had she moved on to other treasures? The guard held his flashlight on Katherine as he came into view. Katherine pointed to her badge, and he nodded to her before rushing off to search another part of the museum.

From the right, a crash then a series of pings mingled with the alarm bells. Katherine crept toward the sound and found the culprit. The brunette stood in the corner facing a shattered glass case, an ivory statue in her hand — probably what she used to inflict the damage. Katherine slinked around the edge of a table in the middle of the exhibit. The woman grabbed an artifact, one of the jade carvings from the broken case, and stuck it in her pocket.

Just before the woman could run off, Katherine lunged. She grabbed the thief around the knees and brought her to the ground.

"Get off me!" The thief struggled, managed to free one of her legs, and kicked Katherine in the jaw. Katherine grunted and dull pain shot into her teeth. The woman wiggled her other leg free and bolted up and out of the room.

"Oh no you don't." Katherine got up and ran after the woman.

A shadow darted into the next room. Katherine followed, but the room looked empty except for the Roman mosaics and sculptures. She must have hidden somewhere. The alarms went silent — maybe the guard had disabled them. Katherine held her breath and listened for movement but heard none.

Then the woman popped up from behind a table, grabbed the bust of a Roman emperor, and threw it at Katherine's head. Katherine ducked just in time and the bust shattered against the wall.

Katherine growled and flung herself at the criminal but landed on the floor. The crook avoided her and ran out of the room.

Katherine pulled herself up and bounded after her toward the museum's lavish entrance, a lobby with sprawling marble floors and large potted trees near the door. The towering walls were wrapped with balconies on all four floors, and chandeliers sparkled down from the ceiling.

But where was the thief?

Katherine pulled herself up and looked around, spotting the woman heading for the elevator. Katherine bolted after her, running with her hand outstretched, and tried to grab the door before it closed. She missed it by mere inches. The dial above the elevator ticked up as the elevator ascended, and Katherine watched it stop on the fourth floor, the top floor of the building. Katherine laughed. What was her plan? There were no exits up there. She'd trapped herself.

The beat cop who had been patrolling the area burst in. He gave Katherine a mean look and charged toward her, then must have recognized her and slowed his pace.

"Where's the burglar?" He looked around, confused.

The elevator doors clanked open above, and the woman's silhouette jumped off the balcony. Katherine gasped. What was she thinking? A fall from that height could kill a person.

The thief grabbed onto a chandelier and swung out over the atrium. Katherine put the plan together — swinging from chandelier to chandelier would take her straight toward a decorative window. And from there, she could kick it out and escape to the roof.

Katherine ran under the madness, crystals raining down and smashing on the floor beside her. The beat cop ran behind her. The woman flew like a trapeze artist. She grabbed on to the last chandelier, flexing her body to swing again, but the ceiling cracked where it was attached. Plaster crumbled and turned to dust as it hit the floor. Katherine, helpless, watched as the structure gave way.

The chandelier fell. The thief screamed as she let go of it and plummeted toward the floor. Thankfully, one of the trees in the entryway broke her fall, and she tumbled down the branches, the leaves cushioning the impact. Then the thief collapsed onto a padded bench near the door. She landed with a *thud*, rolled to her side, and seemed shaken but mostly unharmed. Katherine made it just in time to block the door, spreading her arms like an eagle protecting her nest.

The woman, now covered in scrapes and contusions, managed to get up and run into a room full of medieval weaponry. Katherine followed in time to witness the thief smash another glass case and grab a sword from inside. She held it like a baseball bat and swung it wildly from side to side.

"Put down your weapon." The beat cop held up his hands, showing he meant no harm. The woman stopped for a moment and took a few quick breaths, then lifted the sword again. Katherine's mind spun, wondering if this woman was more than a thief. She seemed to have no qualms about threatening two police officers' lives. What if it wasn't the first time she had drawn a deadly weapon?

Katherine dangled her fingers over her revolver. Would drawing her own weapon cause more harm than good? The threat could aggravate the woman further, possibly inciting her to attack. If Katherine escalated the situation one of them could end up dead. It may be better to let the thief believe she had the upper hand.

Katherine waited, watching the sword swing. The thief slowed her movements; her arms must be getting tired. If Katherine timed it right, she could lunge when the sword was up and tackle her. She watched a few more swings. Back and forth. Back and forth.

Katherine pounced.

Chapter Fifteen

"So I'm chasing the guy, and he's scared. I mean terrified," Henry recounted his adventure to the few officers who would listen. He and Peterson had just arrived back at the station with their thief, a man named Franklin Green. Once they got Green locked in a holding cell, Henry shared his story with the night crew. He couldn't contain himself, acting out the scene as though he was on stage, complete with boisterous hand gestures and overdone facial expressions.

"He's shaking. I'm right behind him and he knows he ain't getting away. He crawls up on the roof and I swing up there after him. I look him right in the eye and say, 'End of the line, pal. No one escapes Officer Williams.' The guy is backing up, shaking his head at me, begging for mercy. Then the moron backs right off the roof. Good thing a truck full of salad was idling out there. That fall must have spooked him good because he took off, but I wasn't gonna let him get away that easy. I pounced on him and got him in handcuffs. He put up a hell of a fight, but you know me, boys. I don't give up. Now instead of breaking into windows, he's sleeping behind bars."

"There is no finer officer on the force than you, Williams." Peterson gave him a thumbs-up.

The other officers cheered, clapping Henry on the shoulder and giving their accolades. Sure, his story had a little extra flavor added to it; nobody wanted to hear the boring, watered-down truth. As excited as he was to tell the guys at the station, he was more excited to tell McAlister. Tomorrow he would saunter into the lieutenant's office and give him the good news. While Dell was letting criminals slip through her fingers, Henry was getting them off the streets. Now who deserved a detective badge?

A crash echoed from the ground floor, sounding as if someone had just kicked in the door. Everyone froze. Voices argued in the distance and feet hit the stairs in staccato rhythms. The officers all slid their hands onto their weapons, waiting to see what would come through the door.

"Maybe Murphy caught the guy who broke in across the street. You heard the alarms earlier."

Henry glanced back at his colleague and hoped he was right. He hadn't been at the station when the alarms chimed but Murphy knew what he was doing. With him on patrol, a burglar didn't stand a chance.

The door flew open and, to Henry's surprise, revealed Dell wrestling with a struggling brunette. She kept trying to wiggle out of Dell's grasp, but to no avail. The handcuffs kept her off-balance, and Dell's pushing forced her toward the interrogation room.

"Get off me, copper!" The woman bucked and almost headbutted Dell, but Dell dodged the attack. Henry ran over to them and grabbed the woman's arm.

"I got her." Dell's eyes lit up with fury aimed at him. Henry took a step back from them but followed Dell and her prisoner into the interrogation room.

"Where's Murphy?" Henry asked.

"He's watching the museum." Dell pushed the woman down into a chair, then scowled at Henry. "If you really want to help, you can take notes." She kept one hand on the writhing crook and threw a notepad at Henry with the other. Dell bent down to the woman. "Name."

"Let me go. Please! I didn't do anything."

"That's for the judge to decide. Considering I caught you red-handed, the decision should be easy." Dell held up a green stone carving then set it on the table.

"Please, you gotta let me go. You don't understand—"

"Name. Now. Or we'll add resisting arrest to the charges." Dell stood nose to nose with the suspect, pointing in her face. "I'm not asking again."

"Rita. Rita Davis."

Henry scribbled the name down. Rita's lip quivered. Her beady brown eyes squinted even as they filled with tears.

"How long have you been in the thieving business, Miss Davis? Did Walter get you involved in the scam, or is it the other way around? That's right. I know about your accomplice. Walter Smith, or is it Carson? Or something else entirely? The man who worked at Bailey Jewelers and left the door open for you. The same man who took a guard job at the museum you just robbed, isn't that right?" Dell growled out her words. This dame must have really gotten under her skin. Now that Henry had a moment to take in her appearance, he noticed the bruise forming on her chin and the crystals in her hair. What the hell had happened to her?

"We never wanted to steal those pearls, or the art, or anything else for that matter. We don't have a choice." Rita shook in her seat.

"That's a lot of hooey and you know it. How would you like it if your little boyfriend went to prison? And what about the Boss? You're in cahoots with one of the biggest crime lords in the city, aren't you?" Dell slammed her hands on the table, startling her suspect.

"Dell!" Henry's voice boomed. "May I see you outside?"

Dell backed away from Rita, who whimpered in her chair. Henry nodded toward the door. Dell turned on her heel and exited, and he followed her.

"What is going on in there? Are you okay?"

"I'm fine." Dell glared at Henry.

"No, you're not. You can't treat a suspect like that."

"She's not a suspect. She's a criminal. I caught her stealing, and I bet she's done worse things than that. She threatened me."

"Still, you gotta keep your cool."

"How can I with scum like her running around the streets working with the seedy underbelly of this city? We might not have even scratched the surface of her crimes."

"Why don't you go home and get cleaned up. I can take care of her," Henry offered.

"No. It's my collar. I'm taking care of this."

Dell was clearly in distress. Maybe the altercation across the street was too much for her to handle and she needed a man to take over. Poor gal ought to have a hot bath and a good night's sleep.

"You're right. It's your collar. You did all the real work. From here it's just clerical. Look, I know I have the handwriting of a boozed-up monkey, but I can take a few notes and get a doctor out to look at her injuries, get her into a holding cell for the night. It's standard stuff I can handle for you."

Dell looked down at herself. "I am a mess, aren't I?"

"I've been saying that about you for years. Now go on. Scram."

"I'll get cleaned up once I get her processed. Move." Dell shoved Henry out of her way and stepped toward the interrogation room door.

Henry put a hand on her shoulder. "Seriously, Dell. Go home. You're in no fit state to work."

"You don't have the authority to send me home. I outrank you. If anything, I should send *you* home. In fact, that's exactly what I'll do. Get out of here, *Officer.*" She stretched out his title, a reminder of his low status on the force compared to hers.

Henry refused to let her win.

He slipped into the interrogation room. Before Dell could follow him, he shut the door and twisted the lock. She jiggled the knob, then pounded her fist against the barrier, shouting indistinctly.

Rita had stopped crying. Henry sat down and took the notepad and pencil. "Tell me what happened."

"I never meant for it to turn out like this. I made some mistakes, and everything got worse, and now..." Her tears welled back up.

"You get mixed up with a bad crowd?"

"I owe a lot of money to a really bad man." Rita's voice trembled and her head dropped.

Henry leaned in, concerned. Perhaps this dame wasn't stealing to be selfish. She could be in real trouble. "Who is he? Did he threaten you?" He scratched his notes down.

"Yeah, he threatened me and my boyfriend, Walter. He said if we don't pay him back..." Rita sobbed.

"It's all right. You can tell me."

"If we don't pay him, he'll have us killed."

"That's very serious."

"He'll send the Spider after us." Rita went wide-eyed.

Henry leaned back as the compassion he felt a moment ago drained away. Unbelievable. This broad was lying right to his face, trying to manipulate him into feeling bad for her. Did she really think she could trick an officer of the law with that obvious lie? The Spider. Ha. What a bunch of baloney.

"Let's go."

"What?" Rita tipped her head to the side.

"Let's go to your holding cell. Come on."

"Wait, you're gonna protect us, right? Me and Walter?"

Henry shook his head in disbelief. "Get up. Let's go." He motioned to the door.

Rita stood up, finding her balance.

Dell stood in the hallway, red-faced but calmer than she had been. She followed Henry to the holding cells and made sure Rita was processed on her watch. Once the dame was locked up, Dell went home.

Henry went back to the interrogation room and looked at his notes. He didn't even bother writing down what Rita had said about the Spider. Ridiculous. He tossed the notes onto Dell's desk, then gathered his things and headed home himself.

Chapter Sixteen

Loretta Jones stood on the rickety coffee table in their small apartment. Jack played the role of an audience member as Loretta rehearsed for her audition that night. Loretta shuffled her feet to the rhythm though the table creaked beneath her. As the sun went down, so did her confidence.

"You don't think I'm a little off on that C-sharp?" She scrunched up her face with concern.

"No, I think you sound beautiful!" Jack's eyes sparkled as he beamed at her, and heat rose to Loretta's cheeks. Of course, Jack had nothing but compliments. He loved her. If money wasn't so tight, he probably would have asked her to marry him by now. She wasn't worried about *his* opinion.

But Al Harris might hear the imperfections.

Al was one of her regular customers at the diner, and he owned a club called the Razzle Dazzle. Loretta had never been there, but according to Al, the place needed to move in a new direction. His current headliners weren't bringing in crowds. Loretta had begged for a chance to audition, and nearly dropped the coffeepot in his lap when he obliged. With all the other canaries in town trying to make it big, landing a singing gig in Nolaton had seemed impossible. Now, finally, she had a chance to show off her skills. And to be a headliner, no less! A nervous bubbling rolled through her. This could be her big break. Or it could be a disaster. She had to be sure her performance was perfect.

"Let me run through it one more time." Loretta started to dance.

"I'd listen to you sing all night if I could, but I don't want you to be late." The table gave a low groan. "I also don't want you to break the table." They both laughed. Jack got up and gave her his hand; she took it and hopped down.

"Will you help me pick a dress to wear? I've got it narrowed down to my favorites. Hold on." Loretta ran to the closet and grabbed her picks. When she came back to the living room, Jack had planted himself back on the couch. She held up a black sequined dress with short, draping sleeves; knee-length, with a bit of a flare to the skirt. She shook her hips against the fabric to show how it moved. Jack grimaced.

"Too much?"

"I like it." Jack forced a grin. Loretta stifled a laugh. Her mother always said that the worst liars made the best husbands. Loretta could hardly wait to make Jack hers.

"Tell the truth." Loretta tried to give him a stern look, but Jack's expression was so darn cute that she broke into a smile.

"It's a bit showy. I don't want this Al guy to get the wrong impression." He had a point. The dress was low cut. An idea struck her and she laughed to herself as she ran back to the closet. She took out a satin nightie with lace trim.

"How about this, then?" She held it to herself, trying to keep a straight face.

"I'm not sure. Better try it on." Jack giggled and scooted closer to her.

Loretta, still holding up the lingerie, sauntered up to him. She caressed his cheek and peered into his eyes. "I will as soon as I get home."

Jack turned pink. Loretta set down the nightie and picked up another dress. This one was a navy blue ankle-length gown with long sleeves. The sleek material would hug her body without revealing too much.

"What about this?"

"That's a winner."

Loretta changed into her outfit, then she sat in front of her vanity and made sure her blonde curls were set. She applied an ivory cream, a shade lighter than her natural skin tone, then dabbed bright pink rouge on her cheeks. Pale gold eyeshadow brought out the yellow flecks in her eyes. She took out her mascara bar and brush, getting her lashes as big as they could be. She went over the thin-plucked lines of her brows with a dark pencil, accentuating their length. She painted a bright red lipstick onto her bottom lip and a deeper red onto her top lip, creating a stark cupid's bow.

"You look gorgeous." Jack walked up behind her and put his arms around her. "You're gonna knock 'em dead."

"I love you to the moon and back, Jack." Loretta leaned into his hug. When they released each other, she stood in front of their floor-length mirror.

"Something's missing." Though the dress looked nice on her, the plain outfit would not grab attention and she needed to make an impact on Al. A few cheap necklaces hung inside her closet, but none of them would stand out enough. An idea struck her. She pushed her dresses aside in the closet and found it. A silk scarf, the same dark blue as her dress, with little white roses on the edges. She stepped in front of the mirror and tied it around her neck. At first, she tied her knot too tight and it pinched her skin. She loosened it allowing most of the silk to drape. There.

She grabbed her handbag, gave Jack a kiss, then ran out the door.

Loretta stepped off the trolley. She fluffed her hair and looked around, drinking in the moment. Sirens rang in the distance. Buildings in this area had fallen to disrepair. A beat-up truck idled next to her. It certainly wasn't the classiest part of town, but it was a start. A sign glowed above her, the words alternating, taking their turn illuminating the street. Some of the bulbs were burned out, but she could read what it said. "RAZZLE" then

"DAZZLE" over and over in a steady beat. Loretta almost started dancing to the rhythm.

She walked toward the entrance and smoothed out her dress where the delicate fabric had gotten wrinkled on the trolley ride. She straightened her scarf and fixed the draping. A dolly full of boxes crashed into her leg, almost knocking her to the ground, and one of the boxes fell. Glass shattered and a man swore.

"Watch where you're going, lady!"

"Sorry. I should've..." She looked up at his face and her stomach clenched. Now that she thought about it, that truck had looked familiar. Of all the people to run into before her audition, it just had to be him. Her ex-boyfriend. He must be delivering cases of his small-batch whiskey to the club. "Tom?"

"Loretta?" His eyes narrowed and his jaw jutted out but he said nothing more.

Loretta shrank away and her shoulders tensed. Why him? Why now? She didn't need the guilt or the memories, not before her big moment.

"Do you know how much money is running down the drain?" Tom pointed to the liquid trickling into the sewer. The potent smell of the liquor made her stomach turn.

"I'm sorry, Tom. Can I help you clean up?" Loretta bent down to pick up broken glass.

"You've done enough." He glared.

She backed away, then ran inside the club. No need to get caught up in the past. Her future was ahead of her. According to the clock above the bar, she still had five minutes to find Al's office. She rolled her shoulders back and held her head high.

There weren't many people in the club. On stage, a magician locked his assistant in a box so that only her head and feet showed. The magician presented a large saw to the audience and to Loretta's surprise, he began cutting right where the assistant's hips should be. He pulled the box apart, yet the assistant wiggled her toes and bobbed her head as if she was still in one piece. The audience applauded and Loretta did too. She pictured herself up there on that same stage wearing elbow-length gloves and an elegant gown, her voice carrying over the music to an entranced audience.

Then she felt a pair of eyes on her. Slowly, she turned her head and met the gaze of the handsome bartender, whose face broke into a sultry smile. Loretta felt herself blush; though her heart belonged to Jack it was still flattering to be looked at. She stepped over to him.

"What'll you have?" The bartender — "Lou" according to his nametag — made a cocktail and stuck a lemon wedge on the rim of the glass. He set it down in front of a woman who stood at the bar, but his eyes never left Loretta. The woman sipped her drink and walked away.

"Oh, I don't drink, but thank you for the offer. I'm auditioning for Al Harris. Do you know where I can find him?"

"That's right, he said he had a singer coming in. His office is in the back, just through there." Lou pointed down a dark hallway. As he did so, two women walked up to the bar. One was tall and lanky, easily the tallest woman Loretta had ever seen. The other was short and stocky. Both had on copious amounts of makeup and wore long, sparkling gowns. Loretta recognized them from the poster in the window. The MacDougall sisters, otherwise known as Cream and Sugar — the current headliners.

"Hey, Candace. Hey, Shirley. Can you show this lovely lady to Al's office?" Lou gestured to Loretta.

"Sure. Aren't you a pretty thing? I love that scarf," Candace said in a low purr.

"Thank you."

The women seemed nice, which only made Loretta feel worse. Did they know she might be their replacement? Or that they were getting replaced at all?

"Come right back here with us." Shirley beckoned her into the shadows.

"You sure you don't want a drink? I make a mean Sazerac." Lou winked at her.

Loretta knew he was just being polite, but she did not want to think about whiskey. "No, thank you."

"Whip up a couple of 'em for us, Lou. We'll be back in a minute." Candace winked back at him. Loretta and the women walked down the hallway. At the end was a door with a plaque that read "Al Harris — Owner." Loretta trembled as she approached it.

"Are you nervous to sing for him?" Candace looked at her with concern. Maybe they did know she might be their replacement. Why, then, were they being so kind?

"A little." Loretta's voice quivered, which only made her more apprehensive. Would her voice be steady during her song, or would she clam up and blow her chance?

"You'll do fine. Just relax and show him what you got." Shirley did a playful dance as if she were the one auditioning.

"Knock 'em dead, sweetheart." Candace patted Loretta on the shoulder, then the women left her and walked back toward the bar. As Loretta approached the door, she could hear voices inside. Al sounded upset.

"You better hope I don't run out. If I lose business over this—"

"I'll make it right. I promise. Can you at least pay me for what I delivered?" It was Tom. Loretta squirmed. Not only had she broken his heart a year ago, but now she'd got him in trouble with a client.

"I'll pay you when you deliver in full. Next Tuesday, bring the extra case. Until then, you're not seeing a dime."

"Come on, Al. It was an accident! Have I ever shorted you before?"

"Not that I recall."

"Can't you at least throw me a quarter so I can have supper?"

"Not until I get my full shipment."

A chair scratched against the floor. The door flew open. A seething Tom pushed past her, recoiling when he saw her. He paused for a moment behind her and Loretta held her breath as she anticipated an outburst. Instead, he turned back around and kept walking away.

"Hey, Loretta. Come in." Al sat at his desk. Tension still hung thick in the air.

"Hello, Al." She stood in front of his desk and folded her hands, waiting for him to give direction. He stared at her. She cringed. He had said it was all right to call him Al when he came into the café, but maybe in this setting, he preferred a more formal greeting. Before she could apologize, he spoke.

"Well, are you gonna stand there all day, or are you gonna audition for me?" Al chuckled. His stomach stuck out in front of him and shook when he laughed. Good, he wasn't upset with her.

Loretta forced a smile, though her stomach fluttered with nerves. "Should...should I start?"

"Go for it." He adjusted his glasses and leaned back in his chair.

Loretta cleared her throat and began to sing. She started softer than she meant to, then took a deep breath and pushed more air under the notes. Her hips swished from side to side as she started to sink into her performance. Her hands flared out in front of her and she bobbed them to the beat; she even hit that C-sharp. Her confidence soared enough on the last few bars that she threw in a few trills. All in all, she was happy with the performance. As the last note faded, she hoped Al felt the same way.

He stared at her, his mouth gaping open. Was he impressed or horrified? Loretta set one foot back and dipped into a curtsy. Al applauded.

"That was sensational! You've got a set of pipes on you."

"So I got the gig?" Her legs felt like jellied eels.

"Loretta Jones, I want you to be our new headliner."

Loretta squealed, bouncing up and down with delight. Jack would be so excited. She couldn't wait to tell him. "Thank you, Al!"

"Whoa, now wait a minute, I *want* you to be our headliner, but I need you to do something else first." The light left his eyes. He tipped his head down and leered at Loretta.

She felt nervous, but not the same electric spark she had felt before the audition. Now freezing water flowed through her insides.

Al took a box out from under his desk. He pulled out the contents, a cream-colored see-through dress with a high hemline. The sheer fabric tumbled over his arm as he held it up for her to see. "I got this out of the costume room earlier and I want you to try it on for me. Might be a good look for your act."

Loretta's shoulders tensed. She didn't want to wear a dress that revealing on stage, and especially not now, alone in a room with a man she barely knew.

He got up and placed his hand on her jaw, then gave her a soft, unwelcome caress. "What's wrong, doll? It's just a costume. If you're gonna bring in a crowd, you've got to look the part." He held the dress up to her and ogled her figure. He ran his hand down her side under the pretense of smoothing the fabric. Loretta's heart pounded with quick, blank beats. Al pushed his body against hers. His whiskey breath invaded her nose, making bile rise to her throat. She swallowed hard to force it back down. She wanted to run, but fear clamped onto her ankles and held her in place.

Al bent close and whispered in her ear. "I'll make you a star, darling. Don't you want that?" He ran his hand up her back. She shuddered. "You do me one little favor, and I'll put your name in lights." Al took one hand off her but kept the other firmly in place. With his free hand, he unbuttoned his pants.

Loretta averted her gaze, but Al wrenched her head around and peered into her eyes. She snapped her lids shut, unwilling to look at his reddening face. His heavy breathing filled her ears, mingling with the distant clatter from the bar and footsteps in the hallway. He grabbed her with both hands again, his fingers digging into her arm. She tried to lurch free but couldn't escape.

"Come on, doll. Do me a favor." He gripped her tighter.

No. She would not let him overpower her. If there was any chance for her to get away unscathed, she had to find her strength. She let her rage boil over and snarled at him.

"Let go of me!" She stomped on his foot.

He cried out in pain and released her. She ran to the door but stopped as he called to her.

"Wait! I'm sorry, sweetheart. I shouldn't have done that. It won't happen again, I swear. You'll be my headliner, right?" His words came out in a childish whine as he scrambled to button his pants. His eyes pleaded forgiveness, then went blank again. "Right?" The question came out with an edge, a current of anger flowing underneath.

Loretta's courage faltered and words failed her. Al pounded his fist on the desk, sending a stack of papers flying. "Answer me."

A bolt of terror ran through Loretta. She ran from his office, through the club, and out the door to the alleyway. She needed air. The stars glistened against an inky sky, but Loretta had never found them less inspiring. Her mind raced.

What would Jack say? Did she have to tell him? Jack didn't need to know. She could say she didn't get the gig. Did she even want it anymore? No, not here, not for *him*, but she still wanted to sing. This might have been her only shot. No other club owner would even give her a chance to audition, let alone offer her the gig. Al only had because...*oh no*. Because he knew her from the diner, the one he ate at every day. She would see him there and would have to serve him. Push down the memory of his wandering hands and whiskey breath while she topped off his coffee.

Whether she worked there or at the Razzle, she could not remove him from her life. And maybe...if she took the singing job, some other club owner might scout her out and hire her. Some nice club owner who would treat her well. The Razzle was just a foot in the door, a start to her career. She would call Al tomorrow and accept the job. It was a smart career move after all.

Her stomach was a void, a black hole where joy used to reside.

She pushed the last few minutes out of her mind. No need to dwell. She found a payphone on the corner and put in a nickel.

"Hello?" Jack's voice bounced on the other end.

"Hi, honey!" Loretta's stomach unclenched. His voice warmed her like a sip of tea.

"How did it go? Tell me everything." He sounded so eager, so excited for her.

The words tumbled around her mouth. She wanted to tell him the truth, to lay it all out for him and hear him say that everything would be all right. That it wasn't her fault, that she didn't do anything wrong. That she didn't have to work at the Razzle or see Al ever again. But she couldn't put the burden on Jack. Everything would be better for both of them if she gritted her teeth and took the job.

"I got it!" She did her best to sound excited.

Jack cheered. "That's wonderful! I knew you'd get it. Say, let's have a special dinner tomorrow night to celebrate."

"I'd love that. I'll be home soon, all right?"

"Not soon enough. I love you."

"I love you too." She hung up the phone. Her body felt weak with the lie, like her limbs were made of rubber. Blood rushed to her head, pounding in her ears. She didn't tell him. She wouldn't ever tell him. She would forget it ever happened.

Then her scream punctured the stillness of the night as hands grabbed her scarf from behind and pulled.

Loretta's throat closed, collapsing under the pressure. She gasped for breath, but none came. She scrabbled at the scarf, tried to tug it away from her windpipe, but her strength fell short. Her lungs tried to expand but folded instead as she was pulled to the ground.

The stars disappeared one by one, as her vision went black.

Chapter Seventeen

Henry dragged himself off the couch where he had slept. When Benny moved in, Henry had given up the only bedroom so that his brother would feel more at home. Henry kept his belongings in heaps on the living room floor. He rubbed his eyes and let them adjust, taking in the state of his apartment. He did his best to keep the place dusted and free of clutter, but with the two of them crammed into the small space, messes built up fast.

Sleep had eluded him most of the night. Benny was still coming home late and leaving at odd hours. Henry assumed he broke the rules and found a job, but wherever he was working, they treated him like a dog. Henry would plan a nice meal for them, then Benny would disappear for the night. He played hooky from school. He didn't show up for a football game on Saturday. Benny loved football. It didn't make any sense.

Dell's temper had kept him awake too. She completely mishandled that collar. Intimidating a suspect was against protocol, and it was only right that the lieutenant should hear about her treatment of Rita Davis. He should also know that Henry had solved his big case, and that he had done it within the confines of the police handbook. As soon as he got to the station, he would find McAlister and lay it out for him, but right now his focus was on Benny. He got up and banged on the bedroom door.

"I want you up and ready for school in five minutes."

Benny groaned inside the room but did not respond.

"I'm not leaving this doorway until I hear feet hit the floor."

Benny stomped over to the door and flung it open. "I'm up. Can I have a little peace and quiet now?" Benny ran his hands through his messy brown hair.

"You haven't earned peace and quiet. Get dressed. I'm taking you to school." Henry marched over to his pile of clothes in the living room.

An ironing board had permanent residence in the middle of the living room. Henry took a uniform from the clean clothes pile. He stretched the shirt over the board and misted it with water, then heated up the iron on the stove. He ran the hot metal over the fabric, fighting each wrinkle as he pressed.

"You're not even dressed. Why are you rushing me out the door?" Benny buttoned his shirt but had missed a hole near the bottom, so the garment sat skewed on his small frame. Benny sighed and undid his work, then started the process again.

"Because when I say you've got five minutes, you take twenty. Do something with your hair before we leave." His ironing got sloppy, pushing more wrinkles into the fabric than he pressed out as he stared at his brother. Benny looked rough. His eyes could barely stay open, and his sallow skin had a greenish tint. "You didn't sleep much, did you?"

Benny shook his head.

"What's going on, pal?" Henry set the iron down and walked over to his brother.

Benny refused to look him in the eye. "Nothing. Just homesick."

"Whatever this is, it ain't homesickness. Did you take a job somewhere?" Henry put his hands on his hips the way his father always had when lecturing him. Benny said nothing. "All right, you don't have to tell me, but it ends today. Wherever you're going, whatever you're doing, it's over. Tell them you quit."

"Can we go now?" Benny whined.

"After you comb your hair."

Henry stepped into McAlister's office. He told him everything that happened, citing each infraction from the handbook. How Dell had run her own surveillance and snuck into the museum with no backup. How she'd shouted in the suspect's face and slammed her hands on the table, bringing Davis to tears.

McAlister listened with his fingers tented, and when Henry finished his story, the lieutenant nodded to show he understood.

"I already got the rundown from several sources on what happened last night. I'll talk to her."

Henry waited, expecting more of a response. McAlister shuffled a few papers on his desk and seemed to think the conversation was over. Henry cleared his throat.

"Something else on your mind?" McAlister shoved the papers into a file. Henry tried to catch his eye. McAlister must have picked up on it and gave Henry his full attention.

"I solved Darwood's old case. Franklin Green is off the streets." Henry stood up straight and smiled.

"Good work." McAlister looked back down at his file.

"You said once I solved it, we'd have a conversation about the promotion."

"Then let's have a conversation. Dell solved her case—"

"Yeah, like a lunatic!"

McAlister shot Henry a look. "Do not interrupt me, Officer Williams. She keeps the badge, but I will talk to her about her behavior. If you're so concerned about her methods, then you can assist her on her next case."

"But, sir, she's—"

"You're dismissed." McAlister picked up his documents and started reading.

Henry cursed under his breath, then headed to the break room for a cup of coffee. From down the hallway, he saw Dell walk into the station. She wore that sour expression that pinched up her features, and the bruise on her face was the same purple color as the bags under her eyes. She got into the break room just before he did, dug in the cupboards, and pulled out the red coffee cup. Henry grumbled. She got the badge and the good mug. He got diddly-squat.

"Good morning, Sunshine. You look awful." Henry meant for his teasing to be playful, something he'd say to any of the men on the force. Dell rounded on him, splashing coffee out of the pot as she did so. She rolled her eyes and grabbed a rag.

"That's Detective Sunshine to you. And thank you. That's just what a lady wants to hear." Bitterness clung to each word, which Henry resented. She wanted to be treated like one of the guys, but only when it benefited her.

She cleaned up her mess and emptied the pot into her cup. Henry pushed past her to start a new pot of coffee. As he measured out the grounds, he turned to Dell.

"By the way, McAlister wants a word with you about your big collar." He grinned, excited for the scolding she was about to receive. Dell stormed out of the break room toward McAlister's office. Henry got the coffee brewing, then poked his head out of the break room and caught that puff of red hair disappearing behind McAlister's door. Henry skulked over and pressed his ear to it, ready for the show to begin.

"Sit down." McAlister snapped his fingers. A chair scraped against the floor. "I just had a chat with Williams. I hear you got our museum thief off the streets."

"That I did." Dell sounded satisfied with herself. The nerve of her, sounding so proud of what she'd done.

"One thing bothers me. I can't find the page in the handbook that says to go busting into crime scenes on your own and tackling suspects when you're not even assigned to the case."

Henry smirked. McAlister must be winding up to lay into her. He rubbed his hands together in gleeful anticipation.

"I'm sorry, sir. I saw her lurking outside the museum and then alarms went off — I just knew it was the same woman who robbed Bailey Jewelers."

"You didn't know beans. You had a hunch. You could have been hurt or killed. Your actions caused irreparable property damage. You didn't bring backup — like you never even used your supporting officer on the Bailey case. On top of that, you intimidated a suspect in custody. That's not how we operate." McAlister banged his cane against the floor as he shouted.

"I got tough with her, but I didn't have a choice. She was damned near impossible to catch and uncooperative once I got her here."

"I don't care what she did. That's not how we treat our suspects."

"She tried to stab me with a sword!"

"What do you think you signed up for, Dell? Did you think this job would be easy, that every criminal would happily hop into handcuffs without a fight? You're the cop, the one with the training. You're the one who's supposed to keep the situation under control. If I get wind of this happening again, I won't just demote you. I'll have no choice but to fire you."

Henry sucked air through his teeth. McAlister always played favorites with Dell; Henry hadn't thought she'd wind up in this much trouble. Sure, he wanted the detective spot, but he didn't want her to lose her job. Then again, maybe she deserved a sacking.

"Why don't you fire me now?" Dell was choked up. Had the lieutenant made her cry?

"Because despite all that, a criminal is in custody and Davis may be able to give us information about the Boss. I don't always approve of your methods, but damned if you don't get results."

Henry's sympathy faded. *She gets results, huh? And I don't?* It sounded like her job was safe, at least. He went to check on the coffee.

"Hello?" A timid young man stood just outside the station door grasping an envelope in his hand.

"Something I can help you with?" Henry waved the man inside. Coffee would have to wait.

"I, um, well, I'm not sure what to do."

"Let's talk in here." Henry guided him toward one of the interrogation rooms. Usually they kept those rooms dark, with only a spotlight to intimidate the suspect, but Henry didn't want to make this guy more anxious than he already was. He switched on a light, which filled the room with warmth. They both sat at the table.

"I think I...I need to make a missing person report." The man looked as if he might burst into tears. Henry remained calm and hoped his demeanor would help put the man at ease.

"What's your name?"

"Jack Lewis." He took sharp breaths as if he was trying his best not to fall apart.

"Nice to meet you, Jack. I'm Officer Williams. You said someone has gone missing?" He kept his voice calm and soothing.

"My girl, Loretta Jones. She didn't come home last night." Jack barely got the sentence out. His eyes were rimmed with red.

"Any chance she had too much to drink and stayed out late? Maybe she's coming home this morning?" It happened often enough. People would get too rambunctious and pass out at a friend's house but forget to call their loved ones to check in. Henry hoped that was the case this time.

"She wouldn't do that." Jack clenched his jaw. Why had that upset him so much? "Sorry." Jack relaxed back into his chair. "She just...that's not who she is anymore. She had this big audition to replace the headliners at the Razzle Dazzle. You know the place?"

"I'm familiar with it." Henry winced. He had only been there once; when he was new in town, a gal he'd been seeing had insisted on going there. It wasn't exactly a high-class establishment. Then again, neither was the gal.

"Loretta called me after, and said she got the job. Then she said she'd come home, but..." Jack trailed off. He stared into the distance, not able to find the rest of the sentence. Henry, staying professional, brought the conversation back to the facts.

"What's in the envelope?"

Jack sprang back into reality and flipped open the top of the package. "I brought a couple pictures of her. I thought that might help with the search. You can put up posters or, well, I'm not sure what you do." Jack handed over a few photos of a young, gorgeous, blonde woman. Henry shuddered. A pretty girl alone in a rough part of town like that? He had seen too many cases start this way and those didn't tend to have happy endings.

"What was she wearing when you last saw her?"

Jack thought for a moment. "A long blue dress, and blue shoes."

Henry made a note of that. "Thank you for coming in, Jack. We'll take it from here." He took down Jack's contact information, then showed him to the door.

Once Jack was gone, Henry started toward McAlister's office to give him the missing person information but stopped outside Dell's office first. A twinge resonated in his stomach like a plucked guitar string. The lieutenant had given her a real dressing-down. Maybe he ought to apologize, even though it irked him to do so. If they had to work together, he'd like to start on good terms. He knocked on her door.

Chapter Eighteen

Katherine shrank into the chair in McAlister's office while he chewed her out for her antics last night. The adrenaline rush of catching Rita Davis had kept her up all night, and now she struggled to focus. She had to stay alert, though. McAlister deserved her respect and full attention. He softened as he praised her for getting a criminal off the streets, even if he didn't like how it happened.

"Thank you, sir." Relief washed over her. Her job was safe and the detective badge was still hers, for now. McAlister sat down.

"I get where you're coming from, Dell. Back when I was a run-of-the-mill cop, I took risks and broke protocol too, but I learned my lesson the hard way.

"When I was about your age, I caught wind that a shipment of stolen goods was heading to the harbor. My partner didn't think the tip had merit. He thought it was a diversion for a bigger crime. We argued and decided to investigate separately. He stayed at the precinct while I snuck off to the docks. Foolish, in hindsight.

"My hunch was correct. An unmarked ship rolled in. I hid behind some old crates while the Boss and his cronies checked out the goods. Fur coats, God only knows what animal they came from."

"The Boss? You got that close to him?" Katherine pictured a young McAlister with a head full of hair slinking around near the biggest crime lord in Nolaton. Even back then, the lieutenant must have been unshakeable.

"He wasn't as big of a player at the time, but still a known criminal. A dangerous one at that. I won't lie to you, Dell. I was terrified, but I wanted to be the one to take him in, get justice for everything he'd done to the city.

"I stepped out from behind the crates. A few of his henchmen ran, but I kept my sights on the Boss. He whistled and two guys came out of nowhere — they took my gun, held me down while the Boss came over with a crowbar and bashed my knee. I nearly blacked out from the pain.

"They pushed me into the water. Have you ever tried to swim with a broken leg? It's not easy. By the time I made it to shore, they were gone." McAlister looked down at his bum leg. "Doctors couldn't get it to heal right so I couldn't do much as a beat cop after that. I was stuck at the station pushing papers. Sure, I've made it up the ranks, but the Boss took away the part of the job I loved. Don't get me wrong. I understand why you went after Davis last night, but I'm telling you it's not worth it to pull that sort of stunt."

"I understand, sir." Katherine let the story wash over her. She got the point — follow the handbook and stay safe — but she couldn't help wondering…if McAlister's ambush had gone differently, perhaps the Boss would be behind bars right now instead of running a crime ring. Sure, McAlister's attempt at stopping the Boss had gone sour, but that didn't mean it wasn't worth the effort. The story hadn't scared her like McAlister intended. If anything, it strengthened her resolve. So what if she got injured or even killed? Her job was to keep Nolaton safe, no matter the price.

"Listen, Dell, I'm not happy about how you handled your first case, but I got another one for you. I'm assigning Officer Williams as your support whether you like it or not. You two will make a good pair."

Katherine couldn't imagine any scenario where she and Williams made a good pair. McAlister probably just wanted him around to keep an eye on her, but if Williams knew what was good for him, he'd stay out of her way.

McAlister handed her the case file, then dismissed her.

Katherine trudged back to her office and a thought struck her. How had Williams known that McAlister wanted to speak with her? Had that little fink ratted her out?

She shook off her annoyance and read over the details of her new case. A body had been found outside the Razzle Dazzle. Katherine wrinkled her nose as she read the name of the club. She had been there once or twice many years ago with some girlfriends from the theater. The place was a dive. Then again, her memories of those nights were quite fuzzy. Maybe it wasn't as bad as she remembered.

According to the crime scene investigator's report, the woman had no purse or pocketbook on her. She may have been robbed before or after being killed. Katherine took out the photos. A woman's body lay in an alley, her limbs falling at odd angles. Another murdered prostitute, perhaps? No, her clothes were modest, and her makeup was tasteful.

A dark line snaked across the victim's neck. At first, Katherine thought it was a cut, but upon closer inspection of the photograph, it looked more like a bruise. The poor thing must have been strangled. She leafed through the file and found the coroner's report, which confirmed her conclusion. The autopsy revealed small hemorrhages in her eyes and at the base of her tongue consistent with ligature strangulation — the use of an object rather than hands. Scratch marks on her neck and tissue under her fingernails showed that the victim had tried to rip the object away. Katherine thought of this woman's last moments, desperate for breath and clawing for life. Whoever put her through that hell would not go unpunished.

Katherine looked back at the photograph noting the size and shape of the bruise across the woman's neck. The bruise would mimic the object she had been throttled with. Katherine agreed that this could not have been manual strangulation, otherwise the bruise would look like handprints. But what had she been strangled with? A shoelace perhaps, or a necklace?

That wasn't right. Though the dark line was the most prominent part of the mark, the bruise extended lightly above and below.

Someone knocked on her door.

"Come in." She spoke politely just in case it was McAlister. The knob turned and an offensively eager face appeared in the doorway. Williams. He leaned on her door frame, holding an envelope in front of him.

Katherine scowled and raised an eyebrow at him, hoping he would take the hint and leave her alone. "What do you want?"

"I thought we could discuss our case." That obnoxious grin of his spread further across his face.

"*Our* case? You mean *my* case?" Clearly, he needed a reminder of the hierarchy.

Williams stuck out his arms, waving away her comment. "Hey, McAlister wanted me to give you a hand—"

"Keep your hands to yourself. I don't need help." Katherine pointed out the door, imploring him to walk away.

"Don't be like that." Williams waltzed into her office and set the envelope on her desk.

"You didn't have to tattle on me." Katherine glared at him, surprised by how hurt she felt. It wasn't as if she and Williams were friends, but for him to go out of his way to get her in trouble...

"I'm sorry, okay? Can we get to work already?"

Katherine kept glaring at him but nodded. She spun the folder around and let him see what McAlister had given her. He looked perplexed, then opened the envelope he had brought in. "Look at this." He handed her a photo of a glowing young blonde who, sadly, looked familiar.

"Wait a minute." Katherine picked up her photo of the dead body as Williams came around her desk to stand beside her. Katherine held the pictures out, looking back and forth between the two. Side by side it was unmistakable.

"Same gal, right?" Katherine angled the photos toward Williams. As angry as she was with him, solving the case was more important than their feud.

"Same gal. Her boyfriend just came in to report her missing. Said she went to an audition last night to replace the headliners at the Razzle Dazzle, and never came home."

"That's where the body was found." Interesting. Could her death have been about the audition? Maybe someone didn't want a new act coming in. Who was the headliner these days? Katherine couldn't believe that those MacDougall sisters would still be there; their routine had been tired ten years ago.

Williams put his hand on her desk to get her attention. "Here's what we'll do. I'll go down to the Razzle and investigate—"

Katherine scoffed. How dare he try to call the shots. "Excuse me? I'm the detective here. I'll decide who does what."

"McAlister never said you were in charge. He wants us to work on this together." Williams spoke to her like she was a child.

"I outrank you. It's implied that I'm in charge." How could he not see that?

Williams spoke out of the side of his mouth. "Do you really think you ought to be?"

"What was that?"

"Leadership might not be your strong suit. If I remember correctly, you couldn't even process that thief on your own."

Katherine shot up out of her seat. "I had the situation under control—"

"You had me taking notes like some kind of secretary before you went nutso on her, isn't that right? I had to clean up your mess by myself?"

"Get out."

"Gladly." Williams walked out, without a glance back at her.

Katherine balled up her fists as she sank into her chair. She could have handled Rita Davis on her own, and she could handle this case on her own. That arrogant bastard didn't know what she was capable of.

Her shoulders were so tense they almost reached her ears and Katherine forced them back down. She pushed Williams's pigheaded attitude from her mind, then looked at the cases side by side. The victim had a boyfriend, Jack Lewis. Poor guy. He'd have to come in to identify the body. Katherine was certain it was the same girl, but at this point she couldn't afford to ignore protocol.

Katherine turned her chair and stared out of her window into the street. Would she ever get the respect she deserved? Would the men on the force see her as one of them? In the end, did it matter? Katherine trusted herself and respected herself. Maybe that was enough.

She turned back to her case file. Time to call Jack Lewis and break his heart.

A few hours later, Katherine came back to the station after a gut-wrenching trip to the medical examiner's office. Jack had identified the body as Loretta Marie Jones, age twenty-two. Katherine's heart fell with that familiar weighty emptiness. No one should ever have to lose someone they love.

"Sir, I've got something to show you." She lingered in the lieutenant's door frame with a file in hand, the tension of their last conversation tightening around her. She explained her findings so far and laid out the photos Jack had brought next to the photo of Loretta's body.

McAlister stared at the photos. Katherine hoped he wasn't already cooking up criticism.

"Too damn young. What was she doing there?"

He wasn't picking apart her work. Katherine wiggled her fingers, willing herself to relax. "She wanted to be a jazz singer. The last time Jack saw her she was on her way to an audition with Al Harris, the owner of the Razzle Dazzle."

"She was auditioning *there*?" McAlister scowled. "That place is…" He couldn't seem to find appropriate words. Katherine was sure several inappropriate ones were circling his mind.

"Not the best place to start a respected career," she finished for him. "Have you ever seen their headliner show there? Cream and Sugar?"

"I wouldn't step foot in that joint, but I've heard about them. They're not still doing that act, are they?"

"I called the Razzle; they haven't changed a line since opening night. Loretta was auditioning to replace them."

"Maybe they didn't like the competition." Half a smile spread on his face.

"I can't imagine they did." She mimicked his expression. The tension ebbed as her confidence grew. McAlister had promoted her for a reason, and one slipup wouldn't get her fired. "I'll go there tonight and question the lovely ladies." She collected her photos and turned to leave.

"Have Williams meet you down there." McAlister seemed to think she needed a reminder, as if she would forget his command to work with her least favorite officer. She would have gladly left Williams at the station but was in no position to disobey her superior.

Katherine slowly turned around. "Yes, sir." The words broke through her clenched teeth.

Lights flashed from the sign hanging on the dingy building; the rain did little to cleanse the decades of filth from the brick. The words "RAZZLE" and "DAZZLE" shined backward in the street puddles, distorted by the ripples and missing bulbs. Wet trash spilled out from the alley, old papers and wrappers sticking to the curb.

Williams stood in front of the club holding an umbrella. He had a bored expression, which made Katherine wonder how much energy he would put toward solving the case. Would he allow their feud to interfere with the investigation? She hoped he was better than that. "All right, Detective. You're in charge. Where do we start?"

Katherine balled up her fist at that smarmy attitude. Maybe he needed a reminder of her higher status. "*We* don't start anywhere. I'll go question Al Harris and the current headliners, while you..." She grabbed him by the shoulders and guided him to the yellow rope cordoning off the alley. "...stand right here and look pretty." She pinched his cheek, mimicking an overzealous aunt, then walked toward the club entrance.

"That's it? That's all I get to do?"

"That's it. Now hop to it." She snapped her fingers as if expecting him to jump into action, chuckling under her breath. Williams's face twisted into a frown.

"You can't be serious. It's freezing out here!" He hunched his shoulders and fell into dramatic shivers.

"Are you questioning a direct order from a superior?" Katherine feigned surprise at his challenge. He grumbled.

"No, ma'am."

"Come on. I'm not that cruel. You can take notes while I ask questions." Katherine motioned for him to follow her inside. He bounded over to her, probably trying to get to the entrance before she changed her mind.

Katherine shook out her umbrella, then opened the Razzle's front door. A coating of grime transferred from the handle to her palm, and she wiped it off with her handkerchief. Her boots peeled from the floor with each step. How many years' worth of spilled drinks she was walking through? The room had a humid haze that smelled of stale cigarettes. Several round tables sat in front of the stage, and only a handful were occupied. The clientele hunched over their cocktails, taking sips here and there with slack-jawed ambivalence.

On stage stood a balding, middle-aged man, his face lit up by a spotlight. He told a few crude jokes, which the audience mostly ignored. The man tugged on his collar, clearly fazed by the lack of laughter.

"Don't worry, folks. You don't have to listen to me anymore. Here they are, the gals you've been waiting for — the magnificent Cream and Sugar!" He gestured to the side of the stage and two women walked on. One was slender and quite tall for a woman, the other short with a potbelly. Both had squeezed into sequined dresses, their hair bound in elaborate updos. They stood near the edge of the stage and broke into a tap number. The song was jaunty, but the ladies were not. They performed as if it was a punishment. The number finally came to an end as the women shook their hands toward the audience, and unenthusiastic applause issued from the few occupied seats.

"Welcome to our show!" The short woman flung her arm up.

"We're so glad to see your lovely faces." The tall woman gestured to the right side of the room.

"We're glad you showed up too." The short woman pointed to the left side of the room.

"I'm Candace MacDougall," said the tall woman.

"I'm Shirley MacDougall," said the short woman.

"But for you," they said together, "we're Cream and Sugar!" They shimmied their chests at the front row.

"Cream? More like skim milk! You don't have an ounce of fat on you." Shirley pinched Candace's ribs.

"Aw, Sugar, you're too sweet. Say, have you heard the one about the priest and the aged salami?" Candace winked at the audience.

Katherine didn't want to hear the end of that joke. She looked around, hoping to find someone who could point her to the owner. Just as she was about to approach the bartender, a man walked out from the back hallway and started to circulate. He went up to a couple at the bar, asking if they were having a nice time, his booming voice filling the room. They nodded and lifted their drinks. He made his way around to the tables and spoke to a group there.

"Don't these ladies put on a fabulous show? Are you enjoying yourselves?"

They nodded.

"Good, glad to hear it. I'm Al, the owner. If you need anything, just ask." He noticed Katherine and his eyes bugged out.

"Well, hello!" He slicked his hair back with his palm as he approached her. "What a treat to have such a beautiful woman in our audience tonight. Are you here to see the show?"

"Actually, I'm here to see you. Mr. Harris, I presume?"

"Yes, ma'am, but please, call me Al. What can I help you with this evening?" Al looked a little too eager, and Katherine showed her badge. "I'm Detective Dell. I need to ask you a few questions about a young lady who auditioned here recently." Katherine took out her notebook and tried to hand it off to Williams, but Williams was preoccupied watching the act. He was so busy chortling at the dirty punchlines, Katherine had to whack his arm with the notebook to get his attention. Williams turned to her and snatched the notebook from her hands as his face drooped.

Al's enthusiasm faded and he looked chagrined, like a schoolboy who got in trouble with the teacher. "Of course. Ask away."

"What's the difference between a camel and my ex-boyfriend?" Shirley said from the stage.

"Somewhere private, if you don't mind," Katherine said to Al.

Al's office felt more like a converted broom closet. The walls were white and relatively bare other than a few old posters, including one of Cream and Sugar's opening night. In the photo their eyes sparkled, full of hope. Katherine wondered when that sparkle had faded. It certainly wasn't there tonight. Al sat behind the pinewood table he used as a desk and gestured for Katherine to pull up the rickety-looking chair in the corner.

"I'll stand, if that's all right."

Williams stood at attention behind her with the notebook open and pencil poised. Maybe her threat to make him stand out in the rain had earned her some loyalty.

"Suit yourself. Oh, where are my manners? Can I get either of you a beverage? We've got beer, wine, or Lou could whip you up a whiskey sour. That's one of our specialties. Feels good to offer our whole beverage selection legally, I'll tell you that!"

"No, thank you." Even if she wasn't on duty, Katherine wouldn't take a drink from him. If the glasses were as clean as the rest of the place, she'd give herself botulism. She turned to Williams, who shook his head, declining a drink as well.

"Of course, doll. I just couldn't forgive myself if I didn't offer." Al set his elbows on the desk, then set his chin in his hands. He looked like an expectant audience member, waiting for Katherine to dance for him. She crossed her arms over her chest.

"Mind if I ask my questions?" It wasn't a request. She shot him a look that said she meant business.

Al sat up straight. "Fire away."

"A young woman by the name of Loretta Jones came to your club last night, auditioning to be your new headliner, correct?"

"Yes, yes, Miss Loretta. What a lovely young girl. Sweet as an angel, with a voice to match." Al's gaze drifted past Katherine as though he was deep in thought.

"So her audition went well? You offered her the job?"

Jack had confirmed this, but Katherine wanted to hear Al's point of view.

"It went better than well! That girl would have been a star and made me rich in the process. She sang one song for me, and I hired her on the spot." Al gestured wildly as he spoke.

"'Would have been' — so you're aware that she's deceased?" Katherine put on her most menacing expression and Al squirmed. Williams's pencil scratched away behind her.

"Awful, isn't it? Someone found her right out there." Al pointed toward the wall, in the direction of the roped-off alley.

"What time did she arrive and what time did she leave?"

"Oh, she got here at nine o'clock and left ten or fifteen minutes later."

"You said she sang one song for you, but she stayed for 'ten or fifteen' minutes? That would be an awfully long audition song. What else happened during her visit?"

Al's cheeks turned red and he shifted in his seat. Was he growing uncomfortable with the questions, and if so, why?

"Nothing noteworthy," he said at last, "just discussed the expectations of the job."

"So you didn't hear or see anything suspicious last night after she left?"

"Heavens no! To be honest, I had a bit too much of the giggle juice. I went upstairs after her audition to sleep it off."

"Upstairs?"

"Yeah, my wife and I have an apartment above the club. Speak of the devil." Al huffed and gestured toward the door.

Katherine turned. A woman stood in the door frame, looking disheveled. Her dress hung from her scrawny frame, revealing a small line of cleavage. Makeup was plastered onto her face, but it couldn't disguise the bruise under her eye.

"What do you want, Vicki?" Al snapped at her.

"Sorry to interrupt. Aren't you gonna introduce me?" She looked Katherine up and down, then panned Williams and smiled. Al let out a frustrated sigh.

"This is Detective Dell and, uh, I didn't catch your name, sir."

"Officer Williams. Pleasure to meet you, ma'am." Williams nodded toward Vicki, who blushed in return.

"There, you've been introduced. Are you happy now?" Al waved his hand, dismissing Vicki from the room. She giggled and let herself in instead.

"Oh, Al. Don't be like that. Detective, huh? What's the bit?"

"Bit?" Katherine asked.

Vicki circled Katherine as if checking out merchandise in a shop. "You've got a dancer's body, that's for sure. Oh, I get you! It's a cop-themed burlesque act. How fun! I did burlesque in my younger days. You can pretend to arrest someone in the audience each night. You'll draw a crowd." Vicki straightened Katherine's suit coat, taking a moment to inspect it. "I'd go with a more traditional costume, though. You know, dark blue with the brass buttons more like his." She pointed to Williams. "Do you dance too, honey?"

"Ah, Vicki, they are real police officers. They're investigating the murder in the alley last night."

Vicki's mouth dropped and she hurriedly took her hands off Katherine. "Golly, I'm sorry! So you're a real copper, huh?" Vicki smiled, seeming eager to hear more.

"Any particular reason you're interrupting us?" Anger underscored Al's words, and Vicki hunched over just a bit as if cowering away from her husband.

"The whiskey guy was here. He wanted to see you, but I took care of it." She stuttered out her words.

"What are you driving at? The whiskey guy wasn't here."

"Yes, he was." Vicki put her hands on her hips.

"He only delivers on Tuesdays. Today is not Tuesday, sweetheart," Al said condescendingly.

"I know what day it is. I'm not an idiot." Vicki changed her tone to match his.

"What do you mean you took care of it?"

"He only dropped off four cases yesterday, and he stopped by today with the fifth one. He said he hadn't gotten paid, so I gave him cash from the register."

"You did what? That's not how this business works!" Al was shouting now.

Katherine and Williams glanced at each other while the couple argued, and Al must have noticed their discomfort. "Vicki, may I speak with you in the hallway?" Al spoke through gritted teeth.

"Of course, dear." They stepped outside the door, but Katherine could still hear their conversation. Williams scribbled down a few lines.

"Did I give you permission to talk to the whiskey guy?"

"I came down for a cocktail and ran into him. What? I'm not allowed in the club?"

"I'd prefer if you stayed upstairs."

"You'd prefer it if I never left the apartment."

"Damn right. Maybe then the place would be clean."

"I'm not your servant, Al. I'm your wife."

"Some wife you are, always running off to your sewing circle or your book club. When's the last time you made me a hot meal?"

"When's the last time you deserved it?" Vicki screeched her words.

Katherine heard a loud thud against the wall, followed by a slap, and a whimper. She gasped and sprang toward the door to stop Al from causing any more damage. Maybe he had put that bruise on Vicki's face earlier. Williams turned to join her, but the altercation ended before either of them could intervene.

"I'll deal with your mess. You go upstairs and put a goddamn roast in the oven."

"Wait, Al. I'm sorry! I didn't mean to upset you. Please don't be mad at me."

"Get out of my sight." He opened the office door and Vicki's footsteps echoed in the hall as she hurried away.

"Sorry for the interruption, Detective. Did you have any more questions?" Al's charming smile returned. Katherine recoiled. How could a man switch from beating his wife to flashing his teeth that quickly? Katherine did her best to remain professional, though inside she seethed.

"That's all I needed from you, Mr. Harris. I'd like to speak with the MacDougall sisters. When will they be done performing?"

Al checked his watch. "They'll be off stage in about half an hour. Feel free to enjoy the show until then."

Katherine figured she would sit in the audience until the show was over. She walked into the bar with Williams at her heel and there, at one of those round tables, sat Vicki. She had a cocktail in one hand and a cigarette in the other. She lifted the cigarette to her lips and took a listless drag. Puffy, red eyes showed under her running mascara. She noticed Katherine and waved her over. Katherine gestured for Williams to follow and approached her table.

"I'm sure you're busy, but can I talk to you for a minute?" Vicki indicated the chairs across from her. "I'm sorry you had to see that." The mark on Vicki's cheek had already turned a painful shade of pink. She put her hand up to cover it and Katherine took a seat.

"No need to apologize. I've seen a lot worse in my line of work."

Vicki squirmed in her seat.

"You don't think..." Vicki trailed off.

"Think what?"

"...that he killed that girl?" Her eyes begged for answers.

"He's not a suspect at this time." Although, after that hotheaded display, Katherine had started to wonder.

Vicki heaved a sigh of relief. "I thought you were here to arrest him or something. The thought of losing my Al...of him going to prison..." She took a swig of her drink. "He's not a violent person. He's a good man."

Katherine winced at the assertion. A good man would not hit his wife. Ever. "You know, the police are only a phone call away if things get out of hand."

"It's not like that. He's my husband. I vowed to obey him. He has to let me know when I get out of line."

"I realize it's none of my business, but your husband shouldn't leave marks on you."

"You sound like my kids. They don't talk to Al anymore." Vicki swirled her drink, clearly saddened by the estrangement. This stung Katherine as she thought of her own strained relationship with her father. At least her father wasn't violent, only insensitive and obtuse. This was no time to dwell, however.

Vicki went on. "They don't get it, and you don't either. It's my own fault."

Pulling Vicki from her delusion seemed impossible. If she believed that Al was right to treat her that way Katherine wouldn't be able to convince her otherwise, and the law was firmly on Al's side. Katherine pitied her and wished she could help, but she couldn't force Vicki to see the truth. Perhaps Vicki could be helpful with the investigation, though.

Katherine fired off a few questions, but Vicki had no new information.

"Sorry, I should really get back upstairs. I've let the dishes pile up too long. Thanks for listening to me ramble." Vicki slammed her drink, then scampered away with her cigarette still glowing.

Katherine watched the last part of the show, surprised that the jokes could actually get worse. At last, the sisters sang their final number.

Chapter Nineteen

After the show, the bartender pointed Katherine and Williams to the MacDougall sisters' dressing room. Katherine found the door with two faded paper stars taped to it. One read "Cream," the other "Sugar." The corners of the stars curled forward. Katherine knocked. Williams took a few steps back, probably to keep from getting an accidental peek at a women's dressing room. Katherine knew all too well how awkward a man could feel when he bursts in on a gal while she's changing. She pushed her memory of Joey aside to focus on her work.

"You'll have to come back later, we're about to change our clothes," said a voice from inside.

"Unless you're Clark Gable, then come on in!" said another voice.

"I'm Detective Dell, here with my colleague Officer Williams. I need to ask you a few questions."

A long pause followed, then fevered whispers sounded from within. Katherine pushed the door open, the hinges creaking. Both of the sisters stood looking defeated, their arms outstretched as though waiting to be cuffed.

"Go ahead." Candace tossed her head.

"We know why you're here." Shirley closed her eyes.

"Slap them on. Take us to the station." Candace extended her hands farther toward Katherine. Were they really going to give up that easily?

"So you admit it?"

"We knew the cops would come knocking eventually," Shirley said.

Katherine couldn't believe she was getting a confession so readily. "What you've done is unforgivable. Absolutely vile." Katherine dug out her handcuffs and Williams followed suit.

"Well, I wouldn't go that far!" Shirley sneered.

"Take a look in the mirror, honey. You're not any better than us," Candace said. Katherine grew indignant.

"Me? You know nothing about me, but I'll tell you this — I'm better than a couple of murderers."

Both Candace and Shirley pulled their hands back, eyes widening. "Murderers? Who said anything about being murderers?" Shirley placed her hand on her heart, shocked at the assertion.

"What the hell else would I arrest you for?"

Katherine stared at them, and then it clicked. She hadn't seen it before with the makeup and stage lights, but she saw it now — the strategic padding, the cosmetics Shirley used to create the illusion of cleavage, the Adam's apple hidden beneath Candace's high neckline. Cross-dressing was illegal, even for performances, and the people arrested for it were usually not treated kindly.

Katherine took Candace's instruction to heart and glanced in the mirror herself. She had faced plenty of scrutiny as a female police officer. Who was she to judge anyone else for refusing to conform?

"I take it you're not really sisters," Katherine asked, weighing this new information.

Candace and Shirley looked at each other. Neither seemed sure how to respond.

"More like..." Shirley trailed off.

"...close friends," Candace finished.

"Listen, no one is going to jail tonight — at least not because of your outfits." Katherine glared at Williams, challenging him to disagree. She expected him to scold her, remind her to follow protocol and push past her to cuff the performers. Instead, he nodded in agreement.

"We're here to solve a murder. Let's focus on that," Williams said.

"Thank goodness! I mean, that's bad that someone got killed, but good we're not going to jail." Candace fanned her face.

"I've been in jail since I put these torture devices on." Shirley pointed to her high heels, her feet crunched into the ill-fitting leather.

"Should I leave you ladies — um, gentlemen? — to get changed?" Now that Katherine was in the room with them, the pair of veteran performers seemed tame. She had trouble picturing them as ruthless killers.

"It's 'ladies,' and we'll change after you leave. Just give us one moment to get settled." Candace pulled two stools out from under the makeup counter.

"Did you see the show?" Shirley asked excitedly, some of that sparkle from the poster back in her eyes. Nostalgia for her stage days floated over Katherine. She missed that postshow high.

"I did. It was very good." Katherine felt bad for lying, but figured they'd be more cooperative with her investigation if she complimented them. Shirley pulled two buckets of water out from under the counter and set them in front of the stools. The ladies kicked off their shoes and lowered their feet to soak. Both let out a satisfied "Ahh."

"So what happened?" Candace asked. "You said there was a murder?"

"You don't know? A body was found in the alley early this morning." From their scandalized expressions, Katherine suspected they really hadn't known anything about it. They looked at each other, then back at Katherine.

"I had no idea!" Shirley said.

"Nobody tells us nothing around here." Candace folded her arms.

"It was in the evening papers," Katherine said.

"We don't read those rags." Shirley gestured dismissively.

"Who got whacked?" Candace asked.

"A young lady by the name of Loretta Jones. She—"

"Loretta?" Shirley reached for her cigarettes and offered one to Candace.

"Please tell me you're joking." Candace lit a match under her cigarette and puffed, obviously agitated.

"That poor, sweet girl," Shirley said.

"What happened to her?" Candace asked.

Katherine rubbed her temple, growing frustrated by the back-and-forth. "That's what I'm trying to figure out. Were you here at the club during her audition?"

"Honey, we never leave," Candace said.

"Did you see anything out of the ordinary?" Katherine asked.

"Ain't no such thing as ordinary around here." Shirley laughed, and Katherine gave her a warning look. "We didn't see anything unusual." Shirley sank back in her seat.

"You've been the headliners at this club for how many years?"

Shirley looked at Candace and shrugged. "A hundred?"

"Fifteen, if my math is correct," Candace said. "We got hired right after Prohibition started. Remember? Al bought this place the year before, back when it was just a bar."

"That's right. Our old club got busted up, so we came here. Al thought he would lose the place once they made booze illegal, so we suggested he run it as a theater. With us as the stars, naturally!" Shirley batted her eyelashes.

Katherine leaned in, ready to draw out a confession as Shirley had just touched on a motive for murder. "And Loretta was poised to take over as the star if her audition went well?"

"What are you getting at?" Candace narrowed her eyes.

"It seems odd to me that a young, talented woman was hired to take your jobs and gets murdered the same night." Katherine placed her hand on her hip.

Candace and Shirley spoke at the same time.

"You think we had something to do with this?" Shirley asked.

"You think we'd hurt that sweet girl?" Candace went doe-eyed.

"Give me one good reason why you wouldn't." Katherine let a frigid silence permeate the room, hoping to intimidate the suspects.

The women paused for a moment and exchanged glances. Shirley broke the silence. "My bunions, that's why. Sweetheart, we've been doing this show every night for fifteen years. If I have to tell that joke about the 'opposite of constitution' one more time, my brain will explode out of my ears!" Shirley put a hand to her forehead in dramatic demonstration.

"We would gladly give up the spotlight. Honestly, we're exhausted," Candace said.

"Seriously, my bunions could take an eye out. You wanna see them?" Shirley lifted one foot from her bucket.

"Don't be gross." Candace smacked Shirley on the arm.

"We didn't have any ill will toward Loretta. Al wants to take this place in a different direction, and we don't blame him. Our show isn't drawing the crowds like it used to," Candace said.

"I'll let you in on a little secret." Shirley curled her pointer finger, motioning for Katherine to lean in farther. "We've been saving our pennies over the years. With that, plus my inheritance from Grandma Ginger, God rest her soul, we could quit performing right now and buy our own club."

"It's been a dream of ours for a long time. Opening our own juice joint for...well, for people like us." Candace looked concerned. "Maybe I shouldn't say that to a cop."

"I'll leave it out of my notes." Katherine whipped her head around to look at Williams, who crossed out a few lines in the notebook.

"We'd have to stop performing to make it happen, but we can't just up and quit. Al has been good to us and we can't leave him without a headliner. It would be nice to take a break, though." Shirley sighed.

Katherine finished her questions and gave the ladies her contact information. She felt confident that they were not responsible for strangling Loretta, but wouldn't rule out any suspects until she had more concrete evidence. As she and Williams made their way out of the dressing room, she contemplated her findings.

If Candace and Shirley hadn't killed Loretta, who did? Al had certainly made a bad impression on Katherine during their interview, but he had no motive. According to what Candace and Shirley said, he wanted a more mainstream headliner and Loretta was both beautiful and talented — exactly what he was looking for. Something didn't add up.

Williams kept his nose in the notebook and refused to speak to her as they walked out of the club. Katherine didn't care if he was sore at her as long as his work got done. She glanced around the outside of the club, taking in the scene one last time to be sure she hadn't missed anything obvious. Just as she turned to head toward the trolley stop, two figures standing across the street caught her eye.

It couldn't be. She had to be imagining it. Slowly, she turned and looked. Standing there in the shadows were two men, almost identical, down to the matching gray suits. The brims of their hats hid their eyes, but Katherine felt the force of their stares. It was them. The same men she had seen five years ago — the men who had stalked Joey like prey. Katherine closed her eyes, then braved another glance across the street. They were gone.

"Did you see them?" She tapped Williams on the shoulder and pointed to where the figures had just been standing.

"Who?"

"Those men, right over there."

Williams looked over, a confused expression on his face. The street was quiet. There was no sign of them. Had she been hallucinating? No, they had been standing right there under the awning.

The Gray Suits. The men who worked for the Spider.

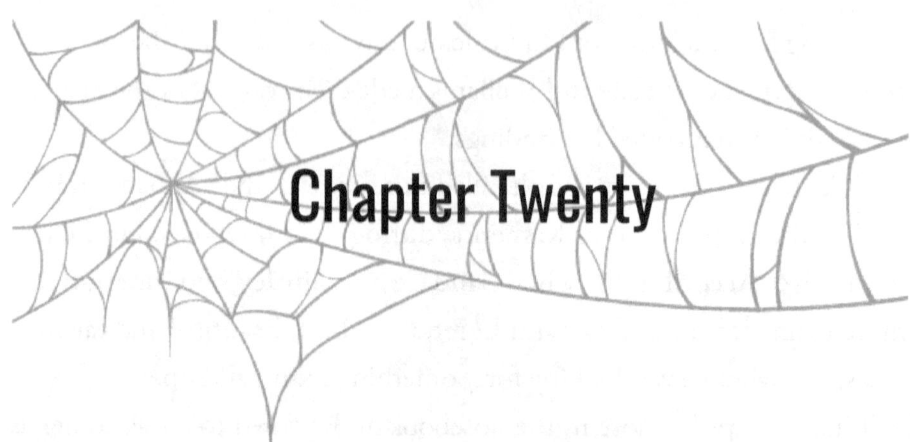

Chapter Twenty

The next morning, Katherine met Williams in the parking lot of the police station. They had arranged to meet Jack Lewis at his apartment. Since their inquiries at the Razzle had come up empty, Katherine wanted more insight into Loretta's life.

"Ready to go?" Williams leaned on the back of one of the department's new Model 18s with keys in his hand. She nodded at him and lit up as he walked around to the passenger side. Usually, the detective takes the driver's seat, but Katherine had expected Williams to argue, saying that he, as a man, would be more qualified to take the wheel. Maybe he finally understood his place and would get in the passenger seat without a fuss. She rubbed her hands together, excited to get behind the wheel, but Williams opened the passenger door and motioned for her to enter instead.

Katherine steamed. He'd never hold the car door for a male officer, and definitely not for a male detective. There would have been no question who sat in the driver's seat if she were a man. She walked up to him, mimicking the grin on his face, and took the keys from his hand. His face fell as she made her way to the driver's side door.

They pulled out of the parking lot in silence. Williams kept glancing at her, but she paid no attention to him. As they drove off, rain sprinkled the windshield, and she watched the drops get larger and more frequent. Williams cleared his throat. Katherine hoped he wasn't going to get her sick. He cleared his throat again.

"Need a lozenge?" She pursed her lips.

"No."

"Then stop doing that. If I have to bring you along, the least you can do is make it a pleasant journey." Silence returned, broken a few moments later by Williams.

"Why do you do that?"

"Do what?"

"Make those mean comments."

Katherine couldn't help but laugh. Had she hurt his delicate feelings? Did he have any regard for how his actions affected her?

"Why are you such a condescending jerk?" She was still upset over his assumption that he'd be driving.

"I didn't know I was a jerk." He leaned against the window, staring out at the road. That was odd. Wasn't he going to fire back with a rude comment of his own? Was he upset, or deep in thought? Katherine wasn't sure how to proceed.

"Well, you are." The words came out harsher than she intended. "Sometimes you are," she added, hoping that would soften the criticism. "Especially since I got the badge over you. I didn't think you wanted it that badly."

"You piss the lieutenant off at every turn, and he gives you a promotion. I do all the right things, follow the rules—"

"And I get results."

"So do I. You think Franklin Green would be behind bars right now if I hadn't taken that case? No. He'd still be out robbing little old ladies' apartments. I've got what it takes to make some real changes in this city."

"And I don't?" Katherine glared at him, then snapped her attention back to the road.

He tented his fingers like he was calculating his next move. "That's not what I meant. I just, well, it would be nice to bring home a little more bacon." Williams spoke his words at rapid speed like he didn't want to say it at all.

Katherine huffed, disgusted by his greed. "Is that all you care about? A little extra pocket change?"

"Well, no, it's just...never mind..." Williams trailed off.

"What? Want to take your girlfriends out to fancier restaurants?" Katherine spoke with a fake haughtiness. A man like Williams would only want a fatter paycheck to impress the floozies, right?

"Not that it's any of your business, but I haven't been on a date in four months." That tidbit lingered in the air between them, leaving Katherine unsure what to do with it. "I need the money because things have changed in my life and...you know what? I don't have to explain myself to you." He hissed his words and hunched his shoulders into a defensive arch.

Katherine's hands tensed around the steering wheel. She had been mad at Williams dozens of times, but she couldn't remember a time when he had been mad at her. Annoyed or frustrated, maybe. Taunting and tormenting, always. But nothing like this. It bothered her more than she thought it would.

"Look, I'm sorry. I shouldn't have..." she started as she pulled up to Jack's apartment.

"It's all right. We're here."

She turned off the engine and Williams got out of the car. The windows were a blur of raindrops, but she could see him tromping up to the apartment. Katherine supposed she'd gotten her wish. She opened her car door herself.

Katherine knocked on the door of apartment 103 and a puffy-eyed Jack Lewis answered. His hair had not been combed and a slight odor emanated from him as if he hadn't washed. Katherine couldn't judge him. He probably felt exactly the way she had after Joey died, like a mechanism in the brain had ceased functioning and the engine stalled. He invited them to enter, and they stepped inside.

"Can I get you some tea or coffee?" Jack asked. He had the same desperate eyes she had seen in her own mirror. Katherine melted. Despite his troubles, he still wanted to be a good host. Though she found the offer endearing, she turned him down, wanting to focus on the case instead of beverages.

"Do you mind if I take a look around?" Williams asked.

"If it will help figure out who hurt Loretta, you can look through anything you'd like." Jack began to tear up. Williams began his search. Jack sat on the couch and indicated for Katherine to join him. She sat and took out her notepad.

"I don't know how much help I'm gonna be."

"Any information you have will be of great help. Did you notice anything unusual when Miss Jones left for the audition?"

"She was nervous, but who wouldn't be? This was going to be her big break." Jack pulled at the threads of his couch cushion.

"Have you ever been to the Razzle Dazzle?" Katherine looked at him out of the side of her eye. Jack must have picked up her meaning.

"I know it's a seedy joint, but Lo was over the moon. I wasn't gonna stop her from pursuing her dream."

"Whoa!" Williams poked his head around the corner. Katherine snapped to attention. He held out a velvet box. Inside was a glimmering diamond ring. The center stone was larger than Katherine's. She squinted around the room, taking in the shabby furnishings. A "Cliff's Market" apron embroidered with Jack's name hung from the front door. The coffee table was poorly constructed and had several scratches. Even the walls were bare. Something didn't add up. These were not people of means. How on earth could Jack afford a ring of that caliber? Did he have to borrow money to buy it? Did he borrow from the wrong people?

"Jack, forgive me for being rude, but how did you afford a ring like that?"

Jack managed a smile. "It's fake. Just glass. I told Lo I'd buy her a real one someday, but I gave her that as a placeholder. The band is too big, though, so she couldn't wear it. I was gonna get it resized." Jack's eyes drifted to the floor, yet he seemed to be looking several miles away. Williams closed the box and went back to searching.

"Can you think of anyone who would want to hurt Loretta?"

Jack thought for a moment. "We're not the most popular people in the building. Some of our neighbors don't want to live next to an unwed couple."

"Has anyone made threats?"

"Not directly, but we get dirty looks and comments."

"From whom?"

"Everyone in the building."

Williams finished his search, though it yielded nothing. Katherine thanked Jack for his time, then beckoned Williams to the hallway. If the neighbors had been that abrasive toward Jack and Loretta, perhaps one of them had taken their hostility too far. She planned to knock on every door in the building to weed out any possible suspects.

"I don't have time to knock on twenty doors. I promised I'd meet Peterson—"

Katherine cut him off. "My investigation, my rules." She knocked on the door of the apartment next to Jack's. An elderly woman answered, a strong stench of ammonia flooding out when she opened the door. Newspapers and magazines lay in heaps against the walls. The woman introduced herself as Mrs. Morton and she adjusted her glasses, trying to read Katherine's badge.

"You're with the police department? Did someone complain about my cats?"

"No, Mrs. Morton. We're here investigating..." Katherine didn't want to scare the old woman and changed tack. "...something more serious. Can you tell us where you were on Tuesday night around nine o'clock?"

"You got her pegged as the killer?" Williams mumbled to Katherine.

"No, but she might have information for us," Katherine whispered back.

"I was stuck at the vet all evening. I found Buster pawing at the garbage cans outside and I just had to keep him." Mrs. Morton picked up a gray cat with black markings around its eyes. More cats, about a dozen of them, crawled out of the magazine piles and came to the door. "Little Buster here was in a world of trouble. The vet spent hours brushing out his fur and picking out the lice."

Williams's eyes widened at the mention of lice. He took a step back from the cat and threw his hands over his hair, as if shielding it from the parasites. Katherine stifled her laughter.

"Wait a minute. This isn't Buster." Mrs. Morton squinted at the creature in her hands and the others around her feet. Another gray cat rubbed against Katherine's ankles. "That's Buster!" Mrs. Morton set down the imposter and picked up the real Buster. The imposter ran into the hallway and Katherine tried to catch it, but the cat was too quick.

"Sorry, Mrs. Morton."

"Oh, no worries. Mitsy will be back by suppertime. She'll tell me all about her adventure."

"Thank you for your time, Mrs. Morton." Katherine tried to keep a smile on her face.

They walked to the next apartment and knocked on the door. A man answered, struggling to open his door. His leg was in a cast and the door hit his crutches; he hopped back a few inches to give it clearance. Williams gave Katherine an incredulous look. Katherine ignored him and explained the purpose of their visit.

"That funny couple two doors down? I don't approve, but it's none of my business."

"When did you sustain your injuries?" Katherine glanced at his leg.

"Last Saturday. I figured I know how to ride a bicycle; riding a unicycle can't be that different. I was wrong. Very wrong. I've been cooped up here ever since. Doctor's orders."

Katherine and Williams spent the next hour knocking on doors. The Framples had tickets to a play that night. Mr. Rusket took samba lessons every week at that time. Miss Watters had a promising third date. No one knew anything pertinent to the case.

"Bravo, Detective. Great use of our time," Williams said mockingly as they walked back to Jack's place.

"Hey, now we can cross them off the list."

"I don't know. That Mitsy seemed like a shady character."

Katherine grimaced at him. They knocked on Jack's door and he let them back in.

"Anyone else you can think of?" Katherine asked, desperate for a lead.

"I should tell you…" Jack trailed off. He paced the room.

"Tell me what?"

"I can't." Jack threw his hands up in frustration.

Katherine stood in front of him. She placed her hands on his shoulders, hoping it would calm him. "If you know something that could aid the investigation, I need to hear it."

Jack slunk back to the couch and drooped down onto the cushions. Katherine grabbed her notebook and stuck it in Williams's hands while she gave her full attention to Jack.

"Loretta does have a bit of a past. When I met her, she was with someone else. A fellow named Tom Phillips. He ran some sort of illegal business. Loretta thought she could change him, but when that didn't work out, she came running to me."

"What sort of illegal business?"

"Bootlegging, I think. I don't know the details."

"That's all right. Did this Tom Phillips ever contact you? Threaten you?"

"He found me at work when Loretta and I first got together. Some harsh words were exchanged, but that's all. I can't blame the guy for being angry. He thought I stole his gal, but I didn't convince her to leave him. Lo made her own choice. He left me alone after that. I shouldn't have brought him up. But Loretta is just so sweet, no one else would be after her." Jack put his head between his hands. Katherine sensed he was on the verge of breaking down. Perhaps it was time to leave.

As they left the apartment, Katherine stewed with unease. Something was off, and it wasn't just the tension from her tiff with Williams. On the surface, the case seemed straightforward. Loretta had gone out alone, run into Tom, and he'd taken his revenge for her leaving him. Too often when a young woman was killed, the ex-boyfriend was the culprit. It was the most likely solution.

Katherine tried to stay focused on the facts, but she couldn't shake the memory of those men in the shadows outside the Razzle. What were they doing there? Could they have something to do with Loretta's murder? Unlikely. According to all the interviews and her own experience with Joey, the Gray Suits disappeared once the murder was committed. But why else would they have been there?

Were they spying on *her*?

Chapter Twenty-One

Katherine stared at the calendar on her desk. It felt like just yesterday she had crumpled up the page from October, but now it was the last weekend in November, a full four days since Loretta had been killed.

Katherine and Williams hadn't spoken since their fight two days ago, and she had been running the investigation alone. She'd spent the last two days checking out all the neighbors' alibis. She interviewed Loretta's coworkers at the diner, but her search came up empty. Apparently even the angriest customers calmed down once Loretta stepped in. Loretta's parents couldn't think of anyone who would hurt their daughter. Aunts, uncles, friends, and cousins all agreed: Loretta was sweet as pie. No one could name a single enemy, except for that ex-boyfriend of hers.

If this Tom Phillips had been involved in bootlegging, they may already have a file on him. Katherine walked down the narrow hall to the station's file room. Beige metal cabinets, all of them nearly ceiling height, had been shoved against the unpainted drywall. A row of shorter cabinets sat in the middle. The room was colder than the rest of the precinct, more closely matching the chilly weather outside. Katherine closed the door behind her and tried to ignore the perpetual rattle of the dehumidifier as she opened drawers.

After twenty minutes of searching, Katherine found the file on Tom Phillips. It had been shoved in with the *T*s instead of the *P*s. She wondered if Officer Martin had been the last one to look at it.

She sat back on her heels and flipped through it.

Tom Phillips, thirty-five years old, had been arrested twice in the last ten years for bootlegging, among multiple other infractions. He had a history of getting into drunken brawls. Having met Jack, it was hard to believe the same woman had dated both of them. She must have grown up in the meantime...and that got Katherine thinking, was it possible Loretta had a criminal history of her own?

From what she knew about Loretta, it didn't seem likely. Although, when good people run with the wrong crowd, sometimes they get caught up in the chaos. Katherine opened the filing cabinet labeled *J* and searched the records. Plenty of files contained the last name Jones, but there were no Lorettas. She checked the *L*s just in case. Nothing there.

Perhaps it was time to visit Tom Phillips and hear his side of the story. Even if he was innocent, he may know others from Loretta's past who might have motive to hurt her. Katherine walked out of the filing room and on her way back to her office, passed Williams's desk. McAlister would order her to take him along, but she still didn't see the point of bringing backup, especially when she only wanted to ask a few questions. She was perfectly capable of taking notes on her own and did not need Williams's huffy attitude clouding her day. She walked out of the station and hopped into the driver's seat of a Model 18.

Katherine drove up Tom Phillips's driveway and got out of the car. The air brought the promise of winter. Goosebumps popped up on Katherine's neck, and she shut her coat a bit tighter. The first snow of the season had fallen the night before, and remnants of ice stuck to the ground.

Tom lived on the outskirts of town in a dilapidated two-story shack, and the autumn cold snap had killed off his foliage. Even without leaves, it was clear his plants had been left to grow wild and untended. Browning vines crawled along the ground as if clinging to hope, waiting for spring to revive them. Bushes with thorny branches shot up around the foundation. She avoided their grasp as she walked to his door.

Before she could knock, the door flew open. The man who opened it stank of whiskey but did not seem intoxicated. His stain-covered shirt hung loosely on his wiry frame. His eyes pierced her.

"You can't be here. You have no right to step on my property." His gravelly voice croaked out the words.

She grabbed her badge and showed it to him. "Tom Phillips, I presume?" Katherine placed her hand on her hip.

"In case they forgot to tell you, liquor is legal now. I distribute my product *legally* to bars who sell it *legally*."

"I'm aware of the law." Katherine ignored his rude tone.

"Then why the hell are you on my property?"

"I'm investigating a murder, and I need to ask you a few questions."

"I don't know anything about a murder." Tom was unfazed. He took a step inside and moved to shut the door.

Katherine stuck her hand against it and stopped it from closing.

"A body was found right outside of the Razzle Dazzle early Wednesday morning. The victim's name is Loretta Jones. Sound familiar?"

Tom froze. A vein in his temple throbbed. He was either shocked or scared — maybe a mix of both. His eyes narrowed into slits. Was he processing the news of her death, or plotting how to get away with her murder? Once his cogs stopped turning, he snapped to.

"If you want to question me, show me a police order. Don't have one? Then get off my property." He slammed the door.

Seething, Katherine banged her fist against the door.

"Mr. Phillips? Mr. Phillips? Tom! Open this door!" She knocked a few more times with no response, then stomped over to the window, dodging the spiky plant life in her path. Tom stood in his living room, staring out at her. She rubbed the frost from the pane and put on a charming smile.

"I could get a police order," she called loudly enough to be heard through the closed window, "and come back with five or six officers at my side. I could include a search warrant. I could go to your trial and tell the judge how obstructive you were today. I'm sure you're aware that ex-boyfriends don't fare well in murder cases. If that's how you want to play it, I'll head back to the station right now." She turned on her heel and sauntered toward the car.

The shack door creaked open.

"Wait. You can come in."

"What a gracious host." Katherine winked at him. She made her way back to the door and stepped inside.

Tom took a swig from his flask. "What do you want from me, lady?"

"Answers. Sit." Katherine snapped her fingers at the couch. Tom did as he was told. The greasy cushions sagged under his weight. Katherine sat in the armchair to the left of the couch as it looked cleaner, though not by much. She stared at him for a moment. "Where were you on Tuesday night at nine?"

"I was making deliveries." Tom went pale, and his eyes darted to the side. His fingers drummed on his flask.

"Where?"

"About a dozen different bars and restaurants. What? You want me to name them all?"

"Yes I do, and include the times you arrived and left."

Tom heaved a dramatic sigh and went through his delivery route. Jazzy Jerry's Music Lounge at eight, Coco's Cocktails at eight thirty, The Lobster Shell at nine. Katherine jotted down the names, noting that he hadn't mentioned the place next door to the crime scene. Was that because he hadn't gone there or was he covering his tracks?

"You make whiskey, is that correct?" Katherine glanced at the container in his hand.

"The best in town."

"You ever sell to the Razzle Dazzle? I hear the bartender there makes a mean whiskey sour."

Tom tensed up. "No. Never been there."

Katherine noted his discomfort and thought it may be time for a more straightforward question.

"When did you last see Loretta?"

"I don't know, a year ago?"

"You sure it wasn't more recent than that?" He went silent. He wasn't being truthful, but she couldn't pinpoint the lie. "Let's start from the beginning. When did you meet Loretta?" Katherine used a calming voice, hoping to lull Tom into dropping his guard.

"About four years ago. A friend of mine was throwing a party and asked me to bring some of my product. When I got there, my friend was playing the piano and Loretta was singing. We started drinking. I asked her to dance." Tom took a sip. His eyes glazed, either lost in memory or overtaken by the booze. Katherine needed him to stay focused and pressed on with her questions.

"So it was love at first sight?"

Tom huffed. "You could say that. When we first got together, she had these grand dreams of being a famous singer and traveling the world. She would practice day in and day out. I'd tell her — 'darlin', you're my radio.'"

Katherine thought of Joey and how he used to sing to her. She longed to hear his voice just one more time. "Sounds like you two were happy. What changed?"

"She wasn't landing auditions. I'd try to make her practice, but eventually she gave up on herself. Take a wild guess what she did to kill the pain." He shook his flask in the air. "I make a damn fine whiskey. I can't blame her for liking it so much." He took a few gulps himself. "She'd lie on the couch all day too boozed up to be useful."

"What happened? Did you break it off?"

Tom looked appalled. "Did I break it off? I was ready to spend the rest of my life with that woman. She's the one who..." He closed his eyes and took a moment, then continued. "I thought it might help if she had some responsibilities, something to get her out of the house. I gave her some money to go get her hair done, go grocery shopping. Well, that's exactly what she did. She met that damn stock boy, Jack. He told her how evil booze is."

Tom went into a mocking falsetto. "Jack says liquor makes your insides rot. Jack says liquor makes you lose ten years off your life." He dropped the impression. "Well, Loretta knew it made her into a mess. That was all she needed to give up the sauce for good."

"And that meant giving you up too." The picture became clearer for Katherine. Loretta had gone through quite a rough patch. Tom may have been sweet to her, but his lifestyle had dragged her into despair.

"How could she be with a man who makes this evil nectar? I gave her everything I could. In return, she took every last part of me, then walked out the door when something better came along." The alcohol was definitely affecting Tom now. His eyes drooped, and he slumped lower in his seat.

"When did she break things off?"

"A year ago. I haven't seen her since then." His eyes darted to the side again. He was almost too insistent on this time frame. Was that what he was lying about?

"Can I be alone now?" His head lolled to his shoulder.

"That's all I need."

Katherine walked to her car with an uneasy prickle coursing through her. There was something fishy about Tom Phillips.

Chapter Twenty-Two

Katherine came back to her office after questioning Tom Phillips and settled at her desk. She unwrapped the jelly sandwich she had slapped together that morning and took a bite as she read over Loretta Jones's case file again. Tom was a decent suspect, but she needed evidence. She planned to call the bars and restaurants he delivered to and see if his itinerary matched their version of events. If he really was out making deliveries the night Loretta was murdered, could Katherine prove that he had made a deadly detour?

Or was he telling the truth? Perhaps he had arranged for someone else to strangle Loretta while he created a solid alibi. That brought her back to her Spider theory, and those men who had been watching her outside the Razzle. Maybe the Spider was involved, but then why were the Gray Suits lingering near the crime scene?

Five years ago, when those men stalked Joey, they must have seen Katherine too. Between wedding planning and working at the theater, Katherine was with Joey nearly all the time. Did they figure out she had become a cop? Possibly, but then why hadn't they sniffed her out before? Even as a beat cop she had assisted on a few murder cases, ones she thought could be tied to the Spider. Yet, those men left her alone then. Maybe they learned she had been promoted to detective and were concerned about the power she now wielded.

Or maybe someone had taken a hit out on Katherine. As a cop, she had made plenty of enemies. She couldn't count how many criminals sat in prison cells because of cases she had helped with. Hell, Rita Davis's accomplice was still at large. Maybe he, or Davis herself, had contacted the Spider to exact revenge.

The air around Katherine seemed to pressurize, like invisible hands squeezed her lungs. Should she...would it be worth it...to tell McAlister? Or would that conversation just pry open old wounds?

"You catch that killer yet, Dell?"

Startled by the voice, Katherine jerked her head toward her door. Standing in the frame was Williams, back to his old sarcastic self. He must have gotten over his hurt feelings and she too was ready to set their tiff aside. Katherine shook off her spiraling thoughts and put her sandwich down, then brushed the crumbs from her fingers.

"Yeah, I caught the perp, Al Capone, and Jack the Ripper all at the same time." Katherine flashed him a smile.

"That's good news. Say, McAlister stopped by my desk just now and asked how the case was going, then he chewed me out when I told him you were running it yourself." Williams put his hands on his hips like he was chastising a child. How unfair of him. It wasn't as if she had kicked him off the assignment.

"You were too busy pouting about our last conversation to talk to me, so yes, I continued on without you. What was I supposed to do? Let a killer run free because my supporting officer was having a tantrum?"

"Well, I'm not gonna get in trouble with the lieutenant again. Fill me in. Any more leads?"

Katherine scrunched up her face as she resigned to cooperate. Williams and McAlister had her cornered. She would have to play nicely. She filled Williams in on her visit with Tom.

"He was nervous to speak with me, like he was hiding something."

"Doesn't have the best track record with the police, does he? It could be that cops make him uncomfortable even when he's not doing anything wrong."

"This wasn't your everyday cop anxiety. Fidgety hands, bulging eyes. Why would an innocent man act that way?"

"Why would a man wait a whole year after being dumped to kill his ex-girlfriend?"

The timing had struck Katherine as odd too, though it hadn't cleared Tom's name in her mind. In some cases, ex-lovers came back for revenge years later.

"I don't know what would have triggered him to kill her now. I do know he wasn't honest with me." Katherine wanted to share the rest of her theory, that the Spider could be involved, but wasn't sure how to proceed. She didn't want to launch into her whole sob story about Joey; the details were too personal. Even admitting she believed the rumors about the Spider came with risks.

None of the other officers believed the Spider existed. They would jokingly toss out the theory as a solution to a murder case at their monthly staff meetings or tease about sending the Spider if one of them owed the other lunch. If she told the full truth, Williams might tell the rest of the force and make her the object of ridicule, even more than she already was. Maybe instead of sharing her true opinion, she could casually float the idea past him.

"So, it was either Tom Phillips or..." She paused, gathering up her courage and figuring out how to word her theory.

"Or?" Williams circled his finger in the air, indicating for her to continue.

"Or maybe Tom hired a hitman to kill her."

"Why would he hire someone instead of doing the dirty work himself?"

"He already has a record and wouldn't want his prints on the scene. Why not hire someone with experience?"

"Someone like the Spider?" Williams laughed and wiggled his fingers like spider legs. Katherine stayed silent, amazed that he made the joke by pure coincidence and hurt by his mockery. Williams slowed his finger wiggle then dropped his hands. "I'm just kidding. I don't actually believe in that lunacy."

Lunacy, huh?

"It might not be as crazy as it seems on the surface. I know it sounds strange and the murders don't seem connected, but why would all those people lie about being followed by the men in gray suits?"

"To get their name in the paper." He had a point, she had to admit.

"Sure, but what if there was more to it than that? Listen, when we left the Razzle and I saw two men across the street? I know you're gonna think I'm bananas, but it was them, the Spider's henchmen."

Williams stared at her as if waiting for her to burst out laughing and say that she was teasing him. When she kept a straight face, he burst out laughing instead.

"Even assuming those rumors have any merit, how would you know what the Spider's henchmen look like?"

Katherine cringed. She could abandon the endeavor right now, fake a giggle and say she was messing with him, but if the Spider had anything to do with Loretta's murder, her supporting officer should be made aware. She would have to peel off another protective layer and let him in a bit further.

"Because I've seen them before." Saying it out loud turned her stomach.

"You feeling okay? You're not making any sense." Williams looked genuinely concerned.

"I'd rather not dive into the details, but trust me, I know what those men look like and that's who I saw."

"In the dark for about five seconds before they disappeared?" Williams sputtered, losing his words for a moment, then pointed outside. "Look out the window and tell me what you see."

Begrudgingly, she got up and turned toward her window. People milled about, heading into the museum or the restaurants farther down the block. Williams came over and stood next to her.

"What do you see there?" He pointed across the street. Two men in gray suits had just come around the corner. They spoke excitedly to each other and waved at a couple who passed by. "And what about them?" Another pair of men came out of a bakery. They were roughly the same height, and both wore gray wool coats. One took a bite of his pastry while the other handed him a napkin. "Men in gray suits aren't too hard to come by. You saw two men at a juice joint. They looked familiar. That doesn't mean the Spider is real."

Katherine fumed over his patronizing speech. He was being purposely obtuse, and Katherine would not stand for it. She whipped around to face him.

"Think whatever you want; I'm running my case the way I see fit and it's something we should look into at least. You want to help? Fine. But I'm the detective in charge, and we're doing things my way."

"I do want to help, but I'm not chasing after some fictional boogeyman."

A voice in the back of Katherine's mind cautioned her to be rational, but the silent scream that radiated in her chest drowned it out. "Then I'll do it on my own. Thanks for stopping by." She waved her hand toward the door. Williams shook his head and started to walk out.

If Katherine wanted to keep the lieutenant happy, she had to grit her teeth and work with Williams. "Wait," Katherine called after him in her best attempt to sound cordial. He turned around and took a step back into her office. "McAlister wants us to work on this together. We need to respect that."

"Then we're going to do this my way. Does saying that make me a condescending jerk?" Williams leaned his hand on the door frame.

Maybe her words earlier had affected him more than she thought. "Yes, it does." Even if her words hurt, he needed to hear them. "And since this is my case, I have an assignment for you. Call these places and make sure Tom Phillips really delivered at these times." She ripped the list of her notebook and shoved the page in his hand. "Oh, and shut the door on your way out, will you?" She pointed toward the exit. He kicked the door open wider as he left, looking her right in the eye as he did it. *That little...*Katherine didn't care what he thought about her theory. She didn't care what anyone thought.

She flipped through the pages of Loretta's file, taking another look at the photo of the corpse. Here was this glamorous young woman, ready to show off her talent. She had taken the time to apply makeup and curl her hair but wore a plain outfit — a simple blue dress and matching shoes. Nothing memorable. Katherine thought of the flashy clothes and showy accessories she had seen when shopping for her suits. Loretta would have wanted to look in vogue for her audition, and this outfit screamed "plain Jane." Was something missing? She found Jack's number and dialed. He picked up.

"Jack, it's Detective Dell. I need to know what Loretta was wearing the night she was murdered." Silence followed. Perhaps she should have prefaced her question with the usual pleasantries. Too late for that now.

Jack broke the silence and stuttered out a response. "She wore a blue dress and, uh, a nice pair of shoes. Her handbag."

"Anything else? Jewelry? Accessories?"

"No jewelry, but she wore a silk scarf. A blue one, with white flowers on the edge."

Katherine checked the photo again to be sure. Loretta hadn't been wearing a scarf when she was found. Was that the Spider's stolen trophy? Katherine's pulse sped up.

"Jack, I'm going to ask you something very important. In the days before Loretta died, did you ever notice anyone following her?"

"What do you mean?"

"I know this sounds strange, but did you see two men hanging around?" Katherine simmered with nerves as she waited for his response.

"Are you saying she was two-timing me?" Jack sounded choked up.

"No! Nothing like that." Katherine felt awful about the mix-up. "I mean men in gray suits watching where she went, keeping tabs on her."

"Well, I didn't see any men around." He paused for a moment. "Is that something I should be concerned about?"

"You're safe, Jack. Don't worry. Thank you for your time." Katherine hung up the phone. She was more confused now than before the call. The missing scarf meant that Loretta's death fit the Spider's usual pattern, but then Jack would have seen his spies. Was it possible that they had stalked Loretta, but Jack hadn't noticed?

What would McAlister say? He would tell her to keep pursuing Tom Phillips as a suspect. Loretta's scarf could have blown away in the night, or someone stumbled across her body and stole it for themselves. For all she knew, a stray dog could have ripped it off.

Time to refocus. She took out Tom's criminal records. As she flipped through the pages, she noticed something she had missed before. Stuck to the back of one of his mugshots was a note — during Prohibition, another officer had compiled a list of places where Tom sold his whiskey. Right there in the middle, it said "Razzle Dazzle." That little creep. He said he'd never been there.

Katherine grabbed the notes from her visit with Al. He'd yelled at Vicki about paying off the whiskey delivery man for an extra crate, missing from the previous night's run. That meant whoever supplied the Razzle's whiskey now had been there the night Loretta was murdered. She picked up the phone and dialed the Razzle. The bartender, Lou, answered and confirmed that Tom Phillips was their go-to guy for whiskey and that he had delivered on the night in question.

So…not only had Tom been to the Razzle before, but he was there regularly. Maybe he found out she got the job, and he didn't want to see her around, so he strangled her.

Perhaps this wasn't a Spider case after all. That made it easier to work with Williams. She walked over to his desk and explained her findings, showing him the note from the file.

"So don't bother calling those bars, I already got what I need."

"Welcome back to reality, Dell," he said with his classic toothy smile. Katherine wanted to smack it off his face, but she refrained. She deserved that condescending grin. He had good insight sometimes, and who knew, he might even prove useful. "I'll try to be less of a jerk, but I'm not making any promises." Williams winked at her. A smile threatened the corners of her mouth.

She told him about the missing scarf.

"Loretta was strangled, right?" Williams held his hands up to his throat.

It clicked for her. "What if she was strangled with that scarf?" Katherine had been so focused on the scarf as the Spider's stolen trinket that she hadn't seen what was right in front of her. The bruise across the neck could have been made with a silk scarf if the fabric folded into a crease on impact. The softer bruising around the stark line could have been from rest of the scarf bunching up. She mentally kicked herself for allowing her obsession to cloud her judgment.

"And the killer took it, getting the murder weapon off the scene. Find the scarf, find the killer." Williams looked pleased with his assertion, but Katherine couldn't help poking holes.

"Not necessarily. The killer could have ditched it somewhere. Thrown it away or given it to someone."

"True." Williams looked down, defeated, but must have recovered quickly. His head snapped back up and he smiled. "But if we find it, it's still an important clue. Let's go down to the Razzle and ask some questions. See if anyone found the scarf, or has more information on this Tom Phillips guy," Williams said, then added, "if you feel that's the best course of action, Detective."

Katherine laughed, though she wasn't sure if Williams was being sincere or not. Either way, they had their next course of action laid out.

"For once, Officer, you and I are in agreement."

Chapter Twenty-Three

The Razzle Dazzle looked worse in the daylight. All the dirty crevices between the bricks were exposed. The sign still blinked, but without enthusiasm. The streets surrounding the club were deserted.

Katherine and Williams walked in and went up to the bar. Lou stood behind it, slicing lemons with gusto. Katherine tried to get his attention without startling him, bending down to counter level and waving. The bartender smiled at her.

"You were here the other night, weren't you? Welcome back."

"Yes we were, and I believe you and I spoke on the phone earlier about Tom Phillips," Katherine said.

"We just need some more information about him," Williams said.

Lou's face fell. "Is he in some sort of trouble?"

"Hey, Lou, is Al gone? Oh, hello, Detective." Vicki Harris appeared from the back of the club before Lou could answer, and she sent a timid wave to Katherine. A fresh bruise blossomed on Vicki's face.

"Sorry, Officers. One moment." Lou turned to Vicki, who glanced around, hunching her shoulders. She looked like a mouse on alert for predators. "Al stepped out for a cup of coffee, but he should be back any minute." Lou made a cocktail and garnished it with a lemon wedge, then handed it to Vicki.

"I'll take this upstairs, if you don't mind." Vicki shuffled away, swigging from her drink as she left. Al must have ordered her to stay in the apartment. That poor woman deserved better.

"Don't forget us, Lou!"

"We're in the mood for Manhattans." Candace and Shirley MacDougall emerged from the back hallway. Lou grabbed a bottle and gave an apologetic look toward Katherine and Williams, who nodded sympathetically.

"Hey, it's our detective friend!" Candace waved at Katherine.

"Are we having a party?" a voice boomed from the entrance. Al popped in, apparently jazzed up from his caffeine fix. He beamed at the group and held out his hands in a gesture of welcome. Lou plunked a cherry in each glass then handed them to the Candace and Shirley.

"Every day is a party at this place!" Shirley downed her drink.

"Someday we'll learn to behave ourselves." Candace took a gulp from her glass.

"But it's a lot more fun if we don't." Shirley winked. Candace gave her a light smack on the arm, then guided Shirley out of the room. "Come on. The officers need to do their work." The ladies sauntered back toward their dressing room.

"Wait a moment." Katherine lifted her pointer finger and the ladies turned back around. "Has anyone found a blue silk scarf with flowers on it?"

Everyone looked at each other with crumpled mouths and shrugging shoulders.

"Never mind." Katherine dismissed Candace and Shirley, then nodded to Al. "Good to see you again."

"Likewise. To what do I owe this pleasure?"

"We've got a few questions about Tom Phillips," Williams said.

"You don't think he had something to do with the murder?" Lou said, shock and sadness on his face.

"As a matter of fact, we do." Katherine whipped around to look at him. Did he have evidence that could exonerate Tom? Lou wiped up a splash of vermouth from the bar counter, then gave his attention to Katherine.

"Well, he didn't do it, if that's what you're after. He brought in the crates of whiskey that night, then went back to the office to talk to Al. He left while the girl was still singing. I saw him drive away."

"But he ran into her here?"

"Yeah, he told me he saw her outside and she broke a crate of bottles. He wouldn't kill her over that, though."

Katherine wasn't so sure. Perhaps the pain of losing her to another man combined with the fresh provocation of the ruined product was enough to send him over the edge.

"Maybe he thought twice after driving off. Maybe he turned around to get revenge on Loretta."

"He couldn't have. That old beater truck of his is so loud, I would have heard it on the way back," Lou said.

"Sounds like he's on the level," Williams whispered to Katherine. Damn it. Katherine glanced at Williams, who only frowned in return. She was so close to solving this. What was she missing?

First Candace and Shirley were cleared, now this. If Tom was innocent, then who had killed Loretta Jones?

That evening, Katherine walked up the steps to her apartment, her visit to the Razzle spinning in her mind. She dug in her pocket for her keys, but with a nervous jolt, found it empty. She stuck her hand in her other coat pocket, then scrambled through the folds of her outfit. Had she left them at the station? Or locked them inside the apartment?

Damn it. That's exactly what she had done. That morning, after she had wrapped up her sandwich, she grabbed the paper bag but left her key ring on the counter. She tried the doorknob just in case she had forgotten to twist the locking mechanism. The knob rattled in her hand but did not turn. Sure, she remembered that part at least. Her feet ached and her head felt like it weighed a hundred pounds. All she wanted was to be alone. Have a quick dinner. Listen to the radio. Lie in bed for a while and think.

Kicking herself for the error, she pulled a pin from her hair. How embarrassing; breaking into her own home. The lock clicked and she turned the knob. Her keys sat on the counter, just as she thought. She threw them in her coat pocket so they would be in the right place tomorrow.

Just as she prepared to strip off her work clothes, a phone call interrupted her plans. Vera's merry voice greeted her on the line. Her show had opened to rave reviews, and she was throwing a party at her apartment to celebrate. She insisted Katherine come along.

"Please, Katherine! It would mean a lot to me."

Katherine pressed her hand to her forehead. "I just had a long day at work. Can I celebrate with you another time?"

"Sure, if you want to break my heart."

"You sound like my mother."

"That's not a compliment, is it?" Vera laughed, then got serious. "I think it would be good for you to get out of the house. Come meet some new people. Live a little!"

Katherine cringed at the thought. A party sounded fun, but that heavy, foggy feeling spread through her again. That feeling like she couldn't move even if she wanted to. The overwhelming idea of getting dressed up, putting on makeup, calling a cab, meeting new people...

"I'm sorry, Vera. I can't tonight. Maybe another time."

"When, Katherine? When is 'another time' going to happen?" Vera sounded angry. That wasn't fair of her. She couldn't back Katherine into a trap like this.

"I don't know. When work slows down."

"Work is never going to slow down." Vera's voice warbled. Maybe it wasn't anger Katherine had heard before.

"Are you crying?"

Vera sniffed. "A little. I don't even know you anymore. You never call. I hardly ever see you."

"You're right. I should—"

"No. No more empty promises. You're supposed to be my best friend. You always needed a little nudge to go out before, but now it's like you're tethered between home and the station."

"I'm sorry. I—"

"I miss him too, you know. He meant more to you, of course, but he was my friend. Seeing him there with a bullet in his chest..." Vera fell into sobs. A weight plummeted into Katherine's stomach, coated in a thick film of guilt and exhaustion. She had been so caught up in her own pain, she had never addressed Vera's. Katherine wasn't the only one who had lost someone special when Joey died.

Joey had been like family to everyone at the theater. All the girls had loved him. Most had been sweet on him, though they knew his heart belonged to Katherine. Joey knew he was a terrible dancer, but he pretended to try different moves from the show, badly, to make the girls laugh. If someone had a crummy day, he was there to cheer them up. When Vera sprained her ankle a week before opening night, and she thought she would have to quit the show, Joey set up a chair for her just off stage so she could rest between numbers. She'd been ready to perform when the show opened.

Vera was the one who had found him that day. Katherine had walked to the theater, the sunlight glimmering off her ruby. Joey had been acting strangely, but she had kept the hope that he would bounce back after the wedding. She had been happily planning her wedding hairstyle on her way to the theater that day. Then she'd seen Vera, running toward her, tears streaming down her face.

The rest was blurry. Two police cars and an ambulance idled outside the theater. Her fellow dancers stood out front, hugging and sobbing. A body in the alley, covered in a sheet. Vera hardly got a word out before Katherine ran to him. The police had tried to hold her back, but Katherine broke through. She pulled the sheet back, revealing his lifeless face. His chest had bloomed with red.

On the phone, Vera's voice changed from its usual chiming bells to a reedy howl. "I lost him, and then I lost you too. You don't do anything besides sit alone in your apartment between shifts. You're not the one who died, but you sure aren't living."

Tears fell onto Katherine's lap. "I had no clue you felt that way."

"How did you think I felt, losing a friend, then watching my best friend implode?"

Lost in the selfishness of grief, Katherine hadn't thought much at all about Vera's feelings. She hadn't checked up on Vera after Joey died. Everything had become about her own pain. Her sorrow. But Vera carried pain too, and Katherine needed to acknowledge that.

"You're right. Let me make it up to you. I'll celebrate with you tonight, and we can go out this weekend. Dinner, dancing, whatever you want. My treat." Katherine expected an enthusiastic response. Instead, she got uncomfortable silence. "Are you still there?"

"Yeah, I'm here. Why don't you just stay home."

"No, really, I'll come—"

"I don't want you here if you don't want to be here. Have a good night." Vera hung up the phone.

Katherine fell into sobs. Her heart broke over Vera's anger and the truth she had just laid out. Katherine wasn't living. She was barely surviving. Just getting out of bed each day drained her. She was a terrible, selfish friend.

She looked around her apartment. The floor hadn't been swept in weeks. Her sheets hadn't been changed in who knows how long. Dirty dishes clogged her sink.

If she got a few chores done, maybe she could stop feeling guilty. Vera might be proud of her for that at least. It was a step toward normal living. Her first stop would be the kitchen. A layer of grime had settled over the countertops. She told herself to walk over and start cleaning. Just move her legs. Stand up. Make it happen. Grab a rag and wipe down the counters. Run some water over the dishes. People do this every day.

Something wasn't connecting. Her engine backfired. Her legs wouldn't move. If she couldn't do something as simple as clean her kitchen, how the hell was she supposed to catch a murderer? Her case was falling apart. She was pouring every bit of her energy into work and couldn't even do that right.

Instead of the kitchen, she shuffled to her bedroom. A voice in the back of her mind scolded her for skipping her nightly routine, cold cream and hair rollers, but beauty treatments felt utterly pointless. Why bother combatting pimples and frizz when she would be a failure regardless? It was much too early to sleep, but she changed into her nightgown and lay down anyway.

Did it make a difference if she was awake or asleep? Her night would look the same either way, lying there feeling too much and too little all at once. She forced her eyes open, but they closed again. Sleep won the battle.

She awoke hours later with a start. Katherine thought her dreams must have lingered in the forefront of her mind; that was the simplest explanation for the two pairs of eyes peering down at her. But as sleep fully faded and the room became clear, so did the forms of the men standing next to her bed. The Gray Suits.

Chapter Twenty-Four

Henry came home late at night after a twelve-hour shift, which included an unsuccessful trip to the Razzle Dazzle. Poor Dell was devasted when her only lead dried up, but Henry held out hope they would find the culprit. He chuckled to himself, thinking about her wacko theory — that the Spider had done it. Maybe that was her odd attempt at humor, though the joke had gone pretty far.

He pushed work from his mind and called Benny's name but got no response. His brother hadn't been home in days. At least, Henry hadn't seen him; Benny might have crept in a time or two while Henry was at work. Henry had called his teacher almost every day since he found out Benny had ditched a week of school, and Mrs. Costwell confirmed that Benny was still skipping half his classes. His bed still seemed slept in, at least. What would Ma think about all this? She'd be disappointed in Henry. Big brothers were supposed to protect their siblings, not let them run wild in a dangerous city. But Henry had to work hard, otherwise he might never get a promotion which, according to his bank statements, he needed desperately.

He hung up his hat and let out a deep sigh. A few letters had been crammed in his mailbox. One was a bill from the electric company. Henry winced. He paid what he could toward it, but the balance had crept up over the last few months. Between the new charges and the late fees, he must owe at least twelve dollars at this point. He ripped the seal open.

The usual red stamp warning of late payments was missing. Instead, it read "paid in full." He opened the gas bill, then the water bill. Both were up to date. He crumpled the pages in his fist. Benny. He must have used the wages from his job to pay the debt. A dull ache resonated inside his chest. A fourteen-year-old should not be paying Henry's bills.

A smile spread over his face as he opened the ice box. An apple was missing, along with a chunk of cheese. Benny must have come home at some point and eaten. This small indication of his safety gave Henry a warm sense of peace. He threw together a sandwich — nothing glamorous, just the rest of the cheese and mustard. He opened his mouth to take a bite, then paused at a soft noise somewhere in the apartment. Benny poked his head out of his room and a wave of relief washed over Henry. His brother was safe, right here in front of him. Relief turned to apprehension as Benny's lip trembled.

"What's wrong, pal?" Henry set down his sandwich. Benny heaved as if he might start crying.

"Can I talk to you?" Benny choked out his words.

"Of course. Hey, you want half?" Henry grabbed a second plate and cut his sandwich in two, though Benny did not respond, heading back into his bedroom. Henry followed him. The place was a pit, with dirty clothes scattered on the floor and old newspapers stacked up on his nightstand. Henry wanted to lecture him, tell him to clean the place up, but now was not the time. Benny was upset and Henry wanted to know why. He handed Benny his half of the sandwich, but Benny set it down without taking a bite. Henry sat next to him, then scooted an inch when something poked into him.

A photo album, open to a page of childhood memories. Henry pointed to a picture of the two of them. Benny's toothless smile beamed out from the photo, and Henry was sticking out his tongue. Behind them, the farm burst with foliage.

"Remember that? You were five, so I must have been right around the age you are now." Henry looked at Benny. That little boy in the picture didn't exist anymore. Benny was almost a grown man.

"My first day of school. Ma made you walk with me." Benny smiled, but sadness stayed in his eyes.

"Somebody had to protect you from the bullies." Henry elbowed him playfully.

Benny didn't play along. He took an envelope from his bedside table drawer. "I might still need you to protect me from the bullies."

"Somebody picking on you at school?" Henry puffed out his chest.

Benny shook his head. "Worse. Remember when we went to the parade? We got in a fight because I wanted a job. You were walking in the parade and a man came up to me."

"That tall, skinny guy?"

"Yes. His name is Tony. Sometimes people call him Bones." Henry had heard that name thrown around the station. He didn't remember the details, but Tony sounded like a creep. Benny continued. "He gave me a phone number to call, and we arranged a meeting by the harbor. That's where I met the leader. He likes to be called the Boss."

Henry took a beat to process what he'd just heard. The Boss? The gangland kingpin that McAlister had been after for decades?

"You're not mad, are you?" Benny's eyes grew large. Of course Henry was mad, furious in fact. And terrified. But it didn't matter how he felt. Benny was opening up to him at last; he had to hang on to the moment.

"I'm not mad, Benny. Go on."

"He said I could borrow some money from him to pay our bills, but that I'd have to work for him to pay it back."

"What did he have you do?"

"It started small. Delivering messages. I wasn't allowed to read them, but the Boss said they weren't anything bad. Just payment reminders to people who borrowed money from him. I don't know if he was telling the truth, though. I think he might have been threatening people."

"That wouldn't surprise me." Henry tried to keep his voice calm.

"Then some people who work for him got arrested. One of them was a woman. The Boss said…" Benny trailed off and put his hands over his eyes. He looked so small, a child who needed the comfort of a parent, but all he had was Henry. If only Ma were there to wrap Benny in her arms and tell him everything would be all right. She had a gift for making troubles disappear. Henry put his arm around Benny's shoulders, his best attempt at filling Ma's shoes.

"It's all right. You can tell me."

"He said he wanted to have her killed. And her boyfriend too. Henry, I swear I had no idea that kind of stuff was going on when I took the job. I knew they were shady guys, but I didn't think it was going that far."

Henry's stomach churned. A thousand thoughts circled his mind at once. If he had known his brother was running with the Boss…but it didn't matter now. He needed to stay focused. Henry pushed his fear and anger down to be dealt with later.

"What's in the envelope?"

Benny crinkled the paper in his hands. "Like I said, they wanted to take a hit out on this lady and her boyfriend. There's this one guy who would take the names to the hitman. Or he would deliver it to these guys that work as go-betweens for the hitman. I don't know. I only overheard some of it."

"Do the best you can to remember."

"The guy in charge of delivering the names and information got arrested. His name was Gray, I think. Franklin Gray. Something like that."

"Franklin Green?" The apartment burglar Henry had arrested…that guy had been running around with the Boss?

"Yes, that's it. How did you know?"

"Long story. Keep talking."

"Well, with Green out of the picture, they needed someone else to deliver the hits. The hitman's henchmen keep a low profile, and the Boss is allowed to pick one person to give the location to. He picked Tony to replace the last guy, because Tony's been loyal to the Boss for years."

Henry gulped, pushing down his fear. "How did you end up with the envelope if it was supposed to go to Tony?"

"I stole it from Tony's jacket pocket."

Henry took the envelope. Inside was a wad of cash, two hundred dollars at least, maybe more. Stuffed between the bills, a scrap of paper, which Henry took out and unfolded. Scrawled across the torn page was an address, and two names: Walter Macy and Rita Davis.

Davis. That gal Dell brought in when she'd had her temper tantrum. Davis had said her boyfriend, Walter, would be killed by the Spider. It couldn't be. Henry tried to wrap his mind around the situation. "You stole this from the Boss?"

"I had to. Otherwise, those people would have been killed." Benny's expression hardened.

"Benny, this is really bad. What happens if he finds out you stole it? Is he gonna take a hit out on you?"

"He won't find out."

"How do you know that?"

"Because the Boss already asked me about it and I told him Tony probably lost the envelope. Now he's tossing all his rage Tony's way. I felt bad throwing Tony to the wolves but I couldn't let those two people get murdered."

"So you're safe? You're positive the Boss won't find out it was you?"

"Positive." Benny sounded annoyed by the line of questioning, but Henry didn't care. Henry also didn't share Benny's faith that the Boss would never know who took the envelope. He hoped Benny was right, that the Boss would blame Tony and punish the lackey for his carelessness. Henry decided to drop the subject, digging for more information instead.

Since he wasn't a detective, he didn't know all the details but knew that McAlister was on the lookout for the Boss's main hub.

"Do you know where the Boss's headquarters are?" Henry leaned in, anxious for an answer.

"Well, yes, but that's not why I told you about this."

"You have to tell me where to find him."

"No! It's too dangerous. I only wanted to protect these people — Macy and Davis. I'm not telling you where to find the Boss." Benny jumped off the bed and tried to snatch the envelope from Henry's hands.

Henry stuffed it in his pocket before Benny could get a grip on it. "I'm a police officer. It's my job to take down guys like this. We have a whole force who can help."

"I'm not letting you do that." Benny lunged for the envelope again.

Henry angled away from him, keeping his distance. While he wanted to believe his brother was safe, intuition nudged him toward caution. "Listen to me. Stay here. Lock the doors. Don't let anyone in. Do not leave the apartment. Not for school. Not for nothing. You're staying put until we can be sure you're safe. I'll be back later." Henry jumped up and grabbed the phone and dialed. "Peterson? I didn't wake you up, did I? Well, too bad. Put your uniform on and meet me at the men's prison. We need to talk to Franklin Green."

The guard led them to Green's cell. Green sat on the floor next to his bed, curled up in a ball and rocking gently back and forth. He hummed a childish tune as he rocked; one which sounded familiar, but that Henry couldn't place. Green's eyes widened at the sight of Henry and Peterson, but he stayed tucked in a ball.

"Rumor has it you've been helping the Boss take out hits." Henry leaned against the bars.

"I don't deal in rumors. Only facts." Green showed his rotting teeth.

"Give me the facts, then."

"I'm no rat. Only rats talk to pigs." Green hummed his song. Henry, annoyed, decided to try a different approach.

"Come on, Green. Look what loyalty to the Boss got you. Loyalty to me might get you out sooner."

"Loyalty to you makes me next on the hit list." Green curled up tighter.

Peterson stepped up to the bars. He leaned a hand against them just like Henry. "Then tell me the hitman's name." Peterson spoke with confidence and Henry nodded to him with approval.

Green hissed with laughter. "I don't know the hitman's name. I only deliver the information."

"Deliver it to who?" Peterson asked.

"To the men who take the information," Green wheezed, then a burst of high-pitched laughter emanated from him. Peterson took a step back and grumbled.

"So you have no clue who this hitman is? No idea at all?" Henry glared at the prisoner. Lives were on the line and this criminal had the audacity to laugh about it. Every muscle in Henry's core clamped up with disgust.

"Oh I know who it is." Green started humming again.

"You just told us you don't have the hitman's name. So which is it? You know who the hitman is, or you don't?" Peterson widened his hands in exasperation.

"I know who it is, and I don't have the name. I do have the title." Green hummed his song. Henry was about to burst, sick of the riddles.

"All right. What's the hitman's title then?" Henry tried to keep his voice soft, to lull Green into trusting him.

"I've been telling you the whole time!" Tears built in Green's eyes as he popped with uncontrolled laughter like a child who had too much sugar. Henry and Peterson looked at each other and Peterson's eyebrows knit together, making him look as clueless as Henry felt.

"My colleague and I must have missed the memo. Spell it out for us," Henry said.

"I'm a bad speller, but I'm a good singer." Green hummed louder.

"You're a regular Fred Astaire. What does that have to do with anything?" Henry was at the end of his fuse.

"I get it." Peterson nodded his head. "This guy has lost his marbles."

"Help me out here, Peterson."

"The song he's humming. Listen."

Henry leaned in, listening intently. He sighed as the answer washed over him. "'The Itsy-Bitsy Spider.'"

Green burst into laughter. Henry motioned for them to leave.

"What a nutjob. The Spider ain't real, right? You told me that yourself." Peterson stared at Henry, but Henry stayed quiet. Pieces were fitting together in ways he didn't like. Everyone said the Spider couldn't be real, because there was no meaningful pattern to any of the deaths. They were all different — different weapons, different types of people, different locations. But what if that was the whole point? A good hitman might try to make the kills look unrelated on purpose.

What else had Dell talked about? Those men who supposedly followed the victims. Could they be the men Tony was supposed to meet to deliver the next hit list?

Henry took that slip of paper out of his pocket — the one Benny had stolen, with the address written on it.

"I've got one more stop for us to make."

Henry and Peterson lingered outside an apartment building that matched the address on the note. The unit they sought was on the first floor. The windows were blacked out, and Henry tapped on the glass.

"Police. Open up." There was no answer. Peterson pried the window open and they crawled inside. Shining their flashlights around the room showed them living room walls covered with photos. They looked like photos that a private investigator would take, with the subjects unaware their pictures were being taken. These couldn't be Spider victims, could they? He skimmed over the wall with his flashlight, then continued his search. Two bedrooms, each with a twin-size bed. The closets were full of suits — all charcoal gray.

"Two men living here. You think these guys are hitmen?" Peterson shined his flashlight under the bed in one of the rooms.

"No. Benny said these guys just gather information."

"They're obviously involved in something sinister. Couldn't they have started the Spider rumor themselves? They could off the victims, then pin the murders on a fictional culprit." Peterson's eyes lit up with pride at his theory. Henry hated to dim that light, but Peterson's story didn't add up.

"Look at these suits." Henry pointed his light into the closet. "They're good for blending into a crowd, but don't allow for the agility a hitman would need. Plus a hitman would have more weapons."

"I found a pistol under each bed."

"Sure. You'll find a pistol under almost every bed in Nolaton."

"So what, they're the hitman's secretaries?" Peterson scratched his head.

Henry laughed. "Maybe. That's one way to put it."

Henry wandered back to the living room and Peterson followed. Henry panned his light over the photos on the wall again, this time taking in each image.

"Where are they tonight?" Peterson asked. Henry paused.

"That's a good question. If they're supposed to gather information on their targets, who are they following right now?"

"It could be their night off. Maybe they have dates." Peterson shrugged.

"I hope they do. Everyone deserves someone special, right?" Henry spoke with sarcasm. Peterson must not have caught on that Henry was joking.

"Looking for love, Williams? Got your eye on anyone in particular?"

Henry kept looking through the photos, ignoring Peterson's teasing. His flashlight stopped on one square in particular and his jaw dropped. He ripped the photo off the wall and the pin that had held it in place fell to the floor. The photo showed a young man in a shabby suit and homburg, with his arm around a curly-haired woman. She was younger in the photo and her hair was shorter, but her identity was unmistakable. Her name escaped his lips in a whisper.

"Dell."

"Really? I didn't think she was your type."

"No, you idiot. Look!" Henry showed him the photo.

"What the hell is this?"

Henry stared at the younger Dell, her eyes sparkling as she beamed at the man next to her. Dell didn't talk much about her personal life, but she wore a ring on her left hand. She had been on the force ever since Henry started almost four years ago and in all that time, she had never mentioned a weekend trip or a nice dinner with her husband. If the guy was still around, he would have come up in conversation at least once, right?

Dell had told him she had seen those men in gray suits before. Was it possible that this guy in the photo with her had fallen victim to...to whatever this was? He tucked the picture in his pocket and planned to do more digging at the station tomorrow. He would find Dell first thing in the morning to let her know what he'd discovered.

"I don't know, but I'm gonna find out."

Chapter Twenty-Five

Katherine couldn't move. Her brain pounded against her skull and her muscles stiffened around her bones. The room spun, bed tilting away from underneath her, but only for a moment until the dizzy spell passed. Her bedroom wobbled into focus as a cloth lifted from her mouth. Then terror seized her, a rumbling torrent of acid through her insides. Two identical men stared down at her, their faces blank and empty — like they were cats, and she was a ball of yarn.

The men looked familiar, but not because they had been outside the Razzle that night or because they had followed Joey. It was something about their eyes. She had seen those eyes somewhere before.

One of the men grabbed her wrist, and though his grip was loose, she couldn't pull away. Her weakened muscles would not cooperate. The man who grabbed her bound her hands with satin. She bucked away from him as hard as she could, but he overpowered her and twisted the fabric around her bedpost, trapping her to the frame. The other man bound her legs together and tied them to her footboard. The room lurched around her again before resettling in her vision. That cloth must have some sort of chemical on it. Ether?

Light from the streetlamps below gleamed off metal and flashed into her eyes. The man who had restrained her feet held a knife in his hand. He walked over to his accomplice and they both hovered over Katherine's face. She kicked to get loose from the ties, but the restraints only tightened on her wrists and ankles, digging into her skin. She screamed, and the man with the knife threw his empty hand over her mouth.

"Shh. Wouldn't want to wake the neighbors." He had a deep voice and spoke in a matter-of-fact tone. She stopped screaming and he took his hand away, but she could still taste the salt from his clammy palm. He dangled the knife over her chest in an unspoken but very clear threat.

"Who the hell are you?" Katherine whispered through clenched teeth.

"Just a couple of men with some good advice for you," the knifeless man said, spitting his words.

"How did you get into my apartment?"

"We have our ways."

"She asks too many questions. I could put a stop to that." The man with the knife caressed her jaw with the blade, the cold metal pressing into her skin. How far would the blade delve before he stopped? Katherine gasped for breath, her body trembling as though she was sinking in ice water.

"Now, now. Let's not get ahead of ourselves." The other man pushed the knife away, then grabbed Katherine's left hand. The satin around her wrists stopped her from pulling away as he flipped her ring right side up. "That's a lovely rock you have, Detective Dell."

"Don't touch me," Katherine stuttered in fear. The man with the knife hissed with laughter.

"You're not scared, are you?" He tapped the knife against her sternum, snagging the loose threads of her nightgown with the sharp edge. The risk brought back her strength as adrenaline coursed through her bloodstream. She spat at him. The wad of saliva hit his cheek. He wiped it away with the back of his hand, then bared his teeth. "I knew she'd be a pain."

"And all we're trying to do is deliver a message. Can you do us one little courtesy, Miss Dell?"

"What do you want from me?"

"Just one thing. Drop Loretta Jones's case. Tell McAlister the trail went cold."

"Why would I do that?"

"Because the Spider doesn't want you poking around. Quit investigating the murder and stop hunting for the Spider or you'll be another fly caught in the web."

"I think we've made our point." The man with the knife shoved the rag over Katherine's mouth again. Darkness swirled around her, and she sank into a void.

Katherine woke up the next morning as a sunbeam crossed her face. Her head pounded as if she'd had too many cocktails the night before. But she hadn't gone to Vera's party, so why—

Those men. They had drugged her and tied her up and — she jumped out of bed and ran through the apartment despite the lingering dizziness. No one was there. The front door locks were intact. Had she locked up last night, or had Vera's phone call distracted her? Either way, they could have picked the lock as easily as she had. Nothing had been overturned or stolen. Nothing seemed different at all. Had she imagined those men?

She looked at her left hand. Sparkling in the sunlight, turned right side up, was her ruby. Sickened by the proof of their presence, she twisted the gem back down.

Katherine burst into McAlister's office. She didn't want to put this burden on him, but he needed to know what had happened. He had never given an inkling before that he believed in the Spider, but she had always wondered if, deep down, he saw the truth. She explained about the men breaking in and he responded with a blank stare.

That icy stab hit Katherine in the chest.

"I'm telling you, sir, it was real."

"It sounds like you were dreaming," McAlister said dismissively.

"I *was* dreaming, then the Gray Suits woke me up, tied me to my bed, threatened me, and knocked me out again. They told me point-blank that the Spider was involved with Loretta's murder and to mark the case cold."

"Dell—"

"These were the same men who followed Joey. You have to believe me," Katherine pleaded.

"Nobody cut your locks. Nothing looked out of place this morning."

Katherine held up her left hand. "Except my ring. One of them twisted it and when I woke up—"

"So it turned around in the middle of the night. You're telling me that's never happened before?" McAlister gave her a pointed look.

"I'm telling you that's never happened before." The ring had been too big when Joey had proposed, and he'd had it sized just right for her. It didn't move unless someone touched it.

"It sounds like you had one hell of a dream. You must have jostled it upright while you slept."

Katherine shrank into herself. "I thought you would believe me," she whispered.

McAlister frowned. "I believe what the evidence tells me. Now, I don't think you're lying, but I don't think you're seeing the truth. The more you obsess about this Spider business, the more real it becomes to you. You think about it a lot, don't you?"

Katherine nodded and tears built in her eyes. She blinked hard, desperate to keep from crying in front of the lieutenant. As her watery eyes cleared, McAlister's stony face softened. He got up from his desk and walked over to her, placing a hand on her shoulder, an unusually warm gesture. The icy stab melted at his kindness.

"And you think about Joey a lot too?" McAlister asked. Hearing McAlister say his name brought an odd sense of relief. They hardly ever talked about the man they both lost.

After Joey's parents died, he was raised by his grandparents. McAlister, Joey's grandfather, cherished his grandson more than anyone else. And he had been so happy to hear that Joey had found a gal to marry. McAlister had always been tough to read, even before Katherine became a cop, but she got the impression that he approved of her marrying Joey.

Then Joey joined his parents in death. Katherine had tried to convince McAlister that the Spider had done it, that those Gray Suits had tracked him down. She had told him that all he had to do was let her become a cop, and she would prove it to him. He'd spurned her at first, with harsh words about ballerinas not belonging on the force.

She'd fired back by telling him that dancers were agile and strong. She had come out of most rehearsals covered in bruises. Once, she'd broken a toe the day before a show opened. She still got on stage and twirled with a smile on her face despite the shooting pain. Wasn't that what the force wanted in a cop? An unstoppable, iron-willed athlete who would let nothing stand in her way?

And she'd won, that time. McAlister wrote her that all-important reference letter for the police academy. She had always wondered what had made him take that leap of faith, to hire a female cop, especially one who believed in the Spider. She had never dared to ask directly, afraid that if he thought about it too hard he would realize he had made a mistake five years ago. But maybe it was time to get an answer.

"Why am I here? Of all the men you could have hired, why did you give me a chance?"

McAlister rubbed his chin and gave a deep sigh. He stared past her as if he didn't want to answer. "You're a smart gal, and you've got a good eye for detail. And, frankly, because part of me believes you." He spoke softly as if he didn't want to say it at all.

Katherine clenched her fist and her ruby dug into her palm. He'd let her think she was crazy all this time, and all the while he believed her? Heat built behind her eyes. "Why didn't you tell me?"

"I didn't want you to go chasing ghosts, and I can't let you open a cold case that you're so close to. Still, some part of me thought if I hired you, something would click in your mind. Some murder case would remind you of Joey's and you'd wind up figuring it out. If anyone can find his killer, it's you."

"Is that why you put me on the Jones case? You think the Spider killed both Joey and Loretta?"

"I don't know who killed Joey, but I can't believe he would get involved in some criminal scheme." It was McAlister's turn to tear up. "He would have told me. I have to think that if he was in that big of trouble, he would have come to me and maybe I could have fixed it. It makes more sense that he was being mugged and fought back, then the mugger shot him. Hell, he could have been saving someone else from getting mugged. Joey always stood up for what's right. That story checks out for me, but thinking about him borrowing money from some dirtbag, then getting offed by a hitman... Then again, I don't know where he got the money to buy your ring. I said *part* of me believes you, Dell. There's no hard evidence. But I'll admit, sometimes I wonder..."

"I could get evidence, especially if I have your blessing." She pressed her hands together as if praying, imploring him to consider the offer.

"That's what I'm afraid of. I don't want you to go digging around for something that may or may not exist and get yourself hurt in the process. Or, God forbid, killed."

"I won't."

"You might. There are people in this city who wouldn't think twice about putting a bullet in your head — you get in their way, you end up in the morgue. That's why we have rules in place."

Katherine hung her head. She'd been so focused on her independence that she hadn't realized that he'd been trying to protect her. "I'm sorry, sir."

"You don't have to apologize. No one else on this force is more dedicated than you. That's why I promoted you. You want to protect this city more than any of those morons out there." He nodded toward the bullpen. "Just remember that you're not invincible, and I have your best interests at heart. I want Joey's killer behind bars too, but I'm not willing to sacrifice you to make that happen. Stick to procedure and stick to the facts. When was the last time you took a day off? One where you *didn't* come in to catch up on paperwork?"

Katherine thought back over the last month. She couldn't remember a full day spent away from the station.

"When was the last time you had a hot meal?"

She had gone to bed without supper last night.

"Take the day off. Relax. Eat. Wash your hair."

"I can't. I have to—"

"That's not a suggestion, Dell. It's an order."

Katherine dug her fingernails into her palms as she walked out of the station. McAlister wanted her to relax? Fine. She'd play along. A bakery had opened a block away from the station more than a year ago. She kept meaning to try it but always found herself too busy. Today, she would buy herself a treat. A full stomach might help her think up a plan.

A bell dinged over the door when she walked in, and sweet cinnamon filled her nose. She unclenched her jaw as she took a deep inhale. The place was quite charming. The tablecloths flowed to the floor, cascades of white set against the deep blue wallpaper. Fresh chrysanthemums peeked out of glass vases. Customers at the tables sipped from porcelain cups rimmed with gold.

The man behind the counter loaded blueberry muffins into the display case while another worker took a steaming tray of cinnamon rolls out of the oven. He drizzled icing over them, which melted into the coiled crevices of the buns. Katherine drifted to the cash register to place her order.

The man with the muffins stepped away from the display case and over to the register. He had a pained expression, as if apprehensive about approaching Katherine. She realized too late that she hadn't fixed her hair in her rush to leave the apartment this morning, and she hadn't done her makeup. Yesterday's pinned-up curls drooped and fell from her head. Her old mascara was probably smeared under her eyes. She'd thrown on the first dress she'd grabbed from the pile on her chair, and she stuck out in this fancy tearoom like the proverbial sore thumb. She forced a smile to show that she was harmless. The baker's face only contorted further.

She ordered a cinnamon roll and handed the man two dimes. Her treat arrived on a gold-rimmed plate. She took a seat near the window and devoured the first layer, the icing sticking to her fingers. A little voice in her mind told her to get a napkin, but her rumbling stomach drowned it out. To hell with proper manners; she picked up the roll and took a bite. Icing smeared her cheek. She wiped it away with her hand, then filled her mouth with another bite.

As she chewed, two men walked into the bakery. One of them had a familiar face. Gray hair crept up his temples and his glasses slipped down his thin nose. He looked over at her with horrified surprise. "Katherine, is that you?"

That was when she recognized him. "Avery Thurgood?" she shouted with her mouth full. Her reporter friend from the *Nolaton City Gazette*. She fell into laughter, careful not to spit out her confection, but relieved to see the one person who might actually take her seriously. She ran over to Avery and hugged him close. Oh, thank goodness for Avery. She could give an account of the break-in, and he would surely fly back to his office and get it into the evening paper. Though part of her wanted to pass out from exhaustion, excitement flowed through her as well. The man Avery was with shuffled a few feet away from them, and Avery peeled Katherine from his jacket.

"I hardly recognized you. You look..." Avery declined to finish his thought but introduced Katherine to his colleague. "Mr. Applebaum and I are working on an article about the winter festival."

Mr. Applebaum let out a nervous chuckle. Katherine's off-putting appearance must not have made a great impression. "With weather like this, the skating rink will be ready in no time."

It had snowed last night, and a few flakes still danced on the breeze. Katherine hadn't even noticed until Mr. Applebaum pointed it out.

"That's very nice. Avery, I need to talk to you." She pulled on his sleeve, but he yanked his arm back.

"Can it wait? I'm conducting an interview."

"I was attacked last night. Those men, the Gray Suits, they broke into my apartment—"

"Why don't we get you a cup of coffee." Avery led her to the register, away from Applebaum.

"I don't want coffee. I want you to listen." Katherine tried to catch his eye, but Avery stared ahead at the man working the register.

"Two coffees with cream, please."

"I don't take cream in—"

"Let's sit here." Avery plunked her down at the nearest table, far from her cinnamon roll. Why was he being so obstinate, ignoring her dire need to be heard? He took the coffees and gave one to her.

She took a sip to be polite, but the cream left a slimy film on her tongue. She set the cup down with no intention of picking it up again. "Avery, look at me. Those men—"

"I can't do this now. Mr. Applebaum is the editor-in-chief's father. He'll have me chucked out of the *Gazette* if I don't stay in line."

"I'm sorry to hear that, but this is important."

"I want to get your story, just not now. Can I call you this week and set up a time?"

Katherine stood up and buttoned her coat, ready to leave the tearoom. "I thought *you* of all people would understand the urgency."

"Sit down. What do you want me to do?" Avery sighed with exasperation. Katherine remained standing, hurt by his callous disregard.

"Print an article to warn everyone in the city that a detective was attacked by criminals in her own home. If it can happen to me, it can happen to anyone. People have a right to know how dangerous—"

"All right, all right. We'll get something drafted. I just can't do this today." He looked over at Mr. Applebaum, who tapped his watch.

"Of course. The winter carnival is a much more pressing issue. I'm sure the Spider will adhere to your schedule. Thanks for the coffee." She pushed her full cup toward him, sloshing some over the side. Avery jumped up to avoid the spill.

Katherine stormed out of the bakery. The image of her attackers hovering over her kept replaying in her mind, with their creepy smiles and leering eyes. If no one would help her stop the Spider and those minions, she would have to do it herself.

Snow squeaked under her boots as she wandered the city streets, heading nowhere in particular. She couldn't go back to the station — McAlister had made that clear. She could go home, but what would she accomplish there? Every out-of-place noise would startle her and each footstep up the concrete stairs would strike her with fear. No, she couldn't sit at home all day expecting her attackers to reappear. With nothing else to do, she went over the details of the Jones case. If she could solve it quickly enough, maybe she could save her own life.

Loretta's body had been left on display in the alley — her scarf and handbag were missing. It screamed "Spider" to Katherine. Yet in the weeks leading to Loretta's murder, her life had remained the same. A fake engagement ring, a small apartment, no flashy new cars or lavish vacations.

No sneaking around or keeping secrets. According to Jack, she went to work each day and came home her usual happy self.

The police had investigated dozens of cases that Katherine had tied to the Spider, but no cops had ever reported being personally threatened before. Why now? Was she getting too close to the answer? Or was there something different about Loretta's murder? Maybe no one had taken a hit out on Loretta. Maybe the Spider wanted her dead for personal reasons, then staged the body to look like a stick-up gone wrong. The Spider's skills at secrecy had covered these crimes for this long, so why not keep the pattern the same?

If it was personal, then what was the reason for killing her? Did the Spider want to keep her quiet or get revenge for something she had done? Could Tom Phillips be connected after all? He was the only one at the Razzle with a motive to kill Loretta. Lou had given him an alibi, but maybe Lou was just protecting his pal. He had smart business reasons to keep Tom out of jail — he specialized in whiskey cocktails and Tom's product was his most popular liquor. And they'd known each other a long time. Lou had been the bartender at the Razzle Dazzle for years, which meant he was selling cocktails while Prohibition was in effect. Certainly not the worst crime, but a crime nonetheless.

Wait a minute. Katherine paused. Tom had been running a criminal enterprise during the years booze was banned. He might know all the underground scum in town. Maybe they'd come to him wanting more than whiskey.

Maybe Tom was the Spider. Did that really make sense, though? Why would the criminal underground of Nolaton City use some rumrunner as their hitman? What was she missing? The details didn't quite add up. She needed more information, and she knew just where to look.

Chapter Twenty-Six

Katherine took one of the Model 18s from the station parking lot and pounded on the gas pedal. Trees and houses swam past the window, but she stayed focused on what lay ahead. Somewhere in Tom's house she would find Loretta's scarf — and if she was lucky, a whole lot more. If he really was the Spider, he would have a collection of the trinkets that he'd stolen from the victims. Little trophies to remember each kill. Katherine's stomach turned.

She stopped a block away from his house and looked for his truck, but it wasn't parked anywhere nearby. Good. He was gone.

She tried to look casual as she walked up the street. Just a friendly woman out for a stroll. A thin layer of snow covered the ground, and ice formed in patches where it had melted and cooled.

Tom's house was dark inside, confirming that he was out. She decided to sneak in through the back and avoid the neighbors. How embarrassing would it be if one of them called the cops on *her*? She sauntered up to the house on the concrete walkway, which, thankfully, Tom must have shoveled that morning. Any footprints she made would melt in the sun that now shined on his backyard.

A screen door hung off-kilter from its frame. Katherine pushed it aside and went to work on the real door. She took a pin from her hair, and a whisper of frizz escaped its grasp. With a bit of wiggling, the pin fit into the keyhole. Listening for the tell-tale clicks, she scraped metal on metal until at last the lock popped open.

She tiptoed inside, first one foot, then the other, and closed the door behind her. Maybe it was her training or a mix of guilt and nerves, but even though the house was deserted, she still felt the need to keep quiet. As a starting point, she chose his bedroom. That was where most people hid their secrets. She looked under his bed first, finding nothing but dust. The closet contained only clothes and shoes, none of which appeared to be from the Spider's victims. She tapped the walls and floor, looking for a hidden compartment. Nothing.

She moved on to the basement. The space was unfinished and cramped; no hidden compartments there either. Besides the utilities, not much else would fit.

She slinked up the stairs to the attic. The second story was half the size of the first, and the floors buckled under her feet. She treaded cautiously as she searched the room. Tom didn't have much stored up there. Broken barrels that stank of old liquor had been shoved in the corner. A busted lamp and a few old pieces of furniture sat propped against the far wall. Boxes, maybe a half dozen, were strewn around, and Katherine opened them. They contained old photo albums and childhood memorabilia, nothing suspicious. His ragged teddy bear wasn't going to help her case. She kicked the boxes aside.

To her right was a door that she suspected led to a storage room. Her suspicions were confirmed as she pushed it open, but again, she found very little inside. Hoses and tubes — most likely brewing equipment — collected dust on a shelf. Old gardening shears lay rusting in the corner. Some auto mechanic tools. Katherine cursed, then an idea struck her. Maybe the trinkets weren't hidden in the house.

In order to supply all those bars with whiskey, he would need a hell of an operation. Fermenting tubs, a large still, dozens of barrels for aging, a bottling setup. It's not as if he could run that business from his tiny shack. Even after Tom got arrested for bootlegging, the cops couldn't find his distillery. He must own another property, a barn perhaps? Katherine would have to investigate, maybe tail Tom until he led her to the spot. And there, she might find his trinkets.

She began her descent to the lower level, then froze at the sound of popping gaskets and a rumbling engine. The engine cut, then Tom's front door opened. Damn it. Tom must have come home. She tiptoed back up the stairs then stood still against the closest wall, her pulse pounding against her eardrums.

The attic stairs creaked with each of his heavy footsteps. If Katherine didn't find a better hiding spot, she would be caught. She darted into the storage room, left the door cracked open to see what he was doing, and held her breath.

Tom looked around the attic, then turned his sights to the storage room. Katherine realized her mistake. Tom's old beater truck must need a repair, and she had hidden with his tools. Katherine searched for a better hiding spot, but other than the shelves, the room was bare. She looked at the window — was it big enough to crawl through?

She pushed it open, thankful that the frame stayed silent. She hoisted herself up and wrapped one leg around the edge. All she could stand on was an ice-covered patch of roof. She flung her other leg over. Her feet fell from under her, but she caught the window frame with her hands. She scrambled to find her footing, but the unforgiving sheen of ice rejected her. Then her hand slipped off the window frame, her sweaty palms betraying her. She grasped on and dug her fingernails into the rotting wood.

Tom opened the storage room door and though Katherine tried to duck, she couldn't hide the hands that kept her secured to the window. Tom stuck his head out the window, fire in his eyes.

"Well, I'd call the police to report a break-in but it looks like they're already here." He clamped on to her wrists. *Oh no.* He could fling her from the roof, leaving her injured or dead. Katherine let out a squeal and tried yet again to gain traction under her feet. Instead of throwing her from the window frame, Tom pulled her toward the warmth of the attic. She had no choice but to let him drag her like a limp ragdoll. Once inside, she sprang to her feet and dangled her hand near her revolver. He had just saved her, but that did little to put her at ease. Any of his neighbors could have seen him if he shoved her off the roof. Perhaps he still planned to kill her but wanted to get her somewhere private first.

"Calm down, lady. I'm not going to hurt you." He held his hands up, showing he meant no harm.

"But you've hurt others, haven't you?" A blinding rage took hold of Katherine. If Tom really was the Spider, she would show him no mercy.

"I've never hurt a soul unless they attacked me first. Is that what you mean? The bar fight from six years ago where a guy twice my size shoved me into a pool table? Of course I hit him back."

Was he toying with her or did he really not know what she meant?

"Were you at the Razzle Dazzle the night Loretta Jones was killed? Don't lie to me like last time."

Tom squirmed, caught off guard by her vehemence. "Fine. Yes, I was there. I made my usual delivery, then I left to finish my route."

"You realize this doesn't look good for you. You said you'd never been there before."

"Invading my house doesn't look good for you. And how would it look if I'd told the truth? I'd have been arrested on the spot. You said it yourself — it's always the ex-boyfriend, right?" Tom crossed his arms defiantly.

"It looks a lot better when you're honest." Katherine gritted her teeth. Tom glared at her.

"Did you see Loretta when you were there?"

Tom glowered as he nodded.

"Not a pleasant interaction, I'm guessing?"

"Nobody wants to run into an old girlfriend." Tom refused to look Katherine in the eye.

"There's more to it than that, isn't there?"

Tom contorted his face into a sneer. "If you insist that honesty is an advantage, I'll tell the truth. She ran into my dolly and broke those damned whiskey bottles. She's the reason I lost product and didn't get paid that night."

"Why, that must have made you angry." Katherine spoke with mock surprise. She had him cornered — it sounded like he'd just told her the motive behind the murder. Now all she needed was a confession. And she needed it badly. After the stunt she just pulled, breaking into a suspect's home, she could lose her badge. If she had any chance of catching the Spider, it had to happen now. She would squeeze the truth out of Tom no matter how long it took. "Am I right? You went to the Razzle to do your job and you saw the woman who broke your heart. Then she goes and breaks your bottles too. That burned you up, didn't it?"

Tom's face went red. "Yes! I mean no. I mean...I didn't kill her, if that's what you're getting at."

"Yes you did. And you've killed plenty more people, haven't you? Making the crimes look like muggings, taking trinkets from the bodies, getting paid once the job is done."

"Have you lost your mind? What are you going on about?" Tom had the audacity to laugh at her. Katherine rounded on him, trapping him in the corner of the storage room. He tried to back away from her but had nowhere to step. His mouth formed a terrified circle, and his eyes grew large. Good, he should be afraid. He should feel the same fear that Joey endured as he bled out in the alley.

"Admit it. You're the Spider."

Tom's face contorted with confusion and he blinked at her.

"Listen, I've never killed anybody, and I would have never hurt Loretta no matter how much she hurt me. I love her and you don't hurt people you love."

Katherine drew back, surprised by the heartfelt speech. She watched his face, looking for the usual signs of trickery, but there were none. No trembling hands or drumming fingers, no nervous laughter or quickened breath. He continued on.

"Even after she left, I'd dream about her coming back, saying she had made a mistake. I knew the odds were stacked against me, but I'd imagine her knocking on my door and saying she left Jack, that she missed me too much and couldn't stay away. That sounds stupid but a man can't help how he feels. When you told me she died, it was like a punch to the chest. All I wanted was for her to be happy. I swear to you, I never meant her an ounce of harm." His eyes peered into hers with a sincere longing for the woman he lost. Katherine believed him, as much as it broke her heart. Now her career lay in his hands, and she had to convince him not to report her for breaking in.

"I'm sorry I came here and put you through this. And I swear to *you*, if you keep this quiet then I will do whatever I can to find Loretta's killer. But if you tell the police I broke in—"

"The last thing I want is more cops prowling around. No one needs to know you were here, but I'd appreciate it if you let yourself out now." He pointed to the storage room door.

"Of course." She ran out with Tom following about ten paces behind, probably making sure she actually intended to leave. She let herself out through the front door and darted to the car without looking back.

She got in the driver's seat and the keys jingled as she turned on the engine. Her foot should be hitting the gas pedal, but it didn't. She couldn't move. That feeling — the lack of feeling — came over her. The emptiness filled her and she sat like her gears were rusted and wouldn't turn.

Tears welled up in her eyes. What had she just done? She'd broken into a suspect's home and searched without a warrant. She put her career on the line to chase a hunch, exactly what McAlister had told her not to do.

She gasped for breath as tears rolled down her cheeks. Her chest tightened and her lungs refused to fill. She was desperate for breath, her heart racing and her chest burning like her body was about to fail. Like this sudden attack could end her life.

No. Nothing was wrong with her, physically. The stress of it all threw her into panic, but she could fight through. Her lungs would take air whether they liked it or not. She balled up her hands into fists and took a great gasping breath. Relaxing her fists, she let the air back out. Flexing and forcing air into her chest, she felt a sense of calm take hold. Her breath came naturally again, and her heart rate slowed.

Once calm, Katherine drove the car back to the station, then walked home. She climbed the stairs to her apartment and lay on her bed, staring up at the ceiling. Tears streaked her face and soaked into her hair. One thing was clear: she couldn't continue like this.

The Spider had been operating for fifteen years or more. If no one had found this killer, what made her think she could? Despite her promise to Tom, she didn't know if she had the skills to find Loretta's attacker. Maybe she should do what the Gray Suits had suggested. Designate Loretta's murder as a cold case. Walk away and give up on ever finding the Spider.

Chapter Twenty-Seven

The next day, Katherine sat at her desk typing up her notes on the Jones murder, not that she had much to say. No evidence other than the ligature marks on her neck and the missing scarf. No leads. No clue who the Spider could be.

She took a red ink pad and a rubber stamp from her desk drawer, one that said "cold case" in bold letters. The threats from her attackers hovered over her like a boulder ready to crush her. Mark the case cold, or the Spider will come for you.

What harm would it do to give up? Loretta was already dead. Jack had already lost the love of his life. Nothing could bring her back. No one would help Katherine track down the Spider.

She rubbed her eyes, trying to shake the emotions. A heavy clunk on her desk got her attention. She peered over her hands and saw the red mug, her favorite, filled to the brim with mud-thick coffee. Black, just the way she liked it. Williams stood in front of her with a worried expression.

"Where were you yesterday? I found something I wanted to show you, but I must have missed you."

That caught Katherine off guard and irritated her. Why on earth was Williams so eager to see her? It's not as if this man, who so adamantly denied her theories about the Spider, could offer anything relevant. And why had he placed his coffee so close to her? Was he bragging about getting the good mug?

"McAlister gave me the day off." Katherine shuffled papers on her desk. Maybe if she looked busy he would leave her alone. Instead, he pushed the mug farther toward her. Had she misread his intentions? "Is this for me?" She pointed to the steaming cup.

"You look like you need it. Rough night?"

"Rough week. Rough month." If she was being honest, rough five years. She picked up the coffee and took a sip. Maybe it was the lack of sleep, but it was the best cup of joe she'd ever had. Warmth spread through her, dampening the horror she felt at her situation.

"Dell, I don't mean this as an insult, please don't take it the wrong way, but you don't look so good." Williams leaned away from her as if expecting her to lash out. When she remained silent, he continued. "You look like you haven't slept in days."

"I haven't slept well since...never mind. You wouldn't believe me." She hung her head.

"Try me." He perched on the edge of her desk, and since he was being so amiable, Katherine didn't mind him taking up her space.

The story poured out of her. The men breaking into her apartment. The threats they had made. Her theory about Tom, breaking into his place. Her search coming up empty. Williams would run to the lieutenant, and she would be escorted out of the station with her things boxed up. It didn't matter anymore if she kept the detective badge; Joey's killer had escaped her grasp.

"There. You win," she concluded with a sigh. "Go tell McAlister. He'll fire me, and you can have my job."

Williams stared at her. Silence permeated the room. Why wasn't he speaking? Was he trying not to laugh at her, or was he working up a lecture?

"I owe you one hell of an apology." Williams's face hardened and Katherine tried to read his expression but found herself stumped.

"What for?"

"For calling you crazy. Those men broke in and threatened you?" He sounded angry, like he wanted to defend her.

"Yes." Tears clouded her vision, and she willed them not to fall.

Williams set his hand on hers, his touch a surprising comfort. "We're not giving up, Dell. I found something two nights ago, and I think it's connected to the men who attacked you. From what I saw, the Spider has to be real."

"So you believe?" Katherine popped her head up and stared at him.

"I believe."

Katherine let this soak in. Another officer understood the threat that lingered over Nolaton. She felt a burden lift from her back, like her voice had finally become loud enough to echo from the station walls. Like she'd earned her badge. She wiped her eyes, ready to continue the investigation. "I'd like to see what you found."

Williams dug in his pocket and pulled out a photograph. Katherine gasped and took it from him. It was a picture of her and Joey strolling down Maple Lane. Joey's smiling face sent daggers shooting through her chest. That must have been the day they'd gone to the bakery to choose their wedding cake.

"Is he your husband?" Williams shrank away as if he had already guessed the answer.

"He was supposed to be." She took a moment, swallowed hard, then pushed her feelings back down. Now was not the time to wallow. "Where did you find this? Who took it?"

"I'll show you."

Katherine drove them to the apartment while Williams directed her. As she pulled up to the curb, Williams pointed at a first-floor unit and stuttered.

"They had blackout curtains up before." The curtains had been taken down from the windows, and they could see straight through the glass. Williams got out of the car and Katherine followed. They stuck their faces up to the pane and saw, well, nothing. The whole place had been emptied. Williams jimmied the window open, and they slipped inside. Every room was empty, everything gone from the walls. The men must have figured out someone had been in the apartment.

"I swear it was here. All the photos were on this wall held up with thumbtacks." Williams pointed to the living room wall, which was covered in tiny pinpricks.

"Now how are we going to find them?" Katherine fought the hopelessness that wanted to take hold. Williams tented his fingers over his lips.

"You're not gonna like this, Dell, but there's someone we should talk to. Someone who might know a thing or two about the Spider."

Katherine and Williams walked into the prison's visitor's center downtown, took a table near the entrance, and waited. After a few minutes, the alarm buzzed, and the door opened. There, much to Katherine's chagrin, was Rita Davis, handcuffed and escorted by a guard.

Rita sat at their table but said nothing, her expression impossible to read.

"Hello, Miss Davis," Williams said in an overly cheerful tone, probably an attempt to break the tension, but he was not successful.

"You here to scream at me again?" Rita leaned back in her chair.

"Are you going to threaten me with a sword again?" Katherine scoffed.

"Tough to do that given the situation." Rita lifted her chained hands. "Is there a reason for your visit, or is this just a social call?"

Katherine decided to play nice. She would rather get information from Rita than fight with her. Pride would have to take a back seat. "I'm sorry for the way I treated you."

"You should be." Rita glanced out the window at the prison yard, then sighed. "All right, I'm sorry I tried to stab you with a sword."

"We're just here to ask a few questions," Williams said.

Rita looked suspicious. "What do you wanna know?"

"After your arrest, when it was just you and me at the police station, you mentioned the Spider, remember?"

"And then you shoved me into a holding cell. Yes, I remember."

"Do you know who the Spider is?" Katherine's heart pounded in anticipation.

Rita paused and looked down at her handcuffs. "I didn't think any of you cops believed in the Spider."

"Some of us do." Williams nodded at Katherine.

"Do you know who it is, Miss Davis?" Katherine tried to stay calm but was desperate for name, a lead, a hint. Anything.

"No. I know the Spider ain't just a rumor like people say, but I don't know who does the killing."

Williams deflated, probably feeling foolish for bringing them there just to hit another dead end. Katherine's mind spun, wondering if Rita could offer more information. "You know something, though, don't you?"

"I've known a lot of dangerous people for a long time." Rita's eyes narrowed.

"You know the Boss, right?" Katherine knew she had to tread the topic lightly. Rita may still be loyal to the crime lord and could mislead them on purpose.

"All too well. He's the bastard who got me into this situation. That's what I was trying to tell you when I got arrested. I was only sixteen when I met the Boss and he tricked me into borrowing money from him, then made me steal whatever he needed as a way of paying him back. He always said he would let me go once the debt was paid, but no matter how much I gave him, it still wasn't enough. If I threatened to quit, he said he would send the Spider after me. And he'd done it before. I met some of his other thieves and they had the same story. They'd try to leave and wind up dead in an alley."

"How...how long ago did you start working for him?" It was a long shot, but had she ever crossed paths with Joey? If Joey had borrowed money from the Boss like Rita did—

"Four years ago."

Joey had already been murdered by the time Rita started working for the Boss. Katherine swallowed her disappointment.

"You don't happen to know where the Boss's headquarters are, do you?" Williams asked.

"As a matter of fact, I do."

Williams spun his finger in the air, imploring her to give up the information, but Rita folded her hands and refused to continue.

"If you can tell us, I bet we can make things easier for you. We could talk to the DA about knocking some time from your sentence. Deal?" Katherine extended her hand for Rita to shake.

Rita snubbed her. "No deal."

"Miss Davis, an opportunity like this doesn't come knocking every day. All you have to do is give us some information," Katherine said.

"I know that."

"Then give Detective Dell what she needs." Williams patted the table as he spoke. Katherine couldn't help but smile at Williams's use of her full title. Maybe she had finally earned his respect.

"And what happens if you go after him and botch the operation? If the Boss finds out who squealed, it ain't gonna be pretty for me."

"We can protect you," Katherine said.

Rita grunted but otherwise stayed silent.

"We're offering you months, maybe years of your life back. What else could you possibly want?" Williams threw his hands up in frustration then steadied himself. "Think of all the people you would help if the Boss was no longer in business."

Rita let out a scornful laugh. "There's only one person I care about helping."

"Who?" Katherine gazed at Rita, searching her face for answers. She couldn't mean herself or else she would take the deal, and there was more behind her eyes than self-preservation. A hint of love and longing broke through Rita's tough expression.

"Walter?" Williams asked, and Rita nodded. Katherine put it together. This Walter fellow must be more than an accomplice.

"He's not just a partner in crime, is he?" Katherine asked.

"He's my partner in everything, the love of my life, and he is in danger. I've checked the obituaries every day and so far, I haven't seen his name, but I don't know how much longer that will last. I think the Boss has our neighbors spying on us and if he gets wind that Walter is fleeing town, he'll have one of his lackeys kill him right then and there. And if Walter stays in town, even in a jail cell, the Spider will get him. But if he can get out, even just across Nolaton's border, the Boss can't touch him."

"Why not?" Williams asked.

"Nolaton is his territory, but the neighboring cities are run by other gangs. The Boss wouldn't send his hitman out there and risk starting a turf war. I want him taken out of the city safely. I don't care where he goes, only that the Boss's goons don't find him on his way out of town."

Katherine and Williams looked at each other. Williams shook his head.

"Our jurisdiction ends at the city limits. We'd have to coordinate with other towns' forces, especially seeing as Walter's a wanted criminal. And we'd have to figure out a place for him to stay. I don't know if—"

"He could stay with his brother in Lavendale. Or he could serve jail time in another town for all I care...please just get him out of Nolaton." Rita picked at her fingernail as she waited for a response to her plea.

Katherine wondered how much trouble she would get in if she took Walter out of town without official permission. Was that trouble more important than a man's life? Her job was to keep people safe, and sometimes that meant working outside the bounds of the police handbook. As far as Katherine knew, Walter wasn't violent or posing a threat to anyone's life; he simply got caught up in a bad situation while trying to help the woman he loved. Now Katherine had a chance to save him from the same killer who took Joey from her. How could she say no to that? Katherine gave Williams a determined look, imploring him to cooperate. With a sigh, he nodded his agreement.

"I can do this for you, Miss Davis, and I can look into transferring you to a prison in another town as well." Katherine figured if the Spider could get Walter in one of Nolaton's jail cells, then Rita's current cell wasn't safe either.

Rita tipped her head in confusion, but her eyes sparkled with hope. "You can?"

"If you tell me where the Boss's headquarters are."

"Got a pen and paper?" Rita held out her cuffed hands as Katherine dug for her notebook. Katherine handed over her pencil and a blank page torn from her notepad. Rita wrote down the location of headquarters and told them where to find Walter. As she handed it back to Katherine, she said, "Promise me you can do this?"

"I promise."

"Thank you." Rita's eyes welled with tears.

They said their goodbyes, then Rita was escorted back out of the visitor's center. Katherine flagged down a guard who had been standing in the corner with his arms crossed. She asked to borrow a phone — official police business — and he guided her to an unoccupied office instead of the public payphone so she could have privacy. Williams stood next to her as she picked up the receiver and dialed McAlister's number. The lieutenant answered on the first ring.

"Sir, it's Dell. I found out where the Boss's headquarters are." She hoped he wouldn't pry into her method of obtaining the address. Her hopes were dashed as he bellowed into the phone.

"How the hell did you get that?"

She mulled over her options. If she told the truth, he may try to stop her from bringing Walter to safety and force her to arrest him instead. Knowing McAlister, he'd give a speech about how well-protected the Nolaton men's jail cells are and dismiss Rita's claim that the Spider could kill Walter while in custody. Katherine didn't want to lie; she respected McAlister too much. Her best bet was to shirk the question.

"You wouldn't like the answer but trust me, I am doing what's best for the city."

McAlister grumbled on the other end of the line. Had she already said too much?

"*Can* I trust you? Last time I saw you, you seemed, uh, on edge."

Katherine assumed he had chosen softer words than he would have normally, and she appreciated that. Yet, her disappointment hung heavy around her. She understood his doubts, but that didn't make it hurt less that she still, after all these years of working for him, had to prove her sanity.

"I'm in my right mind, and I have Officer Williams here with me." Perhaps name-dropping her supporting officer would give her some credibility. "Sir, I swear to you, he and I have the situation under control. You have nothing to worry about."

"I don't know how my newest detective managed to pull this off, but if you really did get the Boss's address, I applaud you."

Pride swelled in Katherine's chest for a moment but was quickly replaced with determination. Now that she had McAlister on her side and up to speed, they had a crime lord to catch. She read the address to the lieutenant, who scratched it down.

"As much as I'd like to go bust down his door, we've got to do some planning. I'll put a team together, get a judge to sign off on a warrant, and we'll raid the place tonight — midnight."

Katherine agreed that she and Williams would meet the team outside the Boss's headquarters before the raid. That gave them plenty of time to find Walter beforehand.

"And, Dell, whatever it is you're up to, please be careful."

"I will, sir."

She hung up the call, then walked out of the prison with Williams at her side. Katherine pulled out the slip of paper Rita had written instructions on how to find Walter in Shantytown. She hopped into the driver's seat and they made their way there.

Chapter Twenty-Eight

Katherine cut the engine on the edge of Nolaton Park. What had once been a field lush with green grass was now a barren patch dotted with shelters. The snow from two nights before had melted, leaving the land muddy. Katherine and Williams got out of the car and the ground squelched beneath their feet. Katherine took out Rita's instructions.

"From the plum tree, their shelter is eight rows up and twelve houses toward the center." Katherine glanced around, then pointed toward a squat tree with light, smooth bark. No leaves or fruit had survived the cold snap, but Katherine recognized it anyway. Her parents had a plum tree in the backyard when she was little, though it had withered and been removed many years ago. "Over here." She nodded for Williams to follow her. Once they stood in front of the tree, Katherine began to count the rows.

"Dell, how do you know you're counting right? I mean, these aren't exactly razor straight rows." Williams undulated his hand from left to right, imitating the sporadic placement of the shelters. He was right; the structures were not sitting in perfect rows like houses would be. People had set them wherever there was room. "We can't go calling his name or knocking on any random door. Remember, the neighbors might be spying for the Boss."

Katherine was concerned as well and could only make her best guess as to where the rows started.

"I think she means we need to count the eight closest to the edge then turn 90 degrees and walk straight to the twelfth. And she said theirs is made of cardboard next to one made of tin. We should be able to find it." She tried to force a confident smile but Williams still seemed uneasy. Her fake smile faded. "We have to try something."

"Let's hope we wind up in the right spot."

They walked from the plum tree and counted out eight structures, then turned into the jagged row. Katherine counted as they went farther into Shantytown. Some of the shelters had holes, probably from weather damage or mice, that had not yet been patched. Inside of one, a family huddled near a small fire built in a cooking pot. In another, a man slept, covered in newspapers for warmth. He woke with a start and saw Katherine through the soggy opening, then hid under the papers. He must have assumed the park officials called the cops to bust up their neighborhood and take them away. It wouldn't be the first time Shantytown had been dismantled and rebuilt. Katherine wanted to reassure the man they meant him no harm, but the damage was done. With a heavy heart and a new appreciation for her warm apartment, she walked on.

They arrived at the twelfth shelter in, not even a quarter of the way into the neighborhood. The structure was made of cardboard and sat next to one made of tin, just like Rita said. Katherine, hoping she had the right place, tapped on the cardboard but got no response. She tapped it harder, then a face popped out of the tin structure next door.

"Coming to arrest that lowlife?" the man sneered, apparently delighted to have his neighbor carted away by police.

"Go back in your home, sir." Williams waved the man away. The pesky neighbor glowered at Williams but did as he was told and crawled back inside. Katherine tapped Walter's door again, then lifted the flap. A man curled up under a blanket in the corner.

"Walter?" Katherine whispered. He looked emaciated, with sunken cheeks and worried eyes. He saw them and backed away farther into the corner.

"Who are you?" He looked back and forth between his intruders, but with no hint of anger, only fear.

"It's okay." Katherine put on a smile and held out her hands to defuse the tension. "I'm Detective Dell and this is Officer Williams. We're here to help."

"We're here to get you out of the city safely." Williams spoke in hushed tones so as not to be overheard.

Walter's demeanor changed. The fear subsided, replaced by hostility. "I'm not leaving her. If the Boss finds out I skipped town, she'll be his next target."

"That's for us to worry about. Since she's in danger, we may be able to transfer her to a different facility, but right now getting you to safety is top priority," Williams said.

Katherine considered telling Walter about the raid, how a team of trained cops would bust down the Boss's door nine hours from now, stopping the crook from taking the hit on Rita. She had to keep it quiet, however. It wouldn't be smart to give any civilian that level of inside information, and it could be especially detrimental if a meddling neighbor were eavesdropping. And she couldn't be certain the raid would be successful. She would have to convince Walter a different way.

"The best thing you can do for her is leave. How do you think she would feel if the Spider got you? What kind of hell would that be for her?"

Walter thought for a moment but stayed silent. Katherine continued talking.

"I know how she would feel. Empty. Sad. Guilty. Most of all, lonely. I know because that's how I feel every day. Don't put her through that. She asked us to take you to safety. For her sake, please come with us."

Walter's shoulders relaxed away from his ears. He looked near tears but got up and left the shelter. Perhaps Katherine had gotten through. Maybe he saw in her the same fear and longing that he felt. They walked toward the car. Behind them, Katherine heard a shuffling sound. She turned and saw that pesky neighbor leaving his home and walking the opposite direction. Was he the one spying for the Boss? She quickened her pace and hoped she was just being paranoid.

When they got to the car, Walter got in the back seat, while Williams took the passenger seat and Katherine drove.

They pulled onto the highway and sped past the harbor, and through the industrial part of town. After another ten or fifteen minutes on the road, their surroundings changed. Instead of skyscrapers in the bustling city, thin trees stretched toward the clouds in the stillness of nature. In the distance, a hand-painted wooden sign read "Now Leaving Nolaton."

Katherine drove toward it, but something in the mirror caught her eye. A black Roadster merged into the lane behind them. It sped up and rode close to their back bumper. Katherine checked her speed. She was just above the legal limit, and this other driver had no business getting so close.

The Roadster slammed into them. Katherine's chest smacked into the steering wheel, her head whipping forward then jolting back. Williams grabbed on to the dashboard and steadied himself while Walter ducked down in the back seat. Katherine peered at the other car in the rearview mirror. The driver grimaced at them through the windshield. Could he be one of the Boss's lackeys? Had that damn neighbor gone and ratted them out?

The Roadster rammed into the police car again and Katherine's neck ached from the impact. The Model 18 lost traction and the trees whirled around them as the car spun across the road, ending up facing the opposite way. Katherine growled. She jammed her foot down on the clutch, pushed the gear shift forward, and stomped on the gas.

"What are you doing, Dell?" Williams shouted as the car sped up and threw his arms over his face.

Katherine crashed the front of her car into the car that had been chasing them. Good thing the police department just got new models. While her front bumper took deep scratches, the Roadster's round headlights shattered, and shards of glass rained onto the street.

As the Roadster smoked, Walter popped up and pumped his fist. The man in the Roadster curled his lips into a menacing smile, then pulled out a pistol. Thinking fast, Katherine threw the car in reverse and sped backward toward the city border. The man fired his weapon but missed them by inches, then fired again. This time the bullet smashed into their windshield and got lodged in the laminated glass, fracturing most of the pane.

Katherine slammed her foot onto the gas pedal, blasting them backward, and turned the wheel side to side, zigzagging their car to make it a harder target to hit. The Roadster careened forward while the man fired twice more. Katherine veered just as the bullets whizzed past her window.

Williams let out a guttural roar that Katherine had never heard from him before. He pulled out his revolver then leaned out his open window and fired. His bullet struck the driver's side tire of the Roadster, which hissed and flattened. The lackey's car spun off the road and smashed into a birch tree. The driver must have pounded the gas pedal; the tires reeled but could not gain traction in the mud and fallen leaves.

Katherine cranked the Model 18 around to face the hand-painted sign. She glanced in the rearview mirror to make sure the lackey had not gotten back on the road. He was still spinning his wheels in the dirt.

Walter stayed crouched in the back and Williams rolled up his window. Katherine simply stared out through the unbroken chunk of windshield in front of her. They passed Nolaton's border shaken, but uninjured.

Katherine checked the rearview mirror every few minutes to be sure their pursuer wouldn't make a miraculous recovery and reappear on their tail. She also kept glancing at Walter, who now sat upright in his seat but stared forward with worried eyes. As trained cops, she and Williams were prepared for dangerous situations. Walter, however, had probably never experienced something so terrifying. She wanted to reassure him, but no words of comfort came to her.

After about thirty minutes, the group fully relaxed. Williams lamented that the car didn't have a radio, but the department's budget probably wouldn't cover that sort of gimmick. Katherine too found herself desperate to fill the silence. Now that Walter seemed more at ease, she had a few questions for him.

"I don't mean to sound insensitive, but does the Boss usually put that much effort into keeping his thieves in town? Does he always send an armed man after the runners?" She took a look in the mirror and noted Walter's uncomfortable expression — knitted eyebrows and pursed lips. A twinge of guilt hit her in the chest, but she needed as much information as she could gather. She didn't expect Walter to know everything about the Boss's organization, but any information he provided could prove useful during the raid that night or during a trial afterward if they could gather enough evidence.

"I've never met the man, but Rita told me how he runs things, or at least as much as she knows. Most of his thieves only last a few months, then they refuse to cooperate. At that point, he tells them they aren't allowed to leave town, though most of them don't have enough money for a life on the run anyway. They stick around Nolaton hoping the Boss was making an empty threat, then two or three weeks later, they wind up dead in an alley."

"Killed by the Spider, right?" Katherine looked back at Walter, who nodded. "But Rita worked for him for years. How did she last that much longer than everyone else?" Katherine glanced at Walter again, pleased to see a smile emerge on his otherwise doleful face.

"Rita is as stubborn as they come; she does not quit. The Boss kept telling her that she would pay off her debt eventually as long as she did his dirty work. She knew if she left the enterprise before the debt was cleared, he would send the Spider after her. Plus, she believed that there was a dollar amount that she would hit and then he would set her free. As if at some point he would tip his cap and allow her to walk out on him."

"You don't believe the Boss had a dollar amount in mind?" Katherine picked up on Walter's scornful tone.

"I find it odd that after four years, after everything she has given him, that it still won't cover what she borrowed. He kept making excuses about interest payments and fees that he charged on the loan, but I think he was lying to her. I don't think he ever intended to let her go. Any of his other thieves would quit without a second thought, but Rita always showed up."

"So he valued her loyalty?"

"Very much so. He had her stealing for his best client and wouldn't let any of his other thieves fill that client's requests. The fellow would place the strangest orders, like all the teapots from a china shop or three violins from an antiques dealer."

"Or all the pearls from a jewelry store?" Perhaps this client started the whole chain of events that led to the Bailey Jewelers break-in.

"Exactly. The Boss really wanted to keep this guy happy and Rita was the only one he trusted. I have no idea who the client is, but once the Boss started working with him, that's when he brought me on to help. And that's when the threats ramped up. The Boss told Rita that if she tried to quit on him, he would have me killed first so she would feel the agony of losing me. For Rita, that was a bigger threat than her own death."

Katherine understood why. If she could trade places with Joey... She didn't want to dwell on that. This conversation was too important.

"Wait a minute," Williams said. "So the Boss lends out money on the front end, hires a hitman on the back end. That's a lot of cash flying out the door."

"I don't know the details, but between all the robberies and burglaries, I have no doubt he's turning a profit. Maybe he loses money on some of his thieves but makes up the difference on others."

Katherine turned to Williams, who seemed satisfied with that answer. She thanked Walter for the information, and he nodded in return. As the car fell silent, Katherine stewed on the questions Walter couldn't answer. Who was this client with all the eclectic requests? And how did the Boss make sure his business stayed out of the red? He must have a system to track who owes what and how much they have stolen. How much is he paying for the hits? And what vile things does the Spider do with the earnings? She shuddered, unwilling to board that train of thought. Perhaps some things are best left unknown.

By the time they arrived in Lavendale, the sun was hovering above the horizon. Lavendale was much smaller than Nolaton. The buildings were shorter but had larger windows, which reflected the glow of the fading sunlight. People wandered about without worry, heads held high. They didn't hunch their shoulders the way the people of Nolaton did, a protective stance to avoid unwanted attention. Though Lavendale seemed safer, it wasn't perfect. Outside of the steak houses and nail salons milled people holding up signs asking for work.

Walter directed them to his brother's apartment on Seventh Street. When they pulled up to the brick complex, Walter gasped. A man stood on the sidewalk with a cardboard sign that read "Will Work for Money or Food." The man looked like Walter; they even had the same sunken-eyed appearance of someone who didn't get enough to eat.

"That's Ricky. My brother."

Katherine pulled over and Walter got out of the car. Ricky looked surprised at the sight of his brother.

"What are you doing here?" Ricky threw his arms around Walter but still held on to his sign. Between the Model 18 and Williams's uniform, it must have registered with him that Walter was being escorted by cops. "Are you in some sort of trouble?"

"That's one way to put it. I was hoping to stay with you, but I'm guessing that's not an option now."

"I got evicted last month after I lost my job. Seems like no matter how hard I work, I'm the first to be let go when the layoffs come." Ricky and Walter exchanged knowing looks. "I'll let you know as soon as I'm back on my feet, but for now I'm sleeping on a friend's couch. All the shelters are full and a ritzy town like this one doesn't have the best resources for people down on their luck."

They said their goodbyes and Walter got back in the car.

"You don't happen to have another relative to stay with?" Williams asked with trepidation.

Walter shook his head. "My parents still live in Nolaton, not that they want anything to do with a criminal like me."

"No aunts or uncles? Grandparents? Cousins?" Williams snapped his fingers as he tried to come up with solutions.

"Nobody close enough to take me in."

They had driven all this way and now they had no place for Walter to stay. Well, there was one place she knew of, but Katherine's skin crawled at the thought of asking them for assistance. Her parents lived on the outskirts of Lavendale and had a large house; they could spare a bedroom for a stranger in need. But would they be willing? They weren't big on favors for anyone, let alone those they saw as beneath their station, and would see the situation through a selfish lens. What rumors might circulate if someone saw Walter living there? What would the neighbors think?

Katherine would have to convince them that Walter's life was more important than their social standing.

"I have an idea, but it's a long shot." She filled the men in on her plan. They agreed it might not work but was worth a try. Katherine merged on the road and drove toward the sea.

Chapter Twenty-Nine

Katherine drove past the iron gate and pulled up to the house, parking right outside the front door. The Dells lived in a two-story dark brick manor with a turret on the east end overlooking the ocean. The spikes of the chimneys imposed upon the tree line. White-capped waves splashed on the rocky shore. Katherine yearned to stomp on the gas pedal and zoom away. Seeing her parents, especially with such a large favor to ask of them, brought out every instinct to flee.

"Wow! Dell, you grew up here?" Williams took in the sight of the estate with childlike wonder. Katherine envied his excitement. It would be nice to see this place through his eyes. All she saw were lonely holidays, and unattainable expectations.

"It's not as glamorous as it looks." She stepped out of the car and frigid breeze whirled around her. Mother appeared in the doorway. Father stepped into view next to his wife.

"Katherine?" Mother tapped her hands on to her cheeks, showing how delighted she was to see her daughter, though Katherine wasn't sure if the gesture was genuine. Walter and Williams got out of the car.

"Who on earth are these men?" Father stared at the intruders with the same look he used to give Katherine growing up — confusion mingled with anger, and a hint of disappointment.

"A colleague and a friend," Katherine said. Mother may chastise her later, but Katherine tossed good manners aside and skipped the formal introductions. They could deal with that once they were out of the cold. "May we come in?"

"Not until you park that monstrosity out of sight. What were you thinking, driving this clunker up to our front door?" Father pointed to Williams. "And you. Why would you let a lady operate a vehicle? You're a police officer. Surely you know how to drive."

"I...uh..." Williams's stuttering did not yield an answer. Katherine handed him the keys.

"Park it around back. I'll meet you inside."

Father went inside, presumably to meet Williams and Walter at the back entrance. Katherine walked up the stone porch steps and Mother held the door open for her. As she stepped inside, the scent that had haunted her childhood, her mother's favorite potpourri, invaded her nose and sank down deep in her lungs. Dried rose petals mixed with clove made her want to run back outside to the fresh ocean breeze, cold weather be damned. Instead, she slinked farther into the house as her mother invited her to the parlor.

They had redecorated. The original mahogany remained, curving around the home in the form of baseboards, crown molding, and built-in shelves. The walls, however, had been painted a dusty blue, a far cry from the golden floral wallpaper she had grown up with. The furniture had been replaced too; instead of the old leather Chesterfield sofa and matching tufted chairs that used to fill the space, Katherine now sat on a streamlined striped couch the same color as the walls. The unforgiving cushion pressed into her back. The place did not feel like home with all the changes, though it never really did even with the old décor.

"It looks lovely," Katherine said to her mother, hoping to defuse some tension. Her mother smiled and began listing where each item was purchased, but was interrupted as the men walked into the room. Williams panned the space with that idiotic open-mouthed glee, as if he'd never been anywhere so magnificent. Katherine fought the urge to roll her eyes at him.

Father took the chair closest to the fireplace. Mother asked the guests to sit, and they took the empty spots on the couch next to Katherine. Then Mother gave a mild lecture on etiquette. Since it was the first time the men had visited her home, the polite thing to do would have been to bring a hostess gift — a baked good, perhaps. Both men squirmed and apologized. Mother made a trip to the kitchen and when she returned, glanced pointedly in their direction as she laid out a spread of cookies she had baked herself, and served coffee from an ornate carafe. Gilt-framed oil paintings of Katherine's ancestors lined the sitting room wall, staring down in judgment as Katherine bit into her cookie.

"Darling, may I ask what brings you here? And why these gentlemen have accompanied you?" Mother sat in a chair and took a tense sip of her coffee. Father peered over the top of his cup.

"Of course. You see, my friend here would like a place to stay," Katherine said. "Just temporarily."

"Which friend is looking for accommodation?" Father narrowed his eyes and looked between the two strangers.

"I am, sir." Walter's shoulders tightened as Father's nostrils flared.

"He got in a little situation back in Nolaton and needs to hide out for a bit." Williams smiled, apparently thinking his explanation was helpful. Katherine shot him a look of disdain and his smile faded.

"Is he some sort of criminal?" Mother asked Katherine. Katherine opened her mouth to reply, but Walter spoke first.

"As Officer Williams said, sir, I'm a man who needs some help. If you're unwilling to give it, I understand."

"We're unwilling. And seeing as we were not expecting company for supper, it would be best if you take your leave," Father said, and gave the trio a terse nod. Though Katherine assumed that would be her father's response, it still pained her that he so flippantly dismissed a stranger in need. Her father had everything handed to him from the wealthy generations of Dells who came before him and could use a sliver of his means to help someone in dire need. But his arrogance and snobbery engulfed any shred of empathy in him. Katherine would not stand for it.

"No." Katherine set down her coffee and settled into her seat, feeling her face grow hot.

"No?" Father's face turned red as well. "Your mother and I taught you better manners than that, young lady."

"You taught me manners. I'll teach you compassion. This man needs a place to stay. You have the ability to help him." Katherine leaned toward her father.

Walter raised his hands as if he could push away the tension. "It's okay, Detective. I'll go back to Nolaton and figure out a plan."

"It's not okay," she said to Walter. She turned to her father, anger burning in her chest. "It's not okay to treat anyone that way. It was never okay how you treated Joey like he was beneath you either. And he lost his life." Katherine's breath quickened at the memory. She hadn't intended to bring up Joey; the words had burst out of her before she had a chance to sort them out.

"That's not my fault." Father balled up his fists in his lap. If he really believed he had no part in Joey's death, why was he getting defensive?

"But you're not entirely blameless. For once in your life, do what's right instead of what's proper. Let Walter stay." Katherine stared at her father, watching the wheels turn in his mind and steeling herself for another rejection. Father hissed out a breath, then turned to Walter.

"All right. You can stay in the guest room, but not for long."

Katherine blinked hard, wondering if she had heard him correctly. She looked at Walter, his expression as shocked as she felt.

"I'll be out of your hair as soon as I can," Walter said.

With that settled, Katherine got up and motioned for Williams to follow her. She didn't want to spend one more minute in the thick perfume and bitter atmosphere.

"Where are you going?" Mother asked, disappointment dripping from her.

"It's almost supper time and we've been asked to leave, haven't we?"

Mother looked at her husband with pleading eyes. Guilt hovered over Katherine at the strain she caused between them. Mother always had to play the peacemaker, but it wasn't fair to put that burden on her. Perhaps Father came to the same conclusion. He huffed and relented to the request with a wave of his hand. Mother smiled. "Oh, please stay!"

Though Katherine still wished she could fly away, she felt obligated to join them for a meal. They were family, though they rarely acted like it.

Mother set the elegant table with burgundy napkins on a white linen tablecloth, floral china, and tapered candles. Walter offered to help place the silverware, but Mother insisted that she do it herself. Walter was a guest after all. They sat around the table and Mother brought out thick bowls of clam chowder. Clinking spoons filled most of the silence while Mother attempted polite conversation.

"How do you like being a police officer, Mr. Williams?"

Williams swallowed the bite he had just taken. "Oh, it's swell."

Silence descended upon the table again, grating on Katherine's nerves. Maybe she should have left when she had the chance.

"And what about you, dear? What do you do for work?" Mother directed this to Walter.

"I don't think he's employed, darling," Father whispered to his wife, but loudly enough for the table to hear.

"First thing tomorrow I'll be looking for work and an apartment," Walter replied, looking at them from the side of his eye.

"And what is it you would like to do?" Mother took a delicate sip from her soup spoon.

Walter stared at his bowl as though he was deep in thought. After a moment, he responded. "I'd like to do whatever it takes to support my family. If I ever have a family to support, that is."

"Are you married?" Mother asked. Father shot her an annoyed look.

"Not yet, ma'am. It might be a while before that happens."

Katherine squirmed. If she hadn't chased Rita down, Walter wouldn't be in this position to begin with.

"You'll need a decent job before you get a wife." Father nodded at his own words as if he were offering sage advice that no one had ever heard before.

Katherine slammed down her spoon. "That's not true."

Father whipped a glare at her. "Young lady, I've had just about enough of this attitude. What happened to that boy was a tragedy, but it wasn't my fault. In any case, you deserve better than a janitor."

A piercing fire lit inside Katherine. "I deserve someone who treats me kindly. Who respects me and listens to my ideas. Who makes me laugh. Who gets me medicine when I'm sick, and chocolate when I'm sad. Who dances with me and holds my hand. That's the man Joey was, and it doesn't get any better than that."

Father seethed and Katherine braced herself for an outburst. Mother popped out of her chair with a nervous giggle. "I hope everyone likes lamb." She excused herself to the kitchen, her way of hiding from the conflict. Father turned to Katherine and she glared in return, expecting the worst.

"All right, darling. I'm done trying to convince you. You're a grown woman, and you're free to run your life as you see fit." His reddened face returned to its natural color.

Katherine was astonished. He wasn't going to argue or shout? Mother returned and doled out servings of lamb with mint jelly, along with yams and steamed carrots.

"That's all you have to say?" Katherine stared at her plate, then braved a look at her father. He had lifted a bite to his lips but lowered his fork before eating it.

"I wish you were more like your mother, but you're not. I can't fight against that anymore. It's like fighting against the tide. I can hardly stand how impulsive you are, not to mention that temper of yours! But I'd rather have my daughter in my life exactly the way she is than not have her around at all."

Katherine shut her eyes to keep her tears at bay. Her father had never expressed his feelings like that before. He'd always seemed content to pretend his daughter didn't exist, but maybe he did love her.

"I'd like that as well." Katherine and her father locked eyes for a moment before digging into their lamb.

Williams leaned over to Father. "I get where you're coming from. She's a real firecracker." Katherine shot him a dirty look, but Williams made a show of continuing on. "But she's a heck of a gal, and an asset on the force."

She couldn't tell if Williams meant it or was just trying to be funny, but either way, it was nice to hear. He smiled at her, not his usual irksome grin, but a genuine smile. Maybe he wasn't such a condescending jerk after all.

Mother let out a mighty sob, her victory cry at having the family reunited. She blotted her tears with her napkin, careful not to smear her makeup. With a large sniff, she raised her hand to get the table's attention, then words seemed to fail her. She smiled and shook her head, then said what any good hostess should.

"Save room for apple pie."

On the drive home, Katherine ruminated on the already eventful day and the tasks still at hand. Williams leaned against the window, staring out at the passing woodlands. Katherine bit her lip, embarrassed that her subordinate had witnessed such an intimate moment with her family.

"I'm sorry you had to be there for that." Her words came out like bullets.

He turned to her and smiled. "Why are you sorry? That was a tasty meal and a hell of a show." Katherine smacked his arm. He chuckled and she relaxed into her seat, then checked the time. A quarter to nine, just enough time for them to get back in town by midnight.

Three hours later, the trees disappeared as they approached Nolaton, making way for concrete giants. Their long day was far from over. The raid at the Boss's headquarters still loomed large in Katherine's mind.

Chapter Thirty

It was nearly midnight by the time Henry and Dell got back to the city. The plan from McAlister had said the other officers would be ready to conduct the raid any minute. Dell drove them to the harbor toward the address Rita had given them.

The Boss's headquarters was a warehouse tucked into an alley. Dell slowed as she approached, and Henry looked around, surprised to see that none of their colleagues were there. Had they all hunkered in the surrounding alleys or parked a few blocks away? Were he and Dell supposed to do the same?

"Did they call it off or something?" Henry asked.

"I'm sure they're on their way," Dell said, but her furrowed brow did not give Henry much confidence. The least he could do was lighten the mood.

"I just hope they remember the rules," Henry said with fake concern.

"What rules?" Dell asked.

Henry put on airs. "Well, it's their first time coming here. They ought to bring a plate of cookies." Henry grinned at her and Dell snorted at his joke, then both went back to panning the area.

A cop car drove up the street. Good. They could get started. Except the car sped past the warehouse, sirens blaring. Did the driver get the address wrong? Another set of sirens went off, but the sound receded into the distance.

"Where on earth are they going?" Dell pointed to the car that had just flown past. "Something is off. I'm going to the call box around the corner to see if I can reach McAlister. You wait here in case they show up." Dell popped her door open, nodded at Henry, who nodded back, then took off on foot.

Though Dell had barked an order at him, Henry didn't mind obeying. He hadn't exactly been fair to her when she first got the badge, assuming he would be better at the job. Henry still thought he would make a good detective, but Dell had her strengths too and deserved the respect of her supporting officer.

A shriek burst from the warehouse, like a steam engine exploding to life. Henry whipped his head toward the source, a primal fear pulsing inside him. What the hell could make such a shrill, demonic screech? Against every instinct, Henry got out of the car and crept toward the rusted green door of the warehouse. If his fellow cops ever did show up, they would appreciate him scoping the place out, especially if the Boss had something dangerous inside. Henry pressed his ear against the cold metal. Voices murmured inside, but the barrier muffled their words.

Henry shifted to the window next to the door. It was covered by curtains hung on the inside that blocked his view. Though it would be easier to hear if he pressed his ear against the glass, his shadow might give him away. Instead, he crouched beneath and listened, though most of the words still dissipated before he could make them out

"...still upset! ...allow me to spend all that money?" a familiar voice asked. Henry could hardly believe it, but there was no mistaking the bouncing tones and strict articulation of Mayor Herbert. What was the most respected man in Nolaton doing in a seedy joint like this? Another man spoke.

"...not my job to tell you how to spend your dough." His smoky voice was lower, quieter than the mayor's. That must be the Boss.

"...warning would have been nice. ...can't believe I blew through so much," Herbert said.

The men inside the warehouse jabbered back and forth a bit more, but Henry couldn't hear what they were saying, until Herbert shouted with glee.

"He's even more beautiful than I imagined," said the mayor in the same booming voice he would use for a crowd.

"*She*," the Boss said.

A rumble like the one Henry had heard before echoed through the streets. The Boss laughed then murmured too softly for Henry to understand.

"I'll take her! What is that in her cage? Steak? Did you get a treat, my dear?" Herbert cooed to whatever creature was held captive in there. A rhythmic sound followed, like a wooden mallet hitting the floor. "What's that racket?" Herbert asked. The Boss responded, then the place thundered with screams and more thuds.

"What is this? What are you doing to this boy?" Herbert shouted.

"I'm protecting my business," the Boss shouted back. "If you want to keep benefitting from my enterprise, you'll keep your mouth shut."

"Untie him this instant!"

"No...little rat has proven that he can't be trusted...right, Benny?"

The harbor melted away as Henry went numb and stars filled his eyes. All he could feel was his pulse knocking against his skin. That bastard had Benny.

Dell's frame came into focus and his vision cleared. She walked toward with him a concerned expression, quickening her pace until she stood right in front of him.

"What's wrong?"

Henry couldn't catch his breath to speak, though his lungs pulled at the ocean air as hard as they could. He met Dell's eyes and steadied himself enough to explain what he'd heard.

"They've got my brother." Henry fought the tears that built in his panicked rage. "Please tell me the other guys will be here soon."

Dell looked terrified.

"They called off the raid. McAlister ordered us back to the station—"

"I won't leave until Benny is safe. I'm sorry, I just can't." Henry didn't care if Dell reported him for insubordination. McAlister could sack him over this, but his job didn't matter now, not with Benny's life in the hands of that maniac. To Henry's surprise, Dell nodded her support.

"You don't have to apologize for protecting a loved one. We have to get in there. I can call for backup, but—"

"What if it's too late by the time they get here? I'm getting my brother now!"

Henry jumped over to the door and lined up his foot with the lock, then kicked, putting the full force of his body weight into the attack. The door shook but did not open. He howled with frustration and kicked again. The door burst open.

Henry scanned the room, looking for Benny, but even with the place being damn near empty he didn't see his brother. The warehouse was a gutted shell, a large open space with marks on the floor where shelves must have sat when the place was operational. Dripping pipes twisted along the ceiling. Stacks of boxes looked ready to topple in the far-left corner almost blocking the entrance to an old office. A gleaming desk, way too upscale for the surroundings, had been set in the middle of the room. A panther paced in her cage near the window Henry had listened under. So that's what Herbert had been doting over.

Two men stood in the far right corner near a door with a faded label that read "Storage." Maybe that's where Benny was being held. Henry recognized the mayor and assumed the other man must be the Boss. He was larger than Henry expected, with broad shoulders and a wide stance. With a sneer, the Boss took a revolver from his hip holster and switched between aiming it at Dell and Henry. Herbert whimpered and curled into a ball on the floor, his arms over his head. Henry drew his gun and aimed it at the Boss.

"Give me my brother." Henry's voice shook with anger. The Boss smirked, then aimed his gun square at Henry's head.

"Drop your weapon." Dell drew her gun and kept it poised on the Boss. She stayed near the entrance while Henry circled the dim room, closing in on his target.

"Open that door and give me my brother," Henry ordered.

The Boss laughed, then stuck his fingers in his mouth and whistled. The office door behind the boxes opened. Three large men skulked onto the warehouse floor. One had an underbite, which caused his pointed teeth to protrude, and another had a heavy brow. The third was a musclebound brute who hissed as Henry aimed at the pack.

Underbite lunged at Henry and grabbed on to his revolver. Henry gripped as tight as he could without risking discharging it, then pulled with all his strength. Underbite kicked Henry in the gut, knocking the breath out of him. In his moment of weakness, the revolver slipped from Henry's grasp. Underbite threw it toward the Boss. The Boss bent over and picked up Henry's gun.

"Police issue. Very nice. Better than this old piece of junk." The Boss tossed his old revolver to Eyebrows and took Henry's as his own. "Go guard the entrance. Make sure there aren't any other pigs rooting around."

Eyebrows marched outside and slammed the door behind him. Henry panted as he and his assailant circled each other. Underbite threw a punch, but Henry jumped back. The man's meaty fist missed his nose by an inch. Henry took a jab at Underbite's jaw, cracking his knuckles against the bone. Underbite crashed his fist against Henry's cheek hard enough to leave a heavy mark. The bruise forming under his eye burned and begged for ice, but Henry pushed the pain out of his mind as he took another shot.

Meanwhile, the third man, the towering mass of muscle, had been circling Dell. He picked up a rope near the panther's cage, tied it into a makeshift lasso, and swung it at her. She dived out of the way, but he must have anticipated her movement. He slung the lasso over her and ensnared her, gluing her arms to her body. He tugged her to the ground then took her weapon and pocketed it. Dell bucked against her restraints until the muscled man held her down. She struggled but couldn't get loose from his grip.

Henry punched Underbite again, feeling the man's nose crunch between his fingers. With blood gushing from the broken mass of cartilage, Underbite knocked his forehead against Henry's. Henry's mouth flooded with the sharp taste of metal as the floor wobbled beneath him. Underbite shoved Henry and kicked him behind the knee, sending Henry plummeting to the ground. His kneecaps smacked into the grimy concrete. Underbite dug his nails into Henry's wrists and pulled his arms back, pinning his helpless body to the ground.

"Oh, Benny! I have a surprise for you," the Boss called out in a singsong voice. He flung the storage door open.

Wood scraped against concrete as the Boss dragged Benny into the room. He'd been gagged and he was tied to a chair, his face bruised and bleeding. His head bobbed as if he was fighting to stay conscious. Henry choked up at the sight of him, the boy he swore to protect, mangled.

"Stop this now!" The mayor squeaked out his words. "This is outrageous behavior. Egregious. Unfathomable!"

"It's how I run my business. If someone betrays me, they get punished." The Boss turned to Benny and bent down to his level. "Remember that talk we had about trust and loyalty? Remember what I said? That those are the most important things to me. Didn't I say that?" He spat his words inches from Benny's face.

"You were disloyal. You broke my trust. I worked hard to build this business. I went from scrappy street filth to king of an empire. You think that's easy? You know how hard I worked to keep from going back there?" He pointed to the door to the alley. "That's where I slept as a kid. Nobody tucked me in at night, Benny. I pulled myself out of the gutter, and out of the goodness of my heart, I give the same opportunity to people like me.

"People who got nowhere else to go? They come here. I give them money and work. I give them purpose, Benny. But you're too good for that, ain't you? You want to sleep in your warm little bed and leave the hard work to the rest of us."

"Leave that boy alone." The mayor was still curled up on the floor, but he straightened up a bit. "If I had known this was how you do business, I never would have employed your services."

"Where else would you get such fine merchandise?" The Boss pointed to the panther.

Benny's head drooped and his eyes closed. Dell tried to get to him but couldn't push away from the muscled man pinning her to the ground.

"If you harm one more person, our arrangement will be terminated. You hear me? I will not be a part of this!" Herbert tried to sound confident but whimpered as the Boss crouched down beside him and spoke to him quietly. Henry couldn't make out all of his words, but he seemed to be trying to win the mayor's allegiance back.

Benny raised his head. The commotion must have jolted him awake. His eyes locked with Henry's.

"I'm so sorry," Benny said in his cracking voice. The Boss and the mayor kept talking, paying no attention to the prisoners. "I didn't listen to you. I should have stayed home like you told me, but I came here to quit this job. When I got here Tony was all tied up. I couldn't let him take the fall for me. I told the Boss that I was the one who stole the envelope. But the Boss said it was still Tony's fault for losing it in the first place. He killed him, then had his goons cut out Tony's heart."

"What? Why would they do that?" Henry spat the question with disgust.

"I don't know. They wrapped up his heart, then chopped up the rest of his body and fed it to the panther. But the Boss said, even with Tony dead, he's still gonna kill me."

"I won't let that bastard hurt you." Henry tried to buck away from Underbite but could not get free of his grasp.

The Boss let out an abrasive crack of laughter as if the mayor had offended him in a way he could not fathom. "Fine, Herbert. If we can't make a deal that works for both of us, I've got no use for you."

"But you said it yourself, I'm your wealthiest customer."

"That's why I'd rather keep working together, but I can't meet your demands. So I'll go with the second-best option and have my men rob your mansion. It'll be easy. You won't even be home."

The Boss fired a bullet into the mayor's temple, splattering globs of flesh on the wall behind him. Herbert's body collapsed, blood pooling on the floor around his husk. The Boss shuddered. "I hate doing the killing myself. Messy business. But now that he's taken care of, I have no reason to keep any of you alive."

The Boss turned to Benny and grabbed on to the chair, then dragged it to the panther's cage. Benny's head slammed into the bars.

The Boss leaned down to Benny as he turned the key and unlocked the enclosure. "Bones was so damn skinny; he hardly had any meat on him. Let's give this girl another meal."

Chapter Thirty-One

Rita was escorted back to her cell after her meeting with Detective Dell and Officer Williams. Once the guard closed her cell door, Rita lay in her bed and stared up at the concrete ceiling. She had kept it together while talking to the police, but the enormity of the situation overwhelmed her now. Of all the tears she had shed in her life, none had been this joyous. A knot that had been tangled for years released in her stomach. Walter would be safe. Detective Dell had promised that she would get him out of the Spider's web.

She scratched at the rash that had flared up on her chest from her itchy state-issued uniform. The barrage of white and black stripes was dizzying. It wasn't enough that metal bars kept her from the outside world. They had to wrap her body in fabric bars as well.

The clink of glass against metal brought Rita to her feet. In the cell across from hers, Irma rang her whiskey bottle against the bars. She smuggled in hooch every week in the laundry cart and sold it to her gaggle of followers, a gang of white women who thought their skin color somehow made them superior.

"Hey, señorita." Irma bared her stained teeth.

"Don't start with me," Rita seethed. Irma had tormented her from the moment Rita had been thrown in here. She and her followers had cornered Rita at breakfast on her first day, asking stupid questions about her last name and her parents, calling her every slur their pea brains could think of.

"Got a problem with me, chica? Oh, wait, only half-chica, right?" Irma took a swig from her bottle.

"Go suck an egg."

"Come over here and say that." Irma spat on the floor. The bars of Rita's cell rang with an ear-splitting echo as the guard rammed his club against them. Irma stuffed the bottle under her mattress.

"Mail," shouted a guard. Rita knew the drill — every day he brought a bag full of envelopes around to each cell. As he delivered the contents, he stopped to watch each inmate open her letters. There was never anything exciting in them, just notes from families and bills from lawyers, but the guards had to check.

"Davis, package for you," said the guard. He handed her a box the size of a cookie jar wrapped in brown paper and tied with string. It was lighter than she expected based on the size, maybe a pound if Rita had to guess. The label said, "with love from Walter." What a sweetheart. But why had he sent a gift? It wasn't her birthday.

She untied the string and unfolded the brown paper. Inside was a flour tin, but it was much too light to be filled with flour. She cracked open the top and tipped her head to the side in confusion. The tin was full of white fabric, like medical bandages, with brown splotches. She peeled back a few layers, then screamed.

This was no gift from Walter — it was a human heart. A note inside the box read, "This is what happens when you don't pay your debt. The rest of me is rotting in an alley, but here's a piece for you." Those cops wouldn't find Walter; he was already dead. If it weren't for those monsters hunting her down over jewelry and paintings, Rita would still be with her love and they'd both be alive.

Pain ripped through Rita's chest. She wailed with grief and fell to the floor. The guard entered her cell, picked her up, and put her on her bed.

With a disgusted grunt, he took the heart and closed it back up in its tin, while Rita sobbed into her pillow.

Then he left her alone to mourn.

An hour passed, but it seemed like days. Rita curled herself up in the corner of her bed, covered by her threadbare blanket. Walter was gone. The man she had loved her whole life had been ripped away. Never again would he tell her to be careful climbing trees or hold her hand to stop her from picking at her nails. He would never share the last of a loaf of bread, saving the end piece for her because it was her favorite part. She would never curl up in his arms and listen to his heartbeat as she fell asleep. They would never make a home together or have the children they wanted so desperately. His spirit had left this earth and it was all her fault.

Eventually, the guard came back and tapped on her cell bars.

"Davis, you're on laundry duty. Come on. Get up." She picked herself up limb by limb; each extremity weighed double. Even with the heavy burden of grief pulling her down, she had to do her job. Prisoners didn't get days off.

In the steam-filled laundry, she scrubbed at a tomato sauce stain on an old uniform, but her effort made no difference. The black stripes faded into the white, and holes had opened in the seams. If a garment took enough damage, it went to the junk cart to be fodder for the rag pickers. Rita threw the uniform on the pile with the rest of the battered clothing. Glass sparkled underneath the mass of fabric, catching her eye. A bottle of whiskey — Irma's delivery. Even with her world torn apart, a plot for revenge crept into Rita's mind. It was flawed and downright foolish, but what did she have to lose? If her attempt failed, they would just give her a longer sentence. With Walter gone she had nothing to go back to on the outside. At least in prison she had a roof over her head and three square meals a day.

On the other side of the laundry, Irma hung up clothes to dry, her cigarette dangling from her lips. Rita grabbed the soiled uniform and, finding a split in a seam, ripped off a strip of fabric. Irma looked up at the sound and Rita hid the fabric behind her back.

"What are you looking at, señorita?"

"All the spots you missed." Rita nodded at the hanging laundry. Irma turned to inspect her work and Rita hurriedly tied the fabric around her leg and hiked it high under her skirt.

"Are you blind? I don't see any spots." Irma took a long drag from her cigarette. Ash fell from the end onto a clean towel, and smoke rose from where it had landed.

"Look again," Rita said and pointed to the glowing embers.

"Damn it!" Irma hit the embers out.

Rita slipped her hand into the junk pile and took hold of a bottle. Irma stayed focused on her laundry. Rita tucked the bottle into her makeshift garter for later.

By that evening, Rita's tears had run out, leaving her eyes and chest burning. Her hollow core walked into the cafeteria for her kitchen shift. Inside the large concrete room, women sat with their trays at long tables set in rows. A group walked in and fought with their rivals over the table near the picture window. Rita didn't see why it mattered whether or not they had a view of the barbed wire fence outside. Strange how the rest of the prison went on as usual while she was so deeply wounded.

The other inmates ate their spongey meat loaf and gritty turnips; terrible as it was, it was better than the cabbage soup they had been served for lunch. Rita ate her portion in the back, taking bites in between cleaning tasks, not that she was hungry. She needed to keep up her strength, though. Walter would have wanted that.

Trays piled up next to Rita and she scrubbed them one by one, letting the remaining globs of food fall into the greasy dishwater. From the sink, she could still see a sliver of the picture window. As the sun sank into the earth, the sliver lost its glow. Abandoned by the sun's warmth, Rita made her own heat by scrubbing harder. She glanced over the buffet station every ten minutes or so to see how many tables were still full of people eating. Early on, almost every table was full, but each time she checked, fewer and fewer women occupied the space. The sooner they cleared out, the better.

As the kitchen was about to close for the night, Irma's gaggle lazed in the kitchen smoking cigarettes and swapping raunchy stories. They were supposed to help clean, but made Rita handle the brunt of the work. With the guard preoccupied by his own meal, Irma called her friends over to the pantry where a tea towel hung over a crate. Irma pulled it off with a flourish, exposing the whiskey bottles hidden inside. The women smiled at the sight but smiles quickly turned to frowns.

"Well, I ain't the best at putting numbers together, but that looks like five bottles to me," one woman said.

"She's holding out on us," another chimed in. The women circled Irma.

"I swear I paid for six. I got enough for all of—" Irma took a punch to the jaw and fell to the floor. The women kicked her in the ribs while slinging insults.

In the cafeteria, twenty or thirty prisoners still sat choking down their dinners. Most of them were seated around tables farthest from the kitchen; the lingering smell of boiled cabbage wasn't as potent over there.

Rita made a rough guess and hoped they were far enough away. While the others were distracted with Irma, Rita opened the gas oven. Underneath, the pilot light burned bright. Rita pulled the stolen bottle out from her makeshift garter and uncorked it, spilling the foul-smelling contents on the floor next to her. Then she dangled the strip of fabric into the oven's flame and threw the burning scrap into the puddle. The alcohol ignited.

"Fire!" Rita shouted. The guard slid his tray aside and ran over, cursed, then grabbed a bucket and plunged it into the dirty dish water. He doused the flames but the greasy water only spread the fire further. He cursed louder and went back to the sink, filling the bucket with clean water. With him distracted, Rita snuck a paring knife from the counter and slipped it down the front of her uniform, careful to aim the blade away from her skin. She also grabbed a cast iron frying pan, then ran toward the picture window and smashed the glass with it.

Irma's gang screeched and scattered at the sight of the flames. They managed to grab their liquor before bolting out of the kitchen and into the cafeteria. The women who had still been eating got up and ran, and in their fury to get out, arms hit trays. Clumps of turnip flew up and snowed down on them. Sirens went off around the prison as women climbed through the broken window and worked to rip apart the barbed wire fence. Rita filtered into the crowd — dozens of women who were making their escape. Some tried to jump over the top, but the spikes slashed their palms, forcing them to let go and fall back into the prison yard. Rita dragged herself through the hole that another prisoner had managed to cut on the bottom of the fencing.

She ran from the prison and, though it would take hours on foot, made her way to the harbor. She ducked through the city shadows, her journey a blur of alleyways. Hours felt like minutes and minutes felt like hours. Police sirens filled the air and Rita hoped they would find the other escaped prisoners before finding her. The back alleys and secret ways became familiar as she got closer to the ocean.

She crouched low and took the knife in her hand, her legs burning and muscles aching from running. The entrance to the Boss's headquarters was right ahead and a man lurked outside. Rita stepped out of the shadows. He aimed a gun at her and she held up her hands, holding her stolen knife. His prominent brow knit together at the sight of her.

"Rita? Is that you?" It was Jimmy, one of the Boss's lackeys.

"Yeah, it's me." She kept her hands up while he aimed at her but lowered them as he lowered his gun.

"I thought you got locked up." He scratched his head. Rita looked at her tattered striped uniform and shrugged. Jimmy had never been the brightest of the Boss's employees.

"Well, I'm out now. What's going on in there?"

Jimmy pushed the green door open, and the commotion struck Rita's ears as she peeked inside, shocked by the scene.

A panther pawed at its cage door and the Boss dragged a battered boy up to it. Officer Williams was there, a fresh bruise on his face, shouting in protest. Detective Dell was there too, tied up on the floor. Anger burned brighter than Rita's sore muscles. If they had believed her the night she got arrested, maybe they could have saved Walter. Now it was too late. The sting of grief sliced through her core.

"I heard you got caught by a lady cop. Was it that one?" Jimmy pointed to the woman trussed up on the ground. Rita nodded.

"And I'd like to be the one to off her. Give me the gun." Rita tossed her stolen knife aside and took the walnut-handled revolver from Jimmy's hand. He smirked and stepped away from Rita, giving her space to take the shot.

A cold wind rushed inside of her as she aimed. This wasn't for her. It was for Walter.

She pulled the trigger.

Chapter Thirty-Two

Blood and brains burst from the wound as the bullet sank in. Katherine turned her neck as far as her restraints would allow. There in the doorway, still holding a gun, stood Rita Davis. A thud tore Katherine's attention back into the warehouse as the Boss's body collapsed to the ground. Half of his head had been blown to pieces by Rita's gunshot. A pool of blood spilled from him, just like the one that had formed under the mayor. Katherine retched at the sight of him and the horrific smell of his postmortem secretions, but she kept her sick down.

She wasn't surprised to see Rita. McAlister had told Katherine about the prison break; that's why he called off the raid. Thirty-some escaped convicts took priority over their hastily planned takedown. It made sense that she would come here and take out the man who had made her life hell.

Rita stepped out of sight, probably running off to avoid murder charges. Even if Katherine hadn't been tied up on the floor, her gut said to let Rita get away instead of chasing after her, though something about that instinct felt off. Katherine's entire reason for joining the force had been to catch murderers, so why did she find herself so unbothered, perhaps even supportive of Rita's actions?

Despite committing a heinous crime, Rita had fired that gun out of self-preservation. The Boss had tortured Rita for years, forcing her into dangerous situations, threatening her life, threatening the man she loved. If Katherine had been in Rita's position, she would have shot the bastard too. By killing the Boss, Rita saved all of their lives, and perhaps many more. Katherine couldn't bring herself to punish her for that.

The panther pushed her way out of the cage and gave a mighty roar, filling the warehouse with thunder. Eyebrows ran. Underbite let go of Williams, and Muscles released his grip on Katherine. Both lackeys escaped into the darkness as well.

The panther feasted on the remains of the Boss, pulling off strips of his flesh and swallowing them whole. Blood soaked her face and clung to her whiskers. The panther seemed occupied with her meal for the moment, but this was a wild animal. No telling what she would do next, especially trapped in a room full of strangers. The panther pulled sinew from the corpse. It snapped, spraying blood in its wake.

Williams ran over to Katherine and pulled out his pocketknife. He cut her free from her ropes as quickly as he could before tending to his brother. She slithered out of the ties. As she untangled herself, Williams cut Benny free. Benny couldn't stand on his own, so Williams picked him up and threw Benny over his shoulders. "I need to get him to a hospital," Williams said.

Benny's head lolled; he was falling asleep, but in his condition, he might not wake up. Katherine ran to them and pushed Benny's hair from his eyes.

"It's all right." She stroked his cheek and his eyes popped open. "You have to stay awake, okay?"

The panther growled and they ran for the door, making it outside. Katherine slammed the door shut, at least temporarily trapping the panther inside the warehouse.

"Wait here. I'll call an ambulance and let McAlister know what happened," Katherine said to Williams. Williams simply nodded then sat on the sidewalk with his back against the warehouse, holding his brother to his chest. Before she ran around the corner to the police call box, she glanced back at her friend, amazed that this was the same man who once wanted her booted off the force. Really, they should have been on the same team all along, keeping Nolaton safe and loved ones close.

Katherine knew she and Williams might get in trouble for busting up the Boss's operation alone, even though they only did it to save Benny. She had to report it, however. Two dead bodies and an apex predator prowling around a crime den? They would have their badges revoked if they didn't call that in. Still, she admired Williams for charging in after Benny, consequences be damned.

She took out her key and unlocked the panel of the police call box, then picked up the receiver that hung inside. After she called for an ambulance, she dialed the station. Mrs. Bobern answered and got McAlister on the line. Katherine explained everything that had happened. McAlister, clearly fazed by the news, collected himself on the other end, then affirmed that he would call the coroner and the Nolaton City Zoo's lead animal trainer. He would also assemble a small team of detectives to help search the warehouse for any record of the Boss's nefarious activity.

As Katherine turned the corner and made her way back to the warehouse, she was surprised to see Rita Davis sitting on the ground next to Williams and Benny. They both leaned their backs against the wall of the warehouse, looking away from each other, while Benny still curled up in the crook of Williams's arm. Rita's hands were cuffed in front of her. What on earth was going on? Why hadn't Rita run off with the Boss's other lackeys? Once she got close enough, Katherine caught Rita's eye and saw the tear streaks on her face.

"You killed a bigwig crime lord in front of two cops, and you didn't run off?" Katherine asked.

"I got nothing to run to." Rita hung her head. Katherine turned to Williams, confused. Hadn't they just gotten her boyfriend to safety? Reuniting with Walter struck Katherine as a good reason to flee. Williams simply shrugged.

"She won't say what's got her so upset. I got a pair of cuffs on her at least."

"What about Walter?" Katherine asked Rita.

Rita screwed up her face and spoke through clenched teeth. "Don't play games with me. I know Walter's dead. I got his heart in the mail today, after you left."

Katherine was taken aback. "That's not true. Officer Williams and I escorted him to Lavendale this afternoon. We dropped him off in a safe place this evening, long after you would have gotten the mail. I'm no doctor, but I'm sure his heart was still beating when we said goodbye."

Benny stirred and sat up, though the motion seemed to pain him.

"It must have been Tony's heart. That's why the Boss had his men set it aside."

"Tony Romano? He's dead?" Rita seemed shocked by this, but not saddened.

"Yes," Williams said. "I bet the Boss sent you that heart so you would think he took the hit on Walter. The Boss was just trying to lord his power over you."

"So it was a trick?" Rita's face lit up with hope, then clouded again with anger. "That sick bastard. I don't care if I'm locked up for the rest of my life; I'm *glad* I gave the Boss what he deserved."

Katherine agreed that the Boss deserved his gruesome fate, but based on the handcuffs clamped to Rita's wrists, Williams chose to follow procedure and planned to get her back into a cell. Katherine understood, of course, but wished they could let her go. Then an idea popped into her head, though Williams may not go for it.

"Miss Davis, you've been stealing for the Boss for years, so you must be a fairly accomplished thief, right?"

Rita glared at Katherine, probably assuming Katherine was picking at old wounds just to be cruel. Katherine hastily corrected the misunderstanding.

"I only mean that, theoretically, it would be easy for you to pick my pocket for the car keys."

This time, Williams scowled. "What are you getting at?"

"I'm saying that as police officers it's our job to get her back to prison, but as human beings...come on, Williams. She just saved our lives. The world is better off without that crook running his underground ring. Look what he did to Benny."

Williams followed her command and gazed down at his brother. Katherine could almost feel his heart breaking over the agony his brother had suffered at the Boss's hand. Katherine continued.

"I know we can't just let her go without risking our jobs, but if she slips out of our grasp..."

Williams finished her thought.

"It happens all the time, I suppose. Criminals weasel their way out of an arrest and take off."

Katherine reveled in the irony. The last criminal that had eluded her was Rita Davis herself.

"Wait a minute. Are you saying you'd let me steal a car and get out of town? After the way you chased me down at the museum...I don't get it." Rita tipped her head to the side in confusion. Katherine's stomach swam with guilt.

"I didn't understand the situation then and I'm sorry for going overboard. Now that the Boss is gone, I can't imagine you'd keep stealing or shooting people."

To Katherine's delight, Rita let out a chuckle.

"Of course not. All I want is to live somewhere quiet with Walter and start a family."

"I want that for you too. Have you driven a car before?" It dawned on Katherine that Rita may not even be able to operate the vehicle. Most women were never taught how to drive. Then again, Rita was not the average woman.

"I drove a getaway car a time or two." Rita looked down with a guilty expression, but Katherine was not going to hold her criminal past against her.

Katherine turned to Williams. "We'll get a slap on the wrist, but I think that's well worth it."

Williams paused for a moment, considering the options. Sirens cried in the distance, a reminder that their colleagues were out rounding up escaped criminals. With police flooding the streets and an ambulance on the way, he didn't have much time to decide.

"If we're gonna tell a lie, can't we leave Davis out of it entirely? Let's say *I* shot the Boss. I'll be labeled a hero!" Williams put on that grin of his, until Rita spoke up.

"That won't work. Too many of the Boss's guys saw me kill him and one of them is bound to squeal. Getting killed by a cop would tarnish his legacy and they'll be loyal to their leader even as a corpse."

Williams let out a heavy sigh. "If Detective Dell thinks this is the right course of action, who am I to argue." He dug in his pocket and pulled out his key ring.

"You're doing the right thing," Katherine said as she snatched the keys from his hand. "Well, as right as can be given the circumstances."

Katherine unlocked Rita's cuffs and gave them back to Williams along with his keys, then grabbed her notepad and wrote down her parents' address.

"You should be with the man you love, and this is where you'll find him." Katherine held out the car keys and the note. "Just don't speed; I wouldn't want you getting pulled over."

Rita laughed. Her eyes sparkled with the first bit of real joy Katherine had ever seen in them. She took the car keys and drove off.

A few minutes later, the ambulance pulled up next to them. Once Benny got settled in the back with Williams by his side, the emergency vehicle took off toward the hospital. Katherine leaned against the warehouse wall, waiting for the coroner and animal keeper to arrive. A few detectives would be making their way over as well. Her mind drifted, wondering what heinous details they might uncover inside the Boss's headquarters.

Chapter Thirty-Three

A Model 18 drove up to the warehouse. Crenshaw, the driver, got out of the car and stared at Katherine, awestruck. Hanson came out of the back seat and gave her a similar look of disbelief. Then McAlister popped open the passenger's side door, stuck his cane on the cobblestone, and pulled himself out of his seat.

"So he was right here all along and we didn't have a clue," McAlister said with an eerie calm.

"And Dell was brave enough to bust into the place." Crenshaw strutted up to her and shook her hand with vigor. Katherine, not expecting the gesture, nearly lost her balance. Crenshaw let go and she got back on solid footing, then Hanson came over and gave her a weak handshake of his own.

Katherine hoped it was dark enough that they couldn't see the heat rising in her cheeks as a mix of excitement and embarrassment took hold. For the first time since her promotion, she felt like she belonged in the group, like the detectives had finally accepted her as one of their own. As much as she enjoyed the men giving her credit, she had to give Williams his share of the praise and reminded the men of his contributions.

The men nodded, then looked down the street as a rumbling vehicle approached. The animal trainer arrived with his team, sedated the panther, then brought her out to their armored truck. He promised to give her a good home at the Nolaton City Zoo. The coroner pulled up and began his examination of the scene.

While the coroner worked, the three detectives and McAlister waited outside. Katherine regaled them with the story of the Boss's downfall. Of course, she added that Rita Davis had run off and stolen her car. The men accepted this, and McAlister even gave her a pat on the back, saying it wasn't her fault that Davis got away. Katherine tried not to let her guilt eat at her, knowing that she had in fact orchestrated Rita's escape from Nolaton. The coroner concluded his investigation and had the bodies removed from the scene, recovering Williams's revolver in the process.

When they got the all-clear from the coroner, the detectives and McAlister walked into the warehouse. The putrid smell of the dead body's innards and musk of wild animal still hung in the air but much more faintly than before.

Hanson began sifting through the boxes stacked in the corner while Crenshaw headed into the storage room. Katherine looked over at McAlister, who was standing in the middle of the near-empty space. As usual, his expression was hard to read, but he seemed overwhelmed. After years of hunting down the Boss, he was now standing in the criminal's office. Katherine could not imagine the rush of emotion that would bring. His eyes met hers and he snapped out of his trance.

"Search his desk, Dell." McAlister tapped his cane with authority, then went over to help Crenshaw in the storage room.

She burrowed through the desk drawers and pushed away the junk. Empty ink bottles and old cigar boxes got shoved to the back, while she shuffled the papers forward. Most were blank note pages or old documents from the warehouse. She wasn't surprised; the Boss would not have written down the specific details of his crimes or kept records on his employees like a normal business. Still, she expected to find *something* that could be used as evidence. Though the Boss would not be serving time in prison, his loyal lackeys could. And maybe, just maybe, she would find something that would help identify the Spider.

She opened the bottom drawer and, again, found a stack of useless old documents. As she kept digging, she grasped a smooth binding — a leatherbound book. Katherine pulled it out and scanned its contents. Each page had a series of numbers and letters. Some numbers were in black ink, others in red. Katherine couldn't make sense of the patterns, but it could be an accounting system. From what she knew about the Boss, he had been obsessed with his profits — perhaps this was how he tracked the inflows and outflows of those who had borrowed money from him.

"Sir, you'll want to see this. I think I just found the Boss's ledger," she called to McAlister. He stuck his head out of the storage room and Katherine brought the book to him. Hanson came over and stood next to Katherine while Crenshaw tried to see over McAlister's shoulder. Katherine flipped the book open and held it up to let the men read the contents. Hanson reached over and flipped to the next page, then the next. Crenshaw reached past McAlister to slap Hanson's hand away.

"You're going too fast. Let me see that last page again. Excuse me, sir." Crenshaw squeezed past McAlister in the small doorway of the storage room, then stood on Katherine's other side.

Katherine turned the page and angled the book for Crenshaw to see. He took the book out of her hands and pointed to a ten-digit number at the top of the page scribbled down in black ink. Then he scanned his finger down the rest of the page where shorter numbers had been written.

"Unbelievable. The audacity." Crenshaw poked the page. "After what happened tonight, we know that Mayor Herbert was buying illegal items from the Boss, but here is the proof. Worse than that, he used the city's funds to pay for the goods. See this?" He pointed to the ten-digit number in black. "That's the account number used for Nolaton's bridge project."

"Are you sure?" McAlister asked with a mix of anger and confusion.

"I'll double-check at the station, but I must have seen that account number a hundred times during the bridge collapse investigation. All these other numbers down the page? They correlate to the outflows from the city account."

After their encounter that night, Katherine had wondered if the mayor had been the Boss's biggest client, the one Walter had mentioned on the drive up to Lavendale. Seeing the high dollar amounts and frequency of the purchases solidified that theory.

"Three bridge workers lost their lives so the mayor could have some new toys." Katherine's temper boiled. She thought of that young man with the pipe sticking out of his chest, the one who had taken his last breath as she mopped up his blood. His life had been worth more than anything the mayor could steal.

Another thought struck her. When Mayor Herbert had made his speech at the parade, he told the crowd that he and his wife were celebrating their thirtieth wedding anniversary. Her parents had also just celebrated their thirtieth. That's why her father had given her mother a pearl bracelet — pearl was the traditional gift for a thirtieth anniversary. The pearls from Bailey Jewelers may have been a gift for the mayor's wife.

"Well, that explains this page. What about the rest of it?" Hanson snatched the book from Crenshaw and pawed at the pages. Though he whipped through them quickly, Katherine peered over and saw a pattern emerge. A series of pages in the middle of the ledger looked similar — the top margin contained a series of three letters. Then lists of dollar amounts in red or black ink were scrawled underneath; at least she suspected they were dollar amounts since that would match with the mayor's page. Next to each of those amounts was a six-digit numeral.

"May I see that?" Katherine held out her hands and Hanson plunked the book into them. She studied a few pages, trying to make sense of the Boss's strange accounting method. One page in particular caught her eye as familiar details emerged. The letters on top read "JRC" and the next line had a six-digit code: 061229. Next to that, in red, was written "200." Could JRC be Joseph Robert Callaghan? He could have borrowed $200, then bought her extravagant ring with it. The six-digit codes could be dates, in that case. 061229 translated to June 12, 1929. The day he'd proposed. Maybe he'd borrowed the money, bought the ring, and asked her to marry him on the same day.

Other rows in the ledger had six-digit codes and dollar amounts in black. Each started with 06, 07, 08, 09, or 10, and ended with 29. June through October in the year 1929. Those dates must be when he paid part of the money back to the Boss. Awful images flashed into Katherine's mind as she contemplated what Joey had done to get back into the black. Stolen valuables? Mugged people on the street? Done unspeakable violence? It didn't matter now. She wanted to remember him for the wonderful person he had been, not the mistakes he'd made.

The numbers in black added up to almost $1,800, much more than he had originally borrowed. Walter had speculated that the Boss forced his debtors to pay back more than they owed. He might have been right.

The second to last line started with the six-digit number 100529, so October 5, 1929, if Katherine's assertions were correct. It was right around then that the Gray Suits first appeared. Next to it in red was a dollar amount of $250. The last line on the page held the number 102429. October 24, 1929. The day Joey was killed. Next to that, in red, the number 250. The Boss must have paid $500 total for the hit, probably half upfront and half when the job was done. Katherine fought the wave of nausea overtaking her. Now was not the time to break down, not in front of her colleagues and with such important work to do.

Though this page obviously correlated to the last months of Joey's life, it didn't prove that the Spider had killed him. She looked through other pages to see if she could match the pattern to other suspected victims of the Spider. GLP was scrawled at the top of one page. Could that be Gabriel

Perkins? His date of death matched the last six digits, and again in red someone had written 250 with another 250 going out a few weeks before.

AAT was on the top of another page. Could that be Alice Thurgood? Again, the dates matched, and the hit had cost $500 paid in two installments. Same with Arthur Fitzgerald and another handful of Spider victims whose cases Katherine had memorized.

"Anything you'd like to share with us, Dell?" McAlister asked. All three men were staring at her, probably annoyed that she had been hogging the book. McAlister would be devasted to learn the truth of Joey's past. Though it would rip open wounds for both of them, she couldn't keep it from him.

"Sir, it may be best for us to speak privately." Katherine did not want to show him Joey's page in front of the other detectives.

"Why don't you two work on the pile over there." McAlister pointed toward the tower of boxes in the corner. Hanson and Crenshaw shuffled away toward the stack but kept looking over their shoulders as if trying to eavesdrop. Katherine, as tenderly as she could, explained her findings to McAlister.

"If I'm not mistaken, that means Joey had been working for the Boss and was killed by the Spider."

McAlister looked like someone had knocked the wind out of him as he leaned on his cane and heaved a great sigh. Katherine, concerned he would lose his balance, almost took him by the arm to lead him to the Boss's desk chair. Before she could grab ahold of him, McAlister regained his composure and stood up straight.

"I can't believe my boy would work for such a terrible man, but I think you're right."

Katherine had suspected for years that Joey had been involved in something sinister. She had processed it, accepted it even, and chosen to forgive the man she loved. For McAlister, this revelation was brand-new and must seem impossible to swallow. Seeing the pain in his eyes broke Katherine's heart.

"If it helps at all, I don't think he knew what he was signing up for. He probably thought he could pay back what he borrowed like a normal loan, not get roped into this vile organization. And from what I've gathered, the only reason he had a hit taken on him was because he tried to quit."

"But what did he do when he was serving the Boss? How many unsolved crimes in our file room were committed by the man I raised as my son? Makes me sick to my stomach." McAlister put a hand up to his reddening face and Katherine wondered if he was hiding tear-filled eyes. Katherine wanted to throw her arms around him and hug him, show him that she thought of him as family, even though they never got the chance to be. It wouldn't be appropriate though, and she didn't want to embarrass him in front of Crenshaw and Hanson, who kept peeking over. Instead, she kept her distance but tried to say something that would console him.

"It makes me sick too, but I refuse to let those last few months define his whole life. He was a good person who made mistakes."

"Aren't we all?" McAlister dropped his hand back down to his side.

"I know I am." Katherine had made more mistakes in her life than she would care to admit. McAlister swallowed hard and wiped the water from his eyes, then put on his usual terse expression.

"So there really is a Spider, but who is it? You've been looking into these cases for years. Any leads?"

Katherine took a second to compose herself and switch back into her professional mode. She shook her head, desperately wishing she could give a better answer.

"All I know for certain is what the Gray Suits told me: that the Spider killed Loretta Jones. But they also told me if I keep investigating her murder, the Spider will kill me." Katherine stared at McAlister, a man she had always admired and looked to for guidance, but saw only fear in his expression.

"I'm sorry I didn't believe you about those men breaking in. I'll take you off the Jones case."

"No!" The command burst out of Katherine before she could stop it. She softened her tone. "I mean, please, sir, I would rather keep working on it. If anyone can catch the Spider, it's me."

"But for your own protection—"

"The Gray Suits told me to mark the case cold and I didn't. They'll have me killed regardless of who's assigned to the case. What are we going to do, leave the Jones murder unsolved?"

"Of course not." McAlister seemed offended by the assertion, which was exactly what Katherine intended.

"Then trust me and let me do my job."

McAlister groaned and dismissed the argument with the wave of his hand, no doubt aware that Katherine would not give up the fight. "Fine. The case is still yours, but I'm telling every officer on the force to keep an eye on you. If you're going after a murderer this dangerous, you'll need protection."

"Don't do that. I can handle this on my own." Katherine cringed at the thought of her colleagues coddling her.

"Hogwash. Nobody could handle this by themselves."

"I've got Williams helping me." Katherine wanted to make it clear she didn't intend to work completely unaided; she just didn't want the entire precinct breathing down her neck.

"That's not enough. Dell, you are in real danger and there is no shame in getting help from the people around you. I know the guys on the force act like baboons half the time, but they'll look out for you in a situation this serious. You work on a team, so use that to your advantage."

Katherine contemplated this, and though it pained her to admit it, McAlister was right. She had felt isolated and ostracized by the whole precinct ever since she started working there, but now was the time to put those feelings aside. Asking for help was not a mark of weakness;

if anything, it was a show of strength. She was still the lead on the investigation but being in charge did not mean being alone. The more help and protection she had from those around her, the better her chances at finding the Spider. She would not let her pride stand in her way.

"I will, sir."

McAlister nodded, then resumed his search in the storage room. Katherine turned on her heel and went back to searching the Boss's desk. As she leafed through the papers in his top drawer, her mind drifted to the Spider. Even with McAlister's blessing, how the hell was she going to figure out the identity of Nolaton's most infamous killer?

Chapter Thirty-Four

The next morning, Katherine sat at her desk with the ledger open in front of her and the comfort of her favorite red mug in her hand. All of her bottom-drawer files related to Spider killings were stacked next to the ledger. Katherine had been working through the pile, matching the victim's initials to the pages in the Boss's book. She thought that if she could find a set of initials in the ledger that did not match any of her files, she could find a matching murder case in the file room or at another precinct, and it may give a clue to the Spider's identity.

She had also looked for a page with LMJ at the top, Loretta Jones's initials, but couldn't find one. Either Loretta's hit had not been taken out by the Boss or, as Katherine suspected, no hit had been taken at all. She still held on to the theory that Loretta's murder had been personal, but why? What connection did she have to the Spider?

Katherine took a slow sip of coffee, the only thing keeping her eyes open after a sleepless night. It felt odd coming into work as if it were a normal day, as if she hadn't watched a bullet careen into the skull of a crime lord only eight hours prior. As if her skin weren't shining pink where the rough rope had dug into her flesh when she was tied up. Katherine rubbed her tender forearms, feeling the pain points where the bruises were forming, though they were hidden by the sleeves of her suit coat.

She pulled herself out of last night's memories as she slurped the dregs of her coffee, then plunked the mug down on her desk. The leatherbound ledger still confounded her, even with caffeine in her system. She scowled down at the book. It was the most concrete evidence of the Spider's existence that she had ever found, yet it gave no indication as to who the Spider could be. Not that she had expected to find the Spider's name and phone number in the margins.

A knock sounded on her door.

"Come in," Katherine said, ungluing her eyes from the ledger. Much to her surprise, Williams opened her office door. She assumed he would take the day off to spend with Benny and let that giant bruise on his face heal. Her shock must have been obvious. Williams let out a gentle laugh.

"It's all right. You can say it. You've never seen me look more handsome." Williams put on his cheesy grin.

"With your face looking like a rotten turnip, who could resist?" Katherine pretended to swoon over him, placing her hand on her heart and letting out a high-pitched sigh. Once their laughter died down, Katherine asked, "How's Benny?"

"Still at the hospital, but the doctor says he'll be fine after a few days of rest. I figured I'd let him sleep, come here, and catch up on things. McAlister says you found something interesting last night."

"That's one word for it." Katherine spun the ledger around for Williams to see. He pulled up a chair and scanned the pages while Katherine explained the numbers.

"Geez, each hit cost $500? That's ten times my rent!" Williams looked puzzled. "What does the Spider do with all that dough?"

Katherine had wondered the same thing abstractly before but found the concept too awful to dwell on. Now that they had a solid dollar amount to work with, Katherine's imagination dared to enter that territory.

"The Spider kills three people a year on average, so we'll call it $1,500 annually. Then again, those are just the hits we know about. There could be more."

"Is that all the Spider lives on, or is there another source of income?"

Katherine pondered this, though it made her ill to think about where the Spider lives, eats, sleeps, and, if Williams was right, works. Williams continued.

"And what about those men in gray? Do they get paid from the $500?"

A detail that had gnawed at Katherine floated to the forefront of her mind. Those men, she had seen them twice now. Once outside the Razzle after their first visit, and once — the memory sliced into her gut — hovering over her bed after their second visit to the club. Could that be a coincidence, or was someone at the Razzle sending their goons after her? She shared her theory with Williams.

"The Spider could be working at the Razzle, I suppose." He nodded in agreement.

Katherine's stomach twisted at the thought. She had always imagined the Spider as a faceless shadow, an enemy sewn together from scraps of her fears. But it was possible that this enemy was someone she had already met in person. She looked at the ledger with page after page devoted to victims. Who at the Razzle could have committed these atrocities?

"What about those Cream and Sugar gals?" Williams asked. "They said they had enough money to open their own place. Did they get all that money legally?"

"Maybe not, but they also wanted to have a replacement lined up before they quit as headliners. Loretta would have been a perfect fit, so why kill her? Lou the bartender has been there for years and with how few customers he gets, I doubt he makes much in tips. How does he keep afloat?"

"I'm guessing Al had to pay him pretty good to keep him quiet during Prohibition."

Al. Katherine churned the name over in her mind. During Prohibition, a lot of speakeasy owners were in with the mobs and gangs that ran rampant in Nolaton. The gangsters would offer protection in exchange for cash or favors. Maybe Al agreed to work as the Boss's hitman for $500 a pop and protection for the Razzle. Something about that didn't add up.

Katherine had dismissed Al as a suspect before, but only because she couldn't figure out his motive for killing Loretta. She might have missed something, though. Perhaps there had been more to that audition than she thought. Al had quite a temper; she'd seen it. If Loretta had done something to upset him, he could have killed her in a fit of passion. She was the one who had broken Tom's whiskey bottles — did Al find out she was to blame? Would that upset him enough to kill her? Or did something else happen that night? "What about Al? Working as a hitman on the side would explain how his grimy little club has survived over the years."

"Could be." Williams nodded. "Hey, if the Razzle had been shut down a few times during Prohibition, wouldn't their financial records have been confiscated?"

"And they might still be in the file room. Good thinking, Williams."

They both headed toward the file room and went inside. The temperature outside had dropped severely and the concrete room had an unforgiving chill. Katherine snapped her hand back from the freezing handle of the metal cabinet labeled *R*. She reached out again, prepared for the cold this time, and opened it. After a bit of searching, she found six leatherbound ledgers similar to the one the Boss used. She gathered them up and handed half to Williams.

As they walked back to her office she said, "Now it's possible that these are cooked books. If he had been funneling illegal gains into the club, odds are he would fake his accounting."

"That's true. And this won't cover the whole history of his business, only what he had on hand when it was seized. We might not see an influx of cash if there were no Spider killings at the time."

Though the exercise may prove futile, Katherine still thought it was worthwhile to go through the books. If Al was dumb enough to account for the $500 in hit money in his business ledgers, they would have a good piece of evidence to build a case around. *If* he was the Spider. Katherine still wasn't convinced.

Yet, after spending three hours poring over the details, a surprising pattern emerged. The books covered the period from December 1930 through September 1931. Arthur Fitzgerald had been killed during that time, April 8 to be exact. Alice Thurgood had been killed that year on August 12. Al kept receipts totaling how many drinks were sold and how much money was in the bar register at the end of each night. Most nights, only thirty or forty drinks were sold. The profits reflected those sales. Then some nights the amount in the register jumped but the number of drinks sold didn't.

Fifty extra dollars would show up for five nights in a row, starting on the date the Spider got paid the initial $250 fee. Then it would happen again starting on the date of the murder. Katherine matched the dates again just to be sure and found that the cash jumps lined up with Spider strikes.

"What an idiot! Who would keep records of their criminal activity like this?" Williams slapped the ledger in his hand.

"An overly confident killer who didn't think he'd ever be caught." Katherine boiled with rage. Al Harris had played innocent, complimenting her looks and offering beverages, all the while holding back his dastardly crimes. She squeezed her ruby into her palm vowing to bring Joey justice. "This won't be enough to arrest him, but we can at least confront him and, if we're lucky, get him to confess." Katherine thought of her talk with McAlister last night, how she should rely on her team instead of forging ahead on her own. "Let's bring this to McAlister and see if he'll send some guys to search the Razzle for the Spider's trinkets."

"If we find those, we'll definitely have enough evidence to make an arrest."

Katherine nodded as a surge of determination coursed through her.

That afternoon, Katherine walked into the Razzle Dazzle with her coat shut tight to keep out the cold. Williams had volunteered to carry the ledgers and came in after her shivering with an armful of books. As the door swung shut behind them, the chill vanished, but the tension remained.

Lou, as usual, stood at the bar making a cocktail. Vicki Harris leaned on the counter waiting patiently as Lou stirred the contents and jammed a lemon wedge on the side of the glass. Lou looked up and waved at Katherine and Williams. Vicki turned and waved to them as well, then sipped her drink.

"What brings you two back in here?" Vicki asked with a smile. The door swung open, letting in another draft of freezing air. Officer Peterson and two other uniformed cops stormed in. A judge had signed off on a search warrant and they had clearance to retrieve any item that matched the description of a Spider trinket. Vicki's smile faded upon seeing them break off and search the club. "What's going on?"

Poor Vicki. She hadn't done anything wrong but her life would be upended if they could prove that Al was a murderer. He would go to prison, most likely for life, leaving Vicki worse off than a widow. Katherine could not let her compassion slow her down, though. If Al was the Spider, he deserved to be thrown in a cell.

"Is Mr. Harris in? We'd like to speak with him." Katherine kept her face straight, shirking all pleasantries. Vicki pointed down the hallway and mumbled.

"He's in his office."

Katherine nodded for Williams to follow her as she marched to Al's spot. She flung the door open and stomped over to Al's desk. Al cowered as she smacked her hands down on the pine, leaning over and glaring at him. Williams shut the door then slammed the stack of ledgers down next to Katherine's left hand. He stood by her side with his arms crossed like a bodyguard.

"Um, hello, Detective." Al barely spoke above a whisper. He was scared, exactly what Katherine wanted. Katherine did her best to steady herself. A shaky voice and tear-filled temper flare would not get her the truth, only ridicule from a man like Al. She had to remain calm and shove her emotions down to be dealt with later.

"If you confess to the murders now, it'll be easier on all of us." Katherine pulled back from the desk and folded her arms, mirroring Williams.

"I'm sorry, did you say murders? Plural?" Al cocked his head to the side as if he didn't understand the word. Katherine bit down on her tongue to keep from exploding, then released it to answer to question.

"Yes, murders plural. Loretta Jones. Arthur Fitzgerald. Alice Thurgood. Joseph Callaghan." Katherine choked up on Joey's name and cleared her throat before pressing on. "And too many others to name. All victims of your side business, isn't that right?"

Al stared at her with squinted eyes. Katherine couldn't tell if he was confused or about to lash out. She kept a close watch on his movements.

"We've got the proof right here." Williams patted the ledgers. "You laid it all out for us."

"Are these my old ledgers?" Al pointed to the stack.

Katherine ignored his question. "Let's dig in, shall we?" She reached over and flipped open the first ledger to the page they had marked. She held out the book for Al to see then placed it open on his desk and gave it a violent push toward him. "Notice anything odd?"

Al caught the book before it slid into his lap, then muttered to himself as he stared at the numbers. "That can't be right." He slid his adding machine over and started punching in numbers, his fingers clicking on the keys while a roll of paper unfurled from the top. He ripped off the loose paper that had popped out and matched it to his old ledger.

"Off by fifty dollars, right?" Katherine raised an eyebrow to look intimidating. Al nodded.

"Either you're really bad at math, or you thought you could slip a little extra cash into the register and no one would notice." Williams flipped to the next page for Al to see. "Try this one."

Again, Al's fingers flew over the keys and again, found a fifty-dollar discrepancy.

"Now this is only ten months' worth of records. You've got other ledgers tucked away somewhere, don't you? Let's see them." Katherine circled around to stand next to Al. The only storage in his office were two short filing cabinets shoved under the table that served as his desk. He opened one of the makeshift desk drawers in a swift motion, probably making a show of cooperating as if that would help him get out of trouble.

Inside the drawer, Katherine saw three or four ledgers shoved in the back, but in front of them was a balled up cream-colored sheer fabric almost like a bridal veil or thin window dressing. Why would Al have either of those things in his office?

"What is that?"

Al turned beet red and let out a nervous puff of air. "I forgot that was in there. It's nothing. Just a costume piece."

"Do you usually keep costumes in your office?" Katherine reach in and pulled out the sheer dress with the high hemline, more of a lingerie piece than a costume, in her opinion. Williams looked at it sideways then averted his eyes in embarrassment. Katherine dropped the dress down out of sight but held on to it.

"No, we have a costume room down the hall. But sometimes things get misplaced..." Al trailed off but Katherine didn't need to hear the end of his sentence. A costume room — of course! That sounded like the perfect place for the Spider to hide trinkets. Katherine was no stranger to the disarray of a theater's costume storage.

In her dancer days, she would often have to rush back between performances, wading through a mess of chiffon and taffeta to find a dropped earring or lost shoe. She imagined the Razzle's costume room to be an explosion of old sequin gowns and cheap jewelry. All the real jewelry and garments the Spider had taken would blend into the chaos.

Unless a person knew exactly what they were looking for. Peterson and the other cops needed to know about this room and to pay special attention to it. They would probably find it on their own, but Katherine couldn't risk them overlooking it.

"Williams, stay here and keep going over the records. I'd like to see this costume room for myself." Katherine threw the sheer dress back into Al's drawer then curved around the table and into the hallway.

Down the hall to the left was the door to Candace and Shirley's dressing room, but to the right was another door, cracked open but dark inside. That must be the room Al had mentioned. As Katherine approached, the door slammed shut.

Odd. Maybe one of the cops had already found it. Katherine tiptoed toward the door, turned the brass knob, and pushed it open.

A dingy light bulb hung from the middle of the ceiling. Its muted glow illuminated the center of the small storage room but left the corners shrouded in black. Had that light been on before or had someone just clicked it on?

Rows of dresses hanging on garment racks took up most of the room, though several gowns had fallen on the floor. Shelves full of haphazardly placed accessories lined the walls and the floor was littered with old costume pieces that must have cascaded off the piles. A large trunk in the center of the room had scraps of soft fabrics spilling out from under the closed lid. Cobwebs clung to most of the surfaces.

"Hello? Detective Dell with the Nolaton City Police," Katherine called into the stillness. "Anyone in here?"

No response. The officers had no reason to keep quiet, which meant they were not in there searching and the door hadn't closed on its own. Before she could hunt for the Spider's trinkets, she needed to be sure no one dangerous was lurking in the shadows. Katherine took out her flashlight to inspect the dark corners.

She shined her light into the unseen patches of the costume room. Both corners at the front of the room were clear so Katherine slipped to the back, first checking to the right, then the left. A collection of wigs sat on mannequin heads perched on a wall shelf. Below them, a pair of eyes glimmered at her from the darkness.

Katherine gasped, then realized who it was. Curled up in the corner was Vicki Harris.

"I didn't mean to startle you." Vicki held up her hands apologetically, then picked herself up from the floor.

Katherine smiled at her, the pity she felt for Vicki returning in full force. "That's all right. What are you doing back here?" Katherine had a theory, even before she answered. Most wives would be by their husband's side at a time like this, but that must be the last place Vicki wanted to be. She was hiding from the commotion and anger that Al's possible arrest would cause.

"The cops are searching our apartment upstairs. They said they think Al is a murderer." Vicki spoke with disbelief. "I...I didn't want to get in the way, but I didn't know where else to go," Vicki said, confirming Katherine's assumption.

"This might be hard to hear, but if we can gather enough evidence, your husband is going away for a long time. I know how awful that sounds, but it could be a good change for you. He won't be able to hurt you anymore." Katherine reached out her hand to help Vicki up. Vicki took it, then collapsed into Katherine, holding herself up on Katherine's shoulders as she sobbed. Katherine held her tight in an attempt to comfort her, Vicki's bony frame poking into her. This poor woman had suffered far too long.

"You really think he killed all those people?" Vicki threw her arms around Katherine's waist and buried her tearful face into Katherine's shoulder. This amount of contact with a woman she barely knew made Katherine squirm, but Katherine didn't have the heart to push her away. As monstrous as Al was, and had been to her, Vicki must still have trouble viewing him as anything other than her charming husband.

"The evidence is pointing squarely in his direction. I'm sorry, but I believe your husband is the most prolific hitman in the history of Nolaton, the Spider." As Katherine held her, she looked over Vicki's shoulder into the corner where Vicki had been sitting. Though barely visible in the dim light, Katherine could just make it out. A scrap of blue silk with little white roses lay in a crumpled pile against the wall. Loretta's scarf? It matched the description Jack Lewis had given her over the phone. Al must have thrown it all the way to the back of the room after he killed her.

Other things were there as well — a gold watch draped across the scarf, possibly the one stolen from Gabriel Perkins. A pair of shoes laid next to it, ones that could have belonged to Arthur Fitzgerald. A bracelet, a fountain pen, a fur wrap — all of them were items taken by the Spider. Katherine's stomach lurched as her eyes landed on a round box. The lid was partway off and sticking out of the top of the box was a well-worn gray homburg.

Joey's hat.

Vicki sobbed on her shoulder, but Katherine's attention fixated on the pile. It was all wrong. Joey had died five years ago; Loretta mere weeks. Al wasn't throwing the items back there as he obtained them. They were out of order, and from where she was standing, she couldn't see any cobwebs.

"Vicki, what were you really doing in here? Did you collect those things from the shelves?" Did Vicki know about her husband's crimes? Was she trying to hide his trophies to cover for him?

Vicki picked up her head from Katherine's shoulder but still clung to her waist. She stared into Katherine's eyes, their noses inches apart. Vicki's eyes changed. The light left them. They were like windows to an empty house.

A rush of cold wind ran up Katherine's spine as she remembered those men hovering over her bed. Their eyes had the same soulless vacancy.

That's why they looked familiar, they had Vicki's eyes. Her mind raced through the possibilities. Were the Gray Suits Al and Vicki's sons? Was that why they worked for the Spider, to help their father make a profit? But Vicki said it herself, their children no longer spoke to Al. They wouldn't help him with a criminal enterprise. Then why—

Vicki slipped Katherine's gun from the holster and aimed it at Katherine's head.

"My boys told you to drop the investigation, but you wouldn't listen. Well, congratulations, Detective. You've caught me. Now all you have to do is get out of the Spider's web alive."

Chapter Thirty-Five

"What I don't understand is why you wrote the cash amounts in the ledger. If you wanted to launder your hit money through your business, why not forge the receipts too?" Henry stifled a laugh as he brought up this oversight to Al.

"I didn't have any hit money to launder. Honestly, I don't get what you keep accusing me of. I've never killed anybody. I wouldn't dream of it!" Al curled up his lip in a confused glower. Henry, disgusted by Al's lies, wished he had enough evidence to slap his cuffs on the killer's wrists. While the other cops searched for hard evidence, Henry would have to draw out the truth, get Al to unburden himself of the crimes.

"Drop the act and admit it already. You've been running a business on the side to keep this one afloat. Getting your boys to hunt down people with debt hanging over their heads, then sweeping in and killing them. You're the Spider."

Al stared at Henry, unblinking. Henry simply stared back, waiting for that all-important confession. Instead, Al burst into laughter. Henry felt his gut light up with rage seeing this monstrous man laugh about the murders that had plagued Nolaton. But then he realized how ridiculous the accusation would sound to someone who didn't believe the Spider existed.

"That's a good one. Who put you up to this? Was it Lou? Ha! I'll have to think of something to get him back with."

Henry snarled, sick of Al's laughter and still itching to cuff the bastard.

"This isn't some schoolyard prank. As an officer of the law, I'm telling you the Spider is real and the evidence points in your direction."

That shut him up. Al deflated, sinking into his chair as his eyes glazed over in fear.

"I thought that was a story meant to scare teenagers or something. I swear on everything holy, I am not the Spider."

"Why would anyone else take the exact amount of cash the Spider got for a hit and slip it into your register here at the Razzle? Nobody but you would benefit from that."

"No, no one else would. Well, no one except..." Al let out a grunt of disbelief. "That can't be right. Unless..." Al leaned over onto his desk and plunked his elbows down, then ran his hands through his thinning hair. He took large gasping breaths. Henry was worried the man might collapse in front of him.

"Do I need to call an ambulance?"

Instead, Al sat up straight but kept his pained expression.

"How does it go again? The story about the Spider? There's two guys who stalk the person they want killed, right? And the guys, the Suits or whatever their called, they're twins, aren't they?"

"They have been described as looking similar, could be twins. Why?"

"My wife and I have twin boys, well, not boys, adults at this point. They haven't spoken to me in a decade, but my wife is close with them. She's the only other person who would benefit from my business staying out of the red."

"Are you saying Mrs. Harris is the Spider?" Henry once again found himself having to force down laughter. How could that tiny, frail old woman be a hitman?

"She always worries about money. Maybe she took it upon herself to solve our financial woes. Plus she's sneaky and stronger than she looks."

This theory swam in Henry's mind, the believability of it ebbing and flowing like ocean tides. Vicki Harris — it was easier to imagine her baking a pie than strangling a person. Then again, he would have said the same about Dell if he didn't know her better. Dell had the strength to bring a grown man to his knees, and she would take just about any damn risk to get what she wanted.

Maybe Vicki had that same fire burning inside of her. Maybe her small frame and unassuming nature was the very thing that made her a good hitman. She could flash a smile and mewl in her high-pitched voice; her victims would never suspect that she intended to end their lives.

Or maybe Al was cruel enough to pin his crimes on his unsuspecting wife. Henry had seen the way Al treated her, like a punching bag with no free will of her own. Was Al pinning his own transgressions on an innocent woman? Henry pressed on with his questions.

"That doesn't explain how that extra cash flowed into your till unnoticed. You're telling me your wife slipped it into the register and you conveniently overlooked it?" Henry had a hard time buying that any business owner could be so lousy at basic math. Al flushed pink and looked down at his folded hands, ashamed.

"Sometimes I have a few too many whiskey sours and by the end of the night the numbers all blur together. I count up what's in the register and trust Lou to keep track of the drinks sold, so I assume the numbers match. You must think I'm an idiot."

Henry did think that, but also still had trouble picturing Vicki as a killer. One detail in particular gnawed at him, especially since it didn't add up to either of the Harrises being the Spider.

"If Mrs. Harris only took those hits to keep the club running, then why kill Loretta Jones? Her singing would have brought customers in droves from what you've said."

Al cleared his throat as he turned a darker shade of pink, then looked up at Henry with a coy shrug.

"I've, uh...I've got a theory about that. I had a few cocktails in me during Loretta's audition and, well, man-to-man, you know how it is when you get a pretty girl alone." Al gave a knowing smile.

Henry knew exactly what to do with a pretty gal behind closed doors, but only if the gal gave the go-ahead. Over the years, he'd had his share of dates who wound up spending the night at his apartment, but that was different. Loretta was not Al's date. She was auditioning for a job, pursuing her passion. From what Henry knew, she planned on marrying Jack Lewis. Why would she throw that away for a romp with Al?

"You mean to tell me she found you so irresistible she was willing to have an affair with you?" Henry stared at the stumpy, balding man, who shrank into his chair.

"Well, it was more like...part of the deal. I'd do her a favor by giving her the job; she'd do a favor for me in return." Al spoke as if this was common, like that was how deals were struck every day.

"And Loretta was fine with that arrangement? Totally willing to comply?" Henry found that hard to believe. Al's face melted into a frown.

"It took some convincing—"

"Convincing or coercion?"

"Nothing even wound up happening! She ran out of here before I could..." Al snapped his mouth shut and a flash of guilt shined in his eyes.

"Before you could violate her?" Henry spat his words. Al seethed, baring his teeth like an attack dog ready to pounce.

"That little tart paraded around in front of me at the diner for months, bending down in her skintight uniform to pour my coffee, giggling at my jokes. Then she comes up to me one day, lips all pouty, begging for a chance to audition. What was I supposed to make of that? I did what any red-blooded man would do and took my chances with a gorgeous broad. If she wanted me to zip my pants back up she could have said something."

"Sounds like she was doing her job as a waitress, and then tried to get a better job working for you. You turned it into something vile." Henry's insides boiled thinking about how scared and powerless Loretta must have felt with Al drooling on her.

"This ain't about what I did, remember? You're after a killer and I think my wife is to blame. Vicki is always sticking her nose in here unannounced. I bet she popped in and took one look at Loretta then went nuts with jealousy."

It seemed easy for Al to use his wife as a shield, forcing her crimes to the forefront of the conversation and hoping his own crime slipped away unnoticed. Henry would make sure that Al did not get away with his indiscretion.

"Even if your wife did something far worse, that doesn't excuse what you did. Exposing yourself to a woman is against the law."

Someone knocked on the door then cracked it open. Peterson stood in the door frame and took a glance around the small office.

"Where's Detective Dell? The guys and I found something upstairs."

Henry stepped over to Peterson so they could speak in whispers and not be overheard by Al.

"What did you find?"

"A whole slew of weapons in a hidden compartment under the bed. Pistols, knives, all sorts of stuff."

That helped build a case against Al or Vicki Harris, though Henry wasn't sure which one seemed more likely to be the killer. Vicki could have strangled her in a jealous rage, or Al could have done it since he didn't get his way with Loretta. At least Henry knew Al was guilty of one crime.

"Good find. Say, have you ever arrested anyone before?"

Peterson shook his head, clearly confused.

"I've assisted but I haven't done it myself."

"Well, now's your chance." Henry explained Al's misdeed, and Peterson glared at the club owner. "I'll find Dell if you want to slap a pair of cuffs on him."

Without a word, Peterson marched over and took out his handcuffs.

"Oh, come on! I didn't do anything wrong."

Peterson ignored Al's protests and made him stand up. He put on a stern expression as he clicked the cuffs in place. Henry gave him a proud nod before making his way down the hall to the costume room. Dell had said she wanted to see it for herself, and he assumed she'd still be there searching for clues.

He found the only other door besides Al's office and the ladies' dressing room. As he pushed the costume room door open, a powerful odor clogged his nose. A sweet floral perfume mixed with the metallic bitterness of blood.

Chapter Thirty-Six

Vicki stood in front of Katherine, the gun aimed at her forehead.

"You're the Spider?" Katherine tried to wrap her mind around the revelation. Mousy Vicki Harris, a cold-blooded killer? The woman she had pitied had been the one who took her love away.

Katherine's body pulsed with fear. Her heart rammed against her chest. Her last heartbeats.

No. It couldn't end this way. Vicki needed to be brought to justice. To pay for what she had done. Katherine's mind raced. There had to be a way out. She stared down the barrel of her own gun. Why hadn't Vicki fired?

The answer dawned on her. "You're not going to shoot me. The sound would attract too much attention."

Vicki adjusted her grip, keeping the barrel aimed at Katherine. "You think I won't shoot?" Vicki's voice trembled. After all the murders she had committed, killing Katherine should be easy, but Vicki was out of her element.

"Your boys didn't plan this murder for you; not so easy to cover your tracks without them, is it? If you shoot, every cop in this place will come running."

"You're right." Vicki's face twisted with rage as she unloaded the revolver and scattered the bullets on the floor. She tucked the empty gun into her dress. "I'll have to kill you quietly and dump your body later." Vicki dove at Katherine, tackling her to the floor.

Katherine tried to get out from under her but was trapped. "I can't shoot you, but I could strangle you. We both know I'm good at it." Vicki pushed her hands onto Katherine's neck and closed her grip. Dull pain shot from Katherine's neck up to her skull and into her shoulders as she gasped for breath. Her eyes felt like they would swell and burst from her head. Flecks of light swam in front of her, clouding her vision.

As Katherine struggled to breathe, the enormity of the situation washed over her. At last she knew who had killed Joey, but if Vicki succeeded, she would join him in death. She thought of Williams, part of her wishing desperately that he would come and save her. She pushed the thought aside. She wanted him here to fight by her side, but she had the strength to do this alone.

Katherine forced a short burst of air into her lungs, then her eyes darted around the room as her vision momentarily cleared. Under one of the clothing racks, a mousetrap sat primed with a piece of moldy cheese. She would have to reach for it slowly to keep from calling attention to it and to keep the mechanism from crashing down on her fingers. Her hand snaked away from her body as she felt for the wooden base. It was too far away to reach. Sweat beads formed on Vicki's forehead. She snarled and pressed her hands further into Katherine's flesh. Katherine stretched her arm farther, hoping her attacker would think her movements were involuntary. Her vision clouded again as her consciousness started to slip away, but she focused on the trap, forcing her mind to stay active.

She stretched her arm just enough to tap the corner of the trap and knock it closer. With a wave of relief, she grabbed it and snapped it onto Vicki's arm. Vicki gasped with pain and let Katherine go, scrabbling to remove the trap. Katherine drove the palm of her hand into Vicki's nose, and both felt and heard it snap.

Vicki, now delirious from pain, held her hands to her nose. Katherine rolled out from under her then shoved Vicki to the floor and pinned down her shoulder. With her right hand, Katherine grabbed a handful of Vicki's hair and pulled, causing Vicki to screech but keeping her immobile. The question that had plagued her for the last five years came bounding out.

"Why did you do it?"

Vicki strained to speak while Katherine wrenched her head to the side.

"I had to protect my family! We would have been out on the street if I hadn't taken those hits."

"You don't get to protect your family by destroying someone else's." Katherine let go of her hair and punched Vicki in the jaw.

Vicki groaned from the impact, then with a growl, grabbed Katherine's shoulders and threw her off. Katherine crashed into a dress rack, bringing the whole thing down with her to the ground. She struggled to untangle herself from the garments, sequins scratching her hands. Vicki stood over her as if victorious, half a smile stretching across her battered face. Thinking fast, Katherine kicked her in the stomach and Vicki doubled over with a grunt.

Katherine popped up and grabbed Vicki's wrist. All she had to do was the cuff the woman and the ordeal would be over. She reached for her handcuffs, but Vicki wriggled her arm free and punched Katherine in the mouth.

Katherine stumbled into the pile of trinkets, metals and gems jabbing into her back. The room spun around her and her mouth flooded with a coppery liquid. She spat a wad of red onto the floor next to the pile. Vicki lunged on top of her, stole the cuffs, and threw them across the room. Katherine felt around for anything she could use against Vicki. Her revolver handle poked out of Vicki's dress, but even if she could wrestle the gun from Vicki, the bullets were out of reach.

Then she got her hand around a leather loop — the strap of a high heel. She raked it across Vicki's face, the corner of the heel slicing her eye. Vicki howled and clapped her hands to her face, blood trickling between her fingers.

Loretta's scarf was within reach and Katherine grabbed it, then clawed at Vicki's wrist until she had a grasp. Working quickly and fighting the adrenaline-fueled tremors, she tied Vicki's hands with the silk. Vicki struggled against the tight restraints, her fingers turning purple. With Vicki bound, Katherine grabbed her gun, but before she could get to the bullets, Vicki shoved her toward the center of the room.

Katherine fell, stumbling out of the dark corner, and landed against the trunk full of fabric. Her head cracked against the edge. Stars flooded her eyes and her skull pounded with pain.

When her vision cleared, Vicki stood above her again, and a malicious grin spread across her face. She held an oversized perfume bottle in her bound hands. Katherine nearly found herself laughing. What was her plan? Spritz Katherine to death?

Vicki smashed the bottle, which broke into jagged shards of glass. The floral scent overwhelmed the room, choking Katherine with its thick musk, and the plan became clear. Vicki picked up a piece of glass and pressed it to Katherine's throat.

"It's over, Detective." Vicki's lips curled into a smile. Katherine tried to push her arms away but Vicki pressed hard and the edge of the glass grazed Katherine's neck. She felt her skin split and a warm gush as blood spilled from the wound.

But Vicki was wrong. It wasn't over. Katherine kneed Vicki in the stomach, then wrestled the glass from her. She rolled on top of her and held the shard to Vicki's jugular while her other hand squeezed her neck. One slice and the woman she had been hunting for five years would be dead. No longer could she hurt people for her own selfish gain. The world would be better without her.

The door burst open, letting in a rush of fresh air, and Katherine gasped. Williams stood there, mouth gaping. "Don't do it, Dell."

"She's the Spider! She killed Joey."

"Put the glass down. Please, Dell. You're not a killer."

His words tumbled in her ears. Rita Davis had killed her tormenter and Katherine had supported her fully.

This was different, though. Katherine was a cop, and she had to hold herself to higher standards. Her job was to protect and serve, not take lives. Pushing the glass into Vicki's neck, letting her blood flow, would ensure she couldn't hurt anyone else. But could Katherine live with her choice?

No. She had the power to bring real justice to all the people that Vicki hurt, to make this woman rot in cell for the rest of her miserable life. It's what McAlister would want her to do. It's what Joey would want her to do. Katherine wailed and threw the glass shard to an empty corner where it shattered.

Williams ran over and examined Katherine's wounds. Blood had trickled from the cut on her neck down her arm and Williams reached for a cotton dress to clean it up.

"It doesn't look too deep but keep this pressed here to stop the bleeding." He tucked the old garment against the injury then Katherine gathered the fabric in her hand and held it in place. Williams turned to Vicki and clicked his handcuffs onto her wrists. He removed the silk scarf to be kept as evidence.

"Will you take her outside? There's something I need to do." Katherine looked at Williams. He seemed confused but nodded and led Vicki out the door. Once Katherine was alone, she waded through the mess to the pile of stolen items that Vicki had been hoarding.

She pulled the cover off the hatbox, exposing the contents. Joey's old hat looked exactly the way she remembered. She took it out of the box, then cradled it against her cheek.

After all these years it still smelled like him, a mix of leather and earth. She caressed the fabric, remembering how he would playfully tip the brim. She remembered his laugh, the way his eyes squinted when he smiled. The bubbles that would course through her body at his touch. The way his lips melted onto hers.

She sank to her knees and let her tears soak into the homburg.

Chapter Thirty-Seven

December arrived on a wave of ice storms, yet the residents of Nolaton fought through the cold to put up Christmas decorations, making the frosted city sparkle with lights. Katherine watched them glisten in the falling snow on her way to work.

One week ago, after they got Vicki Harris into handcuffs, Peterson had seen two men idling in a car outside the Razzle Dazzle. Two men in gray suits. Vicki later confessed that she had called her boys as soon as she saw the team of cops begin their search. She planned to grab all the stolen purses and trinkets, then hightail it out of town with them. Instead, Peterson and the other cops arrested the Gray Suits and sent them to the Nolaton City men's prison.

Katherine stepped into station and shook the snowflakes from her hair. Before heading to her office, she made a stop at the evidence locker. She stared at the Spider's trinkets, which consumed an entire shelf. Vicki was locked in a maximum-security cell at Kinghill Prison, more than two hundred miles from Nolaton. This array of evidence would ensure she stayed there.

McAlister joined Katherine in the cramped room. He glanced over the whole shelf before his eyes landed on Joey's hat. He seemed to be debating what to say, or if he should say anything at all. Katherine had trouble finding the right words too.

"You really did it. I couldn't be prouder of you." He shook his head in disbelief at the items on the shelf.

"I couldn't have done it without you." Katherine nodded to him.

McAlister dropped his chin. "I suppose you'll be quitting the force, now that the Spider's behind bars."

Katherine pondered this. She had become a cop to find Joey's killer, and she'd accomplished her goal. What more was there to do? She looked at the ruby sparkling above her palm. The Spider was behind bars, but that didn't rid the city of murderers. She still had killers to catch.

"I'll quit the force once there's no more crime in the city." She smirked at him. For the first time in five years, he gave her a genuine smile.

"Then you've got a long career ahead of you." His face hardened again. "Now, normally I wouldn't do this, but we've got enough evidence here to put the Spider away for good. Even if one of these trinkets were to go missing, we'd still have plenty to go on. I wouldn't be upset if you decided to keep something off that shelf." He nodded to Joey's hat, then he turned and walked out of the room.

Katherine picked up the homburg. Joey's scent was already fading from the wool. He was gone and no amount of obsession would bring him back. Keeping his old hat would only hurt her, drag her back into the fog. Blood still pumped through her veins and she should enjoy the life she'd been given.

It was time to let go of her grief.

She set the hat back on the shelf, but McAlister did say she could take one item. She picked up Alice Thurgood's opal necklace. Avery should have it, along with an apology for her behavior at the bakery that day. She slipped it into her pocket. Before leaving the evidence locker, she ran her finger along the brim of the homburg.

She had to let Joey go, but she wanted to say goodbye.

Katherine stood at the edge of the graveyard. With Christmas only a few weeks away, she had brought a bouquet of red and white roses. She started toward Joey's grave, then turned when a figure caught her eye. Standing by a row of newer graves was Jack Lewis. He stared down at a tombstone.

"Jack?" she said as she approached.

He turned, startled. "Oh, Detective Dell. Hello." He tried to smile but couldn't quite manage it. He turned back to Loretta's gravestone. Katherine's heart ached for Loretta, for the both of them. The circumstances of her death were completely unfair. All this talented young woman had wanted was to build a career, and lust, greed, and jealousy had stolen that from her. Jack looked at the bouquet in Katherine's hand.

"Flowers. That's a good idea. I should have brought her some."

Katherine unraveled the ribbon that held the stems together. She picked out the white roses and handed them to Jack. Joey would have preferred the red ones anyway.

"Careful of the thorns," she said as he took the flowers. Tears filled his eyes.

"Thank you," he said. She nodded, then gave him space, rewrapping the ribbon around her remaining flowers. Her feet sank into the snow as she walked to Joey's grave.

"Hi, Joey." She laid the flowers down. The pain of losing him was still there; it always would be. The anger, however, had subsided.

"I'll never stop loving you, Joey. I think it's time for me to let go, though. You've probably been looking down at me, begging me to move on. I'm finally ready to listen." She kissed her fingertips and touched the grave marker, then she slipped the ring from her finger. Her first thought was to leave it on the ground where he lay, but then she looked behind her at the church. Why waste this lovely ruby when it could do some good in the world?

The wooden doors of the chapel squeaked as she opened them. Just inside sat the offering box, with a slot cut in the top. The money went to feed the hungry. Katherine took one last look at her ring, then dropped it into the box.

As she made her way to the trolley stop, she made a vow. No more wallowing in self-pity or guilt. She would take care of herself and fight the fog. Eat well and get enough sleep. Take days off. Keep her apartment clean. Visit friends and family. Go to ballet class. If her work schedule allowed, she might even dance on stage again. She would cling to moments of joy whenever she found them and remind herself often that she deserved to be happy. She would live. Really, truly live.

Epilogue

Rita and Walter now lived in Lavendale and planned to never step foot into Nolaton again. Walter had found a job at the local university, cleaning classrooms and shelving books in the library. His earnings were meager, but it was steady work and the university offered a ton of benefits. Walter could read as many library books as he wished, and often came home with a heavy stack of science texts or heroic sagas. Best of all, the institution provided cheap housing to students and staff. Walter rented a small first-floor apartment. Ricky collected enough cash doing odd jobs that he could help pay rent and had his mattress in their living room. Though water stains hung on the ceiling and frost crept up the windows, it was better than the cardboard shack they left behind.

Rita worked with an organization that fed the homeless. The pay was lousy, but so were her job prospects, and they had been willing to take a chance on her. She wouldn't let them down.

Three days before Christmas, Rita came home after her shift smelling of broth and sweat. A string had been run from one end of the living room to the other and Ricky was hanging wet clothes on the line to dry. He greeted her with a mischievous smile, then went back to the laundry. What had him in such good spirits?

Walter was in the kitchen boiling a pot of water. A bag of uncooked pasta sat next to the stove for that night's supper. Rita wrapped her arms around his waist, and he returned the hug. Over his shoulder, she noticed a bouquet of wildflowers lying on the table.

"These are beautiful." She let go of Walter and went over to the table, picking up the flowers and breathing in their sweetness.

"The horticulture department was going to throw them away. I didn't want them going to waste." Walter wouldn't meet her eye. Why was he acting strange?

Rita pushed that thought from her mind, took a water glass from the cupboard, and placed the flowers inside. As she arranged the blossoms, Walter nodded to Ricky through the kitchen door. Ricky nodded back as if they shared a secret.

"I'm going out for a bit. Job hunting." Ricky slipped on his shoes and left the apartment.

"That was odd." Rita put her hands on her hips. Walter's neck disappeared into his shoulders. "What's going on?" Rita asked firmly.

"Well, there is something I've been meaning to ask you, but I don't have..." He picked a tiny white bloom from the bunch in the vase, and tied the stem into a circle. "I know it's not much, and I'll get you a real one as soon as I can, but this will have to do for now." He bent down on his knee and held out the flower. "Rita, will you marry—?"

"Of course I will!" He slipped the makeshift ring onto her finger, positioning the flower where a gemstone would be. "And this ring is perfect. Forget all that stuff about buying me a real one. I've got you, and that's all I need." She pulled him up and kissed him. His warmth engulfed her as he kissed her back, his lips a familiar comfort.

Life was far from perfect, but this was the first step to life they always dreamed of.

Henry looked at his brother with pride, then back at the road. Benny scribbled on a notepad in the front seat.

"What are you working on?" Henry asked.

"Just catching up on math homework." Benny smiled up at Henry.

After Benny had mostly healed from his injuries, he and Henry had made a deal. As long as Benny's grades stayed up, he could work on the weekends. A new theater was opening in town, and they were hiring people to help with renovations. He was working his first shift this Saturday morning. Everything Benny earned would be put aside for schooling. Henry still struggled to pay the bills, but wouldn't for much longer. After Mayor Herbert's death, the city of Nolaton had scheduled a special election to replace him, and Detective Hanson was running. Win or lose, Hanson planned to retire right after the holidays and that left a detective spot open. McAlister had already announced that the badge would go to Henry.

They pulled up to the club. The old sign lay in the alley. Most of the bulbs had shattered, but their pattern spelled out "Razzle Dazzle." A new sign now took its place. Each bulb lit up in turn and the flashes raced across each word. "Cream and Sugar's Show Hall."

"Ready?" Henry asked. Benny wrote a few more numbers, then set his notebook on the dashboard. He gave a sharp nod.

"Ready."

They walked into a mad rush of color and smiles. New paint now replaced the old peeling wallpaper, and the gold trim reflected the bright house lights. A glittering curtain hung behind the stage, and workers ran in all directions with bolts of fabric or new chairs.

"Not bad, huh?" Shirley MacDougall held out her arms to demonstrate, as if holding the place on platters.

"Amazing what a little elbow grease can do." Candace MacDougall glanced around as if she couldn't quite believe the transformation.

"Where do I start?" Benny stood at attention and waited for orders.

"Why don't you help Lou clean behind the bar," Candace said. Lou popped up from under the bar counter and sent a friendly wave to Henry. Henry waved back.

Tom Phillips stood behind the bar as well, unloading whiskey bottles onto the new glass shelves. Benny marched over.

"Let me know if that boy gives you any trouble," Henry said. Candace laughed, and Shirley waved away the comment.

"There's no way he can cause more trouble than we do." Shirley winked.

Katherine dug through her cupboards and found her cleaning supplies. Dust flew up from the floors as she swept. She scrubbed her kitchen counters until they shined. Her bathroom got a bath of its own.

After a full afternoon of housework, she beamed at her progress. The little apartment now looked like a home. The fog of her anxiety billowed away, leaving her with an internal glow. Even her houseplant, back to getting regular water and sun, had begun to turn green. With her dustbin in hand, she walked over to her wastebasket and saw the corner of the envelope.

The invitation had been buried under the mess on her coffee table and in her cleaning frenzy, she had thrown out the whole pile. She pinched the corner of the envelope and rescued the letter from under an orange peel. She tipped the dustbin into the trash, then read the invitation once more and considered her options. The party started at seven o'clock that night, and she could bring a guest. She could think of no one else she would rather have by her side. She picked up the phone and dialed.

"Hello?" said a voice on the other line.

"I still owe you a glass of wine, don't I?" Katherine said.

"You owe me at least three by now," Vera said.

"Well, if you join me for a party tonight, I can make it up to you."

"Promise you won't run off in the middle to catch a criminal?"

"I promise."

"No working at all?"

"Not even a little."

"Where is the party?"

Katherine closed her eyes, anticipating Vera's response. "It's the annual Christmas party...at the station."

Vera hummed with disapproval. Katherine added, "There's free booze."

"All right, I'll be there."

Katherine entered the station wearing a new dress. The neckline draped becomingly, and burgundy satin caressed her hips. Christmas was only three days away, and though it was dark outside, the party provided a much-needed lightness. She smiled at her colleagues in their finery; even Mrs. Bobern wore a floor-length black gown that showed off her figure. Katherine complimented the dress and the Christmas decorations.

"It was nothing." Mrs. Bobern waved her comment away. Katherine knew she was being modest. It must have taken her all day to set up. The desks had been pushed aside, creating a dance floor in the center of the room. Garlands draped from the ceiling, illuminated by lights of every color. Red bulbs and gold tinsel dangled from the Christmas tree set up near the evidence locker. The break room counters overflowed with Christmas cookies, and bottles of liquor covered the lunch table. Katherine and Vera each poured themselves a glass of wine.

Williams and Peterson walked in, and the men froze when they saw Katherine and Vera.

"You're here," Williams said, excitement in his voice.

"Hello." Peterson stared, mesmerized by Vera. Vera giggled in a way she only did around men she found handsome, high-pitched with a hint of nervous crackle. Katherine introduced them, trying not to laugh at Vera's flirtations. "Would you like to dance?" Peterson held out his hand. Vera looked at Katherine.

"She's all yours. Just have her back by midnight and no funny business." Katherine winked while Vera's mouth fell open in embarrassment. Vera smacked Katherine's arm playfully, then grabbed Peterson's hand and pulled him to the dance floor. Williams poured himself a glass of scotch.

"I brought you a present but I didn't know if you were coming tonight, so I set it in your office." Williams seemed embarrassed or nervous but he had no reason to be. Katherine knew the gift was simply a gesture of friendship, one she greatly appreciated.

"I got a present for you too. It's in my desk drawer." She led Williams back to her office, then took a small gift out of her desk. She had wrapped it in brown paper and tied it with a ribbon.

"It's not much." She handed it to Williams. He opened it. For a moment, he stared at the contents — a toy detective badge, the kind children wore while playing cops and robbers. Katherine squirmed as she waited for his reaction. She'd meant for it to be funny but maybe she had hurt his feelings instead. "I figure you'll be getting a real one soon, but this can hold you over until then."

Williams doubled over in laughter and Katherine heaved a sigh of relief. Williams held up the toy badge and pinned it to his lapel. "I love it. Now open yours." He slid his gift to her. She tore the paper off and inside was a bright red coffee mug, just like the one they always fought over. This mug, however, was engraved with the words "Detective Dell."

"There, now it's got your name on it."

"Thank you!" Katherine adored the gift.

"Would you like to dance? You know, since our dates abandoned us." He held out his hand.

"I'd love to." She put down the mug, swigged the rest of her wine, and set the empty glass down on her desk. They stepped out of her office onto the dance floor, swaying to Benny Goodman's new hit song. They only stopped for a moment when Officer Martin fell into the Christmas tree.

Vera and Peterson glided over to them.

"You know you're standing under the mistletoe?" She giggled and pointed at the ceiling. Katherine and Williams looked up at the plant hanging there, red berries surrounded by green leaves.

"That's holly." Katherine nodded up at it, and Williams feigned a dramatic sigh of relief. Vera gave Katherine a look of disapproval and Katherine mocked her with a similar expression.

Calm washed over her as she joked with her friends. As they danced, she looked out one of the office windows. The stars glistened over Nolaton. The sun had set as early as it would all year, but going forward the daylight would last longer. Little by little, the light would carve more space for itself, and each new day would be warmer and brighter than the last.

Thanks for Reading!

I hope you enjoyed my debut novel. Please consider giving this book a quick rating or review, even if it is just a few words. I am grateful for every bit of feedback I receive, and it helps other readers decide whether or not this book is for them.

To hear about my upcoming releases, visit www.ecpecha.com and subscribe to my newsletter. Your email will not be shared or sold, and your inbox will not be filled with useless spam. Thank you!